Betrayed—By Her Own Passions . . .

She was still sitting on the bed when the door opened and Joaquin came through.

"What . . . what do you want?" Reesa asked. Her fear of the dashing young rebel who had saved her from the renegade rapists seemed unreasonable now. Still . . .

Joaquin smiled, his dark brown eyes flashing. He tossed his sombrero casually to one side, then began unbuttoning his shirt. "Easy, my *muchacha*," he said. "I'm not going to hurt you."

Reesa watched, paralyzed, as he undid the great silver buckle of his belt, then let his breeches fall.

"I am a handsome man, no?" he asked softly. Reesa turned her head away from him. "I know this is true because many women have told me I am," he went on. "So why can you not say so?"

"I'm afraid these circumstances don't permit it."

Joaquin laughed quietly, then reached down and put one hand on the edge of the blanket.

"No!" Her cry was short and ineffectual. She pulled the blanket back in place.

Joaquin bent over and kissed her gently on the lips. His kiss was tender, and Reesa felt the heat rising, as if he were kindling the flames within her. *No*, she thought, *I'll not be betrayed by my own body.* But even as her mind formed the words, waves of desire flooded over her. . . .

Harry

STORM of DESIRE

Paula Fairman

PINNACLE BOOKS • LOS ANGELES

STORM OF DESIRE

Copyright © 1979 by Script Representatives, Inc.

An original Pinnacle Books edition, published for the first time anywhere.

First printing, February 1979

ISBN: 0-523-40474-3

Cover illustration by Bill Maughan

Printed in the United States of America

PINNACLE BOOKS, INC.
2029 Century Park East
Los Angeles, California 90067

This book is for
Ann Kearns,
a bouyant voice
in a
Sea of Silence

Chapter One

Had Miller Flowers but known the indignities to which his daughter was nightly subjected, he wouldn't have continued to send her with the crew orders for the midnight train. Reesa was a voluptuous young woman of eighteen, and she couldn't help the fact that men found her beautiful. She had black hair, the color of burnished ebony, coupled with green eyes to make a rather unusual but striking combination. Her face was dusted with a light spray of freckles, an effect which enhanced rather than detracted from her beauty. And as she pushed through the crowd to stand near the twin steel ribbons that connected Albuquerque with civilization, her full breasts and well-rounded derriere would attract awkward and seemingly accidental touches.

Miller Flowers, who had returned from the battle of Shiloh minus one leg, found that he was also a widower with an infant daughter to raise. He had been Reesa's sole parent since she was three months old, and he still looked upon her as a young, innocent child. Young she was, and thus far innocent as well. But Reesa was no child.

Despite the pinches and grabs she had to endure, there was an excitement to meeting the midnight train that Reesa relished. There was always a carnival atmosphere about the crowd: laughter, good-natured joking, the constant cry of drummers who hawked their wares to midnight customers, and, usually, music from guitars or an occasional band.

What Reesa liked best, however, was the approach of the engine. The whistle could be heard first, far off and mournful, a lonesome wail that never failed to send chills through her body.

"Here she comes," someone would shout, and the laughter and talking would grow subdued, as if everyone consciously gave the approaching train center stage.

Those gathered at the platform would move toward the track, and there was an increased sense of excitement in being pushed and shoved so close to the brink of disaster. Reesa would stare down the track, waiting for the train. The first thing to come into view would be the light, a huge, wavering, yellow disc, the gas flame and mirror reflector shining brightly in the distance. That sighting would be closely followed by the hollow sounds of puffing steam, like the gasps of some fire-breathing, serpentine monster. As if to add to the illusion, glowing sparks were whipped away in the black smoke clouds that billowed up into the night sky.

As the train pounded by, Reesa could feel her very body throb in rhythm with the engine's powerful beat. She watched the huge driver wheels, nearly as tall as she was, and the white wisps of steam that escaped from the thrusting piston rods, and she felt herself drawn to it as a woman is drawn to her lover. The engine rushed by, with sparks flying from the pounding drive wheels, and glowing hot embers dripping from its fire box. Then came the yellow squares of light that were the windows of the passenger cars. The cars would flash by, slowly, and finally grind to a halt with a shower of sparks and a hissing of air from the Westinghouse air brakes.

When the train was completely still, Reesa would stand there for a moment, feeling her body bewilderingly alive, yet hauntingly hollow, as if craving something more. It was a bittersweet sensation, and Reesa allowed herself to drift with its pleasurable waves, though a small, unheeded voice often cautioned against it.

After the train was completely stopped and the doors to the cars started coming open, the spell was broken. The train was no longer something sacrosanct, but had become an ordinary tool of commerce. Reesa came out of her reverie and walked along the side of the train, headed for the engine.

Sam Norton was the engineer, and as Reesa approached his cab, she could see through the window the maze of pipes and valves that were Sam's controls. She also saw Ollie, the big Swedish fireman. He was grimy with soot, and sweaty, and he breathed hard as he sat on a bench to grab a breath of fresh air and rest his powerful, but aching muscles.

"Hello, Miss Flowers," Sam called down.

"Hello, Sam," Reesa replied. "Did you have a nice trip?"

"We didn't get away from Trinidad until six-forty-five," Sam said.

"But you made it here on time. You must have really run fast."

"Sometimes better'n fifty-five miles per hour," Sam said proudly.

"Ve haf' the superintendent on board," Ollie said. "Sam vas showing off."

"Do you have our orders, girl?" Sam asked.

"Yes, here in this envelope," Reesa said. She strained and stretched, reaching up to hand the envelope to Sam. The action brought her dress tight against her body, and those who were standing nearby took visible notice of the curves, thus accented.

The envelope slipped from Reesa's fingers and bounced under the engine.

"Allow me, miss," a man's deep, resonant voice said.

The man who spoke was a stranger to Reesa. He was tall and dark, and well-dressed in a russet brown jacket and brown riding breeches tucked into highly polished boots. A ruffled shirt did nothing to hide his powerful chest, nor did the jacket detract from his broad shoulders. His eyes were a warm brown, and Reesa noticed with some surprise that they nearly matched the shade of his jacket. He had an easy smile and a handsome face, and Reesa couldn't

4

help but feel a quickening of her pulse as she looked at him. Her reaction surprised and frightened her somewhat, and she found that for a brief moment she couldn't speak. Finally she found her voice.

"I fear I'll cause you to soil your clothes, sir," Reesa said.

"Then I shall wear the grime as a medal of honor for having served you," the man replied. He handed the envelope to Reesa, then smiled as she stretched to hand it up to the engineer.

"You are staring, sir," Reesa said, flustered.

"Yes," the man answered easily. "And I'm enjoying every minute of it. Fully as much as you are, I suspect."

"Sir, you are impertinent!" Reesa exclaimed, indignantly, but her cheeks flamed in embarrassment, giving credence to the man's comment.

"I apologize; I meant no disrespect," the man said. "I was taken by your charming ways, and meant only to speak honestly. Please forgive me if I offended you."

"Miss Flowers, this here is Ted Foster," Sam said from the cab of his engine. "He's goin' to build this here railroad clear on to the Pacific Ocean."

"You're Ted Foster?" Reesa asked. For she had heard of him, as had everyone in Albuquerque. The news that a new railroad, the Southern Continental, was going to connect Albuquerque with Phoenix and San Diego, was on everyone's lips. But that a man so young could do all this? Ted Foster couldn't have been more than twenty-eight.

"I see you've heard of me," Ted said. "I also see that I don't come up to your expectations. You, on the other hand, are everything I was told you are."

"You've heard of me?"

"Of course," Ted said easily. "You are Reesa Flowers, the beautiful daughter of the man who is going to be my superintendent of station masters and telegraphers."

"What do you mean? Papa hasn't said anything about changing jobs. He has a good job with Western Pacific as station master of the Albuquerque Station."

"I'm sure your papa will want to work for me when I ask him," Ted said. "I intend to raise his salary to three times what he now makes. That should interest him, don't you think?"

Reesa drew in her breath. That would raise her father's salary to sixty dollars a week. At that rate he would be able to retire in one more year and go back to Missouri the way he'd always dreamed. Reesa had no personal desire to return to Missouri, but she wanted it for her father, since she knew that was what he lived for.

"Do you think your father would be interested?" Ted asked again.

"Oh, I'm sorry," Reesa said, when she realized he was talking to her and she was paying no attention. "Yes, yes, I think he would be."

"Fine. Perhaps you can intercede on my behalf if it becomes necessary."

A yard worker approached them and stood back quietly, waiting for recognition. Ted saw

6

him, smiled broadly, and stuck out his hand. "My name's Ted Foster," he said. "Who are you?"

"Arnold Blair, sir," the man replied, surprised that he had been asked. "I've come to tell you that your private car has been detached from the end of the train and pushed onto a sidetrack."

"Good. Thank you, Arnold. I appreciate that."

Reesa was impressed with the way Ted spoke to the man. Many, she knew, would have barely acknowledged him. They would have completely overlooked him as merely another piece of railroad equipment. Ted had taken the time to introduce himself, and learn the man's name, then use it.

"That was nice," she said after Arnold had left.

"It was nice of them to take care of it for me," Ted agreed.

"No, I meant that you took the time to speak with him."

"Friendliness is an investment, Miss Flowers," Ted said. "One which costs little, and often gives great returns. Like now, for example. I'd like to make a friendly gesture and invite you to join me in my car for a small drink before I turn in. Would you be interested?" Ted saw the shock in Reesa's eyes and he laughed. "No? Very well, then perhaps some other time. In the meantime, Miss Flowers, I bid you good night."

Ted gave a small bow, almost mocking in its

lack of movement, though made gracious by his style.

"Good night, Mr. Foster," Reesa said.

As Reesa left the train, the image of Ted Foster stayed with her. She could still see his broad chest and wide shoulders, and the even, white teeth that smiled at her from the tanned, handsome face.

Reesa's innocence went as far as her virginity. No man had known her, though there were many in Albuquerque who had privately vowed they would pay any price for the privilege. Reesa, though still a virgin, already knew herself to be a woman with a passionate nature. Sometimes, unbidden, erotic thoughts played their temptations in her mind. As she was completely without experience, there was no form or substance to these fantasies, but there was an insistent longing for something more.

There were even times when she secretly enjoyed the attention of the men in the crowd and their gropings, and took a measure of pride in the fact that she could stir men so. But such feelings were rare, and were always followed by a sense of guilt. Reesa was determined to dominate the sexual side of her nature. She realized that decent women were not ruled by their passions, but controlled by their minds, and she vowed to keep her lustful feelings in check.

But even as she thought of her determination to he pure of thought, she found herself thinking of Ted Foster. The throbbing feelings in her body that were stirred by the arrival of the engine seemed, somehow, to intermix with

8

thoughts of the handsome young man. She felt a spreading warmth in her body, and a weakness in her knees. No man had ever made her feel this way. What was it about this one that affected her so?

Chapter Two

Reesa braced herself for the onslaught of pinches and pats, then worked her way back through the crowd to the station house. She had learned long ago that it was much better to ignore them than to try to brush them away, because slapping at them only inspired the abuser to grab her wrist.

The station house to which Reesa was hurrying was a small, wooden building. In front there was the station master's office and waiting room, while in the rear there were small, but comfortable living quarters. That was home for Reesa and her father, and Reesa took a great deal of pride in making it an attractive place to live. She had bright splashes of color in the curtains and cushions, fresh flowers when she could get them, and Currier and Ives prints on the walls.

"I'm back, Papa," Reesa said cheerily, as she stepped into the front office. Miller Flowers, her father, was sitting at the telegrapher's table. The instrument was clicking, but Reesa, who had learned telegraphy from her father, knew that it wasn't important. It was only a time and line check, and needed no answer. One pants leg of Miller's trousers was flat, denoting an empty space. The leg that should have been there had been buried in the backyard of a small schoolhouse near Corinth, Mississippi, along with the thousands of other limbs lost during the battle of Shiloh.

"Papa, how many times do I have to tell you to keep that pants leg rolled up? When it flops loose like that, it could trip you and you could get hurt," Reesa said. She knelt in front of her father and began rolling up the pants leg.

"You're a fine broth of a daughter to be havin' around, Reesa Flowers," Miller said, rubbing his hand through her black hair affectionately. "Sure, 'n' 'tis a shame your poor ma never lived to see you become such a beautiful child."

"I'm no longer a child, Papa," Reesa replied. She thought of the feelings Ted Foster had stirred in her. Certainly those weren't the kind of feelings a child would have.

"Don't be in such a hurry to grow up, lassie," Miller cautioned. "Age comes upon a person soon enough without a body rushing it."

"The girl is right, Miller. She's full grown now," a voice said.

Reesa and her father looked up to see Superintendent Percival Bodkins standing in the doorway. He was forty-five, overweight, and balding. He carried a solid gold pocketwatch, and wore the fob stretched across his vest as a badge of rank. He had a leering eye and a lech-

11

erous smile, and frequently found excuses to stop by and "leave a message for Miller" when Reesa was there alone. Reesa remembered now that Ollie had said the superintendent had been on the train. She didn't like him. His very presence could make her feel uneasy.

"Superintendent Bodkins," Miller said in greeting. "I didn't know you were in town."

"Came in on the midnight train," Bodkins said. "I've some business discussions with Ted Foster tomorrow."

"Ted Foster?"

"He's here, Papa, in Albuquerque," Reesa said excitedly. "I just spoke to him."

Reesa wanted to tell her father about Ted's offer, but she had no desire to talk about it in front of Bodkins.

"Is he really going to extend the track on to San Diego? I thought Western Pacific was going to do that," she asked.

"Western Pacific has the exclusive right-of-way across the desert," Bodkins said. "It was granted to us by the United States government. But it would be foolish at this point for us to build out in the wasteland. So, we are going to allow young Ted Foster to try."

"I can't see Western Pacific just giving up like that," Miller said. "What's in it for them?"

"Ted Foster gets a grant of sixteen thousand dollars per mile for every mile of track he builds. We are giving up our right-of-way for one half of his government grant. In addition, we have exclusive shipping rights for all materials across our tracks, and extensive track rental agreements for equipment that stands on

12

Western Pacific property." Bodkins laughed. "There's not a chance in the world he can do the job."

"Then why is Western Pacific willing to sell him the right-of-way?" Reesa asked.

"Quite simple, my dear," Bodkins said. For every mile he does build, we will get eight thousand dollars."

"That doesn't sound fair," Reesa said.

"It's the way of business," Bodkins replied. He put a fat hand on Reesa's shoulder and squeezed. It made Reesa's flesh crawl. "It's a hard world you're growing into, girl."

Reesa twisted out of his hand, trying to make it look like the natural movement of walking over to the window. It wouldn't do to antagonize Bodkins unnecessarily, although if her father took Ted Foster's offer, then Bodkins could just go soak his head from now on as far as Reesa was concerned.

As Reesa thought of Ted Foster, the joy she had anticipated of telling her father of the job offer was deflated. If Bodkins was right, the dream of a new railroad would never be more than just that . . . a dream.

"Who brought the train in, lass?" Miller asked.

"Sam Norton."

Miller reached for his crutches. "I think I'll walk down and say a word or two to him. Sam 'n' I have been friends since we worked on the Cairo and Fulton Railroad in Missouri back before the war."

Reesa was afraid that Bodkins would hang on to talk to her if Miller left, so she yawned

13

and pretended sleepiness, though in fact she would have preferred staying awake until after the train left.

"I'm going to go on to bed, Papa," she said, yawning and stretching. "I'm really bushed."

"Well, I guess I'll see who's out and around," Bodkins said. "I hope it isn't too late to get a hotel room."

Reesa knew that Bodkins was hinting for Miller to invite him to stay with them and she held her breath.

"It's never too late," Miller said. "I'll find a place for you. They've always got room for one more in the hotel."

"Good night, Papa," Reesa said with a thankful smile.

"Good night, my darlin'," Miller answered. The twinkle in his eyes told Reesa that he had understood her plight, and had taken care of it.

After the two men left, Reesa turned down the lantern, then went into her bedroom just off the office. She undressed in the dark so she could look through the window at the train without being seen.

The train was surrounded by people, and the windows of the cars shone bright yellow. Inside there were people moving about, and she wondered about them—who they were, and where they had been.

Almost unbidden, Reesa's eyes traveled down the length of the train and over to the switch track. There she saw the long, nearly dark shape of Ted Foster's private car. A dim light glowed from a shaded window at one end. His bedroom? Reesa pictured him in his bed, perhaps dressed in a silk smoking jacket, having a drink and looking over the reports and papers on his new adventure. It was very exciting, and she wondered what it would be like to be there with him, lying under silk sheets and snuggled up next to him.

Reesa's face flushed hot. Had she actually thought that? She closed her eyes tightly and forced the image out of her mind.

Reesa turned from the window and walked over to her bed. She slipped the camisole off, and for just a second felt the silken sensation of the air against her nude body. It was a pleasant, sensual and, Reesa knew, unnatural feeling. She reached for the nightgown, reluctantly but with a sense of propriety, and started to put it on.

Suddenly her bedroom door opened.

"Well, hello, Reesa," Bodkins's bulk nearly filled the doorway. He looked at her naked body, clearly visible in the dim light from the lamp in the office, yet made even more mysterious and beautiful by the subtle shadows the lighting evoked. The spade of red hair at the junction of her legs picked up the light from the lamp and glowed, as if concealing a well-banked fire. The effect was startling to Bodkins and he stared pointedly.

"What are you doing here?" Reesa gasped. For a moment she was too shocked, too frightened, to cover herself.

"I was looking for your father," Bodkins said. He came on into the room, his eyes still riveted to that most intimate spot.

15

"Well, he isn't here," Reesa snapped. She slipped the nightgown over her head.

"I'm sorry," Bodkins said. "I thought perhaps he would be."

Bodkins made no effort to leave. In fact, he came even closer to her and Reesa could hear the wheezing of his breath. In the dim light she could see a thin line of perspiration beads on his upper lip.

"You can see that he isn't here, so would you please leave?" she demanded indignantly. How dare this buffoon invade her bedroom!

"Am I disturbing you?" Bodkins asked inanely.

"Yes. As you can see, I'm about to go to bed."

"Alone?" Bodkins asked, giving a short laugh as if making a joke.

"Mr. Bodkins, please," Reesa said, fear beginning to creep into her voice. "Go away now. What would your wife think if she saw you? Or your daughter? Your daughter is as old as I am."

"She's one year older," Bodkins said automatically. He reached out for her, but she drew back quickly. She moved between the bed and the wall, then realized her mistake. She was trapped there.

"I can make things nice for your father," Bodkins said, almost pleading. "And for you," he added. "I can give you nice things if you will do nice things for me."

"Please don't touch me," Reesa said quietly.

"Just be nice to me," Bodkins said again. "Do nice things for me, and I'll do nice things for you. We'll make each other feel good." He started toward her, moving in between the bed and the wall, keeping her trapped. Reesa saw a bulge in the front of his pants, and he started undoing the buttons of his trousers.

"Mr. Bodkins, my father will be back any second."

"No, he won't," Bodkins said breathlessly. "He and Sam Norton are having coffee in the restaurant. It's one hour before the train leaves, and your dad will be there that long, at least."

"You planned this!" Reesa gasped, suddenly realizing the fact.

"Yes," Bodkins said. "I planned it. I've watched you, I've seen how you flaunt your body around, showing off your young flesh, driving men mad. And now I aim to do something about it."

"No, get away from me!"

"What do you want? Money? I'll give you money. How much do you want? Ten dollars? Twenty? One hundred? You name it and it's yours."

Reesa's eyes were drawn like a magnet to the front of Bodkins's pants. His fingers released the buttons, then went inside. The palms of Reesa's hands grew sweaty, and she held her breath in fear . . . and fascination, waiting . . . waiting for what?

"Look what I've got for you, girl," Bodkins said.

He held it in his hand, a one-eyed serpent, fascinating and ugly, revolting—yet tempting.

"No," she said, quietly. "Please, Mr. Bodkins, don't do this."

Bodkins moved to her, then put his hand on the neck of her sleeping garment. He started to pull it away.

"Please, don't tear it," she cried.

"Then take it off, girl," he ordered.

Reesa was unable to control her shaking. It was caused by fear, yes, but there was something else, another emotion just as violent. It was excitement!

Reesa closed her eyes and began removing her gown. With her eyes closed, she couldn't see the pallid, sweating face of the man in front of her. In her mind's eye, the man who stood there was not Bodkins, but Ted Foster! The soft, night air caressed her skin, turning it to silk. Her nipples hardened quickly, and she felt a warm dampness starting from within.

No! I will not let this happen! I am not like this!

The words were a piercing scream . . . to Reesa only. For they were formed in her mind and never given voice with her tongue.

Reesa felt Bodkins against her. His hands found her breasts, and though they were clammy, awkward and inept, she imagined them to be Ted's hands, and her own long-smoldering, barely controlled hungers caused her body to react with a response that both thrilled and frightened her.

Bodkins was pushing against her, trying to gain entrance into her tight opening.

For a moment, Reesa's mind regained control

18

of her passions and she held her legs together, refusing to help him. But even while fighting against him, the banked fires threatened to break out, and she felt the overwhelming need of her body beginning to overcome the dictates of her mind.

There was no skill or finesse on Bodkins's part. He was still clumsily trying to effect penetration when it happened. Suddenly, and unexpectedly, a quick, sharp, spasm of pleasure racked Reesa's body. It was small and not accomplished under anything like the conditions of her fantasies, but it was the first and therefore bewildering and satisfying, wonderful and frightening, all at the same time. She shuddered violently.

"Quit struggling against me, girl," Bodkins demanded through clenched teeth.

Thank heavens he doesn't know! Reesa said to herself.

Somehow she found the strength to push him away, and her sudden shove caught him by surprise. He fell against the foot of the bed, and she took the opportunity to run from the corner where she was trapped.

"'Allo, Sam, by gum, you be in there now?" a voice called from outside.

Reesa recognized the voice. It was Ollie, the fireman who had come in on the midnight train. "It's Ollie," she said, a smile of relief passing over her face.

Bodkins, who had stood up from the bed, now stopped in his tracks. A look of fear came into his eyes. He turned toward the door nervously

19

and Reesa saw a sudden deflating of his manhood.

"You'd better leave now, Mr. Bodkins," she said quietly.

"He'll go away when he doesn't find Sam," Bodkins whispered.

"Leave now, or I'll scream. Ollie is my friend, and he is a very strong man."

"Sam, vere you be?" Ollie shouted again.

"You wouldn't scream," Bodkins said. "I could make it very difficult for your father."

Reesa drew in a breath, preparatory to screaming.

"All right, all right, you've made your point," Bodkins said. "I'm leaving."

"Perhaps you'd best tell Ollie where Sam is," Reesa said. "And don't come back, for I shall be sleeping with a gun," she warned.

Bodkins finished rebuttoning his pants. He started to leave, but just as he got to the door he turned to look at her. He tried to salvage some face. "I don't think you'll be too good for me when the time comes to review your father's performance. His promotion depends on the review I give him. You'll be beggin' me for it then, little Miss High and Mighty."

After Bodkins left, Reesa locked the door, then returned to fall across her bed. She did not put her gown back on, but lay there in the dark, in the nude. Her heart was pounding furiously as she realized how close she had come. It was a realization that terrified her.

And fascinated her.

And disgusted her.

What was it about her body that betrayed

her resolve? Why, even with such a revolting person as Percival Bodkins, was the cold cloud of fear edged with the white hot fires of desire?

Chapter Three

Reesa said nothing about Bodkins to her father at breakfast the next morning. But she did talk to him about Ted Foster.

I'm afraid the lad's in for a bit o' disappointment," Miller said.

"Why?"

"Bodkins is right. Without money to develop the land, he'll lose it. It's a shame to see such dreams go for naught."

"Maybe he can do it," Reesa suggested.

"No, lass. There's just no way. And besides, what has your interest so aroused?" Miller asked. He smiled. "Oh, you did say you saw him. He must be a handsome man."

Reesa blushed and looked at her plate. Her father had been closer to the truth than he realized.

"It's just that he's going to offer you a job," she said.

"Ted Foster is going to offer me a job?" Miller asked in amazement. "As what?"

"As superintendent of the line. And he'll pay

you three times what you are making now,"
Reesa said.

"Three times you say? Faith, 'n' 'tis a shame
the lad can't afford to do it. For that would be
a fine job, I'm thinkin'."

"Perhaps he can, Papa," Reesa said. "If what
I've heard of Ted Foster is true, he isn't likely
to be the kind of man who would throw money
away."

"He's a dreamer, lass," Miller said. "And
sometimes a dreamer becomes so blinded with
the glory of his vision that he loses sight of the
reality. 'Tis dangerous to get caught up in another man's dreams."

The telegraph instrument started clicking,
and Reesa recognized the call.

"Do you want me to take the message,
Papa?"

Miller laughed. "Sure 'n' if someone saw you
handlin' my instrument now, I'd be out a job
for teachin' a woman the science. You pour me
another cup of coffee, lass, 'n' I'll take the message."

Miller walked over to the table where the instrument sat, and flashed back a message that
he was ready to receive. Reesa poured another
cup of coffee and took it to her father, then
stood by him as the message came clacking over
the wire:

Message to Ted Foster from Titus Le-
land/ stop/ Agree to the terms you pro-
pose/ stop/ Will provide such financial
backing as is required to make the railroad
a reality/ stop/ As per our agreement am

sending my son Warren as liaison between us/ stop/ Good luck on our new venture/ stop/ Titus Leland.

"Papa, Titus Leland?" Reesa asked.

"That's what the message says," Miller replied.

"Isn't he that rich banker from San Francisco?"

"Honey, he's much more than just a rich banker. He is one of the richest men in the country. Maybe in the world."

"If he's going to back Ted Foster, then Bodkins is wrong, and Ted Foster does have a chance, doesn't he?"

"I'd say a very good chance," Miller said. He rubbed his chin and looked at the message again, reading it over for the second time. "I'm afraid I'd better tell Bodkins of this. Western Pacific should know about it."

"Why?"

"Don't you see, darlin'? Western Pacific figured that Ted Foster would go broke. I don't think they would have let their right-of-way go if they thought he had a chance."

"In other words, they were trying to cheat Ted Foster, but they are winding up by cheating themselves. Is that it?" Reesa asked.

"I wouldn't put it that way," Miller said mildly.

"Why not?"

Miller scratched his head. "It was just a smart business move."

"Well, Mr. Foster is evidently smarter than

Mr. Bodkins and the Western Pacific," Reesa said.

"I still think I should tell. After all, I'm an employee of Western Pacific."

"You are now. But you are about to become an employee of Southern Continental," Reesa said. "Besides, this message was a commercial message. You are under no obligation to Western Pacific."

Miller tapped his fingers on the table, then looked up at Reesa and smiled. "You are right." He folded the message over and put it in an envelope, then handed it to Reesa. "Would you like to deliver it, darlin'?"

"Yes, I think I would," Reesa said. "And when he asks me if you'll go to work for him, what shall I say?"

"Tell him to come see me," Miller said. "I'll listen to any man's offer."

The wires that were connected to Miller Flowers's telegraph instrument ran up the wall of the station house, then out through a small hole where they attached to a tall telegraph pole. The pole was one of many. Some ran north, along the spur line to Santa Fe. Others ran east along the main track, leading back to Trinidad, where connections were made with Kansas City and points east, or, Denver and points west. The poles stretched for as far as the eye could see, until they were only black dots in the distance.

The twin steel ribbons of track, and the graceful curving of the copper wires between the poles, cut across the desert and mountains,

25

visible evidence of man's invasion. They crossed miles of uninhabited country, and it was very easy for someone to make minor alterations without being seen. Thus it was that a totally unauthorized wire branched off the telegraph poles at an unobserved spot. That wire ran over a system of poles not quite as uniform as the official line, but every bit as effective. The unauthorized line stretched over cactus and rock, through mountain pass and along canyons, until it reached a fertile valley wherein stood a well-ordered ranch known as Rancho Sombra de las Montanas.

Rancho Sombra de las Montanas was the ranch of Don Esteban de Mendoza, the eighth generation Mendoza to occupy the land, on an original land grant made in the year 1610 by Don Pedro de Peralta, third governor of New Mexico. When New Mexico was ceded to the United States, the validity of the original Spanish land grant was questioned, and some of the land was set aside to be given or sold to the railroads. Don Esteban looked on the deal with misgivings. He wrote a strong letter to the United States government and to the president of Western Pacific Railroad, when they began surveying route right-of-ways through his land. The letter was ignored.

Don Esteban was sixty-three years old, and the letter was the strongest form of protest he could manage. But his son, Joaquin, was only twenty-seven, and capable of a much stronger protest. Joaquin had fought for one year in the New Mexico border guards against marauding Indians and bandits who would strike across the border, then retreat back into Mexico. He was a skilled and brave warrior; and it was not in his hot, Latin blood to stand by impotently, while his land was invaded by the railroad magnates of the east.

Rancho Sombra de las Montanas consisted of a main building and several smaller ones. The main building was large and brown, with a red tile roof. A cloister with an arched colonnade stretched from the main house to one of the smaller buildings, and the telegraph line ran into that building where it attached to an instrument. The message that had been received by Miller Flowers was also received by this instrument.

"Joaquin, the message says that the new man, Ted Foster, will have money for his railroad," the telegraph operator said. He handed the message to the handsome Mexican, one of several men who stood behind him.

"*Carajole*," Joaquin swore. "Now we have a new enemy."

"Perhaps the new man can be reasoned with."

"There is no reasoning with the *yanquis* who build the roads," Joaquin said. He crumbled the message in his fist and tossed it to one side.

"Let us destroy the track before the train can bring the new money," someone suggested.

"No," Joaquin said. "The track that they now have does not violate our land. We are sworn only to keep our land from being violated, not destroy that which doesn't offend us."

"But in so doing, we can prevent the money

27

from reaching them, and prevent the new track from being laid," the man reasoned.

"No," Joaquin said. "I don't like that idea."

"Why don't you just take the money?" a woman's voice said.

The men turned to see a beautiful young woman, who stood in the doorway. She had the same flashing black eyes and dark rings of hair as Joaquin, though her hair was much longer and fell in soft folds across her shoulders. Her name was Frederica, and she was Joaquin's sister.

"*Si,* just take the money," one of the men laughed. "It is not that easy."

"Why not? If it comes on a special train, we will know of it," Frederica said. She pointed to the telegraph set.

"My sister has a point," Joaquin said. "Perhaps, we *could* take the money."

"*Caramba,* you mean rob the train?" one of the men asked.

"Yes," Joaquin said. "I think this could be done."

"*Ah, chijuajua,* what a victory this would be over the *yanquis!*" one of the men said excitedly. "Let's do it."

"We will," Joaquin said. "But first, I must ride into Albuquerque. I want to have a look around."

Chapter Four

Reesa stood on the platform at the rear of the special car Ted Foster was using and knocked on the door. She waited for a few minutes, knocked a second time, and called his name. There was still no response. As she started to leave, she heard a noise from within . . . as if someone were scurrying about.

"Just a minute." The voice was muffled, but it was clearly Ted.

Reesa felt embarrassed. Ted Foster was obviously still in bed, probably tired from the long trip. She should have shown more discretion than to come over at this early hour. Besides, it made it appear as if she were anxious, and that was unbecoming a lady.

Reesa wished she could just leave quietly. But the fact that he had answered her made that impossible. She was stuck with the situation, and waited self-consciously.

The door opened and Ted's face peered through the crack. When he saw Reesa he smiled.

"Why, Miss Flowers, how nice of you to call," he said. He opened the door wide and stepped back into the room. "Won't you come in?"

Reesa knew that it would have been more proper for her to just hand him the telegram and leave, but she was consumed with curiosity, so she accepted the invitation. In spite of herself, she gasped when she saw the inside of Ted's private car. She had seen living quarters on wheels before, mostly crew quarters, but never had she seen anything like this. The end of the car where she stood was the living room-dining room. It was paneled in mahogany, hung with rich, red velours draperies, lighted with a crystal chandelier and carpeted with a plush, maroon carpet.

"What do you think?" Ted asked, amused by her look of wonder.

"I've never seen anything like it," Reesa said finally.

Ted smiled. "I don't want you to get the wrong impression of me. I'm not this much of a dandy. But I ramrodded construction on the Central Mountain and brought the road in three months ahead of schedule. This private car was my bonus. It's a bit gaudy for my tastes, and not all that practical, but a man has to live somewhere. Perhaps you've reconsidered my offer?"

"Your offer?" Reesa asked, puzzled by the remark.

"For a drink."

"At this hour? Besides, this isn't a social call, Mr. Foster," Reesa said, feeling a blush stain her cheeks. Somehow she had a feeling that he knew what thoughts she had about him, and his easy confidence irritated her. She had to fight against the feelings in her body, but he took everything with ease. It was unfair.

"If it isn't a social call, Miss Flowers, then what can I do for you?"

"I have a telegram for you."

"Who is it, honey?" a woman's voice called from another room.

A woman? Could it be that Ted was married? She had never heard it mentioned. Surely he wouldn't have invited her for a drink last night if he was married? But if not his wife, who was she?

A door opened and a woman came into the room. She was very pretty in a showy sort of way. She looked to be in her early thirties, with bright blonde hair and blue eyes. She was wearing more makeup than Reesa had ever seen on a woman, and even from across the room Reesa could smell the perfume.

"I'm sorry I took so long, honey," the woman said to Ted. "I was having a bit of difficulty." She looked at Reesa and gave her a flashing smile. "Well, Ted, I must say you work fast. Who is this charming creature?"

"Sally, I'd like you to meet Reesa Flowers," Ted said. "Miss Flowers, this is Sally Millet. Sally stopped by to welcome me here. She's an old friend."

"I'm right pleased to meet you, honey," Sally said. She stuck her hand out and grabbed Reesa's in a firm handshake. She looked Reesa over approvingly. "Say, hon, you aren't looking for a job, are you?"

"No," Ted said quickly. "She's not for you, Sally."

"That's too bad," Sally said, walking around and looking at Reesa as someone would look over a prize horse. "It seems the further west we get, the harder the pretty ones are to come by. I could use her."

"I don't understand," Reesa said. "What kind of job?"

"I run a . . ." Sally started.

Ted cleared his throat and spoke quickly. "An entertainment palace," he said. "You know, girls who sing songs . . . that sort of thing."

"Oh, no," Reesa said. "I don't think I'd do very well. It's all I can do to carry a tune."

Sally smiled. "You're probably right. This wouldn't be the type of work for you. Perhaps you'd better forget that I even asked you." She turned to Ted. "I must be going," she said. "I agree to your terms. I don't like them, but I agree to them. I'd rather have you on my side than against me. How soon can I get started?"

"I hope to get construction underway this week," Ted said. "By the end of next week, End-of-Track will be thirty miles from here, at least. You can begin then."

"Thank you," Sally said. She took a hat from the table beneath a gilt-edged mirror and put it on, looking into the glass to adjust it. She pursed her lips several times and checked the heavy application of lip rouge. Reesa stared at her, fascinated by the woman. Finally, with a smile and a wave, Sally Millet left.

"I'm sorry," Ted said as the door closed behind her. "But Mrs. Millet and I had some business to attend to."

"Mrs. Millet? You mean she's married?"

"Widowed. Her husband was a gambler who had a bad habit of playing poker with five aces. Bad habits can kill you, and his did."

"I've never seen hair that color yellow before," Reesa said. She gasped as if suddenly realizing something. "You don't suppose she *dyes* it, do you?"

Ted laughed. "I'm quite certain she does. Why?"

Reesa pulled the window drapery to one side and saw Sally climbing into an expensive looking phaeton, driven by a liveried driver.

"You said you have a telegram for me?"

"Oh, yes," Reesa said. She shoved her hand into her pocket and pulled out the telegram.

"Thank you," Ted said. He took it from her and pitched it carelessly onto a nearby table.

"Aren't you going to read it?"

"What for?"

"Because. It may be important. It *is* important," she sputtered, then she flushed with embarrassment for having disclosed that she knew the telegram's contents.

"I don't need to read it," Ted said. "I already know it's from Titus Leland. He has wired me his decision, so I assume he has agreed to back me. Had he decided otherwise, a letter would have been quick enough to suit him."

Ted was opening a bottle of wine as he spoke,

and he poured two glasses, then handed one to Reesa.

"Wine, at this time of the morning?" she said again.

"There are men of medicine who recommend a glass of wine for breakfast," Ted replied. "Besides, this is a celebration of sorts. Surely you wouldn't make me celebrate alone?"

Ted touched his glass to Reesa's, and the glasses gave a cheery ring. He smiled at her, and she felt a quick, dizzying excitement akin to that which she experienced when she first saw him. She tightened her grip on the glass and took a deep breath to fight away the dizziness. "No, Mr. Foster," she said quietly. "I won't make you celebrate alone."

The wine was light and dry, and had a very pleasant bouquet.

"Did you tell your father of my offer?"

"Yes."

"What did he say?"

"He will listen to you, Mr. Foster."

"It's Ted," he said, holding the bottle of wine over Reesa's glass.

Reesa covered the glass with her hand and smiled. "No, Mr. Foster, I don't care for anymore, thank you. I'll celebrate with you, but I'll not get tipsy."

Ted pulled the bottle back and poured another for himself. "Then will you strike a bargain?"

"What sort of bargain?"

"I'll not try and get you tipsy if you'll call me Ted."

"In due time, Mr. Foster. In due time."

Reesa finished her glass of wine, then set it on the table. "I really must be going," she said. "I must admit that I felt excited for you when I read that you were going to get the backing you need."

"Then he *did* agree," Ted said, letting out a sigh of relief.

"Why, yes, of course. I thought you knew. I mean the celebration and all," Reesa said, confusion showing on her face.

Ted gave a slow, amost embarrassed smile. "The truth is, Ressa, I was too nervous to look. I just ran a bluff, figuring that if I was wrong, you'd tell me." He laughed. "This is great! I mean really great!" He poured himself a third glass, then offered to pour another for her. "Have one more. This time for real."

"No, one is enough," Reesa said. "Besides, we have a bargain now, remember, Ted?"

"Right you are," Ted agreed. He drained the glass, then set it down and rubbed his hands together briskly. "Well, I've much to do today. And I intend to start with your father. Please tell him that I shall call on him this morning."

As Reesa turned to leave, she glanced through the door from which Sally Millet had emerged. Beyond it was the bedroom, and in full view was the bed, very obviously mussed.

"Oh, that's the bedroom?" Reesa asked in surprise.

"Yes, would you like to see it?"

"Certainly not," Reesa answered in a huff. "I should think one woman in your bedroom in a morning would be enough."

For reasons she couldn't understand, Reesa

suddenly felt a stirring of jealousy. It made her react more sharply than she had intended. After all, she certainly had no claim on what Ted Foster did. Why did it bother her this way?

"I'm sorry you are offended," Ted apologized quietly. "I wish Sally and I had concluded our business earlier so she could have been gone by the time you arrived."

"Business? You call that business?"

"I don't. Sally does," Ted said. "She's a prostitute."

After Reesa left Ted Foster's private car, she walked along the wooden train platform, fighting the stinging in her eyes, trying to keep the tears of anger from welling. How dare he humiliate her that way?

What way? her reason asked. After all, it was she who barged into his house at this early hour. Whatever he was doing, it had nothing to do with her. So why was she so angry?

But Reesa couldn't reason clearly, because reason and logic went hand and in hand. And right now Reesa had put logic aside to be ruled by emotion. Emotion, and those uncontrollable and frightening passions that ruled her body.

Four regular trains daily made the run into Albuquerque: at midnight, nine A.M., noon, and four P.M. It was nearly time for the nine A.M. train, and already a large crowd had gathered at the platform.

The coming of a train, any train, was a public event in Albuquerque. Trains brought visitors, friends and relatives. They brought mail, mail order goods, newspapers and treasures. They were visible proof that Albuquerque, so far from everything, was not totally isolated from the world.

Reesa had observed that the composition of the crowd around each train was unique and identifiable. She believed that she could tell which train was coming, without seeing a clock, just by observing the behavior of the crowds.

The midnight train was the most exciting . . . the crowd was gayer and noisier, as if the coming of the train was the feature attraction at a gala party. The day train-watchers were more business-minded—merchants waiting for their wares, businessmen waiting for appointments—and though there were always vendors selling to the midnight crowd, there were even more during the day.

There was a crowd gathered around one of the vendors: a patent medicine man. Reesa drifted over to watch him and listen to his pitch. He was tall and thin, and wearing a black suit that was badly in need of a cleaning. His long, bony finger jabbed at the air as he spoke.

"Yes, ladies and gentlemen, I have come bearing a new miracle drug that will work wonders for all illnesses. If you suffer from ulceration of the kidneys, loss of memory, weak nerves, hot hands, flushing in the body, consumption, torpidity of the liver, costiveness, hot spells, bearing down feelings, or cancer, this marvelous Extract Buchu will be your salvation. And here is something else this drug will do that no other can. Ladies, do you find that in the secrecy of your own bed at night, you have inability to control your thoughts? These impure thoughts can often lead to solitary practices against nature. And it is a well-known fact that such sinful practices lead to the diseases of dyspepsia, debility of thought, and insanity. If you are having a difficult time controlling lascivious thoughts, Extract Buchu will aid you. How about you, girl? Can I sell you a bottle? Only one dollar."

The medicine man pointed his accusing, bony finger directly at Reesa, and her cheeks flushed hot.

"No," she said. "Certainly not."

Reesa left the crowd with cheeks and ears burning. How could he know what thoughts went through her mind? She knew what he meant by solitary practices against nature. There were times when a strange, sweet aching in her loins called out for something. Until last night, she had never done anything about it. Then last night, even while fighting Bodkins off, her passions had taken control of her body, and she had a glimpse of the forbidden pleasures. She realized that in a way, what she had experienced last night was what he was talking about. But would it lead to insanity?

She didn't know, but it was frightening to contemplate. Fortunately, the whistle of the arriving train interrupted Reesa's disquieting thoughts.

Chapter Five

Murdock Felton was a huge man. He stood six feet, nine inches tall and weighed two hundred and eighty-five pounds. He had flaming red hair and a bushy beard of the same color. His legs were like tree trunks, and his arms larger around than most men's legs. He was section foreman the time the Central Pacific laid ten miles of track in a single day to set the record, and his name was spoken in work camps from the Mississippi to the Pacific. He stepped off the train right in front of Reesa and looked around with a bemused expression on his face.

"You, girl," he said when he saw her. "Would you know where to find Ted Foster?"

Reesa had never seen anyone as large, and she stared in silence for a moment before she replied. Murdock realized that he was awe-inspiring to most people, so he just laughed and held his hand out, spreading the palm open for her.

"This big mitt would make three of yours, I

reckon," he said good-naturedly. "When the good Lord started makin' me, he just didn't know when to stop."

"Oh, I'm sorry," Reesa said, suddenly realizing that she had been staring. "You wanted to know where Mr. Foster is?"

"Yes, ma'am."

"He's in his private car." She pointed to Ted's car, which stood on a side switch.

"Thank you kindly, ma'am," Murdock said. He started through the crowd toward the switch, and Reesa watched him for several seconds. He wasn't swallowed up by the crowd; his head and shoulders stuck up above everyone else's and he moved through as if he were wading in a pond.

"What is Murdock Felton doing here?" a voice asked.

Reesa turned to see Superintendent Bodkins.

"I don't know," she said. Suddenly she remembered the incident of the night before and her face flushed. She turned away.

"About last night," Bodkins began.

"I've no wish to talk about it," Reesa said.

"It was unfortunate that Ollie came along when he did," Bodkins went on. "I'll see to it that we have no such interruptions in the future."

"There won't be a future," Reesa said.

"I think maybe there will be." Bodkins smiled evilly. "You do want your papa to keep his job, don't you? Besides, I can see it in your eyes. You're wantin' it awful bad, girl. You're achin' inside from the wantin' of it. It might as well be me as someone else that gives it to you."

40

"You pig!" Reesa spat, slapping him across the face. Her violent reaction surprised even her, and way down, deep inside, she knew that it was because Bodkins had spoken the truth.

The sound of the slap was loud, and several people turned to look. Bodkins put his hand up to his face and rubbed it gingerly. He could still feel the sting of her blow, and he knew that her hand had left its mark.

"You're playin' with fire, girl," he hissed. "I could have your father's job in an instant."

"You pathetic little worm," Reesa taunted. "Do you think that job holds sway over us? For your information, my father intends to be submitting his resignation to you today."

Reesa regretted saying it almost as soon as the words came out. She put her hand to her mouth as if in so doing she could call the statement back. But it was too late, for the damage had been done.

Bodkins smiled, a slow, evil smile. "That's fine," he said. "See to it that you are all moved out by noon. The rooms where you live belong to Western Pacific, you know."

"By noon? That's impossible, where will we go?"

"You made your bed, girl. But you wouldn't sleep in it." Bodkins laughed at his twist of the metaphor.

Reesa turned away, tears burning her eyes. Why had she spoken out? Now her father had no job, and they had no place to live. It was all her fault.

"Remember, girl, if your papa isn't out of there by noon, I'll have the sheriff run him out," Superintendent Bodkins's voice called after her.

Reesa worked her way through the crowd of people, fighting the urge to cry, blinking rapidly to try and keep the tears in. Here and there she recognized someone and tried to return a greeting, but for the most part she thought only of getting back to the safety of her house. Her house? It's the Western Pacific's house, she thought bitterly.

"Hello, darlin'," Miller greeted when Reesa returned. "Say, look on the table in the kitchen. We got a case of those canned peaches in the mail order. Why don't we have some at noon?"

When she heard her father say the word noon, Reesa could no longer keep it inside. She began crying in earnest.

"Reesa, darlin', what is it?"

Reesa went to her father's chair, then dropped to her knees beside him. She leaned her head against him and wept as if there were no end to her tears.

"Lass, here now, what could be botherin' you so?"

"Papa, we won't be here at noon. I did a terrible thing."

"What?" he asked, stroking her hair.

"I . . . I told Bodkins you would be resigning your position and he got mad. He said we had to be out of our house by noon today."

Miller sighed and rubbed Reesa's head affectionately, comfortingly. "Sure now, lass, 'n' if I did decide to take up young Ted Foster's offer, don't you think by rights it should have been me tell the superintendent?"

42

"I know," Reesa cried, "but I couldn't help it. When he told me you would lose your job anyway if I didn't . . . uh . . . I . . . uh, got angry and the words just came out." She had started to tell her father, then thought better of it.

"If you didn't what?" Miller said, picking up on it immediately.

"Nothing," Reesa said. She wiped her tears away and forced herself to stop crying. "I was just upset, that's all."

Miller moved his hands to the side of Reesa's head and turned it so that she was looking at him. "Tell me, girl, did he make an indecent advance?"

"It's nothing, Papa. It's all over now," she said.

"That bastard!" Miller said. He stood up and grabbed his crutches. "I'm going to have a word with him."

"Papa, no, please," Reesa said. "Leave it alone. Nothing happened."

"What do you mean, nothing happened?" Miller asked, his voice raised now in anger. "*Something* happened. Something bad enough to bring you home in tears. And I intend to have words with the man."

"Please, Papa, you'll be hurt. You know you can't . . . "

"Can't what?" Miller replied. He looked at Reesa. "Honey, I left my leg at Shiloh, not my manhood."

"Please, no; don't go see him," Reesa said. She grabbed him, but Miller pulled away, gently though firmly.

43

"Darlin', I will do this," he said. "If you've no wish to watch, you stay here." He moved quickly through the door, and Reesa watched him through tear-dimmed eyes as he swung angrily on his crutches, hurrying along the station platform, bound toward the crowd to seek out Superintendent Bodkins.

A moment after Miller Flowers left, Reesa heard the door to the front office open, and a voice called for her father. She left her bedroom to see who it was.

"Well, Reesa," Ted Foster said. "It's nice to see you again. Is your father in?"

"Oh, Ted," she cried impulsively. "Ted, you've got to help . . . please!"

"Help? Of course; what is it?"

"It's Papa. He's gone to call out Superintendent Bodkins. I think he's going to challenge him to a fight."

"A fight? Then I take it he's ready to leave his job and work for me?" Ted asked.

"Yes."

"That would hardly call for a fight."

"That's not the reason for it," Reesa said. "It's because Bodkins tried to . . . " She hesitated, too embarrassed to tell him.

"Tried to what?"

"I'd rather not say," Reesa replied. She felt her cheeks burning.

"Never mind, Reesa. You don't have to say. I can read it in your face. I don't blame your father. It's right that he should stand up for your honor."

"My honor be damned!" Reesa shouted. "Don't you know my father only has one leg?

44

And Bodkins is younger? He *can't* fight Bodkins!"

"Evidently he feels that he can," Ted said.

"Oh, Ted, please . . . go stop him. Talk to Bodkins."

"Reesa, I couldn't do that to your father. This is his fight. He'd never forgive me if I interfered."

"Oh, my god, what's happening? Has everyone gone mad?" Reesa said.

"I'll tell you what I'll do. I'll go keep an eye on him. I won't let your father be seriously hurt. But I won't fight his fight."

"Wait, I'm going with you," Reesa said.

It wasn't difficult to find them. The crowd at the station had gathered in a large circle, and there was little doubt as to what was going on inside.

"Hurry," Reesa urged.

"Didn't your daughter get the message right?" they heard Bodkins say as they approached. "I want you out of here by noon."

Reesa and Ted forced their way through the crowd until they stood near the large circle that had been formed by the onlookers. Bodkins and Miller Flowers were facing each other inside the circle. Miller Flowers was tall and lean, his leanness intensified by the fact that he had only one leg. Miller's eyes flashed in anger as he stared at Bodkins.

Bodkins was about five years younger than Miller, and forty pounds heavier. And Bodkins had two good legs. He was smiling confidently, almost eagerly, tauntingly.

"Apologize for your treatment of my daughter, sir," Miller demanded quietly.

"Your daughter is a tramp, Flowers," Bodkins said. "I've no intention of apologizing for anything she may have alleged that I said or did."

Miller brought his left hand up quickly, then slashed it across Bodkins's face in a wicked backhand smash. The blow surprised and stunned Bodkins, and a trickle of blood began coming from his nose. "You . . . you one-legged son-of-a-bitch," Bodkins sputtered. "You think I'm going to let half a man get away with that?"

Bodkins swung at Miller, but Miller caught Bodkins's wrist in his hand. He began squeezing, and Bodkins let out a surprised yelp of pain, then gradually was forced to his knees by the strength of Miller's grip.

"As you can see, Mr. Bodkins, I may have only one leg, but there is nothing wrong with my grip," Miller said.

It was only then that those in the crowd realized that years of supporting himself with crutches had given Miller Flowers' upper torso great strength. They had thought, like Bodkins, that the lack of a leg would render Miller completely helpless. But they, like Bodkins, were wrong.

Bodkins was on his knees now, gasping in pain.

"You apologize, sir," Miller said quietly, "or I will break this arm."

"I apologize," Bodkins said through clenched teeth. "I'm sorry; please let go of me."

46

Miller let go of the whimpering superintendent, then stepped back. "I'll be off Western Pacific property by noon, sir," he said.

As Miller turned to walk away, a cheer rose from the crowd.

"Thank God, he wasn't hurt," Reesa said.

"You do not do justice to your father," Ted replied.

Reesa and Ted turned to follow Miller, and didn't see the signal that passed between Bodkins and two rough-looking characters who were standing in the crowd. They also didn't see the two men drift away and start toward the station house.

But one huge, red-headed man did see them, and he started walking, slowly, just behind them.

The two men waited until they were free of the crowd, then they darted across a switch track whereon stood a line of empty boxcars. They ran on silent feet behind the line of cars, then emerged at the far end, perfectly positioned to waylay Miller Flowers as he returned to his house.

The big red-headed man came up behind the line of cars, moving as silently as had the men before him. He reached the end, then stood there quietly, watching the two as they waited for Miller to approach.

Miller was swinging along the track on his crutches, moving quickly toward the house. Reesa and Ted were several feet behind him, following. As Miller reached the end of the cars, the two ruffians stepped out in front of him, smiling wickedly.

"Well, now, for half a man, you did pretty good," one of the men said.

Miller stopped, then took a half step back. Though the words were complimentary, the tone of voice was not, and Miller sensed danger. "What do you want?" he asked.

"Fifty dollars," the other man said.

"Fifty dollars?"

"Yeah. That's what we're bein' given to beat you up. Now it don't make no nevermind to us, one way or the other. You give us the fifty, 'n' we'll leave you alone."

"I certainly will not give you fifty dollars," Miller said. He braced himself, then saw something that made him lose all hope of defending himself. A huge man, larger than anyone he had ever seen, stepped out from behind the cars and stood behind and between the two men. Miller assumed that he was with the two scoundrels.

"The odds don't seem right to me," the big man said. "Two to one is unfair. "I'll make it two to two, if you gents don't mind."

The two waylayers turned around, and saw that they were looking into the chest of the man who spoke. "What the hell?" one of them said. "Who are you?"

"Murdock Felton," the man said easily. "I guess you got a right to know the name of the man who's going to break your neck."

"Let's go!" one of the two shouted, and he broke into a dead run, his partner right behind him.

Miller began laughing and Murdock joined

him in laughter. They were still laughing when Ted and Reesa approached a moment later.

"Papa, what is it? Why are those men running?"

"I guess they just didn't like our company," Miller said. He stuck his hand out toward Murdock. "Mr. Felton, I'm obliged. My name is Miller Flowers."

"Pleased to meet you, Mr. Flowers."

"Murdock Felton is my track foreman," Ted said, smiling. "You two will be seeing a lot of each other if you decide to work for me, Mr. Flowers."

Miller nodded. "I don't reckon I've got much choice," he said. "I'd be proud to work for you."

"Well, that calls for a celebration. What say we get you folks moved out of your place, then go over to Delmonico's for lunch?"

"Oh, Papa, where are we going to live?" Reesa asked, suddenly thinking of it.

"How about my railroad car?" Ted offered.

"Thank you kindly, Mr. Foster . . . " Miller started.

"It's Ted."

"Thank you, Ted, but we couldn't do that."

"Why not? You were living rent free on Western Pacific property. Just look at this the same way."

"But where will *you* live?"

"I've got ten crew cars arriving tomorrow," Ted replied. "One of them is the car I lived in on my last site. It's quite comfortable and I'm used to it. I'll live there."

"Well, then, if you're certain," Miller said. "I'd be honored to live in your railroad car."

"Good. We'll get you moved into it right away, and I'll stay at the hotel tonight."

"I hate putting you out this way," Miller protested.

"Please don't worry about it," Ted assured him. "I'm going to be celebrating tonight. Chances are I wouldn't wind up in my own bed anyway." Ted suddenly realized what he said and turned to Reesa. "I beg your pardon, Reesa," he said. "I was just mouthing off."

"You owe me no apology," Reesa answered, wondering whose bed he would wind up in. She couldn't stop the unbidden thought from sneaking into her consciousness that she wished it would be hers.

Chapter Six

The largest crowd ever to greet a train in Albuquerque turned out early the next morning for the arrival of the *Honest Abe*. *Honest Abe* pulled a train composed of bunkhouse cars, a rolling kitchen, and a field office, all part of Ted Foster's new railroad. The engine was the first of the new line. It was a beautiful Baldwin 4-4-0 fast passenger engine, with huge driver wheels and a diamond stack. The body was green, and it and the green wheels were trimmed in bright red. All the fittings and the bell were of shining brass. The tender, also green and trimmed in red, had the logo SCRR in huge, gilt letters, denoting Southern Continental Railroad.

As the engine rolled to a stop, the engineer blew the whistle, then leaned out the cab window. He smiled down at Reesa, who was standing on the platform.

"What do you think of her, Miss Flowers? Ain't she a beaut?"

"Sam, *you*? What are you doing up there?"

51

"Me 'n' Ollie pulled the pin on Western Pacific," Sam said, using the railroad slang for quitting.

The big Swede suddenly appeared beside Sam in the cab window, white teeth showing through a soot-blackened face.

"Yah," he said. "Sam 'n' me, 've no stay with railroad when they not do right by such fine man as your papa. And Sam is the best hoghead in the business, so Mr. Foster hire him 'n' me right away."

"Oh, I'm glad," Reesa said.

There was a sudden strange cacophony of voices, and Reesa looked back along the train to see several Chinese detraining. She had heard that Chinese labor was being used in building the Western railroads, but this was the first time she had ever seen a large number of them.

"Ling Cho, you old yellow-skinned heathen, how are you?" Reesa heard someone shout. It was Murdock Felton, walking over to greet one of them, shaking the man's hand warmly. Murdock would have made two of the small Ling Cho, but in terms of affection they were equal.

"You know that Chinaman?" Sam called back to Murdock.

"Hell yes, I know him," Murdock answered. "He was my coolie boss on the old Central Pacific. Best damn slave driver you ever saw. Ling Cho, what are you doing here? I thought you were through with railroads."

"I no like San Francisco," Ling Cho replied. "All Chinamen in San Francisco run laundry or place to eat. I no like either, so I come back to work on railroad. Maybe we do good, set another record same-same like in old days."

"You better believe it," Murdock said. He looked at the group of Chinese workers who were climbing off the train. "Have we got any of our boys back?"

"I no can tell," Ling Cho said. "All Chinamen look same to me," he added with a straight face.

Murdock laughed uproariously, then threw his great arm around the small man's shoulders. "Come on, li'l buddy. Let's you 'n' me go get drunker'n hell."

"Murdock, will they let Chinamen drink at this bar?" Sam asked from the cab of his engine.

"Now, by God, Sam, who the hell's goin' to tell me I can't buy my li'l buddy a drink?" Murdock asked.

Sam laughed. "I can't think of a soul."

"I can't either," Murdock replied. "Come on, Ling Cho, let's go."

Reesa saw Ted moving through the crowd, smiling as he approached her. Reesa returned his greeting, and hoped that he couldn't see in her face what she thought every time she was near him. She was only now beginning to gain a sense of control over the weakness in her knees when he was near.

"Here's your new engine, Mr. Foster," Sam said. He had a cloth in his hand, and he rubbed along the bottom frame of the cab window, polishing an imaginary spot.

"Pretty, ain't she? I'll tell you somethin' else. Me 'n' Ollie had her up to fifty miles an hour on the way down here, 'n' she had a lot left. I wouldn't be surprised if she wouldn't make seventy."

"You're going to get a chance to find out," Ted said. "I want you to kick these cars over onto the spur line, then deadhead back up to Trinidad and pick up a string of cars loaded with new rails. I just got the message that they arrived."

"We'll be back in eight hours," Sam guaranteed.

"Eight hours?" Reesa said in wonder. "That's four hundred and fifty miles. You can't make that speed."

"Miss, with the big Swede here keepin' my fire hot, we'll sing on the iron, you mark my words."

The brakeman came up to the engine to join the group. His name was Potter and he, too, had worked for the Western Pacific before coming to work with Ted Foster. Reesa thought it spoke well for Ted, that he could hire so many good men away from WP on the promise of a dream.

"Potter, we've got to kick these cars free," Sam said. "We're headed back for Trinidad."

"We've got a problem," Potter said.

"What?" Ted asked.

"We can't park our cars on the spur line."

"What? Why the hell not?"

"There's a couple of armed galoots at the switch. The switch is locked closed, and they won't open it. They say they have orders to leave it closed until they get word from the station agent."

"I wonder what the hell this is all about?" Ted mused.

"The two guys on the switch say its something about paying the track rent," Potter said.

"Track rent? That's all been taken care of. We don't have to pay the track rent until we get our first loan payment from Leland."

"All I know is what they said," Potter replied.

"Damnit," Ted swore. He rubbed his hand through his hair and looked at Reesa. "Reesa, do you know this agent? This new guy? What's his name?"

"Yes," Reesa said. "His name is Fred Rule. He was Bodkins's assistant before he came here."

"Rule, Rule," Ted mused. "I've heard of him somewhere, haven't I?"

"He's the one who was found negligent in the cornfield meet outside Dodge City," Sam reminded him.

"Yes, yes; I remember now," Ted said.

Cornfield meet was another way of saying a head-on collision. A train wreck between a west-bound passenger train and an eastbound freight had killed forty-three people near Dodge City, Kansas. Investigation revealed that Fred Rule, the station agent at Dodge City, had received a message ordering him to hold the freight train on a side track until the unscheduled passenger train had passed. But, Rule, who was a petty man, was arguing with a rancher over the bill of lading for a shipment of cattle, and the freight train went right on through. It wasn't until fifteen minutes after the train passed that Rule remembered. He hired a fast horse and tried to chase after it, but arrived to find broken rails and twisted cars scattered on both sides of the track. The field was strewn with the dead and dying, and the sound of hissing steam and anguished screams filled the air.

"What's he doing running a station again?" Ted asked. "I thought they found him negligent."

"They did," Potter said. "He was fined one hundred dollars and returned to full duty."

"And now he's here to plague us," Ted said. "I won't have the money until tomorrow. It's arriving on a special train. I wonder if he'll wait until then?"

"Not likely," Potter guessed. "He's still a stickler for petty things."

"It's always the case with men like that," Ted said. "They can't handle the major things, so they tie themselves down with the small." He sighed. "Well, I guess I'll go see what I can do."

Ted left to talk with Fred Rule, and Reesa began walking around, enjoying the crowd that the special train had drawn. As she stepped down from the platform, a man on horseback galloped by. He was going so fast and came so close to Reesa that she let out a short scream and jumped back, only to trip and fall.

"*Señorita,* are you all right?" The man who spoke was Mexican, dressed in solid black, with silver conchos and a silver buckle fastening a gun belt, which held a pearl-handled pistol. His face was shaded by a large sombrero.

"Yes, I'm all right," she answered, struggling to regain her balance and her dignity.

"Please, permit me to help you stand," the man offered, extending his hand to her. He smiled, and Reesa noticed that he was in his late twenties, extremely handsome in a darkly Latin way.

"Thank you." Reesa took his hand, allowing him to help her up. She brushed herself off with what dignity she could muster.

"I saw the man's face, *Señorita*. If you like, I will bring him here and he will get on his knees to apologize to you."

"No, no, don't do that," Reesa protested. "But thank you for your help, *Señor* . . . I'm afraid I don't know your name."

"Mendoza," the man said. He smiled broadly, then removed his hat and gave a graceful, unaffected bow.

"Mendoza? You are the don?"

"No, *Señorita*, that is my father, Don Esteban Mendoza. I am Joaquin."

"The bandit?" Reesa asked impulsively.

Joaquin laughed. "Some may call me a *bandido*," he said. "There are others who call me patriot. I prefer to think of myself as a simple rancher."

"There is nothing simple about Rancho Sombra de las Montanas, *Señor* Mendoza," Reesa said. "I've heard that it stretches from here to the Arizona territory."

"*Si*, this is true," Joaquin agreed. "You can see why we fight so to defend it."

"I remember now," Reesa said. "You destroyed some railroad equipment, and you shot many men in a surveying party."

"I did destroy railroad equipment, *Señorita*, but only because they slaughtered some of my cattle. But I did not shoot any of the surveying party, though I did embarrass them."

Joaquin laughed, and Reesa remembered the incident. Four men had come riding into town, their legs tied beneath the bellies of their horses, their hands tied to the saddle horn. Their entrance into town had been met with great laughter, because all four men were stark naked.

"You are a wanted man, *Señor* Mendoza," Reesa said. "I've seen the posters on you. What are you doing here? Aren't you afraid you'll get caught?"

"No, *Señorita*. I have come only to scout the enemy. I will go quietly, before anyone knows I have been here."

"But *I* know you are here."

"*Si*, but you won't say anything."

"How do you know I won't?"

"Because, *Señorita* Flowers, I can see it in your face."

"Do you know me?"

"I make it a point to know everyone who has anything to do with the railroad. I know all about you and your father, and I know about Ted Foster and the money he is getting from Titus Leland."

"How do you know that?"

Joaquin laughed. "An interesting thing about the telegraph wires, *Señorita*. If you have a wire and a machine, you can read the taps, even though the message isn't addressed to you."

"That's against the law," Reesa said sharply.

"Oh? Haven't you heard? I am already a wanted man," Joaquin said mildly. He took Reesa's hand and raised it to his lips, then brushed it lightly with a kiss. To Reesa's complete surprise and consternation, a quick thrill coursed through her body. She looked at Joaquin in bewilderment.

Joaquin laughed, then dropped her hand and took a step back. He touched his hand to his hat. "*Adios*, my pretty one."

Reesa watched him walk through the crowd with as little concern as if he were strolling through his own house. She knew she should tell someone. He was a wanted man, an avowed enemy of the railroad. To let him remain free was to invite trouble. But for some inexplicable reason, she didn't want to turn him in.

Chapter Seven

After Ted left the train, he started toward the station house with angry, purposeful strides. As he passed the switch, he saw two men standing there, both carrying sawed-off shotguns. He recognized them as the two men who had accosted Miller Flowers the day before.

"Hey, Foster," one of the men called. "Why don't you send that big red-headed son-of-a-bitch over here to open the switch?"

"Yeah," the other said, laughing. "I'd like to see how the big bastard would act with a load of buckshot in his belly."

Both men laughed and Ted walked by without answering them.

When Ted pushed his way into the station house, he saw Miller Flowers's replacement. Fred Rule was a small man who wore wire-rim eyeglasses and suffered with a nervous tic in his jaw.

"Rule, my name is Ted Foster."

"I know who you are, sir," Rule said easily.

"Why won't you let my cars onto the spur track?"

"I'll let them on as soon as you pay the first month's rent," Rule said.

"Bodkins never said anything to me about paying in advance," Ted said.

"I'm afraid he said something to me," Rule said. He put his glasses on, looping them over one ear at a time, and pulled a message from his pocket. He cleared his throat.

"I just got this over the wire this morning," he said. "WP order number eleven, dated June 15, 1881. 'All rolling stock of any railroad other than Western Pacific must pay track rental fees in advance, at the rate of ten dollars per standing car, per day, one month minimum.'" Rule folded the message up and put it in his pocket, then removed his glasses and looked at Ted. "You have ten cars, Mr. Foster. Your rent for the first month is three thousand dollars."

"Very well, I'll pay it tomorrow."

"No, sir, Mr. Foster. It must be paid today."

"Do you think I carry that kind of money with me?" Ted asked angrily, fighting to maintain his control. "I'll have the funds tomorrow."

"I'm afraid Superintendent Bodkins's instructions were very explicit, sir," Rule said. "I was ordered to collect the rent in advance. That means today."

"Why don't you wire Bodkins and tell him that I paid it? I'll have it for you by tomorrow, and he'll never know the difference."

"I'm sorry. I can't do that."

Ted slapped his hand on the desk angrily.

"All right, you dried-up little bastard. I'll get the money today."

"When you give me the money, I'll open the switch," Rule replied.

Ted stepped out onto the station platform and thrust his hands in his pocket. He knew there would be many more aggravations before he brought this railroad in. This was only the first. It wouldn't do to let it get to him.

A handsome phaeton passed by and Ted saw Sally Millet sitting in the rear seat, shielding herself from the sun with a parasol.

"Hello, Sally," he called.

"Driver, stop," Sally said. The liveried driver pulled the team to a stop, and Sally looked out at Ted and smiled. "Well, Ted, I see your first crew of workers have arrived."

"That they have."

"I hope they aren't all Chinese," she said. "That would be awful."

"Why, Sally, you mean your girls don't like the Chinese?" Ted teased.

"Don't be ridiculous. In this business you don't have any choice as to likes or dislikes. It's just that the Chinese don't spend their money as freely as the others do."

Ted stepped down off the platform and stood by the carriage. "Out to look over the clientele?" he asked.

"If they're Chinese, I've seen them," she said. She patted the seat beside her. "Now, how would you like to check the merchandise?"

"Maybe I would at that," Ted said. He climbed in beside her. "Perhaps the hotel?"

Sally smiled broadly. "Quick," she said to the

driver. "Let's get him there before he changes his mind."

"Yes'm," the driver said.

The carriage rolled through the streets of Albuquerque, and Ted was strangely quiet. Finally Sally spoke.

"What is it, Ted? You aren't taking time out just for a little sex."

Ted laughed. "No, I guess you've got me there, Sally. The truth is, I need something, and I'm going to ask you for it."

"What do you need?"

"I need three thousand dollars," Ted said.

"Are you serious?"

"Very."

Sally turned in her seat to Ted, a look of disbelief on her face. "Ted, how do you plan to get this railroad off the ground if you don't even have three thousand dollars?"

Ted explained the problem to Sally, assuring her that he would have the money the next day when Titus Leland and the special train arrived. "So you see," he concluded. "It's to your advantage to let me have it, just long enough to get started. Because if this thing falls through before it ever gets going, you stand to lose a good deal too."

Sally looked through her purse and pulled out a small cigar. She stuck it in her mouth and lit it before she answered. "You've got a point there. All right, come on up to my room. I'll get the money for you."

"Thanks, Sally. I'm going to owe you for this."

Sally put her hand on Ted's leg and looked at

him pointedly. "I'll take my first payment right now."

"That's a payment I won't find hard to make," Ted said.

Reesa thought about her meeting with Joaquin. There was something he had said that vaguely disturbed her, but she couldn't quite put her finger on it. Then, as clearly as a lightning flash in a summer sky, she realized what it had been. Joaquin said that he had a wire connected to the telegraph lines! That meant that he knew everything that was going on, and he knew it as soon as anyone else did.

If Joaquin knew that Titus Leland was supplying money to Ted's operation, then he also knew how and when it was coming. And that could be dangerous. Ted had to be warned.

Reesa saw the unmistakable bulk of Murdock Felton, and she called out to him, asking him if he knew where she could find Ted.

"Yes'm, I just saw him over at the hotel," Murdock answered.

Reesa hurried to the hotel. Somehow she felt guilty about telling Ted, as if she were betraying Joaquin's trust. But Joaquin had no right to expect her to honor a trust between them. She didn't owe him anything. On the other hand, she owed Ted Foster a great deal. Or at least, she owed the fledgling railroad her loyalty. She had burned her father's bridges behind him. There was no place left for him to go, except Ted's railroad, and if Joaquin meant to destroy it, then she would have to stop him in whatever way she could.

"Hello, Miss Flowers," the desk clerk said, looking up as Reesa went inside.

"Hello, Dan. Is Ted Foster in the dining room?"

"No, ma'am, I just saw him go upstairs."

Reesa started upstairs. Of course, Ted would be here. He spent the night here last night, and he would be moving his things back to the crew car. She would help him and tell him about Joaquin as they worked.

When Reesa reached the second floor landing, she saw a maid about to knock on a door. The maid was holding a tray with a bottle of wine.

"Excuse me, do you know where I might find Ted Foster?" Reesa inquired.

"Why, yes, ma'am. He's right in here," the maid answered. "I'm about to deliver this bottle of wine to him."

Upon sight of the wine, Reesa's mind thrust ahead, exploring avenues beyond innocence, yet short of wantonness. Yesterday, she had drunk a toast with Ted and stopped after one glass. Even so, the small libation had set her pulse to racing and thinned her blood so that a strange heat flowed throughout her body. How much more daring would it be to share an entire bottle with this man!

"I will deliver the wine," Reesa said, "as a surprise."

"But, ma'am . . . "

"You shall have your gratuity," Reesa assured the girl.

"Yes, ma'am" the maid said, surrendering the tray to Reesa.

65

Reesa drew in her breath and knocked on the door. "It's the wine, sir," she called, disguising her voice and swallowing the lump of excitement that had risen in her throat.

"Bring it on in," Ted called.

Reesa opened the door and stepped inside. She was surprised to see that it wasn't a bedroom, but rather the sitting room of a suite.

"Just leave it on the table near the door," Ted's muffled voice called from what must have been the bedroom.

Reesa didn't put the wine down. Instead, she moved quietly through the room and up to the bedroom door. She pushed it open slowly and looked inside, certain that the pounding of her heart would betray her stealth.

"Damnit, girl, he told you to put it on the table," an angry woman's voice said.

There, on the bed, she saw the naked splayed legs of Sally Millet, just as Sally saw her. Ted didn't see her, because he was over Sally, with his face buried between her large breasts.

Reesa let out a gasp and dropped the wine bottle along with the tray.

Ted looked around at the crash of sound. "Reesa! What the hell are you doing here?"

Reesa turned and ran from the room. She knocked over the table where the wine was supposed to be placed; then, crying, pulled the door open and ran out into the hall.

"Reesa, wait!" Ted called.

"I hate you, Ted Foster!" Reesa shouted back at him. She ran down the stairs with tear-dimmed eyes, through the small lobby, and out the front door—right into Joaquin Mendoza's arms.

"You," she said angrily. "Let me pass."

Joaquin pulled his pistol from the holster and held it to her head.

"Now," he shouted past her. "I think I have the advantage, no?"

"What? What is this?" Reesa asked.

It wasn't until that moment that she realized what she had done. The street was full of armed and angry men, and it seemed that she had saved Joaquin Mendoza from a certain hanging. But apparently she had saved him at the expense of her own liberty.

"Let her go, Mendoza," one of the men shouted.

"This I cannot do, *Señor*," Joaquin said. "Now, the *señorita* and I will stay right here until someone is so kind as to bring my horse."

"Don't be a fool, Mendoza, you'll never get away with this."

"My horse, please," Joaquin said calmly.

"Do as he says," Miller Flowers spoke out from the crowd. "Reesa, you just stay calm, honey, and we'll get you out of this."

"What is this? What's happening?" Reesa asked, her mind swirling in confusion.

"Unfortunately, one of the gentleman I ran into before recognized me," Joaquin said. "He told the others, and before I knew it, I was about to attend a lynching party. As the guest of honor. You came along just in time, *Señorita*."

"Let me go," Reesa asked. "I didn't have anything to do with this. I didn't tell anyone you were here."

"It doesn't matter now, *Señorita*," Joaquin said. "I can't let you go. You are my only means of escape."

A man started toward them leading a big, black horse.

"Ah, Diablo, my beauty. I must apologize to you. You will have to carry double. But the *señorita*, she is so beautiful, this is not a chore you will dislike, no? Come, *Señorita*, get on the horse." Joaquin prodded her gently with the gun.

The two of them swung into the saddle, and Joaquin looked back at the crowd. "If anyone comes after me, I shall be forced to put a bullet into this lovely head. I'm sure you agree with me that it would be a terrible waste, yes?"

"If you hurt that girl, all the demons of hell won't keep me from you," Miller Flowers shouted.

"The girl will not be hurt if no one acts foolishly," Joaquin said. "*Adios, amigos.*" He slapped his feet against the horse's side, and they left in the thunder of hoofbeats.

Chapter Eight

Reesa did not fight as they rode out of town, because to fight would only make matters worse. Joaquin rode at full speed, and only after he crossed the Rio Grande did he allow the horse to slow to a walk.

"Get down, *Señorita*," he said.

"You're going to make me walk?"

Joaquin lifted Reesa out of the saddle and put her on the ground, then swung off his horse behind her. "We are both going to walk for a while," he said. "Diablo needs the rest."

"You shouldn't have taken me," Reesa said, after a moment. "They will come after you, and they'll kill you."

"Will you cry for me when that happens?" Joaquin asked, his eyes sparkling as he teased her.

"No, not one tear," Reesa replied hotly.

Joaquin clucked his tongue at her. "Ah, you are a cruel woman."

"And why shouldn't I be? You were willing to shoot me if you had to."

Joaquin laughed. "I wouldn't have shot you, *Señorita*. But it was good that the others thought that I would."

"Are you going to let me go now?" she asked, looking around her.

"I think not," Joaquin said. "I think it is better if you stay with me for a while."

"Well, I certainly will *not* stay with you!"

Joaquin smiled easily. "You have no choice, *Señorita*. You are my prisoner."

Reesa saw riders approaching from the west, and a quick surge of hope flashed through her. They were her rescuers! She looked at Joaquin and saw that he, too, saw the riders. But he was smiling as if welcoming them; then Reesa realized that coming from the west they would have to be his own men.

Four men and a woman reined up just in front of them. The woman was a feminine copy of Joaquin. And she was beautiful.

"Who have you here, my brother?" she asked, looking at Reesa.

"Allow me to introduce you," Joaquin said. "*Señorita* Reesa Flowers, this is my sister, Frederica Mendoza."

"Why did you bring her?" Frederica asked, her eyes never leaving Reesa's face.

"I had no choice. I was recognized. The girl was my ticket out of town."

Frederica sighed, nodded at Reesa, and turned to her brother. "What will we do with her?"

"Take her back to the *rancho*," one of the men said. He looked at Reesa and smiled lecherously. "I know what I can do with her."

Joaquin said something in Spanish. Reesa couldn't understand what it was, but it was sharp and angry, and the Mexican replied in Spanish in a tone of voice just as angry. A few more words were exchanged, then the air hung heavy with tension. Without understanding a word, Reesa realized that the two men were having some sort of confrontation.

"Draw your gun, Lopez," Joaquin said in quiet English. "Draw your gun or ride out of here."

Lopez glared at Joaquin angrily, and for a moment Reesa was certain that he was going to draw his pistol. No one made a sound, looking from one man to the other. Joaquin remained calm, not a tremor in his hands, nor a flicker in his eye. Lopez, on the other hand, began shaking. Sweat popped out on his face. Finally, with an oath muttered in Spanish, he slapped his legs against the side of his horse, turned, and rode away.

"You shouldn't have done that, my brother," Frederica scolded.

"He was a pig," Joaquin said easily.

"And so to defend this *gringo* girl you have made an enemy? You know he will go straight to the railroad."

Joaquin shrugged. "What harm can he do?" he asked.

"He can alert them that we intend to rob the special train tomorrow," Frederica said. "Without the element of surprise, we have no chance."

"Then we will not rob the train," Joaquin said easily. "Besides, as long as we have the

71

girl, we have no need to rob the train. We will hold her until the railroad sends its tracks elsewhere."

"We can't take her to the *Casa Grande*," Frederica cautioned. "*Padre* would not approve."

"You are right. The don, unlike his children, is an honorable man," Joaquin said. "We will take her to the old place."

Joaquin regained his saddle, then reached for Reesa.

"It will be a lighter load if she rides with me," Frederica said. She called Reesa over to her horse, then helped her mount. They started out at a brief trot, Joaquin in the lead, the other two men behind him.

"Was my brother bedding you when he captured you?" Frederica asked over her shoulder.

"Certainly not!" Reesa answered in a shocked voice.

"Why not? Didn't he like you? You are certainly beautiful enough. You didn't make him angry, did you?"

"I . . . it never came up," Reesa answered in confusion. "And if it had, I wouldn't have allowed it."

Frederica laughed. "*Señorita,* save your modesty for the others. I am a woman. I know how it is. We pretend that we are angry, but we are not. We love it as much as the men. We just can't admit it."

"Speak for yourself, *Señorita*," Reesa said angrily.

"Oh, I do, Reesa," Frederica answered. "I have no fear on this subject."

They rode hard for four hours, switching Reesa from horse to horse to keep the mounts from tiring. Finally when Reesa felt as if she couldn't ride another minute, they approached the Rio Puerco, and she saw a cluster of houses along the west bank. The horses rode through the shallow river, throwing water and sand up from the hooves, then onto the other side where they were welcomed by a group of men, women and children.

"What is this place?" Reesa asked, as they dismounted.

"It was our family home for many years," Joaquin said. "Now the don lives in the new *casa*, ten miles from here. He has given these houses over to the families of our *vaqueros*."

There was a great deal talking and wild gesturing, and several times someone would look toward Reesa and laugh. It made her extremely uncomfortable.

"What is it?" she asked. "What is everyone laughing about?"

Joaquin smiled. "They want to hold a party in your honor."

"In my honor? Why? I'm a prisoner here, I'm not a guest," Reesa said.

"My people are happy people," Joaquin said. "It takes little excuse for them to have a party. And if they prefer to think of you as a guest rather than a prisoner, why should you object? They are a generous people."

Reesa started to protest again, but suddenly realized that a party might occupy everyone's attention enough to allow her to escape. She forced herself to smile.

73

"All right," she said. "It might be fun."

"There now, that's the way to look at it," Joaquin said. "After all, *Señorita,* you and I are not enemies, no? It is only the railroad which causes the trouble. Come, we will have our party."

The word spread to the others, and in an amazingly short time, the atmosphere changed to one of gaiety. Tables were placed on a shaded patio, and as if materializing from thin air, they were covered with food. There was much wine in evidence, and soon there was singing and dancing to the music of two excellent guitarists.

"*Señorita, Señorita,* you will strike at the *piñata,* yes?" the children urged.

"What do they want me to do?"

"Break the *piñata,*" Joaquin answered. "Sweets are placed in a clay jar, then tied to a rope. The rope is thrown over a tree limb. You are blindfolded and given a stick, and you try to break the *piñata* while it's moved around by the rope. If you break it, the children win."

"Will you do this, *Señorita?*"

Reesa looked at the children and laughed. "Yes," she said.

The children cheered, and two of the older ones took her by the hand and led her to a tree. She was blindfolded and given a stick. She swung several times, missing every time and bringing forth peals of laughter.

"I will help," Joaquin said.

Reesa felt Joaquin's arms go around her, then take her hands in his. She tensed.

"Easy, *muchacha,*" Joaquin said. "I'm just

74

going to help you break the *piñata*. The children grow restless."

Joaquin swung her arms, and she felt the stick hit the clay jar. There was a satisfying crash, then squeals of delight from the children as the contents rained down.

"You may remove your blindfold," Joaquin said.

Reesa took the blindfold off, then laughed. The music swelled and the party went on.

"Now, isn't this the way to be a prisoner?" Joaquin asked.

A prisoner! For a moment Reesa had nearly forgotten.

"Joaquin, you must let me go," she said quietly. "They will come after me and there will be bloodshed."

"Reesa, there is going to be bloodshed anyway, and there is little we can do about it," Joaquin answered.

"Then you must let me go."

"I cannot," Joaquin said. "I intend to use you to bargain with Ted Foster."

"You're a fool," Reesa said. "You will accomplish nothing this way."

"Perhaps not," Joaquin agreed. "But let us talk of this no longer. Are you hungry? Come, we will eat now."

Reesa walked with him to one of the tables, and Joaquin began preparing a plate. "You must eat something," he said. "It is very good."

Reesa began filling a plate with the highly spiced foods. She looked at the far end of the table and saw someone riding up. The rider dismounted, then walked over to talk to Joaquin.

They were speaking in Spanish, and Reesa couldn't understand them, but she wasn't trying. Her attention was held by the horse.

The horse was standing where the rider left him, less than ten feet away from Reesa. There were no other horses anywhere close, and by now many of the men were pretty drunk. If she could just get on that horse, Reesa thought, she could ride out of here!

Reesa eased on down the table, still putting things on her plate, but now using it only as an excuse to reach the horse. Finally she was right there! She sat the plate down and quietly swung up into the saddle.

"Reesa!" Joaquin called, seeing then what she was doing.

Reesa slapped the reins against the horse, and the horse broke into a gallop.

Reesa was a good rider, and the horse cleared the courtyard before anyone was able to react. She heard Joaquin call her name, then shout to the others, but she thought only of getting away.

Reesa bent low over the horse's neck, riding as fast as she could. She looked around to see Joaquin on Diablo, gaining fast.

"Oh, come on, horse, go faster, go faster," she pleaded.

Joaquin overtook her easily, then reached out and grabbed the reins of Reesa's horse. He got them both stopped. "I'm sorry," he said soberly. "We must go back now."

"Damn it," Reesa cried out in frustration.

Joaquin smiled. "Do not be angry with yourself. It was a good try. But I am the owner of this ranch. Do you not think I would keep the fastest horse for myself?"

They rode back to the party, then dismounted. "Frederica," Joaquin called.

"Yes?" She joined them quickly.

"Our guest of honor tried to leave the party early. Perhaps you can think of a way to discourage her."

Frederica smiled. "I can think of a way. Come with me, *Señorita* Flowers," she said.

Reesa followed Frederica inside the house. They walked down a long hallway, then Frederica stopped just outside a door. "In here," she said.

"In there? What for?" Reesa asked.

"In order that you don't run away again, I am going to remove your clothes."

"You most certainly are not!" Reesa said indignantly.

"Have it your way, Reesa," Ferderica said. "Either I will remove your clothes or one of our *vaqueros* will. Now which will it be?"

"All my clothes?" Reesa asked.

"All of them."

Reesa went through the door into a small room. She looked back at Frederica for a moment, as if making one last effort to plead with her. It was a fruitless effort.

Reesa sighed, then began taking her clothes off. Within a moment she was completely naked, and she handed the clothes to the Mexican girl.

"I can understand why my brother is so taken with you, *Señorita*," Frederica said. "You are a beautiful woman."

Even though Frederica was a woman, she looked at Reesa with unashamed interest and appreciation. It made Reesa extremely uneasy.

"Now, *Señorita,* enjoy the party," Frederica said. She smiled one last time, then took Reesa's clothes and left.

Reesa was alone, helpless, naked, and miles from home. She should have been frightened, but she wasn't. Somehow she was able to set fear aside, and consider her situation with a calm and reasoning mind. She was proud of herself for that.

Reesa walked over to the bed and took a blanket to cover her nakedness. She lay back on it, and was surprised at how good it felt. She had had a trying and tiring day. She closed her eyes and was asleep within a few moments.

Chapter Nine

When Reesa awakened later, she saw that it had grown dark, although the room was brightly lit by the full moon. Reesa sat up in bed and looked around the room. At first she was puzzled to see that she was naked, but then she remembered what had happened. The party was still going on. Reesa could hear the sound of guitar music and maracas, and singing and laughter. Occasionally she also heard gunshots, but knew that they were being fired in fun rather than in anger.

She stood up and crossed the room to try the door. To her surprise it was unlocked. She took the light blanket from the bed and wrapped it around her body, leaving her arms free. Then she pushed it open and stepped out into the hallway. There was no one there.

Reesa's heart pounded fiercely. Perhaps this was her chance to escape! She was determined that this time she would succeed.

She pressed herself tightly against the wall of the hallway and began moving down it very slowly, very quietly, scarcely daring to breathe. There was a sudden burst of laughter from just beyond the window in the courtyard and Reesa froze in fear. She remained still for a very long time, then started moving slowly down the hallway again.

There was an open door midway down the hall. Reesa edged closer, ever closer to it, then tried to slip across.

"Do not try it, *Señorita*," Frederica called from the room. "You will be made sport of by my gallant *vaqueros*."

Reesa felt her heart leap into her throat, and she looked into the room. She could scarcely believe what she saw! Frederica and a man she had heard called Ronaldo were in bed, and both were naked. Ronaldo looked up from Frederica's breast and smiled at Reesa. Reesa stared at them in shock and, to her surprise, fascination.

Frederica laughed. "Would you like to join us?" she asked throatily.

"No," Reesa shouted quickly. She turned and ran back up the hall and into her room with the laughter of Frederica and Ronaldo chasing her all the way. She crossed the room and sat on the bed trembling, half expecting them to follow her and continue their sport in her bed.

Like a mouse in a maze, Reesa looked around to seek another means of escape. The room was small and furnished only with a bed. The bed was covered with gaily colored blankets, such as the one Reesa had wrapped around her. Other colorful hangings decorated the adobe walls. The one window high on the wall, through which the moon was shining, was so small that Reesa wasn't sure she could squeeze through it even if she could reach it.

She was still sitting on the bed when the door opened and Joaquin came through, carrying a lamp. The music and laughter swelled and quieted as the door opened and shut.

"What . . . what do you want?" Reesa asked, fearfully drawing the blanket more tightly about her.

Joaquin smiled, his dark brown eyes flashing brightly in his handsome face. He removed his sombrero and tossed it casually to one side, then began unbuttoning the black shirt he wore.

"Easy, my *muchacha*," he said. "I'm not going to hurt you."

Reesa watched, paralyzed by what she was seeing, but unable to look away.

Joaquin unbuckled the great silver buckle of his belt, then let his breeches fall. Within a moment he stood before her, totally naked.

It was terrifying . . . and fascinating. She noticed a small smile of pride playing across Joaquin's lips.

"I am a handsome man, no?" he asked softly.

"I . . . I wouldn't know," Reesa said. She found the strength to turn her head away from him.

Joaquin walked over to her and set down beside her. He put his finger on her chin and turned her head back so that she was looking at him.

"I know this is true because many women have told me I am a handsome man," Joaquin said. "So why can you not say so?"

"I'm afraid these circumstances don't permit it," she answered, averting her eyes.

Joaquin laughed quietly, then reached down and put one hand on her shoulder and the other on the edge of the blanket. He started to remove it.

"No," Reesa said, her cry short and ineffectual. She pulled the blanket back in place.

"Do not fight me, *Señorita*," Joaquin said. "Do you not realize that I am now your lord and master?" He pulled the blanket from her, then held it for a moment and looked at her. Her nude body was soft and glowed pinkly in the light.

"*Ai, yi, yi*, you are one beautiful woman," Joaquin said, almost reverently, and there was so much conviction in his voice that Reesa felt strangely moved by it.

Joaquin pushed her back gently, then bent over her and kissed her on the lips. His kiss was tender, yet with an urgency that was barely held in check. He moved his hands across her body, and Reesa felt the heat rising, as if his hands were kindling flames within her.

No, she thought. *I'll not be betrayed by my body! I'll not let him have his way with me!*

But even as her mind formed the words meant to stop the spreading fires, her body raced ahead, and waves of desire flooded over her.

"Please," she murmured, as she felt his hand move between her legs into that part which was most sensitive.

Please what? Please stop, or please go on? God help her, she didn't know.

The floodtide of passion rose higher and higher, and Reesa felt her hands moving as if by their own volition. She touched that of which Joaquin was so proud.

"Now ask me, *Señorita*," Joaquin said. "Beg me for it."

Reesa's body ached for fulfillment. She longed to go further.

"Beg me," Joaquin said again. "Beg me to make love to you."

Oh, yes, I want it, I want it, Reesa thought.

But she suddenly realized what Joaquin was saying!

"Beg me, if you want it."

Her body ached for her to say the words, but her mind finally regained control. No! Absolutely no! That would be the final degradation!

"No!" Reesa screamed. She pushed against him and struggled to pull away from him.

Joaquin sat up and smiled down at her.

"No?" he said. "Then I shall find another, more willing *Señorita*. And you, my *muchacha*, can stay lonely and cold in this empty room."

"Go away, leave me alone," Reesa said, now crying.

Joaquin put his hands on her shoulders and again Reesa felt their fire.

"Are you sure you don't want me to make love to you? Your lips say no, but your eyes say yes."

"Please, just go away," Reesa begged.

"Very well," Joaquin said agreeably. "But I'll come back when you ask for it."

"Then you'll never come back," Reesa said.

Joaquin sighed and slipped on his boots and

put on his hat. He stood at the door thus attired, poised to leave.

Despite herself, Reesa nearly laughed at the sight, naked as he was except for boots and hat. "Aren't you going to put on your pants?"

"Why?" Joaquin asked. "As soon as I find a willing *señorita* I'll just have to take them off again." He pointed to the boots. "These I need to keep the cactus out of my feet." He blew her a kiss. "Some other time, *Señorita*."

Reesa fell back on the bed after Joaquin left, then rolled over and cried into her pillow. Her body ached with the pain of longing, and her mind reeled with the shame of wanting. She wanted it, but she would not beg it of him. She would not!

Suddenly she heard shooting outside. Not the occasional shots of the party that she'd been hearing all night, but rapid and angry firing. The sounds of music and laughter changed to cries of fear and rage, and then she heard Ted's voice.

"Save Joaquin for me! If he's done anything to that girl, I'll carve the bastard's heart out!"

There was more shooting and more shouts, then the sound of several horses galloping off.

"Mr. Foster, they're gettin' away!"

"After them, men," Ted shouted. "I'm going to look for Reesa."

Reesa heard noises in the house. Doors were being kicked open, and boots stomped down the hallway. She quailed in her bed; and, seconds later, her door exploded into the room, flying off its hinges in splinters.

Ted stood just on the other side of the smashed door, looking in curiously.

"Ted, oh Ted, thank God it's you," Reesa said.

"Reesa, are you all right?"

"Yes," Reesa replied. In her fear and then excitement over being rescued, Reesa had forgotten she was naked. She made no attempt to cover herself until she saw the strange look in Ted's eyes.

"Oh, forgive me, I . . . " she started, but she could think of no explanation, so she dropped it in mid-sentence and sought to regain some decency if not dignity by covering herself with the blanket. "He . . . took my clothes," she said weakly.

"The filthy beast," Ted spat. "When I catch the son-of-a-bitch, I'll kill him for forcing himself on you."

"No, you mustn't," Reesa said quickly. "Don't kill him, please."

"Why not?" Ted asked.

"He didn't force himself on me."

Ted stared at her for a moment, and a strange questioning look came in his eyes. He looked at the floor and saw Joaquin's pants and shirt, then looked at the bed and saw it mussed. Reesa's nude body was flushed.

"I can *see* he didn't force himself on you," he said flatly.

"What . . . what do you mean?" Reesa asked, not understanding yet what was going through Ted's mind.

"It's obvious, isn't it? Joaquin was wrapped in a serape as he rode off. His clothes are in here, and you say he didn't force himself on you."

"No, Ted, you don't understand," Reesa pleaded.

"I think I understand perfectly, Madam," Ted said. "Joaquin is a handsome man, and you are obviously a woman who appreciates the delights a handsome man can offer. Unfortunately, I didn't realize that in time."

"What are you saying?" Reesa's voice was now tinged with fear.

"Perhaps you would would have preferred the rescue to have been delayed a while longer," Ted suggested. "It's obvious that you and Joaquin had not concluded your business."

"How could you think such a thing?"

Ted stepped up to the bed and grabbed the blanket. "You show Joaquin so much, yet cover yourself for me?"

"Ted, please, you don't understand."

"I understand all right," Ted said.

He jerked the blanket away, and Reesa's nudity was exposed to him once again. She was angry and frightened, and her skin was flushed pink with excitement. Ted gasped in admiration, then quickly stripped away his clothing.

Reesa watched, captivated by the scene unfolding before her, unprepared for what happened next.

Ted pushed her back on the bed, then got over her, straddling her body, staring down at her, his face still contorted with the conflicting emotions of anger, lust and hurt. He moved his mouth down to cover hers with a brutal and demanding kiss, bruising her lips beneath his, stabbing his tongue into her mouth. Then, just as she began responding to the floodtide of passion his powerful kiss was evoking, he pulled his lips away. He held her wrists pinioned to the bed with his hands, and with his knees he forced her legs to spread.

Reesa made a strange murmuring noise deep in her throat, whether of passion or fright she could no longer be sure. She closed her eyes, waiting for his next move, now longing desperately for it, yet afraid of it. She cursed aloud, but knew that it was more against the betrayal of her own body than against Ted.

White heat flooded through her, and when Ted drove himself deep into her, the sharp pain she felt as he entered her quickly gave way to a strange feeling of pleasure. The passion and erotic nature, which had lain dormant for so long, was released. Nevertheless she flailed at his back, in an attempt to fight him off. In reality she was satisfying a hunger and fulfilling a need. It went on and on, and Reesa was lifted to the stars, crying when it was over, only because it was over.

When he had finished, Ted remained on top for some time. Reesa lay unprotesting beneath him, riding with the pleasant feelings, which were slow to leave, lingering on like the heat in an iron removed from the blacksmith's forge. Finally Ted rolled away from her. He stood up and looked down at her, now looking weak and small and used in the bed.

"Reesa, I'm sorry," he said. "I don't know what . . . "

"Please," Reesa said in quiet anger. "Don't say anything to me." She stood up and walked to the other side of the room to be away from him, drawing the blanket around her protectively, the action all the more poignant, because it was too late to help her.

It was then that Ted saw a few spots of blood on the bedcovering. He gasped. "My God, don't tell me you were a . . . a . . . "

"Virgin?" Reesa said it for him. "Can't you even say the word?"

"But that's not possible. I thought you and Joaquin . . . "

"I told you, Joaquin didn't force himself on me. No. I was spared that, only to be raped by my rescuer."

"I'm sorry," Ted said in a choked voice.

Reesa started across the shattered door.

"Where are you going?" Ted asked.

"To find my clothes. I trust, sir, that you are finished with me?"

"My God, woman, don't torment me so," Ted pleaded. "I have said that I am sorry."

Reesa walked down the hall to the room where she had seen Frederica and Ronaldo earlier. She opened a small chest and saw her clothes neatly folded in a drawer. As she took the clothes out of the drawer she couldn't help but notice the uncontrollable shaking in her hands.

Reesa knew it wasn't fear or anger now that caused her hands to shake. It was the still-burning excitement of her experience with Ted. She closed her eyes and gripped the edge of the chest tightly, and felt again the passions that swept through her. She had loved it. Oh, how she had loved it.

But, please, don't let Ted know!

Chapter Ten

The morning light spilled in through the window and the plush draperies of the railroad car, which was serving as home to Reesa and her father. The noises of a train being worked on drifted in, and Reesa found herself slowly abandoning sleep. She stretched luxuriously, feeling the sensuous texture of silk sheets and a warm, sweet ache in her loins. For a moment she drifted with the delightful feelings and thought languidly of the dream she had had the night before.

"It wasn't a dream!" Reesa suddenly said aloud, remembering the scene with Ted. She sat up in bed and felt her cheeks burning with shame. She saw herself in the mirror and stared for a moment. She was struck with the thought that the woman whose reflection looked back at her was not the same woman who had awakened the day before. She was no longer a virgin.

Reesa swung her legs out of bed and walked over to the dresser. She was aware of the soreness in her limbs and, even as she thought of it, she became cognizant of a new dampness between her legs. Reesa examined her reflection closely. She looked into her eyes to see if there was any telltale sign of guilt, but she could see nothing different in her appearance.

"Reesa, girl, will you be sleepin' the entire mornin' away now?" her father's voice called from outside the door.

"I'm up, Papa," Reesa said. "I'll be out shortly."

When Reesa was dressed, she left her bedroom and saw two men with her father. One of them was Ted Foster, and for just an instant, Reesa felt a surge of pleasure over seeing him. But Ted cut his eyes away in embarrassment, still shamed by his despicable actions of the night before, and Reesa was brought back to reality.

"Good morning, Mr. Foster," she said coolly.

"Sure now, 'n' that's all you've to say to the man who risked his neck to rescue yours?" her father chastised her. "I'm thinkin' a more proper thank you would be in order."

"It isn't necessary, Mr. Flowers," Ted put in quickly. "Miss Flowers has undergone quite an ordeal."

"Miss Flowers? Mr. Foster?" Miller said, staring at the two young people. "It used to be Ted and Reesa. What's happened?"

"Nothing . . . it's just as he said. I've undergone an ordeal," Reesa said. She looked at the other man with her father, and thankfully was able to use him as an excuse to change the subject. "You haven't introduced our guest," she said.

"I haven't at that," Miller said. "Reesa, darlin', this is Warren Leland, the son of Mr. Titus Leland. Warren here will be lookin' out for his father's investment."

Warren Leland was a tall, handsome man in his mid-twenties, perhaps a year or so younger than Ted. He had wavy brown hair, insolent blue eyes, and a somewhat world-weary look. He had neither the ruggedness, nor the look of strength about him that one saw in Ted. In fact, Warren's classic good looks were almost feminine. But Reesa sensed something about him—a current of danger seemed to flow through him. She instinctively knew that no man who valued his life would lock horns with the young man before her.

"You are even more beautiful than I was led to believe," Warren said. "And that is quite difficult, because I've heard only the most flattering descriptions of you."

Reesa flushed in embarrassment, but felt pleasure over the compliment. "You are too kind with your words, sir," she said.

"Words are inadequate," Warren said. "I do hope you will do me the honor of dining with me tonight. Of course, this invitation includes your father as well," he added quickly.

"Sure 'n' we'd be glad to," Miller answered for the two of them. "Wouldn't we darlin'?"

"Yes, of course," Reesa said. She had no choice in the matter now; her father had preempted that by his acceptance.

"Wonderful. I shall call for you here at seven

this evening," Warren said. He gave the two of them another wide smile, then turned to Ted. "Mr. Foster, if you would care to show me how you are spending my father's money, I shall be glad to accompany you now."

"Of course," Ted said. "Come along, I'll show you the crew cars, then we'll walk out to End-of-Track. It's only a short walk today, but within a week, we'll have to take a locomotive or go on horseback."

"I find the whole idea of laying track across a desert inconceivable," Warren said. "I feel I must warn you now that I don't share my father's enthusiasm for this project. I intend to keep a very close watch on every penny and hold you absolutely to the contract."

"Not one cent will be squandered," Ted promised as they left the car.

Miller watched them through the door for a moment, then he turned to face Reesa.

"Reesa, darlin', would you be tellin' me what's troublin' you now?" he asked.

"What do you mean?"

"Come on, darlin', 'tis your old papa talkin' to you now. I've raised you alone from a pup, remember? I know somethin's wrong."

"It's nothing, really."

Miller suddenly got a pained expression on his face. "Reesa, girl. That Mexican bandit, he didn't . . . that is . . . well, what I'm trying to say is, did he hurt you in any way?"

"No," Reesa said.

"Darlin', don't make me spell it out," Miller said. "You know what I'm askin' you. Did Joaquin make you do somethin' . . . well . . . that you didn't want to do?"

"Joaquin Mendoza did not rape me, if that's what you mean."

"We'll be thankin' the good Lord for that," Miller said, wiping his brow nervously. "You are a lovely broth of a girl, Reesa, and there's many a man who would take unfair advantage of you if they but could. Faith 'n' you're so young and innocent that you don't even know what I'm talkin' about, I'm thinkin'. But it's somethin' you've always got to be on your guard against."

"I'll be on guard, Papa," Reesa said.

Ted and Warren walked out to End-of-Track, now just a few hundred yards beyond the western limits of Albuquerque, and watched the activity of the men laying the new track. Ties without rails were stretched several hundred feet beyond, already in place. Then forty men, twenty to each rail, would snake the long piece of steel ribbon into place, laying it just so on the ties. They would leave and their places would be taken immediately by others who would swing sledge hammers driving the huge spikes home, ringing out, steel on steel. The railroad was growing right before the men's eyes, stretching out nearly as fast as a man could walk.

The Chinese workers were scurrying about like ants working a hill, each indistinguishable from the other. But one of them, who was carrying a bucket of dirt used for setting the ties, tripped and the dirt spilled over Warren

Leland's polished shoes. The laborer was on his feet immediately, bowing apologetically to Warren, unable to express himself in English.

Warren's eyes grew very cold and his hand slipped in under his coat. Murdock Felton, who was standing nearby, saw the move and let out a bellow.

"Ling Cho, take this clumsy son-of-a-bitch out of here and teach him some manners."

Ling Cho, who had seen Warren's move just as Murdock had, reacted quickly. He shouted something in Chinese and, within a second, the man was surrounded by dozens of his countrymen. They were shouting and cursing him, but more effectively, they were shielding him, for by now Warren, who had removed his pistol, could not get a clear shot at him. In fact, within an instant Warren could no longer tell which Chinese it was who had offended him.

"Don't you worry none, Mr. Leland," Murdock said, walking over to the two men and towering over both of them. "We'll strip the hide off the little bugger."

Warren's face showed that he had been denied his satisfaction, but since it was so adroitly handled, he replaced his pistol without a word.

"Would you really have shot him just for spilling dirt on your shoes?" Ted asked.

"Yes," Warren said easily.

"That doesn't seem like enough to kill a man over."

"He was a coolie," Warren said, as if that justified his action.

"The Chinese were printing with movable

type when our ancestors were still writing on the walls of caves," Ted said.

"Mr. Foster, I hope you don't let your tender feelings for these creatures extend into the work you get from them. I expect to see a full measure of work extracted for the money my father invests," Warren said.

"You need have no fear on that score," Ted replied. "There's not a crew in the world who can outwork this one. Murdock Felton and Ling Cho are the best in the business."

"Ling Cho? A Chinese? You have a Chinese in authority? Over white men?" Warren asked incredulously.

"No," Ted said. "He supervises only the Chinese labor."

A train whistle was heard in the distance and the two men looked back toward town, at the track stretching beyond the town to the other side. There, still a couple of miles away, they saw an approaching train, its stack drawing a pencil line of smoke in the clear, blue sky.

"That'll be another crew coming in," Ted said. "I'd best be getting back to meet them."

"More Chinese?"

"Irish," Ted said. "I don't think you'll care much for them either."

As Ted started back, Warren called to him. "I hope you aren't upset over my inviting Miss Flowers to dinner tonight."

Ted stopped and looked back. "Upset? No, why should I be?"

"It's just that I thought I perceived something between the two of you. No? Well, then there is no problem. Reesa Flowers may prove to be a delightful diversion in this otherwise Godforsaken place."

"Miss Flowers is a big girl and can do as she pleases," Ted said.

Warren smiled, an easy but disquieting smile. "I thank you for your permission," he said. "It will make it easier."

"It is not my permission to give," Ted said. He turned away then and hurried to meet the train.

Reesa was very excited as she readied herself for the dinner that evening. This would be her very first date. In fact, it was really her very first social engagement. She had eaten in the hotel restaurant before, but almost always it had been as a matter of necessity or convenience. This would be the very first dinner she had ever eaten out, just for the purpose of eating out. She wished for a moment that it was Ted who would be eating with them, but almost as quickly as that ungrateful thought arose, she put it aside. Warren Leland, after all, was a very handsome man and a gracious one. She was flattered by his attentions, and she knew that her evening with him would be an event to remember.

Warren was exactly on time and Reesa made a last minute adjustment to her hair as she heard her father letting him into the living room. She pinched her cheeks to bring out the rose glow, then walked out to greet him.

"Good evening, Mr. Leland," Reesa said.

Miller Flowers was in the midst of a story and he was smiling as he was talking. He

looked around at his daughter and the smile left
his face to be replaced by an expression of surprise and awe. It was as if he were seeing his
daughter for the first time. And, in fact, this
was the first time he had ever been aware of
her as others saw her.

Reesa was standing in the doorway wearing
a golden colored silk gown. Miller remembered
when she had sent away for it from the mail
order catalog. It was high-necked, but close-
fitting at the bosom and pinched-in at the
waist, then flaring out into many tiers. Her
skin glowed and her eyes sparkled. A flash of
light sparkled from the dancing ear bobs she
was wearing.

"My God, daughter," Miller breathed reverently. "I have never seen you look so beautiful."
He continued to stare, as if it were a stranger
who stood before him.

"I must say that I agree completely," Warren
said easily. He crossed the room and offered
his arm to her. "I have a phaeton waiting outside. Shall we go?"

"You went to all that trouble?" Reesa asked
in surprise. "It's only a few blocks walk."

"My dear, one does not walk to an occasion
such as this. One arrives," Warren informed
her.

The phaeton was elegantly upholstered, and
Reesa sat back in the luxuriously cushioned
seat and drank in the sights, sounds, and feel of
the evening. Never had she done anything like
this, and she wanted to savor every bit of it.

When the phaeton drew up to the front of the

hotel, the hotel doorman and the concierge met them and helped Reesa out of the carriage.

"I have opened the special dining room, sir," the concierge said.

"Thank you," Warren replied. "Did you prepare the wine I selected?"

"We did, sir, and as you instructed. We have allowed it to breathe for one hour. It is ready now."

"I will decide that," Warren answered.

"Yes, sir, of course," the concierge agreed.

Reese almost gasped when she saw the private dining room. She had glimpsed it before, but never had she seen it when it was laid out for serving. It was the most beautiful room she had ever seen. The chandelier was lighted by gas and it glowed in a soft, gold light, with the hundreds of glass facets exploding in spectrums of rainbow color. The table was covered with a beautifully worked damask cloth and laid with bone china, which seemed to glow from some soft, inner light. The eating utensils were of gold and the wine cups silver.

"I will test the wine now," Warren said.

The concierge snapped his fingers. The wine steward who was standing by poured a little wine in a glass goblet and handed it to Warren. Warren held it up to the light, sniffed its bouquet, then tasted it. Finally he nodded at the wine steward, signaling that it could be served. The steward, with a visible look of relief on his face, poured the deep red liquid into the silver goblet at Reesa's setting.

From the serving of the wine through the

beef tournedos to the peach flambée, Warren supervised everything. It was the most elegant and exciting evening Reesa had ever spent.

"And now, Mr. Flowers, I have a Havana cigar for you, which you may smoke as we take a ride through the countryside to enjoy the starlit scenery of your great Southwest," Warren offered.

Miller laughed. "I've seen enough of the mountains to last me a lifetime. For my money, I'll take the swamps and forests of Southeast Missouri. Why don't you two young people take a ride? But, leave the cigar with me."

"That sounds fair enough," Warren said. "Reesa?"

"Yes," Reesa said. "I'll ride with you, Warren." After all, Reesa thought, the driver of the phaeton will be with them. It won't be as if she were going out alone. And she had enjoyed the evening. To refuse to go for a ride with him now would be an unspeakable discourtesy, to say nothing of discouraging any future attention he might pay her. And she certainly didn't want to do that.

Reesa waved to her father as the driver called to the horses, and the phaeton rolled away from the hotel. The pair of horses trotted easily down the main street, then took the desert road. Within moments the town of Albuquerque lay behind them, little more than a few yellow lights on the desert floor.

"I don't care what Papa says," Reesa said, leaning back and looking out. "I think it is beautiful out here. Look at those stars. There are so many, and they are so bright; it's almost

100

as if they are going to fall on you. Oh, look!" she said, laughing and pointing to a flash of light streaking through the sky. "One of them is falling!"

"I arranged that for you," Warren said easily.

"Where do the stars go when they fall?"

"They aren't really stars, you know. They are meteorites. Little pieces of heavenly bodies falling into the earth's atmosphere from space," Warren said.

"Oh, I wonder what they look like? They must be as beautiful as diamonds," Reesa said.

Warren laughed. "No, not really. They just look like any rock you might find on the ground anywhere. They have one in the museum in San Francisco."

"I would love to see it."

Warren put his arm around her shoulder. He did it so easily and with so little fanfare, that Reesa was barely aware that he had moved.

"Perhaps I'll take you there sometimes," Warren suggested. "Edward," he said to the driver. "We'll stop here for awhile."

"Yes, sir," the driver replied, pulling the horses to a stop. "Mr. Leland, do you mind if I take a walk to stretch my legs a bit?"

"Not at all," Warren answered.

"But it wouldn't be right to . . . " Reesa started, but Warren interrupted her.

"You won't embarrass a man who must answer a call of nature, will you?" Warren asked.

"Oh, no, no, of course not," Reesa replied. "I'm sorry."

The driver climbed down and started walk-

ing toward a large outcropping of rock, out-
lined in the moonlight, about one hundred yards
off the road.

"Did you enjoy the evening?" Warren asked
after the driver was out of earshot.

"Oh, yes," Reesa answered easily. "More
than any evening I have ever spent in my entire
life."

"You will have as many such evenings as you
allow me to provide for you," Warren said.

Warren leaned toward her and kissed her. As
it had been when he put his arm around her, it
was done so quickly and with so little fanfare
that Reesa was unable to react until it was too
late.

The kiss was not demanding in its hunger
and urgency as had been Joaquin's and Ted's,
but it was overpowering in the sensations it
evoked. It was the kiss of one who was skilled,
and thus immensely stimulating, even though
devoid of the raw passion that had been present
with Ted and Joaquin. It left Reesa's senses
reeling and her mind spinning.

"Please," she said, turning her head away,
gasping to recover her breath.

"Very well," Warren said. "I've no wish to
force myself upon an unwilling woman."

"It's not that I'm unwilling . . . I mean ungrateful," Reesa said, correcting herself
quickly. "But I think I'd rather we didn't do
this."

What is it? Reesa asked herself. What was
there about her body that would allow men to
arouse her so easily. First Joaquin, then Ted,
and now Warren. All had caused her body to

flare into the heat of passion. However, all are handsome young men, she reasoned. Perhaps there is nothing unusual in reacting to the attentions of handsome young men. But then, with shame, she remembered Superintendent Bodkins. Even he had aroused passions in her.

Reesa looked into the heavens with despair and saw more flashes from the meteor shower. She was like those meteors, she thought. She could no more control her feelings than those meteors could remain fixed in place. And like the bursts of light of those remote flaming stars, her own passions flared out of control.

Chapter Eleven

The train whistle echoed through the canyons, and Joaquin's horse took a few nervous steps.

"Easy, Diablo," Joaquin said, patting the horse on the neck, calming him. "Soon we will have action!"

Four men came running up the hill from the track, and retrieved their horses from four others who were holding the reins for them.

"Did you grease the tracks well?" Joaquin asked.

"*Si*. The engineer is in for one big surprise when he finds that his locomotive can not climb such a little hill."

"Are you certain this will work, my brother?" Frederica asked.

"It will work. I saw it used in the border wars," Joaquin replied. "The driver wheels will slip on the grease and the train will stop."

"I think it would have been better to put dynamite on the track and explode it under the train."

"And perhaps kill the engineer and other innocent people?" Joaquín said. "They are not our enemies, Frederica. It is the railroad that is our enemy, not the people who ride the trains."

"You have a soft heart," she said derisively.

"And you, my sister, for the beautiful woman that you are, have a heart of ice. Ah, but such is the way of women. It is a well-known fact that the fighting bulls get their strength from their fathers and their blood lust from their mothers."

"There, the train comes around the bend and is starting up the hill," one of the men said.

"Get ready," Joaquin ordered. He pulled his pistol from his holster and checked each of his men. Frederica had her pistol drawn as well.

"You stay here," Joaquin ordered.

"You try and make me stay here," she replied.

The train was traveling at fifty miles an hour when it hit the greased tracks. The pounding drive wheels suddenly began spinning and the train slowed, then came to a complete halt and started sliding backwards down the hill.

"Aiieee, it worked," one of the men shouted happily.

"Now," Joaquin called. "We attack!"

Joaquin led his group of men out of the rocks and down the hill. They fired their pistols in the air as they galloped toward the train. They reached it just as the train slid to the bottom of the hill. The engineer, perceiving what was happening, threw the engine into reverse and tried to back away from them, but Joaquin had anticipated that and the grease was the heavi-

105

est there. The engine stood still even though the wheels spun rapidly.

Joaquin rode up to the cabin window of the engine and, as a warning, fired a bullet into the large steam pressure gauge inside. The cab began to fill with steam. He smiled at the engineer and the engineer closed the throttle.

"That is good, *Señor*," Joaquin called to him. "Now if you and the fireman would be so good as to step down?"

A few cars back, a man leaned out from the vestibule. He was holding a gun and Joaquin shot him, hitting him in the arm. The gun fell to the ground.

"I am sorry, *Señor*," Joaquin called out, "but guns make me nervous. If you'll please return to the car, one of my men will attend to your needs shortly."

"You are Joaquin Mendoza," the engineer said.

"At your service," Joaquin said, giving the engineer a salute. He pointed to the baggage car. "Tell whoever is inside to open the door."

"Open up," the engineer shouted.

The door slid open, and a small man started pitching bags out onto the ground, even before he was asked.

"Gracias," Joaquin said. "You are being most cooperative." Joaquin swung down from his horse and picked up the bags. He handed them up to his sister, and she affixed them to her saddle horn.

"If you will forgive me, I have been most rude in keeping the passengers waiting," Joaquin said. "Come, my *amigos*, we must see to them now."

Joaquin climbed to the first car and kicked the door open and stepped inside. A woman screamed, and a man shouted a curse toward him. He smiled back pleasantly and tipped his hat.

"Buenos dias, Señores and *Señoras."* he said. "My name is Joaquin Mendoza. I have robbed this train, but I am here to tell you that you need have no fear. I have no intention of robbing any of you, and none of you will be hurt."

"What about the man you shot?" someone challenged.

"Oh, yes. For that I am truly sorry, but he was about to shoot me, and I feared that perhaps he could not shoot as well as I. I shot him in the arm only. He may have shot me in the heart, and I would not like that."

A little girl of about five, too young to be frightened, had been looking at Joaquin's scarf, which was held around his neck by a large silver and turquoise slide ring. "Mama," she said, pointing at the scarf. "Isn't that pretty?"

"Hush," the girl's mother said.

Joaquin smiled. "No," he said. "You should never stifle a child's appreciation for beautiful things." He removed the scarf and ring and handed them to the little girl. "To remember me by, *poca Señorita*," he said.

"Joaquin, we are ready to ride," someone called from outside.

Joaquin gave a parting wave to the passengers inside. "I must go now. I wish you a pleasant and safe journey."

Joaquin's horse was brought alongside, and he leaped onto the horse's back, then slapped his legs against the animal's side. They rode along the track for several hundred feet so as not to present a target to anyone on the train, then turned and headed out across the desert, back to the Mendoza ranch.

They rode for nearly an hour before they stopped to rest the horses and themselves.

"Look at how the bags bulge," one of the men said. "I wonder how much money they contain."

"It doesn't matter," Joaquin said.

"Of course, it matters."

"It matters only that this is the payroll," Joaquin said. "That means that the workers don't get paid, and if they don't get paid, they don't work. If they don't work, the railroad doesn't get built. That's all that matters."

"But think of the fun we could have with this money."

"No," Joaquin said loudly. He stood up and walked over to stand near the money, then turned to look at the others. "You know why we do this," he said. "It is not because we are thieves, but because we are patriots. Each of you has been given land by my family, and now each of you has your own interest in seeing that the railroad does not take our lands from us. Think of this and of your families, and of the generations to come who will enjoy your land. It is for this that we took the money, not so that you may get drunk and visit with a whore."

"You are right, Joaquin," said the man who

108

had spoken. "I meant nothing. I was only talking."

"The horses have rested. We must be going," Joaquin said.

The train was late in reaching Albuquerque and the crowd was growing very restless. There was some speculation as to whether or not the train had been involved in a wreck, and some were talking of organizing a posse to ride out and look for it. The crowd was much larger than usual because the work crews knew that they were going to be paid when it arrived. Therefore, in addition to the usual people who met the train, there were a couple hundred workers. The Irish, many of whom had already begun to celebrate, were singing, drinking, and laughing amongst themselves, and the Chinese, who were standing or squatting in groups, were just waiting quietly.

Reesa, her father, Ted, and Warren were sitting in a buckboard, waiting with the others. Murdock Felton and Ling Cho, who were to help Ted with the payroll, were standing beside the buckboard.

"What time is it now?" Ted asked.

"Five minutes later than it was the last time you asked," Warren said, looking at his watch. "It is nine-forty-five."

"Forty-five minutes late," Ted said.

"Maybe Rule has telegraphed back to check on it," Reesa suggested.

"No," Miller said easily. The regulations say wait one hour before telegraphing, and you can bet that Rule will be waitin' the full hour."

"My father's bank in Denver put the money on the train," Warren said. "We've got a telegram to that effect. That means the money is now your responsibility. If anything has happened to it, you'll bear the loss."

"I know, I know," Ted said.

"Mr. Foster, you think maybe something has happened?" Murdock asked.

"I don't know, Murdock. But I'm afraid it has. I can't think of any other reason the train would be this late."

"She's on her way in," a man on horseback yelled, galloping down the track toward the station. "I just seen her light from Lookout Point."

There were cheers from the men who were waiting to get paid, and an excited babble of voices from the others in the crowd. The Chinese remained silent.

"Listen," Ted suddenly said, holding his hand up. "Damnit, there's been trouble, I knew it."

"Why do you say that?" Reesa asked.

"Listen," Ted said again.

Reesa heard it then. The engineer was blowing his whistle, but not in the long, mournful wail, which normally marked the entrance to Albuquerque. Instead it was a series of short blasts . . . the sign of trouble.

The men who were waiting to be paid heard the whistle then and their cheering and boisterousness suddenly died. They had all worked the railroads long enough to recognize the signal for trouble, and it didn't take a genius to figure out what the trouble probably was.

110

"Mr. Foster, what are you going to do about getting us paid?" one of the men shouted.

"Yeah," another put in. "We've broke our backs on this damned railroad, and we're entitled to a fair wage."

"Wait a minute," Ted said. "You don't know that the payroll was taken."

"The hell we don't," another said.

"At least wait until the train gets here and find out," Ted pleaded.

"We'll wait, but if there ain't no pay, there ain't no work."

"That ain't enough by me, gents," one of the others called. "If I don't get paid, I intend to tear up the work I already done."

"Murdock, what do we owe that man?" Ted asked, pointing to the one who had just spoken.

"Twenty dollars, Mr. Foster, same as the rest of them," Murdock answered.

Ted pulled his billfold from his pocket and took out twenty dollars. "Pay him," he said. "Then fire him."

"Yes, sir," Murdock replied, smiling. "I never cared much for that troublemaking son-of-a-bitch anyway."

"Oh, Ted, what if the train has been robbed?" Reesa asked. "How will you handle this mob?"

"I'm interested in seeing that myself," Warren said with a smug smile.

The train pounded into the station with the hissing of steam and the grinding of metal, then came to a stop. Almost as soon as the train stopped, people were jumping off the cars.

"We were robbed!" the first man off the

111

train cried. "Joaquin Mendoza and his men held us up."

The crowd of track workers began shouting angrily.

"Now what are you going to do?" Warren asked.

Ted stood up and held his hands out, asking for quiet. "Men," he said. "Listen to me. There's no cause for alarm yet."

"What do you mean there's no cause for alarm? Didn't you just hear that the train was robbed?"

"Trust me," Ted said. "Murdock, keep the men quiet for a while longer. I've got to check on something."

"All right, boss," Murdock said.

"What on earth do you plan to do?" Miller asked. "We don't have nearly enough money in the safe to pay these men."

"I'll be right back," Ted answered cryptically. He hopped out of the buckboard and walked over to the baggage car. He rapped on the door, and after the door slid open, climbed inside. The door closed behind him, and remained closed for several minutes.

"Do you think you can hide in there, Foster?" one of the men shouted.

"Yeah," another called. "You've gotta come out of there sometime, and that train ain't leavin' until you do."

"Warren, can't you do something?" Reesa asked.

"It's Foster's problem," Warren said. "Besides, I don't have sufficient funds to pay this unruly mob. I'm afraid there's nothing I can do."

The door suddenly slid open again and Ted stood on the edge of the car. He held both hands out for quiet. "Men, I'm happy to report that they didn't get the payroll. We'll begin paying immediately."

A loud cheer went up from the crowd, and Reesa gasped in surprise. "Is he serious?"

"Yes, ma'am," Murdock said, grinning. "I guess our little plan worked."

"What plan?" Miller asked.

"When the money was put on board in Trinidad, it was put into bags marked 'seed.' The money bags were filled with paper. Joaquin and his men didn't get nothin' but four bags of junk."

"Paper!" Frederica shrieked angrily. "The son-of-a-bitch tricked us!"

"Paper?" Joaquin asked in disbelief.

"Look!"

Frederica dumped one of the bags on the ground in front of her brother. He stooped down and picked one of the bundles up. It was as his sister said, nothing but old newspaper, cut in the size of money and secured in bundles. He began to laugh.

"You are laughing," she snapped. "You think it's funny?"

"Yes," Joaquin said. "You've got to give him credit for a sense of humor. He played a joke on us. A brilliant joke."

"He made fools of us," Frederica spat.

113

"Of course, my sister," Joaquin said easily. "That is what a joke is supposed to do."

"Well, what are you going to do about it?"

"About this? Nothing," Joaquin said. "But now that I know our friend has a sense of humor, perhaps he will appreciate a joke of our own sometime soon."

Chapter Twelve

"Reesa, darlin', I've got to take the train into Santa Fe, 'n' I won't be back 'til tomorrow mornin'," Miller said. "But I've a whole pile of paperwork I've been meanin' to get around to, 'n' now I just don't have time."

Reesa smiled. "Papa, why didn't you just ask me to do it instead of putting it off? You know I would have been glad to."

"Still 'n' all, it's not right that I should have you doin' my work for me. I'm the one hired on, not you."

Reesa got on her knees in front of her father and began rolling up her father's empty pants leg. "It just so happens that I anticipated this," she said. "And I've already started, so you go on into Santa Fe and don't worry about a thing."

Miller ran his hand affectionately through Reesa's hair. "'Tis a good 'n' lovin' daughter you are, lass. And a fine wife you'll be makin' some man soon."

115

"Oh, I scarcely think I'm about to get married," Reesa said.

"Darlin', you've growed up right before my eyes. I tell you when I saw you standin' in the doorway that night a few weeks ago, sure 'n' it took my breath away."

"You're just prejudiced."

"No, darlin', I'm just honest. But I'm also confused. Somethin' has happened between you and Ted. I've noticed it; don't think I haven't. It's been goin' on ever since he rescued you."

"Papa, there never was anything between us in the first place."

"Your papa has eyes, girl," Miller said. "And I think I know what it is."

A spasm of fear shot through Reesa. Did he *really* know?

"It's young Warren Leland, isn't it? He's been payin' court to you, 'n' Ted's not takin' to it."

"Papa, Ted is so wrapped up with his railroad, that I don't think he even realizes that Warren is paying attention to me."

"That's probably just as well," Miller said. "Warren seems to me to be a fine man, and a good catch if I say so myself."

"Papa!"

"Now listen to me, darlin'," Miller said. "From the beginnin' of time, it's been a father's duty to make a good match for his daughter. And I'm thinkin' there could be no better match anywhere than Warren Leland. He's rich, and he's a gentleman of refinement and education. Ted, on the other hand, is an adventurer. Like as not if he brings this railroad

116

in, he'll go somewhere else to start over. I've seen his kind before, darlin'. With men like Ted, it's the doin' that's important, and once it's done, they lose interest."

"Well, you needn't have any fears, because Ted has no interest in me."

"How about you? Are you interested in him?"

"No," Reesa said. But even as she spoke, she looked away to keep her father from reading the lie in her eyes.

Miller stood up and reached for his crutches. "Good," he said. "I think it's about time you started encouraging Warren then." A train whistle hooted in the distance, and Miller took his hat from a peg on the wall. "That'll be the mornin' Santa Fe train. I'd best be goin'. You'll be all right 'til mornin'?"

"I'll be fine, Papa."

Reesa watched her father leave, then sat at the desk preparatory to doing the paperwork her father left her. But though she tried to concentrate on the figures, she found that it was impossible. She was thinking about the conversation with her father, and about the two men in her life: Ted Foster and Warren Leland.

Her father was right about Warren. He was a very handsome man, and a gentleman of refinement and education. And he had been paying a great deal of attention to her lately, having taken her out to dinner, to a traveling show, or for a ride at least three times each week for the last month. But, except for the first night when he had kissed her beneath the spectacular aerial display of the meteor shower, there had been nothing physical that passed between them.

At first Reesa had been on guard, lest he try again. Then, when she realized that he wasn't going to try, she relaxed and began enjoying their time together. But of late, she found herself wondering more and more how it would be to make love with him. He seemed to approach everything with a sense of detachment, even his relationship with her. And yet, even so, she sensed that her body would respond to his lovemaking if it ever had the chance.

Then thoughts of Ted began to crowd into her mind. Ted, who was rugged and handsome, ambitious and energetic, had the qualities she most admired in men. She had been hurt and angry that he abused her in such a way, but sometimes in the secret compartments of her own heart, she admitted to herself that she wanted it to happen, had in fact nearly willed it to happen. Could she have fought him off if she had really tried? It was a question to which she had no clear answer. She did wish that there was some way she could resolve the dilemma she felt over the two men.

The door to the engineering car opened and Ted stepped in at that moment.

"Where is your father?" Ted asked. "I must send a message to Denver."

"He's gone to Santa Fe," Reesa said. "He won't be back until tomorrow."

"That'll be too late," Ted said. He sighed. "I suppose I can have Rule send it commercially, and pay the rate."

"That isn't necessary," Reesa said easily. She

118

took the lock from the sending key. "I'll send it."

"You'll send it?" Ted asked, laughing. "Are you crazy?"

"What do you mean, crazy?" Reesa replied.

"I've never heard of a woman telegrapher."

"Well, you've heard of one now," Reesa said. She reached for the message in Ted's hand, but he pulled it back. "Look," she said angrily. "You said it was important."

"I don't know," Ted hesitated.

Reesa started operating the key. The small room of the engineering car began echoing with the metallic clacks as her fingers opened and closed the switch in a rapid series of dots and dashes.

"What are you doing?"

"I'm clearing the lines for your message," Reesa answered. She reached up and took the paper from Ted's hand. "Is this it?"

"Yes," Ted said, letting her have the paper. "I didn't get the timbers for the trestle across Prealta's Gulch."

Reesa sent the message and after a moment, another message came flashing back.

"What does it say?" Ted asked anxiously.

"It says the timber order was killed by Warren Leland."

"What? Are you sure?"

"You heard the message same as I did." Reesa replied sarcastically.

"I don't know telegraphy."

"Why not? You're a man, aren't you? Surely a mere woman can't do something you couldn't do."

119

"All right, I'm sorry about that," Ted said. He picked up the message and stared at it. "Why would he cancel the timber order?" he asked angrily.

"I'm sure I don't know."

"No? I would have thought otherwise."

"What is that supposed to mean?" Reesa asked angrily.

"Just that the two of you keep such close company that I find it hard to believe there could be any secrets between you."

"Well, you are wrong, Mr. Foster," Reesa said icily. "I have one secret which I share with no one. Except you, of course, and it would be rather difficult to keep it from you."

Ted pinched the bridge of his nose for a moment and sighed. Finally he looked at Reesa with eyes that were windows into his soul. It was the most unguarded moment Ted had ever shown Reesa.

"Reesa, I'll carry that terrible thing in my heart till my dying day. I can only hope that you'll find it in your heart someday to forgive me, for I know there can never be anything between us until you do. You are a beautiful and decent woman, and I think any man would be the luckiest in the world to ever know your love."

Reesa's spirit leapt! This was the chance she had waited for, the opportunity for an honest exchange between them. Her heart longed to tell him that she did forgive him, and that *he* was the man who could know her love. But she couldn't do it. A small fear started in her mind, perhaps a fear of rejection, certainly a fear of truth, and it moved over her, pushing the honest reaction of her soul away. The Reesa who was trapped inside her body nearly wept when it heard the words coming from her lips.

"*You'll* never be that man, Ted Foster," she said harshly.

The windows in Ted's eyes slammed shut, and the honest emotions retreated. When he spoke again, his voice was quiet and controlled and showed nothing of the inner man.

"I am sorry you feel that way, Miss Flowers," he said. Quickly he turned back to the business at hand. "Please send a telegram reordering the timber. I must find Leland and see why he canceled the order in the first place."

Ted touched the brim of his hat and walked out the door.

Reesa watched him leave with a sickening, sinking sensation inside. Why had she done that? Why had she spurned the chance he offered her? Had she closed the doors between them forever? Her heart felt as if it would break, and the tears filled her eyes so that she could barely read the order numbers on Ted's timber request.

As Ted rode toward End-of-Track, he thought of the conversation he had with Reesa. He had apologized to her, had begged for her forgiveness and had been spurned for his efforts. Her rejection had hurt him much more deeply than he was willing for anyone to know. More deeply, even, than he wanted to admit to himself. For the truth was, Ted believed he was in love with Reesa Flowers, and often in the quiet, introspective moments he wondered what it would be like to be married to her. Of course, marriage to anyone was out of the question right now. After all, he owed his total allegience to the Southern Continental Railroad. But once the railroad was built, he would be president of the company, and he would be able to afford the luxuries of a big house, a fine carriage, and travel. But with no wife to share these things, such a life would be hollow indeed.

It was those thoughts that had driven Ted to cross the lines of reason when he spoke to Reesa, to lower his defenses against her—only to have it thrown back in his face. He vowed that he wouldn't do that again.

A sudden wind blew up from the west, from the direction of End-of-Track. As Ted rode into the wind he could feel and smell in the breeze the dampness of an upcoming rain. He reined in horse and pulled his poncho from the saddle roll, then slipped it over his head. He examined the track as he spread the poncho to provide as much protection for the horse as he could. Twin steel ribbons, straight as an arrow, shining brightly as they stretched back into Albuquerque, now some five miles behind him, and on to End-of-Track, a good twenty miles in front. Tomorrow the engineering car, which was the headquarters of the operation, and Miller Flowers's quarters car, would be moved out to End-of-Track to set up operation there. The twenty-five-mile run with the locomotive wasn't too bad when it was available, but it was generally too busy hauling materials from Albuquerque to the site to be used for transportation. That meant a long horseback ride every time something came up.

Dark, ominous clouds moved across the gray sky, preceded by swiftly moving tumbleweed and a rolling column of dust. Ted squinted his eyes and pressed on.

The rain was coming in full force by the time Ted reached End-of-Track, and he hurried his horse into the canvas shelter erected for the remuda, then ran over to the mess tent to get out of the rain. He removed his hat and poured water out of the brim and crown, then stripped off the poncho and hung it across one of the tent support ropes. The rain was drumming loudly on the canvas, and here and there it was dripping through, making little pools on the tables.

"Want a cup of coffee, Mr. Foster?" the cook asked.

"Yes," Ted answered. "Thanks."

He turned to look back through the tent opening at the activity on the roadbed. The rain hadn't stopped the work, and the crews were still laying track with a well-established rhythm.

"Here you go, fresh made," the cook said, handing a blue tin cup to Ted.

Ted blew on the coffee to cool it, then slurped a drink through lips extended to prevent burning. He had seen Warren Leland sitting quietly at the other end of the tent when he arrived, but had said nothing to him as yet. Finally he spoke.

"I reordered the timber," he said.

123

"You won't need it," Warren replied, without turning around.

"How else do you propose we cross Prealta's Gulch?" Ted asked. "Lay the track on thin air?"

Warren turned now to face him. "You won't be going through Prealta's Gulch. I told the surveyors to lay a course around the gulch."

"What are you talking about? There is no way to go around it. The mountains north of it are virtually impassable."

"We're going south."

"South! That's right through the middle of Mendoza land. If you think we've got troubles now, you just try that. He'll have the government on his side if we do that."

"The government won't do anything after the tracks are already laid, and you know it. They are so anxious to have a railroad through here that they'll back our play. Besides, my father has enough congressmen on the payroll to insure that there will be no trouble."

"I don't care if he has the President," Ted said. "We are not going south of Prealta's Gulch."

"Foster, I had the engineers prepare the cost estimates for me. We can lay track south of Prealta's Gulch for less than half what it's going to take to go across it."

"No."

"You seem to forget whose money is backing this operation of yours," Warren said.

"I'm using your father's money, Leland, not your ideas. This is my railroad, and we'll build it the way I say or you can take your money and go. I'll find backing somewhere else."

"Oh, yeah? Where?"

"Your father wasn't the only one interested," Ted said. "Now you make up your mind, Leland. You let me build this railroad the way I see fit, or just get the hell out of here altogether."

Warren stood up and began putting on his raincoat. "Very well," he said. "Build your trestle. But you go one penny over budget, and you'll default everything you've got to us. That is in the contract." He smiled. "I've got time to wait you out, Foster. And a pleasant way to pass the time while I'm waiting. I see that the train is about to run into Albuquerque. I think I'll just hop a ride into town and visit Reesa."

"Fine," Ted said. "It'll keep you out of the way."

Warren started to leave, then stopped just before he stepped into the rain. "By the way," he said, "Sally Millet is bringing her girls out to End-of-Track tonight. I thought you might like to know that. Perhaps if you had someone to share your bed, you wouldn't be of such short temper. I know it works wonders for me."

"What do you mean?" Ted sputtered. "Are you trying to tell me that you are . . . that you and Reesa are? . . ."

"Of course not, dear fellow," Warren said easily. "A gentleman *never* tells."

He laughed cruelly, then darted through the rain toward the single passenger car the engine was pulling. Ted watched him with cold fury seething inside. He wrapped both hands around the hot tin cup, so angry that it was several seconds before he felt the heat building up in the palms of his hands.

"Don't let Mr. Leland rile you up none, Mr. Foster," the cook said quietly. "His kind is like a cat. They like to torment people when they see they can get to them, and he's gettin' your goat good."

Ted looked at the cook, embarrassed that his emotions were showing so strongly. Finally he set the cup on the table and reached for his poncho. "I'd better see how the work is going," he said. "Thanks for the coffee."

Chapter Thirteen

Despite the rain there was no dampening of the spirits of the gandy dancers that day. Work songs and laughter competed with the ringing of steel and the blowing of steam for attention. The gandy dancers joked good-naturedly, looked at the sun when they could see it to guess the time, and stared back down the track toward Albuquerque as if waiting for something. Then in the late evening, just before the work day was terminated, they saw what they had been waiting for and they gave a loud cheer.

Sally Millet had rented a crew car from the Southern Continental Railroad, and painted and decorated it so that by the time it arrived at End-of-Track that evening, there was no doubt as to its purpose. The rain had already ended, and the men, many of whom had even bathed for the occasion, queued up in a patient line outside the gaily decorated car, waiting for the door to open. The first man in the line was Murdock Felton.

"Hey, Murdock, it ain't right for you to be first," someone called. "You're so big, you're liable to take one of them girls right out of commission."

"Or else fix 'em so's they can't be satisfied by no normal man no more," another shouted.

"I'm gonna get me two of 'em," Murdock replied, laughing. "That way, one of 'em won't be expected to bear too much of a load."

The ribald teasing went on for a while longer, then the door of the car opened and Sally stepped out onto the platform. The men whistled and shouted, and she smiled and waved at them.

"I don't know," she said. "I may have come to the wrong place. I don't see anyone here who looks lonesome."

"Me, me, Sally! I'm so lonesome as near 'bout to die," someone shouted.

"But you've got each other," Sally said, laughing.

"Are you kiddin'? Have you smelled Jonesy? I need someone who smells pretty."

There was more hooting and laughter, then Sally held out her arms to call for quiet. "All right, gentlemen—and I trust all of you are gentlemen, or you've no business in this line— you are welcome here to enjoy the most beautiful girls in the territory as long as you follow the rules, and here they are. Drinkin's all right, but if you are drunk by the time it's your turn, you'll be thrown out. I've got five girls inside, that means six of you can come in at a time. Five to be with the girls, and the sixth to wait in the waitin' room. You'll have ten minutes

128

with the girls, then you gotta leave whether you're finished or not, so I'd advise you to finish as fast as you can. No choice as to the girl, you gotta take the next one that opens up. As far as the line out here is concerned, I'll expect you to keep it policed yourself. I don't have enough help to take care of any disputes that might come up out here. But believe me, gents, I can take care of anything that might happen inside. Now that's the rules, and anyone as can't abide by 'em, best leave the line now."

"Are you one of the five girls, Sally?" someone asked.

"No," Sally replied. "Sorry, boys, but I've got other plans for my evenin'. Now the first six can come on in."

"Damn it, wouldn't you know I'd be seventh?" someone called.

"Yeah? Well, I'll trade with you. I'm twenty-fifth," another answered.

Ted looked out of the back door of his private car and down the track toward the car Sally's girls were using. He had been sipping whiskey ever since Warren rode away, and by now he was quite drunk. In fact, even as he stood there, he found that he had to support himself on the door frame.

"She can't love that son-of-a-bitch," he mumbled. "Surely she sees him for what he is. But who can tell, who can tell?" he added. "I practically begged her for forgiveness and she turned on me."

Ted drained the last of the bottle, then tossed

the bottle aside, wanting to see it burst into a million pieces. Instead of breaking, it bounced and clattered along the ground.

"Made of steel, just like her heart," he muttered.

"My, aren't we having fun tonight?" a woman's cool voice asked sarcastically.

"Who's that?" Ted asked, staring out into the darkness.

Sally appeared, walking toward him. She smiled, and Ted was so drunk that the smile seemed to leave her face and float through the air preceding her.

"I brought a bottle of good wine, but I needn't have bothered," she said. "You are so drunk now, you wouldn't be able to appreciate it."

"Appreciate it? Sure, I can appreciate it," Ted said. "And you, too, Sally. Come on into my car." He made a grand bow and an elegant sweep toward the car with his hand. " 'Course, it's not fancy. I gave that one up to Miss Flowers so's she would have someplace nice to entertain Mr. Warren Leland, fine gentleman that he is."

"Oh, my God, Ted, don't tell me," Sally said.

"Don't tell you what?"

"Don't tell me you are in love with Reesa Flowers. . . . "

Ted reached for the wine and, when Sally started to hand him a glass, he waved it aside and turned the bottle up to his lips, taking several Adam's-apple-bobbing swallows.

"Not to worry, my dear Sally. I won't tell you that, because I'm not. I don't love her. I don't love anyone. The railroad doesn't leave me time for anyone."

"Yeah, well you keep tellin' yourself that, honey, and maybe you'll believe it." Sally took the bottle from him and poured a glass for herself. "I came to keep you company tonight, but it's obvious that you aren't in the mood."

"In the mood? Yes, I'm in the mood," Ted said. "I may be besotted, but I am in the mood." He began unbuttoning his shirt and slipped it off, then he started on his breeches.

Sally put her hand on Ted's shoulder and ran it along the smooth skin and bulging muscles, then across his chest. "Ohhhh," she said. "Reesa Flowers is a damned fool."

"Who is Reesa Flowers?" Ted asked, pulling Sally against his naked body and smothering her with kisses.

"I'm sure I've never heard of her," Sally answered, returning Ted's kisses eagerly and exploring more of his body with her hands.

Sally had been with many men, and with many who were drunk. She knew from experience that alcohol, when used to the point of drunkenness, usually inhibited a man's sexual capacity. But she was not to be disappointed by Ted. Drunk though he was, he was strong and virile, and as he took her, she rose eagerly to meet him. And such was the pleasure of the love-making that she closed her ears to the cry he uttered just as he finished and right before he passed out.

"Reesa, my love," he gasped.

* * *

"Won't you come in, Warren?" Reesa invited, as Warren stood outside the door of the car.

"Reesa, if possible, you are even more beautiful than ever tonight," Warren said. He took her hand and kissed it, then looked around in confusion. "Where is your father?"

"Papa had to go into Santa Fe this morning," she said. "He won't be back until tomorrow."

"Oh, that's a shame," Warren said. "I'm certain he would have enjoyed dinner with us."

"But perhaps we can enjoy it even more without him," Reesa suggested.

What was she saying? She couldn't believe she was hearing herself say those words!

Warren smiled a slow, hot smile. It was only then that he noticed the table had been set for two.

"I thought, perhaps, I could cook for you, and we could have dinner here tonight," Reesa suggested when she saw him looking at the table. "It would be more private."

"Yes," he said. "I think that would be a marvelous idea."

They ate slowly, leisurely, and though Reesa ate the meal and held up her end of the conversation, the food had no taste and the words no meaning. There was only one thing on Reesa's mind, and it burned into her like a branding iron. She was on a one-way ride, and all she could do was hold on to see where it took her.

After the meal, Warren poured a brandy for each of them. Reesa accepted it with thanks, and drank it quickly to allow its warmth to spread through her and relax the nervousness she was feeling.

"It is good that you chose to dine here," Warren said, after finishing his brandy. He removed his coat and tie and lay them across the back of his chair. It was only then that Reesa saw his pistol holster, not worn at the waist like other men, but nestled under his arm, concealed from view when he was fully dressed. He removed the pistol and hooked it over the chair with the coat.

"Are you sure you want to do this?" he asked.

"Do what?"

Warren smiled a confident smile and put his hand lightly on her cheek, then tipped her face up to his. He leaned over and kissed her. It was warm and tender and knowing, and within a second she uttered a small cry and returned it with fervor.

"Let's go into the bedroom where we'll be more comfortable," Warren suggested.

Reesa got up, and without mind or will of her own led the way. She had already turned the bed down, telling herself earlier that it was to save time when she was ready to retire. Now she knew that mockery for what it was. She had prepared the bed for this moment.

Warren began to undress her then. He did it skillfully, as if all her fasteners and appurtenances were familiar to him. Reesa was mesmerized by his actions, by his easy confidence, his subtle skill. Before she realized it, she was nude and lying on the bed, staring up at him with half-closed eyes and splayed legs. Things were coming to her in a haze now, as if she were dreaming and nothing was real.

Warren stared at her. His mouth seemed too full and sensuous to be a man's, and yet it was capable, as she well knew, of evoking the most exquisite pleasures. It was curled up slightly at each edge, forming a smile that seemed to be mocking.

"You are a beautiful woman, Reesa," he said. "A very beautiful woman."

Warren undressed, and his classic good looks were carried out through the whole of his body. His chest was not as powerful as Ted's, nor as hairy as Joaquin's. *My God,* she thought in a sudden flash of insight. *I've already had enough experience to begin comparing men!* Warren was well-muscled, too, but rather than giving the appearance of a powerful bull, he reminded Reesa of a mountain lion, sleek and feline.

Warren climbed into bed with her and began to caress her, tenderly and skillfully. Then, in something which was first shocking, though later exquisitely pleasurable, he began using his tongue on her neck, shoulders, breasts, and nipples, and then her thighs.

Reesa felt her body filling with passion, and her loins flooding with the dampness of desire. Her hands began to explore his body, touching here with the delicacy of a butterfly's wing, grabbing there with a boldness she wouldn't have believed had she not been so swept up in the ecstasy of the moment.

"Oh, Warren, please, make love to me now," she whispered. "I must have you now."

134

Warren moved over her, then into her, filling her with feelings of pleasure so intense that she cried out from the joy of it. His movements established an easy rhythm then, and she matched him move for move until finally, with a powerful shudder, she felt an explosion of pleasure inside her that completely engulfed her, wrenching a sob of ecstasy from her throat. So lost was she in her own release that she scarcely noticed Warren's own frenzied climax.

She lay beneath him for a while, feeling his weight on her, enjoying the warm and pleasant dampness that filled her. She stroked his shoulder with her hand, and he kissed her again, then rolled over and lay beside her for a while. They were both silent, save for their breathing, which was just beginning to return to normal.

"Warren, do you think I am an evil woman?"

Warren raised up and leaned on his elbow. "No, of course not," he said. "Why would you ask such a question?"

"I enjoyed what we did. I can't begin to tell you how much I enjoyed it."

"I enjoyed it, too," Warren said. "It is meant to be enjoyed."

"But women aren't supposed to enjoy it," Reesa said.

"Nonsense."

"Well, maybe if they are in love with the man. But, and here is the really terrible thing—I enjoyed it even though I don't think I'm in love with you."

Warren began laughing, and he fell back on

135

the bed, laughing so hard he was scarcely able to draw a breath.

"What is it? What have I said?" Reesa asked, the tone of her voice clearly showing that she didn't understand. "Doesn't it bother you that I don't love you?"

"I'm sorry, my dear," Warren said. "It's just that the whole thing struck me as rather funny. Please forgive me."

"I forgive you, I guess," Reesa said. "Though I don't know what I'm forgiving."

"You are priceless," he said. He sat up, then swung his legs over the edge of the bed and began getting dressed. He looked back at her nude body and smiled. "But to answer your question, it doesn't bother me a bit that you don't love me. I'm very flattered that you enjoy making love with me. That's enough for any man, Reesa. Believe me."

"I believe you," she said softly.

But is it enough for me? she asked herself.

Chapter Fourteen

When Ted Foster awakened the next morning, he felt as if track had been laid through his head. He was nauseous and thick-tongued, and his head was spinning like a top. He smelled coffee and was puzzled until Sally stuck her head in his bedroom.

"Good morning," she said. "I've got coffee ready. I take it you won't be wanting breakfast."

"No," Ted said quickly. "No food, Sally, please."

Sally laughed and handed a cup of black coffee to him. "Serves you right," she teased. "My big night, and you are drunk."

"I wasn't much good to you, huh?" Ted asked, slurping the coffee gratefully.

"You mean you don't even remember?"

"Not a thing," Ted said.

"I must say, that is one of the most unflattering things any man has ever said to me," Sally pouted.

"I'm sorry," Ted said.

Sally laughed again. "Don't worry about it. But just so's you'll know what you missed, you and I had a marvelous time. Absolutely marvelous."

Ted laughed and put his hand on Sally's shoulder. "You know what I like about you, Sally? There isn't a hypocritical bone in your body."

"Unlike Miss Reesa Flowers you mean?"

"Who said anything about Reesa?"

"Don't play the innocent with me, Ted," Sally said. "You say you admire me because I'm not hypocritical, so let's at least keep honesty between us."

"All right; you're right," Ted admitted. "I was thinking of Reesa."

"She's no good for you, Ted. She can't accept life for what it is, only for what she thinks it should be."

"Perhaps so," Ted said. He sighed. "Anyway, it's none of my affair, as she certainly made clear to me yesterday." He ran his hand through his hair, then heard steel ringing on steel as spikes were driven home. "Good Lord!" he said quickly. "Are the men at work already? What time is it?"

"A little after eight," Sally said.

"I've got to get back into town and follow up on that timber order," he said. "I've also got to move the engineering car out here. Sally, go find Sam, tell him to fire up the boiler and run me in."

"Do you think you are up to a train ride this morning?" Sally teased.

"I'll hold my head out in the wind for the

whole way," Ted said. "It'll either cure me or kill me. And the way I feel right now, I don't much care which."

Sally laughed and left to deliver the message to Sam as Ted got ready.

Upon awakening, Reesa remembered at once the lovemaking of the night before. Unlike her experiences the morning after she lost her virginity, Reesa was not consumed with guilt and shame. After all, she reasoned, one can only lose one's virginity one time. And that was forever lost to Ted Foster. Anything she did now was her own business.

But even as Reesa reasoned this, she found herself amazed that she could have such a reaction. She had been seduced last night . . . *no,* she told herself with a sudden flash of honesty, *she had done the seducing* . . . and this morning as she thought back on it, she thought only of the pleasure of the moment. Was this what her body had been trying to tell her all along? Was she different from other women? Was she cursed with a passionate nature, one which responds easily and eagerly to lovemaking? Something this important, Reesa knew, would have to be considred for a long while. It was not something to be decided in just a few moments, and certainly not on the morning after.

An hour later Reesa was dressed and down to the depot to await her father's train. She hoped she could meet him and speak to him without giving away her secret.

Near the tracks there was a crowd gathered

around a buckboard, where an itinerant preacher was standing on the buckboard giving a sermon. Reesa drifted over to listen, to kill the time while she waited for the train.

The man was of average size and build with a full head of thick, black hair. He jabbed his finger toward the crowd as he spoke to them.

"And here's another reason why there shouldn't be no trains," the man was saying. "It's done been proven in Arkansas that them heavy trains shakes the ground so that the hogs is kept too nervous to eat. They don't fatten up and folks is goin' without pig meat. The live steam wilts the grass and spoils the pasture and the horses and cows won't eat 'n' there goes your beef. 'N' as if it warn't bad enough for the train to kill pigs, cows and horses, it'll even kill little children what gets on the tracks, 'n' yes, old folks who are goin' to church in their buggy. 'N' hear this. Them steel rails lyin' out there on the ground," he pointed to the track, "draws lightnin' better'n a dog's tail, 'n' ever-'one knows to stay away from dogs durin' a lightnin' storm. Now what'll you think all that electricity runnin' loose in the ground'll do to you? I'll tell you what it'll do to you. It'll make you sturl. You know what sturl means? It means the men folks will all be turned into geldin's, and no more children will be born. And that means the end of the human race. I tell you, folks, what you're seein' here is the Antichrist come in the form of a fire-breathin' steel monster."

"I'll give you this, preacher man," one of the men in the crowd called, "you got guts. Don't you know most ever'one in this town makes their livin' off the railroad?"

"You should all turn your efforts to more godly pursuits," the preacher replied.

Reesa was glad that the preacher wasn't talking about sin. She was on tenuous enough ground with her conscience this morning as it was, without having to grapple with the burden of sin. She turned to leave and saw the engine arriving from End-of-Track. Ted was standing on the platform between the engine and the tender, holding onto the assist bar, leaning out and looking down the track. His powerful arms and shoulders and the determined set of his handsome face said that here was a man who had much more to offer than did Warren Leland. He had a passion for life, and she knew that he would share that intense passion with whomever he chose to love.

It was funny, but Reesa could regard Ted in an entirely different light this morning. Yesterday he had been the despoiler of her virginity, and though she didn't really feel it, some misguided sense of propriety had made her lash out at him. But today she was one affair wiser and one hundred years older. She saw her anger with him for what it was: a sham.

The engine stopped and Reesa walked over to speak to him. She wasn't certain how she was going to do it, but somehow she wanted to make amends for the way she had treated him yesterday.

"Hello, Ted," she said brightly.

"Good morning, Miss Flowers," Ted replied.

141

That's all right, Reesa thought. *He has a right to be angry.*

"If you're going to be in town long enough, I thought you might like to have lunch with my father and me," she invited.

"I have other plans," he said formally. "The engineering car and the car you're living in are both being pulled out to End-of-Track."

"When?"

"Right now," Ted said, turning to one of the men. "Sam, hook 'em up."

"Well, can't you at least wait for my father?"

"I've no time for that," Ted said brusquely. "Look, why don't you just go have lunch with Leland. I'm certain he'll welcome your company."

"I'm certain he will," Reesa said hotly. "You are . . . *impossible!*" she sputtered.

"I've no time for you," Ted added. "I see my trestle timber has arrived."

Ted jumped off the platform and walked down the track toward the flatcars, which were loaded with the large twelve by twelve timbers he would use for constructing the trestle across the Prealta Gulch, and Reesa was left standing alone.

"Ohhh, I *hate* you, Ted Foster," she said between clenched teeth.

The engine, which had brought Ted to town, backed down the track and hooked onto the engineering car that served as the office, and then to the plush, private car that Ted had given over to Reesa and her father for living quarters. After the connection with those two cars was made, it moved back to hook up with the flatcars loaded with timber.

"Miss Flowers," one of the brakemen said, approaching Reesa then. "Sam told me to tell you he would hold the train 'til you got on board."

"Tell Sam to go without me," Reesa said. "I'm going to wait here for Papa."

"Very well, miss," the brakeman said. He turned and gave a signal to Sam, and Sam blew his whistle a couple of times, then the engine jerked forward. Sam gave Reesa a wave as the engine chugged by, and the brakeman swung onto one of the rapidly rolling cars with ease.

The train had gathered speed by the time the last car passed her by, and Reesa saw Ted on that car walking along the top of the load carrying a bill of lading, inspecting his timber. He looked down at her once, then looked away as if he didn't even see her. Reesa stood there, watching the train disappear beneath the ribbon of smoke as it receded in the distance.

"Did he think by taking the car he could stop us from seeing each other?" Warren's voice asked.

Reesa turned, startled, as she hadn't heard him approach. "I don't know what he thought," she said. "And it is really immaterial, whatever it was. I'll continue to do as I please."

"That's a good girl," Warren said. "By the way, we just got word that the train is going to be late. Your father won't be in until this afternoon, so I'd like to invite you to have lunch with me."

"I'd be honored to," Reesa replied.

Warren looked at her knowingly and the slow, hot smile returned to his lips. "It's quite a while until lunch. Perhaps you'd like to join me in my room," he suggested. "I think we might find a way to spend the time."

At first a quick anger rose in Reesa, and she nearly cursed him for his insolence. But she managed to check it. After all, her anger was directed toward Ted, not toward Warren. And though she wasn't really certain in her own mind as to why she wanted to hurt Ted, she knew that this would. And it would serve him right. She returned Warren's smile.

"I think we just might find a way at that," she said.

Prealta's Gulch is a deep, wide canyon that lays its scar across the land for some fifteen miles, stretching north and south. At its narrowest and most shallow point, it is three hundred feet deep and one thousand feet across. But at that point the approach from the opposite side wouldn't allow track to be laid, so the engineers had very carefully determined a location for the crossing, which was designed to give the best approaches from the east and west, with the smallest distance and over shallowest canyon possible under the circumstances.

Survey stakes were placed to mark the path, and as the track was laid, the construction crews followed the line of stakes that were tipped by little blue flags as they stretched out before them like a perfect row of desert flowers.

It was three days from the time the timber arrived until the construction crew had laid track to Prealta. Now the timber cars were backed to the canyon's edge, and the precut timbers were snaked off and placed into position. It was nearly four hours before Murdock noticed something was wrong, and he got on a handcar and pumped his way back to the main camp to talk to Ted.

Ted had a map spread before him, and he was examining routes when Murdock knocked on the door.

"What are you doing here?" Ted asked easily. "I thought you had a bridge to build."

"Boss, didn't the engineers send the numbers in for the timbers to be precut?" Murdock asked.

"Yes, of course they did," Ted replied, looking up. "Why?"

"Well, somebody made a mistake," Murdock said.

"What kind of a mistake? What do you mean?"

"I mean the timbers don't fit. They aren't the right size."

"Are you sure?"

"Boss, you wanna come look for yourself? I tell you the damn timbers aren't right. It's impossible to bridge the gulch where we are with the timbers we have."

"Damn," Ted swore. "I think I know the problem."

Ted had been looking at the map in his crew car, and he stepped out the back door and walked along the track to the engineering car.

Murdock was right beside him. When he reached the engineering car, he saw Reesa and Warren inside chatting and drinking coffee.

"Where's your father?" Ted demanded in an angry voice, standing in the doorway.

"He just stepped out," Reesa said. "Why; what's wrong?"

"He's not the one I want to see anyway. It's all your fault. I should have known better than to depend on you to take care of something like this."

"You haven't told me what's wrong," Reesa said. "And I'll not sit here and allow you to chastise me without even knowing why."

"See here, Foster, I don't like your tone of voice," Warren interrupted.

Ted looked at Warren with cold fury in his eyes. "Get out of here, Leland, before I throw you out. I've no time for the likes of you."

Warren's hand started slowly toward his jacket lapel.

"You move that hand one more inch, and I'm going to lay it across a rail and cut it off and make you a present of it," Ted said menacingly. "Now, do you get out of here, or do I throw you out?"

There was a pregnant moment of silence, then Reesa, perhaps fearing that one or both would be killed, spoke up quickly. "Warren, please leave. I don't want any trouble on my account."

"Warren turned to Reesa. "I will be seeing you this evening?" he asked. "As usual?" he added with a quick look at Ted.

"Yes, of course," Reesa replied. "But please, leave now."

"Until then," Warren said, giving Reesa a small bow. He left the car and walked casually across to his buggy, then climbed in and whipped the horses into a run.

Ted felt his heart in his throat. He had been so angry that he nearly pushed Warren into a showdown—a showdown that he, Ted, wasn't really prepared for. He had no idea how it would have come out, though he wasn't at all certain it would have been in his favor.

"Do you feel like a big man for having bullied him?" Reesa asked coldly.

"Me, bully him?" Ted replied. "He's the killer, not me. If it had come to it, he would have probably shot me and that would have been the end of it."

"He might of shot you, boss, but he'd have been dead before he could take another breath," Murdock said. Ted had all but forgotten the big man waiting outside.

"What is all this about anyway?" Reesa asked.

"The timber order that you telegraphed for me. Did you get it right?"

"Of course I did," Reesa answered. "There was nothing to it. I just asked that they reactivate the order you had already submitted. Why?"

"Because it's wrong," Ted said. "The sizes are all wrong. They made the wrong cuts."

"Don't be blamin' her for that, Ted," Miller Flowers said, returning to the car at that moment.

147

"Have you heard?" Ted asked.

"Aye, I've heard. And I'm about to check on the order to make sure they got it good and proper when I sent it the first time."

Miller laid his crutches on the platform of the train, then swung himself aboard. He came inside and started riffling through the pigeon holes until he found the original message. He showed it to Ted.

"These are the numbers, are they not, lad?"

"Yes," Ted said after looking them over.

"Well then, we'll just wire back to Denver and see what numbers they used, if not these."

Miller removed the key lock and began sending his message. Ted looked at Reesa and saw that she was crying quietly, trying to dab at the corners of her eyes without being seen.

"I'm sorry, Reesa," he said. "I shouldn't have come in here half-cocked like that. I had no right."

"No," Reesa said, "you certainly did not."

"Well," Ted said again, this time more self-consciously, "I'm sorry."

"Boss, you wanna go take a look at the timbers?" Murdock asked.

"Yes," Ted said, more than willing to get away from the awkward confrontation with Reesa.

As he hopped off the platform Murdock said, "I've got the handcar; we can take a run out there."

The two men pumped their way out to the edge of the gulch and saw the confusion the mistake had caused. The workers were all sitting or standing around, taking advantage of

148

their unexpected break. The section leaders had the timbers laid out and were looking at them with puzzled expressions on their faces when Ted arrived.

"Boss, somethin' is mighty wrong," one of the men said.

"I know. Murdock told me about getting the wrong timbers."

"No, that ain't what I mean," the man said. "These here are the right timbers, but they still won't work."

"What do you mean they are the right timbers?"

"This here bridge plan has all the sizes marked on it," the man said. "And we done checked 'em out. The sizes is right."

"Then what the bloody hell is wrong?" Ted sputtered.

"I think I see," Murdock said suddenly. "I don't know why I didn't notice this before."

"What is it?"

"Look, do you see that rock ledge there? When I come out here with the surveyors, that ledge was some half mile or so to the north. Now it's about a half mile south. We're at the wrong spot."

"We can't be! We followed the stakes just like they were laid," the man with the bridge plan said.

"The stakes!" Ted said. "They must've been moved!"

"That don't make sense. Who would move them?" Murdock asked.

"Joaquin Mendoza," Ted said. He cursed angrily. "It'll take us two days to get the surveyors back, and another two days to lay in the corrections. There's no telling how far back the error was made. We may have lost as much as two weeks."

"What'll we do with the men in the meantime?" Murdock asked.

"Start pulling up the track," Ted said. "I can't afford to waste any of it. Take it up all the way back to the main camp."

The section leaders began yelling instructions, and the men, amidst much grumbling and cursing and wondering what they would be asked to do next, began taking up the rails they had just worked so hard to lay.

Ted walked out to stand on the edge of the gulch. He looked out across the wide expanse, and down into the deep valley below. Murdock came to stand beside him and handed him a bottle. "Thought you might be able to use a little snort."

"Thanks," Ted replied. He turned the bottle up and took several swallows, then handed it back.

"What do you think Joaquin's purpose was in doing this?" Murdock asked. "Surely he didn't think this would stop us."

"I don't think he intended it to," Ted said. "I think he just wanted to pay us back for giving him a payroll of cut newspaper."

"I'll bet you're right," Murdock said. "The son-of-a-bitch is probably out there somewhere laughing his ass off."

Chapter Fifteen

Don Esteban de la Mendoza, Joaquin's father, was a citizen of the United States by virtue of the fact that his ranch and all of New Mexico had been ceded to the United States. But though he was an American citizen, he was no less Mexican, and was an adherent of the Spanish customs and the old ways. Thus it was that when Jose, his younger brother, who lived in Mexico, wished to remarry after having been a widower for years, he felt it necessary to visit Don Esteban and secure his brother's blessings.

Jose traveled all the way up from Buenaventura to see his brother, and he brought several of his servants, his bride-to-be and her daughter, and their servants with him. The woman he was to marry was Maria Montoya, a handsome and elegant widow of fine background. Maria's daughter, who also made the journey, was a lovely 18-year-old with flashing black eyes and beautiful white teeth, and a smile that lit up her whole face. Her name was Lyrica, and she

151

had been the object of attention of every eligible man on Sombra de las Montanas.

Don Esteban, his brother Jose, and Jose's fiancée, Maria, were taking the grand tour of the ranch, a journey which would take several days to complete. Lyrica remained at the main house where Frederica and Joaquin held a fiesta in her honor. Amidst the food and drink, music and dance, there were also games, and as a result of the games, a great tension had developed at Sombra de las Montanas. It wasn't an uneasy tension, but rather a sense of excitement as everyone gathered around to see how Joaquin would answer the challenge.

The excitement had started thusly: Joaquin and Ronaldo, who were raised almost as brothers, were, as was their custom on such occasions, playing a game they called "one better." It was a game of such skill that only those two of all who lived on the ranch could play, though when they were younger Frederica had sometimes joined in and, to the chagrin of Joaquin and Ronaldo, had often outclassed them.

Today's game had gone far beyond Frederica's skills, however, and had in fact taxed the limits of both men. Ronaldo had just performed a feat of horsemanship that seemingly assured him of victory on the afternoon. He had placed his horse side by side with Joaquin's horse, then standing with one foot on the back of each animal and holding the reins from each, he rode at breakneck speed through a complicated obstacle course.

Now the pressure was on Joaquin to match him if he could.

"Give up now, my brother," Ronaldo teased. "It will be no disgrace. You have lost to me before."

"But I've no desire to lose to you now," Joaquin said. "And I shan't."

"Very well, match my ride if you can."

"I will more than match your ride," Joaquin boasted. "I will better it."

"How?"

Joaquin went to the table where the food and wine were laid out. He picked up six empty wine bottles, then handed them to a couple of the *vaqueros*. "Place these on the course," he instructed. He smiled at Ronaldo. "I will ride the course just as you did," he said. "In addition I will shoot all these bottles, breaking every one."

"But there are six bottles, Joaquin. That's all the bullets you have in your gun. That means you cannot miss, even one shot. And you'll be standing on the backs of two horses."

"I will not miss," Joaquin smiled.

"I do not believe you can do this," Ronaldo said.

"If I do this, will you concede I am the better man?" Joaquin challenged.

"*Si*, if you concede that I am the better if you miss," Ronaldo replied.

"Done," Joaquin agreed. "But we should have some form of wager."

"What could we wager?" Ronaldo asked. "I have nothing you want."

"I will be the prize," Lyrica suddenly said. "I will go with the winner."

The others whistled and shouted, and Joaquin broke into a big smile. "I accept that wager," he said. "The question is, will my sister allow Ronaldo to accept?"

The others laughed again, then Frederica called out hotly, "Ronaldo may do as he pleases. I certainly do."

"Ah, but not to worry, my sister," Joaquin said, looking at the beautiful young girl who had offered herself as prize. "One short ride and this girl is mine anyway."

"We shall see," Ronaldo countered.

Joaquin pulled his pistol from his holster and spun the cylinder, checking to see that every chamber had a bullet. Then he signaled for Lyrica to approach him. When she did, he kissed her. "That is for luck," he said.

Joaquin swung into Diablo's saddle and rode to the far end of the course, leading Ronaldo's horse with him. When he reached the end of the course, he stood on Diablo's back, then guided Ronaldo's horse into place. He put one leg over onto Ronaldo's horse and stayed that way for a long moment. Finally he gave a shout to the horses, and they broke into a run. He leaned over and bent his legs so that his knees acted as springs, taking up the shocks of the horses as they ran. After he negotiated the first two obstacles in the course, he pulled his pistol and prepared for the six wine bottles.

Joaquin did not hesitate as he approached the bottles. He shot quickly, first to one side of the horse and then to the other, the gun popping six times, then he holstered his pistol in time for the final two obstacles. The horses came

154

pounding up to the finish line and he jumped down.

"Well?" he asked, breathless, "how did I do?"

"You rode well," Ronaldo admitted. "It remains to be seen how your marksmanship was."

"He broke them all!" the two men who had gone to check on the bottles shouted. "A dead hit on each of the bottles."

"*Ai, yi, yi,* what shooting!" Ronaldo said in genuine admiration. He took Joaquin's hand and shook it in congratulations. "You have won, my friend, and I do not hesitate to call you the better man."

"And to the victor go the spoils," Joaquin said. "I claim my prize." He put his arm around Lyrica.

"You have won as well," Frederica said to Ronaldo.

"How have I won?"

"Now you will not feel my anger," Frederica said laughing.

The others joined in the laughter, and they were still teasing Ronaldo when a messenger approached them.

"Joaquin, I have good news," the messenger said. "The railroad was fooled as you said they would be. They have built their tracks right up to the Prealta Gulch, but they cannot build the bridge. Now they must tear the tracks out and build again."

Joaquin laughed at the news, then walked over and grabbed another wine bottle, this one nearly full. He held it over his head and called out to the others: "*Amigos,* let us drink a toast to Ted Foster and to the men who must undo what they have done."

"You mean undo what we did, don't you, Joaquin?" someone shouted.

"Yes," Joaquin said. "They must undo what we did. And now my friend, *Señor* Foster, we are even with the jokes. What passes between us from now on will be no joke."

Joaquin held the bottle out in the general direction of the railroad, then turned it up and took several swallows.

"Are you going to claim your prize?" Lyrica asked softly.

Joaquin brought the bottle of wine down from his lips and wiped his mouth with the back of his hand. He looked at Lyrica. She was as slender as the ocotillo bloom and quite as lovely. He held his arm out for her and she came to him, then they walked together into the hacienda.

Later, after they had made love, Joaquin left the bed and padded barefoot over to the window. The slanting afternoon sun splashed a square of light into the shadows of the corner of the room, and he stood there looking through the window across the rolling ground in the direction of the railroad.

The bedsprings squeaked as Lyrica sat up.

"Is she pretty?" she asked. Her voice was soft and as pleasant as the wind chimes, which the children of Sombra de las Montanas hung in the trees to catch the evening breezes.

"Is who pretty?" Joaquin asked, looking back

at the girl on the bed. She had not yet dressed and sat now with her knees pulled up and her arms wrapped around them. Thus it was that even though she showed the smooth lines of a nude form, her modesty was preserved.

"You know of whom I speak," Lyrica said. "The Anglo girl of the railroad."

Joaquin returned to the bed and sat beside Lyrica. He ran his hand through her long, black hair. "You are such a beautiful girl," he said. "I don't understand why you speak of Reesa Flowers."

"Because you were thinking of her as you stood by the window. Do you deny it?"

"Ah, but you cannot read my mind, Lyrica."

"We have just made love, Joaquin," Lyrica said. "When a man makes love to a woman, she knows things about him that he does not want her to know. I know for example, that you are "The *Anglo* girl of the railroad."

Joaquin rubbed Lyrica's cheek with the back of his hand. "Then you must also know that while we were making love, I thought only of you."

She caught his hand in hers and held it for a moment, then smiled. "That is true," she agreed. "And it is good because I am in love with you, Joaquin Mendoza."

Joaquin smiled. "Do not play tricks with my heart, Lyrica. I am a sensitive man," he teased.

"I play no tricks," Lyrica said. "I am in love with you."

"But how can this be? You offered yourself to the winner of the game. It could have been Ronaldo."

"No," Lyrica said. "I knew it would be you."

"But soon you are going to take a marvelous trip to San Francisco. There you may find another."

"I will find no one there," Lyrica said. "I love only you, Joaquin."

Joaquin stood and walked over to the chair where he began pulling on his trousers. "You are a very beautiful girl, Lyrica, but you are still young. I know how easily the young are sometimes misled. We will not speak of love now. If, when you return from San Francisco, you still feel love, then we will speak of it."

"Is that a promise?" Lyrica asked.

"It is a promise," Joaquin answered with a smile. Now fully dressed, he returned to Lyrica's bed and leaned down to kiss her.

Reesa stood watching as the two Chinese workers poured hot water into the large porcelain tub in her bedroom in the car which she shared with her father. Of all the ornate and plush fixtures of the elegant car, Reesa appreciated the tub the most, and though her father insisted that too many baths were unhealthy, it was Reesa's habit to take one every night when possible.

Steam rose from the water, and it looked so inviting that Reesa could scarcely wait until the two Chinese left so she could slip into the tub. Finally the fixture was sufficiently full for her to dismiss the two.

Reesa had poured a frothing soap into the tub as the water was being drawn, and to this she added a scented toilet water. She hurriedly disrobed, then stepped over into the tub and eased her body down into the bubbles. The steaming water stung her skin, and her body pinkened with the heat as she gave in to the most heavenly feeling.

She soaped and scrubbed until all the desert dust was gone, then stood up and reached for a towel. Her eyes were closed to prevent soap from getting into them, which explained why she was standing there nude, groping blindly.

"I believe you are looking for this," Warren said, handing the towel to her.

"Warren!" Reesa gasped, taking the towel from him and wiping her eyes quickly. She saw him leaning rather laconically against the door. "What are you doing here?"

"I saw the Chinaboys bringing in the water," Warren said, "so I knew you were taking a bath. I figured that would be a good time to come in."

"Well, it's a good time for you to leave as well," she said angrily.

"What's the problem? Your father isn't here. He has gone into Albuquerque with Foster to pick up the payroll. We are alone."

"I don't care," Reesa said. "What right do you have to just barge in here at your convenience?"

"I have the right of prior consent," Warren said easily.

"Prior consent? What is that?"

Warren laughed. "You've already given yourself to me," he said. He put his hands on her shoulders, then let one of them trail down through the soap suds and out onto the upcurving greast. A cluster of suds clung to the nipple, and he brushed them away casually. As he did so, the nipple hardened quickly.

Reesa suppressed a shiver. Even when angered, she was capable of sexual excitation.

"Ah, you see," Warren challenged. "We are alike, Reesa. You enjoy sex as much as I."

If the truth were known, Reesa thought, she probably enjoyed it even more. After all, Warren, for all his skills in arousing her and bringing her to orgasm, entered into sex with a sense of detachment that Reesa found maddening.

"I've no desire to continue this," Reesa said. "There is no love between us, Warren, and without love there can never be anything else."

Reesa stepped out of the tub and wrapped the towel around herself, but even as she did so Warren's arms were around her, his hands sliding down her wet back, pulling off the towel. He moved his mouth over hers and though she wanted to stop him, his knowing hands and skilled kisses caused heat to flash through her body, and she leaned into him.

"Do you see what I mean, Reesa?" Warren said triumphantly. "You are as much a creature of the flesh as I. It is not in your power to deny me."

Warren's mocking words angered Reesa and she pushed away from him, then retreated a few steps across the room. "No," she said. "I'm not like that."

Warren's smile never left his face as he advanced toward her. Reesa tried to retreat further, but the back of her legs came in contact with the bed and she fell across it.

Warren was over her then, already opening his trousers. He spread her legs and entered into her, despite her efforts to fight him off. She was unable to deny the lubricity of her desire and Warren's entry was made easy by that fact.

The Warren who made love to her this time was unlike the man she had known before. Instead of the subtle skills and detached aloofness, he took her with an edge of cruelty she hadn't noticed the other times. He was rough with her, and his thrustings pounded her hard against the mattress of her bed. She tried to protest and pushed as hard as she could against his chest, but he didn't stop and showed absolutely no concern for her. The subtle variations and ways he had used in the past to orchestrate her sensuality and develop her passions were left by the wayside, and he thought only of himself as he ravaged her.

Stripped as he was of the skill of his lovemaking, Reesa no longer saw in him the desirable bed partner she once imagined him to be. The quick flame of passion, which had flared under his first moves, now wilted under his tactless assault, and Reesa bore the incident in quiet, controlled anger.

When Warren finally satisfied his lust and rolled off her to lie beside her, panting to recover his breath, Reesa stood up and returned to the bathtub where she slipped back into the now tepid water.

"Never do that again," she said flatly. She was amazed at her lack of hysteria over the rape, happy to discover that she was at least selective in the sex that she enjoyed. For whereas after the rape experience by Ted, she had had to fight against the continuing emotions in her body, she was now calm and collected and knew only a sense of disgust with Warren for forcing himself upon her.

Warren stood up and smiled the same, laconic smile. "Have no fear," he finally said. "I told you once before that I have no interest in forcing unwanted attentions upon a woman."

"What do you call what you just did?" Reesa asked coldly.

"*Touché*," Warren said. "Though in truth, madam, I believed that your nature was such that you would respond whether you wanted to or not. I was wrong. You are not different from the other women after all. It was my mistake."

Warren closed the door behind him and left Reesa sitting in the tub. She should have been furious with him, but she wasn't. Instead, her heart leapt with joy over what he had said.

She wasn't different from other women after all. How wonderful it was to finally be free of the fear that she was somehow possessed of a hedonistic nature beyond her control.

Chapter Sixteen

It took an entire week to pull up the track and lay it again in the right place. That had the end result of costing three times as much to cover the same territory, since once the track was laid, then pulled up, then relaid, the workers had covered ground three times. It required the same amount of work whether they were laying track or pulling it up, and the fact that they were covering the same ground again meant nothing to them as far as their pay was concerned. They were paid just the same.

But Ted was acutely aware of the increased cost of the operation. And he dispersed practically his entire reserve for equipment and supplies. He was in Albuquerque to take care of such business, and most important to pick up more loan money from Warren Leland. He waited at the bank for Leland and, when Leland didn't show at the usual time, he left the bank to look for him. He found him playing poker in the hotel bar.

Warren glanced up as Ted came into the bar.

He held up his cards and smiled. "Some of your bad luck must be rubbing off on me," he said. "I haven't had a decent hand all morning."

Ted looked around the room. It was full of gamblers, drummers, and camp followers of the railroad. He considered them all scavengers, unable to make their own way, subsisting on the efforts of others. He placed Warren, whom he considered a scavenger of his father's money, in the same boat as the rest.

"It's after ten o'clock," Ted said.

Warren reached into his vest pocket and pulled out a gold watch. He opened the case and looked at it, then looked back at Ted and smiled. "I do believe you are correct. Say, if you can tell time that well, you should get a job with the railroad."

Everyone in the room laughed at the joke, and Ted felt a flush of anger burning his cheeks. "You know what I mean," Ted said angrily. "You were supposed to meet me at the bank."

"Really, my good man? I was supposed to meet you at ten o'clock? For what reason?" Warren asked. He put three cards down on the table. "I'll take three," he said to the dealer, as if the game were much more important than his conversation with Ted.

Ted felt the rage building inside him, and he grabbed the edge of the table and flipped it over. Cards and chips slid from the table to the floor, and the players yelled in protest and jumped out of the way causing their chairs to tumble as well, adding to the noise and confusion. Warren stood up slowly and turned to face

164

Ted. He adjusted his jacket so that it hung open slightly, allowing him access to the gun he wore on the shoulder holster.

The motion didn't go unnoticed by anyone in the bar, and they moved quickly out of the way, giving the two men room.

"That's the second time you've braced me, Leland," Ted said quietly. "Don't do it a third time."

"Give me cause to do it again and I'll go through with it," Warren replied just as quietly. "You wear a gun sometimes. The next time I'll make certain you are armed. Now what is all this about?"

"You know damned well what it's about," Ted said. "I have an agreement with your father. A business agreement. He is advancing money for the construction of the railroad. Your only function is as messenger boy, to carry the money from him to me. I was due a payment at ten o'clock this morning and you weren't there."

"You are due no such payment," Leland replied.

"What do you mean, I'm due no such payment," Ted demanded. "The agreement is that at ten o'clock every Monday morning, I will draw funds based on the miles of track I laid the week before."

"And what secures that loan?" Warren asked.

"The government grant," Ted said.

"Precisely," Warren replied. "The government grant, payable when you cross the territorial line, will recompense you for the total track mileage. They will not pay you for the miles of track you laid twice. Therefore, I have made the decision not to advance you any more money until enough progress has been made to once again earn credit toward the government grant. My father has put me in charge of this, and I know he will abide by my decision."

"I see," Ted said quietly. He felt a sinking sensation in his stomach as he realized what was happening.

Warren chuckled, then pulled a long thin cigar out of his pocket. He stuck it in his mouth at a jaunty angle and held fire to it. Finally, when his head was wreathed in blue smoke, he spoke. "However, we may be able to work out something. Would you like to come to my room with me? Or do you want the whole world to listen to your business?"

Ted looked around the room to see that the dialogue he and Leland were having was being very closely followed.

"I'd like to go to your room," Ted said.

"I thought you would."

Warren Leland's room was actually a two-room suite on the second floor of the hotel. It was the finest suite in the hotel and, in fact, the finest suite in the entire city. When Ted saw the creature comforts of the room, he understood why Leland spent most of the time in Albuquerque and came out to End-of-Track only every other day or so.

"Would you like a drink?" Warren invited, holding up a bottle.

"No," Ted said. "It's a little early."

"Very well, I was just trying to be hospitable," Warren said. He put the bottle down and looked at Ted through the cloud of smoke from his cigar. "I've got the money you need," he said. "But it's going to cost you."

"Cost me how?"

"First, you are to transfer final control of construction policy to me. That means how we build and where we build. Secondly, I'll have my accountants establish a rate of stock exchange. For every dollar I provide above the original agreement, you'll transfer stock into my name."

"Those are pretty harsh terms," Ted said.

"Nevertheless, they are my terms," Warren replied.

"I'll have to think about it."

Warren smiled. "Take your time, Foster. But if you don't go along, you are going to lose everything. This way, at least, you'll manage to salvage some interest in the railroad, if not maintain control."

Ted looked at Warren and at the smug expression of confidence on Warren's face. He saw the cigar at its jaunty angle and wanted to knock it right out of his mouth. Instead he tried to put what he hoped was a very calm expression on his face. "I'll let you know," he said.

Ted kept the problem to himself for the rest of the day. He worked down at the depot, checking incoming shipments of rails and ties as if nothing had happened. Finally, he took the last train back to End-of-Track, spending the entire three-hour trip atop one of the box cars, watching as the sun set over the magnificent landscape, underlighting the purple clouds with gold and bringing fire to the mountains. It was a soul-inspiring sight and brought some degree of perspective, if not a solution, to his problem.

It was dark by the time the train reached End-of-Track. Ted could see campfires going on both sides of the track. He could hear singing around the fires of the Irish workers. There was a high-pitched chatter coming from the fires of the Chinese workers, and he knew they were probably engaged in their incessant gambling, their one vice.

Lights were coming from Miller Flowers's car, and he looked at it, feeling a little tug at his heart as he thought of Ressa. She was so beautiful; how had they gotten off on such a poor footing? Anyway, things certainly seemed to have cooled between Reesa and Warren Leland for some reason. It had been well over a week since he had seen them together, and for that he was thankful.

Ted looked over the rest of the camp. The work train—sometimes called the perpetual train because it was always on the move—sat just behind the freshly laid track. The train was pushed by the engine, which sat at the furthermost point back on the track. In front of the train, at the point closest to the construction, several flat cars bore the tools and a blacksmith shop. Next came the crew cars, each one eighty-five feet long, with interiors lined with triple tiers of bunks. The tops of the crew cars sported tents, and there were hammocks slung beneath them. In all, some 400 men were billeted this way. After the crew cars came the dining car with a single table running its full length. The dining car, which augmented the mess tents, fed in shifts of fifty men each, with three minutes between shifts to allow the tin eating plates to be cleaned. They could be cleaned in three minutes because they were nailed to the table and swabbed out with a hand mop. The dining car was followed by the kitchen car and storeroom. The outside of the kitchen car was festooned with quarters of beef, provided by the company herd that grazed nearby. Occasionally, the beef would be augmented by freshly hunted buffalo, and quarters of that meat would hang red and glistening alongside the quarters of beef.

After the kitchen car came the engineers' car, the office or brain-center of the entire operation. It was here that Ted made his own office, and here that Miller Flowers kept them all in contact with the outside world through the telegraph key. Behind the engineers' office, there was a caboose, which Ted was using as his living quarters, then the car in which Miller Flowers and Reesa lived, then Sally's car, then several flat cars that were used for the daily trips back for new rails and ties. On each side of the track, there were tents erected by the camp followers: a preacher, a doctor, a saloon keeper, a general store, a hotel of sorts, and a mess tent to supplement the dining car.

It was a heady feeling to be in charge of an operation this large, and Ted felt a pang of remorse over the prospect of losing it.

"Ted, lad, come in and have coffee with us." Ted had been standing just outside Miller's car, and Miller's voice snapped him out of his reverie. He looked up at the old man. "Thanks, Miller, I just may do that," he agreed.

Reesa poured the coffee for them, then took a cup herself and sat with them. She was pleasant to him, as he was to her, and he was glad that the tension that had lately existed between them was temporarily suspended. His situation was too painful at the moment to accommodate friction between them.

"Why so pensive, lad?" Miller finally asked after they had sipped coffee in silence for several minutes.

"I may be losing everything," Ted said without fanfare.

"Oh? Why?"

Ted explained the costs incurred by having to tear up the track, then lay it a second time. Then he told them of Warren's offer.

"So either way, I figure to be out of it soon," he finally concluded.

"Reesa, darlin', you'll be handin' me a bit o' the Irish sweetenin' for the coffee, if you please," Miller said, to cover his shock.

Reesa handed a flask of whiskey to her father, and he poured a generous amount into his coffee, then added an equal portion to Ted's cup. He put the cap back on and sighed.

"Have you got any ideas, lad?" he asked.

"Not a one, I'm afraid."

"Oh, Ted, what are you going to do?" Reesa asked. "This is your dream. You can't lose it after having come this far."

Ted looked at Reesa and smiled. It had been the first bit of honesty to pass between them for a long while, and he felt warmed by it.

"Thanks," he said. "I appreciate your concern, but I don't know yet what I can do."

There was a knock on the door then, and Reesa got up to answer it. The giant figure of Murdock Felton stood on the other side.

"Ma'am, did Mr. Foster come back on the train?"

"Yes, he's in here," Reesa said. "Won't you come in?"

"Well, I've got Ling Cho with me, ma'am" Murdock said, and only then did Reesa see the diminutive Oriental standing behind him.

"Mr. Cho is welcome as well," Reesa said. "In fact, if you'd like, I'll boil some tea," she added.

"Thank you, missy, I don't wish to bother," Ling Cho said.

The two men came in, and Ted stood to greet them.

"We got troubles, boss," Murdock said.

"What more?" Ted asked.

"The survey engineers say we are going to have to blast our way through Fence Lake Pass."

"I thought they said we wouldn't have to," Ted replied. "That's why we decided to cross there instead of Pie Town."

"I thought so, too," Murdock said. "But they've changed their mind."

"That's all I need," Ted replied glumly. "Do you have any idea what blasting engineers are going to cost us?"

"Chinese do blasting," Ling Cho said quietly.

"Ling Cho, I don't want to sound negative, but it's a pretty sophisticated operation to handle dynamite. It takes a tremendous amount of skill."

"Chinese have skill," Ling Cho insisted. "Chinese invented blasting."

Ted laughed. "I guess you're right about that. Murdock, what do you think?"

"Boss, if Ling Cho says them little fellas can handle dynamite, then I say let's give it a try."

Ted ran his hand through his hair. "All right; I guess we got nothing to lose. Your Chinese can try it," he agreed.

"We do good job for you," Ling Cho said gratefully. "You see."

"Come on, little buddy, we better go now," Murdock said. "We got some plannin' to do."

"You know, I would hate to let them down almost as bad as I would hate losing the railroad," Ted commented after they left.

"Maybe things'll work out all right," Reesa said hopefully.

Ted smiled. "Hang on to your optimism, Reesa, right now it's about all we got."

"Ted, when do you get the government grant?" Reesa asked.

"As soon as I lay continuous tracks to the Territorial Line," Ted answered.

"Could you borrow from anyone else against that money?"

"I'm afraid not," Ted said. "The money that isn't committed to Titus Leland is committed to Western Pacific. I have nothing left to borrow money against. It's a shame, too, because I believe Pacific Trust Bank in San Francisco would lend me money if I had some collateral."

"What about the equipment? The engines, the cars, the tools?" Reesa asked.

"Most of the cars are leased from Western Pacific," Ted said. "The rest is already committed to Leland."

"But there must be something we could do," Reesa suggested.

"There's nothing," Ted said. "There is only so much money to work with, and we've used it up." He stood and stretched. "I've had a rough day. I think I'll go to bed and sleep on it. Maybe I'll get an idea in the morning."

"You'll be havin' our prayers, lad," Miller promised as Ted started to leave.

"Thanks," Ted said. He looked at Reesa. "And thank you," he added.

"For what? I haven't been of any help."

"Yes, you have," Ted said. "More than you realize. I needed someone to talk to tonight, and you were kind enough to listen. Good night."

"Good night," Reesa replied.

She stood at the door for a moment after Ted left.

"Well, lass, I've not seen you that gentle with the young man in a long while. Could it be that some of the original feelings for him are comin' back to life?"

"They never died, Papa," Reesa said. "They were just held back."

173

Chapter Seventeen

Reesa sat up long after her father had gone to bed. She had no idea what time it was, but realized it must be quite late because she heard no sound from the workers outside and knew they must all be asleep.

At first Reesa stayed awake because she was too upset to go to sleep. Then, more to pass the time than to actively look for a solution, she began reading the government regulations pertaining to the requirements to qualify for a Congressional Railroaders' Building Grant. For the construction of the Central Pacific, there had been a government loan of $16,000 per mile of flat land and $48,000 per mile of mountain land crossed, along with a land grant of ten miles to either side of the track. But that had been during the great rush to link the Pacific and Atlantic oceans. Now the government was less generous. The maximum grant was $16,000 per mile, regardless of the type of terrain the railroad crossed, and land grants were for one mile to either side of the right-of-way only. Reesa knew $8,000 per mile was committed to Western Pacific, and that left Ted with little enough to work with. To make matters worse, the track had to cross a state or territorial line in order for the grant to be paid. In this case, the line had to be crossed by the end of the ninetieth day and that was only twenty-three days away.

Reesa was about to close the book when her eyes caught a supplemental paragraph. At first she read it with curiosity, then with interest, and finally with a growing sense of excitement.

"This is it!" she said aloud. "This may be the answer!"

Reesa held the pages of the book open with an ashtray, then looked at the map on the wall. She searched for Fence Lake Pass, the point at which Murdock said they would have to cross, then ran her finger down the line of mountains until she found Pie Town. "Yes!" she said excitedly. "It will work, I know it will!"

Excitement had built to such a pitch that Reesa was unable to prevent the words from spilling out, and she looked around sheepishly, aware that she was talking to herself. At first, she thought to awaken her father and tell him of what she had discovered, but then decided to take it directly to Ted. After all, he was the one who would have to make the ultimate decision.

Reesa was wearing her nightgown and robe, and she started to go to get dressed, but was too excited to take the time. Besides, her robe was modest enough, she decided.

Reesa closed the book and stepped outside. The desert ground was spotted with piles of glowing coals, all that was left of the campfires. The men were asleep now, resting for the five-thirty wake-up call the next morning. The night air was cool, and Reesa shivered slightly as she clutched at the neck of her robe and hurried back to the caboose, which served as Ted's living quarters. She wasn't sure whether the shivering was from the cold or from the excitement of her discovery.

Reesa knocked on the door. She heard nothing, so she knocked again. Finally, she heard Ted call from inside.

"What is it? Who's there?"

"Ted, it's me, Reesa."

"Reesa? What is it? What's wrong?"

"Nothing. Ted, let me in, please. I must talk to you."

"All right; just a minute."

Reesa waited for a moment longer, then the door was opened. Ted was standing on the other side, wrapped up in a blanket. He looked like an Indian, and she chuckled at the sight.

"Excuse the wardrobe," Ted said. "I was in bed, and I don't own a robe. What is it? What are you doing here this late at night?"

"Ted, I've come up with a way to raise the money," Reesa said.

"What are you talking about? There is no way."

"Yes, there is," Reesa said. She went past him into the darkened caboose. "Light a lamp."

Ted did as she instructed and turned the lamp up. The mantle glowed white and the room was bathed in light. She put the book on his desk.

"Do you know what this is?" she asked, pointing to it.

"Yes. It's the government regulations pertaining to railroad grants."

"I have found an additional four hundred ninety-seven thousand dollars in this book," Reesa said.

"What?" Ted asked, his mouth dropping open in surprise. "What are you talking about?"

"Here," Reesa said, opening the book. "Read this paragraph."

"Exceptions to the above conditions," Ted read aloud. *"Additional funds may be made available in those areas where easement must be purchased from private property owners."* He looked at Reesa. "That won't do us any good," he said.

"Read on," she instructed.

"Railroads which serve military installations may receive additional funding from the Department of War, depending upon the recommendations of the Secretary of War. No, nothing here," he murmured. "Wait a minute, is this what you mean? *One thousand dollars per mile above the basic grant will be allocated for each previously settled community the railroad serves."*

"That's it," Reesa said excitedly. "Look," she added, pointing to the map, which hung on his wall. "You are going to have to blast your way through here anyway. Why not swing south and go through at Pie Town? That way you can pick up Hickman and Tres Laguanas, then Pie Town, Omega, Quemado, Red Hill, and Springerville over on the Arizona side. That's

177

seventy-one miles and seven towns, or four hundred ninety-seven thousand dollars."

"I don't know," Ted said slowly. "Some of those places are nothing more than mining camps, just spots on the map. There may not even be anyone living there."

"But they *are* on the maps," Reesa said. "Ted, if you have to, you could *put* people there."

"How do you mean?"

"You've made Papa your line supervisor. He could put railroad agents and their families in each of those places. They are already listed on the map, so we wouldn't be just creating them to get the money. And if someone lived there, they would certainly qualify as settled towns, even if by one family only."

Ted smiled broadly. "You know, Reesa, that head on your shoulders is as smart as it is pretty."

"Thank you for noticing," Reesa said.

"That you're smart?"

"No, that I'm pretty," Reesa replied.

"I've always known that."

"I haven't always been able to tell," Reesa replied. "There have been times when I made you angry, I know."

"Yes," Ted said. "But only because I was more angry with myself."

He took Reesa's hands in his own, and for a moment she felt a weakness in her knees.

"Reesa," Ted began. "I have been so busy with this railroad . . . consumed by it, in fact . . . that I've been a fool. I've nearly lost the one thing that is more important to me than any railroad."

"And what is that?" Reesa asked, her words barely audible.

"You," Ted said. "Reesa—I, well—damnit; I know I have no right in telling you this, coming right out of the blue as it is, but I love you. I think I've loved you right from the moment I first saw you."

Reesa felt her heart begin to race. He said it! Ted admitted to her that he was in love with her! Her head spun with excitement, and she didn't know whether to laugh or cry.

"Ted, oh Ted, why have you never said anything?" she asked.

"I didn't know how you felt," Ted said. "And there was Warren. You seemed always to be with him."

"Oh, you foolish man, can't you recognize when a girl is trying to create a little jealousy? You were always so busy with the railroad that I was never able to get your attention."

"I'll give you all the attention you can use," Ted said. He put his arms around her and kissed her full on the mouth. The kiss took Reesa's breath away, and she surrendered herself to him. It was a kiss of passion, of soul and of feeling. Despite the obvious skill of lovemaking that Warren Leland possessed, his kisses were ineffectual when compared to this.

Reesa raised her hand to Ted's jawline, placed her fingers lightly on a muscle that seemed to jump under her touch, then moved the hand around his neck to pull him closer. Her mouth opened, and she felt the strength of the kiss growing. She leaned against him as if she had turned to molten metal, melting to his searing kiss, flowing to his strong embrace.

Then Reesa lost touch with time and space as she felt herself being swept up in powerful arms and carried over to Ted's bed. He reached out to turn off the lamp then his strong hands moved over her with surprising tenderness, here opening her robe, there caressing her lightly, delightfully. There were no subtleties, no acquired skills, just passion born of love, and it transported Reesa to an ecstasy unlike any she had ever known.

Finally Reesa felt Ted's tightly muscled thigh against the smooth skin of her leg, and she could see his hairy chest, dark and matted in the dim light, as he moved over her. When they made love, the sights, sounds and textures all blended into a symphony without music, and a ballet without dance, sweeping them along to a crashing crescendo of pleasure.

They lay in each others' arms after they had loved, and Reesa studied the splash of silver that spilled into the dark car from the full moon outside. Finally she spoke.

"I must get back before Papa wakes up and misses me."

"I'll go with you."

"Go with me? Whatever for?"

"I want to tell him what a brilliant daughter he has," Ted said affectionately. "Also, I'm going to ask you to do something for me, and I want him in on it."

"What do you want me to do?"

"I want you to go to San Francisco," Ted said easily.

"Why?"

"I'm going to write a letter, which I want you to deliver personally to Gordon Kinder of the Pacific Trust Bank. I am authorizing you to ask for a loan on our behalf of one hundred fifty thousand dollars, securing it with the new grant money we expect to receive."

"Ted, you want me to ask for a one hundred fifty thousand dollar loan?"

"Yes."

"But I couldn't do that."

"Why not?"

"Why, I wouldn't know what to say, what to do, or how to act! I mean, how will it look for a woman to go in there and talk business with a man like Gordon Kinder?"

"Ah, but you aren't just any woman," Ted countered. "You're Reesa Flowers."

"Well, if you think I can do it . . . but don't you think you should send a wire first?"

"Absolutely not," Ted said. "Reesa, this has to be kept secret. You mustn't tell anyone where you are going or why. And especially not Warren."

"Can Papa know?"

"He's the only one we can tell," Ted said. "Is it agreed?"

"Very well," Reesa said.

The two had been dressing as they talked, and now they were ready to return to Reesa's car. They held hands as they slipped through the darkness, and just before they went into Reesa's car, they kissed once more.

"I'll get Papa," she said, after they went inside.

Reesa left Ted looking at the map and went into the compartment that served as her father's bedroom. He was sleeping soundly, snoring contentedly. Reesa shook him awake.

"What is it? What do you want?" Miller said groggily.

"Papa, wake up. Ted Foster is here. He has something he wants to tell you."

"Can't it wait until morning?" Miller burrowed into his pillow.

"No, Papa. He needs to tell you now."

"All right," Miller said. "Give me a moment."

Reesa returned to the front room to find Ted still studying the map.

"I think we can do it," he said, looking over at her. "The whole secret is going to be in making it to the Arizona line within twenty-three days."

"How long would it take you to make the border if you blast through at Fence Creek?" Reesa asked.

"I figured ten days at the outside," Ted said. "It's only half as far. This way we'll have to push it to make it in time. But I still think we can do it."

"Do what?" Miller asked, swinging into the room on his crutches.

"Save the railroad," Ted said. "I'd like to tell you about an idea that a very smart person gave me."

Ted proceeded to explain Reesa's plan to Miller. He ended by telling of the necessity for

182

Reesa to make her secret trip to San Francisco.

"I see," Miller said. "And you want my permission for her to go?"

"That and something else," Ted said.

"What else?"

"I want your permission to marry her."

"What?" Reesa exclaimed. "Ted, do you mean it?" Her breath was nearly taken away by the unexpectedness of the statement.

"Yes," Ted said. "I mean it. I want you to be my wife. That is if you have no objections," he added quickly, looking back at Miller.

Miller laughed. "My boy, 'tis Reesa who'll be tyin' the knot, 'n' 'tis her you'll be pleasin', not me. She's the one to give the word."

"How about it, Reesa?" Ted asked.

"It's yes," Reesa replied.

"Lord help 'er, she's gone and took a railroad man," Miller said in mock horror. He laughed and then moved to the table to pour himself a drink. "This calls for a celebration," he said. He held up the nearly empty bottle of Irish whiskey and looked at it. "Faith 'n' he's a drinkin' man, too. I'd nearly forgotten the sweetenin' of his coffee. Neither a man's daughter nor his whiskey will be safe with the likes of him around."

"You supplied the daughter, I'll return to my car and get the whiskey," Ted offered, laughing.

" 'Tis no matter. I'd be a poor Irishman without a reserve," Miller said. He moved across the room and opened a cabinet door to remove another bottle.

"Lass," he said as he poured the amber fluid

in to a glass, "I've not been a good Catholic in all the ways I should've. But I aim to see my daughter married in a church. You'll oblige me that?"

"Yes, Papa," Reesa agreed.

"And the children? They'll be Catholic?" Miller asked.

"Ted will have to agree to that, Papa," Reesa said.

"And the grandchildren if you wish," Ted agreed happily.

" 'Twould be nice," Miller said.

"Papa, we aren't even married yet, and you've got our grandchildren in church," Reesa protested.

" 'Tis the duty of a father," Miller said. "Now, when is the weddin' to be?"

"Anytime she wants it," Ted replied.

"We'll wait until the railroad is built," Reesa said.

"You mean you'd be willing to wait that long?" Ted asked.

Reesa smiled. "Yes. When we get married, Ted Foster, I want to be the most important thing on your mind. I've no wish to compete with your railroad for attention."

"There's no competition," Ted said, putting his arms around her and kissing her. "You would win, hands down."

"Oh, Ted, the railroad simply must be successful now," Reesa said.

"It will be, lass," Miller said. "I've got a feelin' that it will be."

Chapter Eighteen

The train ride to Denver was uneventful, and as Reesa had been there once before, there was nothing new in the way of adventure. She made the entire passage lost in the daydreams and fantasies of her future as Mrs. Ted Foster. It was such a pleasant way to pass the time that she took scarce notice of the cinders and dust, or the discomfort of spending the night in a cramped coach car, since there were no sleeping cars available for the Albuquerque to Denver run.

Once Reesa reached Denver though, the situation changed drastically. There she entrained aboard the *Pacific Parlor Express*, a luxurious eight-car train that ran from Kansas City to San Francisco. The *Pacific Parlor Express* boasted two libraries, a hair-dressing salon, two organs, and its own private newspaper. The parlor car was resplendent in plush upholstery, rich hangings and hand-carved inlaid paneling. Reesa, who had been raised as a railroader's daughter, had never seen anything to match the luxury and elegance of the train, and its pure grandeur was enough to bring her out of her daydreaming in order to observe the wonder of it all.

"*Mademoiselle* Flowers?" a uniformed steward inquired as soon as Reesa's luggage was stowed and she had settled into a large, overstuffed chair.

"Yes."

"Welcome aboard the *Pacific Parlor Express, Mademoiselle,*" the steward said. He handed her a menu. "There are seats available in the dining car at eleven-thirty, noon and one o'clock. Which would you prefer?" The steward had an accent, but Reesa didn't know whether it was genuinely French or put on just for the overall effect of elegance.

"I think I will take the one o'clock sitting," Reesa said.

"Would *Mademoiselle* care to select from the menu?"

Reesa's previous experience with meals on board trains had been limited to sack lunches or the very unappetizing fare served at stations along the way. Now she saw a veritable feast offered. The menu featured blue-winged teal, antelope steaks, roast beef, boiled ham and tongue, broiled chicken, corn on the cob, fresh fruit, hot rolls and cornbread.

"I'll have broiled chicken, please," she said, returning the menu to the steward.

"An excellent choice," the steward assured her. "Your table companion will be a *Señorita* Lyrica Montoya. She is a young Mexican lady and exceptionally well-cultured. Do you mind?"

"Mind? No, of course not," Reesa replied. "Why should I?"

"There are those who do," the steward said. "I've had two refuse."

"Then you may schedule me as her dining companion for the duration of the journey," Reesa said.

"Thank you, *Mademoiselle,* that is most kind," the steward said. "Your chicken will be ready at one o'clock. I hope you enjoy your trip."

After the steward left, Reesa looked through the large windows at the beautiful scenery. Huge purple mountains hung in the distance, while in the meadows and plains alongside the track, wild flowers grew in colorful profusion. As the train passed, it gathered the curious at trackside, and Reesa saw hundreds of children waving gaily as they sped along. At first she returned their waves, but soon grew tired from the sheer effort of it and settled back to read the free newspaper offered by the train.

The dining car began serving at eleven, and by one o'clock, when the third call for lunch was issued, Reesa was ravenously hungry.

The elegance of the dining car was in keeping with the rest of the train, and Reesa saw richly paneled walls, plush drapes and upholstery, and flower-bedecked tables. She was met by a waiter as soon as she stepped through the door.

"Your name, miss?"

"Reesa Flowers."

"Ah, yes, your dining companion is already seated. This way, please."

As Reesa approached the table, she saw a young, very beautiful Mexican girl sitting quietly. The girl was wearing an elegant gown of pale gold, and it made her dark, flawless skin even more beautiful. She greeted Reesa with sparkling eyes and a dazzling smile.

"Hello," Reesa said. "My name is Reesa Flowers."

Reesa thought she saw something pass over the girl's eyes—recognition, maybe? But that couldn't be. Reesa had never met this girl. She wouldn't ge likely to forget her if she had. Besides, the look passed away as quickly as it arrived.

"I am Lyrica Montoya," the girl said. "I am very pleased to meet you."

"Lyrica . . . what a beautiful name!" Reesa answered warmly.

The waiters brought their lunch then, and the two women got to know more of each other as they enjoyed their meal. Reesa learned that Lyrica had just become the stepdaughter of a very wealthy Mexican and was being sent to San Francisco by her new stepfather to enjoy a vacation.

"I think he is embarrassed to have me around during the—what do you call it, the early part of the marriage?"

"The honeymoon?" Reesa suggested.

"*Si*," the girl said with a smile. "The honeymoon."

"But it will be such a wonderful thing to visit San Francisco, don't you think?" Reesa asked.

"I have never been before," Lyrica said. "Although I have an uncle who lives there. Have you ever visited San Francisco?"

"No," Reesa said. "This is my first."

"Why have you come?"

"I," Reesa started, then hesitated. "I have come on business."

"Forgive me; it was rude to ask," Lyrica apologized.

"No, not at all," Reesa replied. "It is just business to do with a railroad my fiancée is building. It isn't very interesting, I'm afraid."

"Perhaps we can do something together while we are in the city," Lyrica suggested. "I would very much like to see the opera. Wouldn't you?"

"Yes, very much," Reesa replied.

After the meal, Reesa excused herself and returned to the parlor car where she read for a while, then listened to the steady clicking of the wheels on the tracks. She knew from her long association with railroads that the number of clicks she heard in twenty seconds was roughly equal to the speed of travel in miles per hour. She counted fifty-five clicks.

Reesa looked around the parlor car at the other passengers. They were probably unaware of the speed they were traveling and totally unconcerned over their safety. The comfort of the chairs and the luxury of the car seemed to mock the possibility of an accident. And yet Reesa had seen "cornfield meets," and knew from ghastly observation what a four hundred ton train traveling at nearly a mile a minute could do. An engineer had once told her that such a train generated nearly twice the energy of a two thousand-pound cannonball fired from a one hundred-ton Armstrong gun.

Reesa was probably the only passenger in the car to have ridden in an engine cab. She knew what it was like to see the narrow bright line of rails and the slender points of switches as the train rushed forward at fifty or sixty miles per hour. She had heard the thunder of the bridges and saw the track shut in by rocky bluffs as the train swept around sharp curves. She had also seen it during a dark and rainy night, when the headlight reveals only a few yards of glistening rail, and the ghostly telegraph poles light up, then whip by so fast as to be a blur. Reesa knew full well that by the time the headlight picked up anything, it would be far too late to stop.

And yet knowing all this, she, too, was as content as any of the passengers on board, and in a short while the steady clicking of the rails and the comfort of the reclining seat lulled her into sleep. She dreamed pleasantly of being the wife of Ted Foster.

There was a bustle of activity at the station when the train arrived in San Francisco two days later. It was a huge crowd, but unlike the crowds of people who came to meet the trains at Albuquerque, these people all seemed to have a purpose. There were no fewer than fifteen tracks running under the awning at the station, and a train sat on each track. Out of the awning in the yard, there were more tracks and switches than Reesa could effectively count, and everywhere she saw engines puffing about, making up new trains. Her father had been a train man for his entire life, but Reesa knew he had never seen anything this magnificent, and she wished that he had been able to come with her to share the pure excitement of such a sight.

"Reesa!" Reesa heard someone call, and she looked around to see Lyrica Montoya standing with an attractive Mexican gentleman. "Reesa, have you made plans where to stay? Is anyone meeting you?"

"I am staying at the St. Mark's Hotel," Reesa said. "No one is meeting me. I thought I would hail a carriage."

"My Uncle Carlos is here," Lyrica said. "Perhaps you will allow us to give you a ride?"

"I don't wish to put you to any trouble," Reesa said.

"It is no trouble, *Señorita*," Carlos said, smiling broadly at her. "We will be going right by the hotel."

"Well, I thank you very much," Reesa said.

"Where is your baggage?"

"There," Reesa said, pointing to two pieces of luggage.

Carlos spoke in Spanish and an older man, obviously his servant, stooped to pick up her bags.

"But what about Lyrica's baggage?" Reesa asked.

Carlos laughed. "I'm afraid my sister's daughter brought all of Mexico with her. We have another wagon taking her things."

"I did not know what to bring," Lyrica shrugged, "so I brought everything."

Reesa joined the others in laughter, then followed them through the huge station to the street out front. There dozens upon dozens of carriages sat, and hundreds of people walked by quickly, as if hurrying to make an important engagement. Everyone seemed to be yelling at everyone else, and the noise was deafening. She caught a strong, fishy smell and commented on it.

"We are but a short way from the docks," Carlos explained. "What you smell is the sea!"

"The sea!" Reesa said excitedly. "Oh, I've never seen an ocean. I am going to enjoy this trip ever so much."

"Don't forget we have a date for the opera," Lyrica said. "Uncle Carlos tells me there is one tomorrow night. Would you like to go then?"

"Yes, that would be nice," Reesa answered. "My business with the bank should be concluded by then."

"Fine," Lyrica said. "We will call for you at your hotel tomorrow evening at seven-thirty."

"That would be delightful," Reesa replied.

Chapter Nineteen

During the heyday of building rails across the country, there were those smart, if somewhat unscrupulous men, who realized that more money could be made in building a railroad than in actually running one. The government advances and land grants were so generous as to invite speculative building when indeed no railroad was actually planned. The land was divided up into profitable parcels and sold, tracks were shoddily laid across land that dishonest surveyors certified to qualify for the government money, and the get-rich-quick schemers left the Comstock Lodes and flocked to the railroads.

Perhaps, the most grandiose scheme of all was the Credit Mobilier scheme. Credit Mobilier was a construction company organized by the directors of Union Pacific Railroad. The railroad paid for all work through Credit Mobilier, which set its own charges for goods and services. Of the seventy-three million dollars that poured into the Union Pacific construction funds, no more than fifty million dollars went for actual cost. The remaining twenty-three million dollars were divided among the principal stockholders of Credit Mobilier: a brilliant and zany man named George Francis Train; Thomas Durant, one of the principals of the Union Pacific; Oakes Ames, a United States Congressman, and Schuyler Colfax, Vice-President of the United States.

The Credit Mobilier bubble burst in the summer of 1872, however, and the days of high-handed railroad financing had ended. From that day forward, there was very little of the get-rich-quick appeal to railroad building, and backing was much more difficult to obtain. Thus it was that the letter, which Reesa carried with her to present to Gordon Kinder of the Pacific Trust Bank, had a complete accounting of all funds acquired and expended by the Southern Continental Railroad, as well as the anticipated route of travel that would increase the government grant.

Reesa had the letter in her purse as she stood in the lobby of the Pacific Trust Bank. She had asked a clerk for permission to speak with Gordon Kinder, and now cooled her heels as the clerk held a whispered conversation in the back of the room. Reesa was aware that the men in the bank were staring at the upstart woman who would invade their domain, and she tried not to return their stares or to show embarrassment over being the center of their attention. Finally the clerk returned.

"You may see Mr. Kinder," he said.

"Thank you."

Gordon Kinder was a portly man with a thick curving mustache over drooping jowls. He stood as Reesa approached his desk, walked around it, and held a chair for her to be seated. "Now, Miss Flowers, what can I do for you?" he asked after he returned to his own chair.

Reesa opened her purse and removed the envelope she had been given by Ted.

"Mr. Kinder, I believe you recall a Mr. Ted Foster who came to you a few months ago concerning a loan?"

"Ted Foster. Yes, he's building a railroad somewhere I think. Texas or Arizona."

"New Mexico," Reesa said. She handed the envelope to Kinder. "Here is a complete accounting of the operation to date. We've made excellent progress, but now we find that we need an additional one hundred and fifty thousand dollars."

"One hundred and fifty thousand?" Kinder repeated. He read the letter carefully, then read it again. "That isn't an excessive amount. That is, if it offers our depositors a fair chance of return. Tell Mr. Foster I will be happy to speak with him."

Reesa felt a sinking sensation in the pit of her stomach. He hadn't even understood that *she* was asking for the money. She took a deep breath and tried again.

"He won't be able to come see you, Mr. Kinder," she said. "If we are to get the government grant that we are using to secure this loan, we have to lay track across the Arizona line by a set deadline. Ted can't leave the construction. That's why he authorized me to apply for the loan."

Kinder looked up in some surprise. "You? You're a woman."

"Yes, Mr. Kinder, I'm a woman," Reesa replied. "But, as you can see by Ted . . . Mr. Foster's letter, he has complete faith in me and in my ability to negotiate this arrangement."

"I don't know," Kinder said, laying the letter down. He ran his hand under his sagging chins. "It's not that I personally have anything against doing business with a woman, you understand. But I've got my depositors to worry about."

"You would not be doing business with me," Reesa said with a sigh. "You would be doing business with Ted Foster. I am just his messenger."

"But you are a woman, Miss Flowers."

"You keep telling me that," Reesa said. "Look," she added in a frustrated tone of voice, "have you ever made a loan on the strength of a telegram?"

"Well, yes, of course."

"Then you are doing business with whoever delivers that telegram to you," Reesa said. "And sometimes that's a mere youth. Am I right?"

"Yes."

"Then just regard me as the bearer of a telegram. But for certain reasons of confidentiality, Mr. Foster didn't wish to use the telegraph system."

Kinder picked up the letter and looked at it again, rubbing his chins once more. "Very well,

Miss Flowers, I'll have a bank draft made out to you for one hundred fifty thousand dollars."

"I would like it in cash, please," Reesa said.

"Cash? But, Miss Flowers, that's a great deal of money for a woman . . . for anyone to be carrying."

"I realize that," Reesa said. "But I have the cloak of secrecy in my favor. And we must have cash as we are working against a deadline and would not have time to convert the draft into cash."

"Very well," Kinder said. "How do you propose to carry that much money? It won't fit into your purse, and I wouldn't recommend carrying it in one of our bags."

"I brought a portmanteau," Reesa said. "I shall carry the money in that." She pointed to the leather case, which sat by the railing near the clerk's desk.

"It will take a few minutes," Kinder said, excusing himself. "That's a lot of money to gather together."

When Reesa left the bank one half hour later. with the weight of the one hundred and fifty thousand dollars pulling at the suitcase, she had such a heady sense of accomplishment that she didn't even notice the closed coach across the street.

"There she is," Lyrica said, pointing her out to the two men who sat with her. "I am certain that she has the money in that bag. You may keep whatever money there is. Just don't hurt her."

"You're a queer one, girl," one of the two men said. Both were *Anglos,* and rather desperate looking men, one with a large scar on his face and the other with a patch covering one eye. "If you don't want any of the money and you don't want her hurt, just what do you want?"

"I was told you'd do a job for me without question," Lyrica said.

"She's right, Jake," the man with the scar said. "What the hell do we care why she's doin' this? If there's money in that bag, it'll be payment enough. And there sure as hell ought not to be any problem in takin' it away from 'er."

"Remember," Lyrica warned again. "She is not to be harmed in any way."

"What if she puts up a fight?" Jake asked.

Lyrica laughed. "Can't two strong men handle one woman who fights?"

"Not to worry; we'll take care of it all right. I was just wonderin', that's all. Come on, Emmett. We got work to do."

The coach tilted as the two men got out, and one of them turned back to look through the window. "This here'll be the last time you'll ever see us, ma'am. I want ta tell you it's been a pleasure doin' business with ya."

"Good day to you, sir," Lyrica said. She signaled for the coach driver to pull away and left the two men standing beside the street.

Lyrica had been left to guard Reesa's purse one night on the train while the latter went to the ladies' lounge. She read the letter and realized that here might be a way to stop the hated railroad from cutting through the Mendoza land. Such an accomplishment would certainly make Joaquín take more notice of her, maybe even return the love she felt for him. There was needed only a way to take advantage of her knowledge, and that way presented itself when she was taken on a tour of the waterfront.

"There are desperate men here who will do anything for money," her uncle told her as the carriage rolled past the waterfront saloons. "They are drifters, robbers, miners who have lost their claims, men with no hope nor ambition beyond the next day. It is not an area where one should long idle," he added. He spoke to the driver, and the driver whipped the team into a trot.

This morning, saying that she was going to the Museum of Art, Lyrica hailed a closed coach and returned to the waterfront. She found the desperate looking men lounging outside a saloon, and offered her proposition. She would provide them with information, which would allow them to acquire a great deal of money. All they had to do was take it. She wanted nothing other than the money, to be taken.

As the coach rolled down the street, Lyrica turned her head to keep Reesa from seeing her. For just a moment she regretted the whole thing and almost yelled at the driver to stop and pick Reesa up before the robbers got to her. After all, she had gotten to know Reesa on the train, and she liked her, despite the fact that she was jealous of Joaquin's feelings for her. But no, Reesa wouldn't be hurt, and the money wouldn't be a personal loss. It would affect only Ted Foster and his railroad. And in that Lyrica knew that she was doing a noble thing.

Reesa had chosen the St. Mark's Hotel because it was only two blocks from the Pacific Trust Bank. She increased her pace in order to cover the two blocks as quickly as possible. She was perfectly safe; it was broad daylight and no one knew what she had in the bag. But, nevertheless, she would feel much better once she reached the hotel.

As she approached the alleyway just before the hotel, a man lurched out of it. At first he frightened her, not only by the suddenness of his movement, but also because he was a frightening apparition to behold. He was large, unkempt and unshaven, and wore an eyepatch over one eye. But the man was staggering about, and he held an empty wine bottle to his mouth as if trying to milk one last drop. Obviously the poor wretch was a wino, just coming awake from last night's intemperance.

"Hey, missy, would you buy a poor man a drink?" the man slurred, staggering toward her. He reached for her as if pleading, and Reesa's attention was so focused on him that she didn't notice until the last instant the second man hiding in the shadows. He jumped out at her and pulled a canvas sack down over her head. She tried to scream, but the scream was muffled by the bag. She felt a rope being wound around her tightly, and then the portmanteau was wrenched from her grip. Next there was a sharp pain as she was struck on the head, and everything went black.

Chapter Twenty

When Reesa regained consciousness, she found that she was tied and gagged and lying in a crude bed of some sort, the canvas sack gone from her head. The room seemed to be moving, and she could hear creaks and groans as if from stretching rope and flexing boards. A dimly lit lantern cast flickering shadows across the room and, as she examined her situation she saw, in addition to the bed where she lay, a table and chair, a chest, and a shelf with a handful of books. She was also cognizant of a very strong and most unusual odor. It had a bit of a fishy smell to it, though not so overpowering as to be unpleasant.

Reesa heard the rattle of chains. That sound she recognized immediately, having heard chains being used to secure cargo on trains.

"Cap'n, the anchor's aweigh," a voice called.

"Aye, we'll stand off Alcatraz Island for the night, Mr. Simpson."

A ship! She was on board a ship!

Reesa tried to cry out, and strained against

the bonds which held her, but she was unable to make more than a pitiful whining sound. She made no progress against the ropes whatever.

Reesa felt the throb of the ship's engines and realized they were moving, leaving for no telling where. My God, what would she do? What was going to happen to her? She thought of Ted and felt heartsick.

The money!

Reesa tried again to call out, but could manage nothing. She was suddenly aware of a painful bump on her head and realized that the money had been taken. What would Ted do without the money to operate? And how did she get here, and why was she here?

The door opened and a man entered. He was short but muscular, and looked like a solid block of granite. He was bald, but more than made up for it by the full set of chin whiskers. His mouth was clean shaven, however, with no mustache above and nothing below until far down on the chin. The light in the room was not bright enough to allow Reesa to determine the color of his eyes.

"Well, I see you are awake, Miss Martin," the man said.

Miss Martin? Who is Miss Martin? Reesa thought. That's it! There's been a case of mistaken identity. She shook her head rapidly, and the man removed the gag.

"I guess we can take this off now," he said. "After all, we are in the middle of the bay. There is very little chance of anyone hearing you."

"Who is Miss Martin?" Reesa gasped as soon as she could speak.

"Oh, I see . . . you're going to plead mistaken identity, is that it?"

"I am not Miss Martin," Reesa said. "My name is Reesa Flowers. And I can prove it."

"And precisely how do you intend to prove it?" the man asked. "You have no identification on you. Do you have family in San Francisco?"

"No," Reesa said. "I'm from New Mexico."

The man laughed again. "New Mexico. That's as good a place as any, I suppose. Now suppose we quit playing games, Miss Martin."

"Who is this Miss Martin you keep calling me?"

"All right, if you must hear it recited, Miss Martin, I shall accommodate you. Your name is Abigail Martin, and you are from Boston, Massachusetts. You worked as a governess in a private girls' school and—must I go on? Do you realize by now that I know who you are?"

"But I'm not who you say I am," Reesa insisted.

"Look, Miss Martin," the man said gruffly. "You kidnapped four of those little girls, extorted money from their parents, and then killed them. There is no place in the civilized world where you can hide. Two Pinkerton men traced you to San Francisco and caught you yesterday. They put you on board my ship because it was the next one leaving for Boston."

"But that isn't true!" Reesa insisted. "My name is Reesa Flowers. I came to San Francisco yesterday to borrow money for my fiancée's railroad. I left the bank with the money and two men accosted me. They took the money, and now I find myself here in this place. I don't know who you are or why you are so willing to believe that I am this Miss Martin you speak of, but I am Reesa Flowers."

"It is widely known that you are a persuasive woman," the man said. "But you'll find that I can turn a deaf ear to your lies."

"What is your name?" Reesa asked.

"I don't see why that should concern you."

"My God, sir, I am your prisoner! My life is completely in your hands! Am I not even to know the name of the man who may kill me at any moment?"

"You need have no fear on that," the man said. "You'll be taken back to Boston for a fair trial, that I promise you."

"Captain . . . I assume you are the captain of this ship."

"Aye, madam, that I am."

"Captain, if I am who you say I am, wouldn't it make more sense to send me back by train? After all, a train can travel from San Francisco to Boston in ten days. How long will it take you to reach Boston?"

"You've a point there, and I raised the question myself to the Pinkerton agents," the captain answered. "But they explained that the trains'll not carry you without extradition papers, and by the time those are signed you'll likely have made good your escape again."

"And you believed them?"

"I neglected to tell you, Miss Martin," the captain said coldly. "One of the little girls you

204

killed was my own sister's daughter. I'll not be takin' a chance on your gettin' away again. That's for sure."

Reesa began crying quietly, big tears sliding down her face.

"The cryin'll do you no good," the captain said. "I'm immune to such pleadin'."

"Am I to be kept tied for the entire journey?"

"I'll untie you as soon as we are to sea," the captain said. "We'll spend the night anchored just off Alcatraz Island and get underway with the mornin' tide."

The despair of her situation nearly overcame her, and Reesa let out a pitiful cry and strained against the bindings once more. This time her effort succeeded only in throwing the blanket, by which she was covered, to the floor. Evidently during the struggle, her dress had been badly torn, because now that the blanket was removed, she realized that one of her breasts was exposed to the captain's view. She saw his eyes drawn to her breast. It was smooth and creamy with the nipple erect and gleaming in the soft light.

"My God, you're Satan's own daughter, that's for sure," the captain said. "He spared no pains to make you beautiful."

"Please," Reesa said. "I am not who you say I am. Please, at least cover my bosom."

The captain made a small animal-like sound deep in his throat. Reesa looked up at him and saw in his eyes the reflection of the flame of the lamp. The burning flame seemed visible evidence of his desire.

" 'Tis not my own doin', girl," the captain said. He pulled the top of Reesa's dress down, exposing both breasts, then pulled the bottom of her dress up, exposing her bloomers. He jerked the bloomers down so that from the waist down, she was naked. "When evilness such as you possess comes in the body of a woman as beautiful as you, 'tis more of a temptation than a mere mortal can withstand. It is Satan's way, as you well know."

"Please," Reesa begged, as the captain began removing his own clothing. "You are making a mistake, captain. I am not who you say I am."

"Shut up, you vile creature," the captain spat. He was completely naked now, and he climbed onto the bed with her, looming over her like an apparition from hell.

When Reesa felt the captain's full weight upon her, she wanted to scream, but knew to do so would be useless. He entered into her brutally, and that which had brought her only pleasure before now brought her pain. It was so acute that it was all she could do to keep from crying out with the agony of it. How different this was from the passionate response to Ted, the sensual response to Warren, or even the aching hunger she had felt for Joaquin. Now there was only the obscene desecration of her body, painful and degrading beyond imagination.

Finally the captain let a grunt escape from his lips and shuddered once as he finished. He withdrew with as little fanfare as he entered; then, turning his back to her, began dressing quietly.

"Captain," Reesa said quietly. "Describe these so-called Pinkerton men to me."

"I don't wish to discuss it any further, madam," the captain said.

"Did one of them have an eye patch?"

"Yes."

Reesa sighed. "He was one of the two men who robbed me."

The captain turned back toward her, then seeing the proof of his brutality in her abused body, he looked away in shame.

"This Miss Martin," Reesa went on, seeing the captain's shame and hoping to take advantage of it. "Do you have a picture of her?"

"No," the captain said. "But a very good description of her."

"Describe her, please."

"She's a beautiful young woman of nineteen or twenty, known to have very winning ways about her. She has brown eyes and red hair."

"Red hair? My hair is black," Reesa said.

"Madam, we are all aware of dyes which can change the color of a woman's hair," the captain said.

"But, Captain, surely *you* of all people should know the color of my hair. Look again."

The captain looked at Reesa's hair.

"No," Reesa said quietly. "Not there, for the hair on one's head can be changed by dye. There is another place where the hair is the natural color."

"Madam, surely you don't intend for me to . . ."

"Captain, you *raped* me," Reesa spat. "Are

you now too sensitive to even see if you had the right victim?"

The captain took the lantern from the wall and moved it over the bed, causing the shadows in the small cabin to twist into grotesque shapes. He held the lantern over Reesa's stomach and looked at the junction of her legs. There was, glowing ebony in the lamplight, the small triangle of hair which proved Reesa's statement.

"Oh, my God," the captain gasped.

"Do you believe me now?" Reesa asked.

"Oh, my God." the captain said again. "What have I done?"

"You have made a mistake," Reesa said.

"Oh, what am I going to do?" the captain cried.

"Do? Why, you are going to let me go," Reesa said.

"No, I can't," the captain said. "Don't you see that?"

"What?" Reesa felt a new fear knotting at her stomach. "Why not?"

"Because now I'm guilty of abduction and of rape. If I let you go, and you go to the authorities, I'll lose my license. I may even be put in jail."

"Captain, do you intend to add murder to your other crimes?" Reesa asked.

"Murder?" the captain asked. "No; who said anything about murder?"

"The only way you are going to keep me here is to kill me," Reesa said. "I've no intention of staying on board this ship."

"I've got to think." The captain walked

across the room and put both hands on the desk and leaned against it for a moment. "I've got to think of something," he repeated.

"Put me ashore," Reesa suggested. "I don't know who you are. I don't know which ship this is. How can I hurt you?"

"I . . . I don't know," the captain said. Finally he looked back at her. "I'm going to put you ashore on Alcatraz Island."

"Where is that?"

"It's right here in the bay," the captain replied. "You can catch a ferry in the morning. By then I'll be gone."

"Thank you, captain," Reesa said quietly.

The captain quickly untied her and as her wrists were released, she began rubbing against the rope burns gingerly.

"I was given $250 for your passage to Boston," the captain said. He pulled an envelope from his pocket and handed it to her. "I'll give it to you."

Reesa was working on her dress, but was unable to effect a modest enough repair to the damaged bodice. There was no way to keep her breast covered. "Have you something I can wear?" she asked.

"Yes," the captain said. "Forgive me, yes." He opened the chest, removed a bulky sweater and handed it to her. She slipped it on gratefully.

"Come," the captain said. "I'll put you ashore."

"Is there an inn or some lodging on the island?" Reesa asked.

"A inn? No, there is nothing," the captain answered.

"You mean I have to spend the night in the open?"

"I'm sorry," the captain said. "It's the only way."

On deck Reesa saw the type of ship she was on. It had one mast forward and one aft and a huge smoke stack right in the middle of the deck. A large paddle wheel protruded from each side of the ship. Under other circumstances, she might have found the vessel fascinating. Until now she had seen only pictures, or Currier and Ives prints of such ships.

"Mr. Simpson, lower a boat away," the captain ordered.

"Aye, aye, cap'n. Will you need a crew?"

"No. I'm going to put the lady ashore. The fewer of our men she sees, the better off we'll be."

"Cap'n, you mean you aim to let her get away?"

"We've made a mistake, Simpson," the captain said anxiously. "I no longer believe this woman to be Miss Martin."

"Then perhaps we should take her back to . . ."

"I'll make the decisions," the captain interrupted gruffly.

"Aye, aye, sir."

"And make ready to sail. We'll get underway as soon as I return."

"Cap'n, the tide is not yet in."

"We're not waiting for the tide," the captain said. "We're sailing immediately."

"Aye, aye, sir," Simpson said.

Reesa followed the exchange with disinterest. Her only thought now was to escape from this ship. If it meant that she would have to spend the night on some island that she had never heard of, then so be it. She intended to get away before the captain changed his mind.

The captain said nothing as they rowed from the ship to the dark island. There were only the sounds of the oars dipping water and rubbing against the oarlock. Finally she felt the boat scrape against the bottom.

"Step out over the bow, madam, and you'll scarcely wet your feet," the captain said.

Reesa did as she was instructed without saying a word, and no sooner was she out of the boat than the captain began pushing off for the return trip to the ship. He said nothing more to her, nor did she speak to him. She was thankful to be rid of him.

By the light of a full moon overhead, Reesa walked through cold water, which was only an inch or so deep and then reached the rocky, but dry shore. She climbed up a small path until she reached a level place, then she turned to look back at the sea. The boat was nearly returned to the ship, and already smoke was coming from the ship's stack. It was a completely black silhouette, and Reesa knew there would be no way she could ever identify it.

"Who is there?" a voice suddenly called.

Reesa felt a spasm of fear and turned toward the voice.

"Identify yourself at once, or I will shoot," the voice said.

"No, don't shoot," Reesa said.

"Advance and be recognized."

Reesa moved hesitantly toward the voice.

"Halt," the voice said.

Reesa saw a man moving toward her carrying a rifle. As the man got closer, she noticed two things about him. He was quite young, and he was a soldier.

"Good Lord, it's a girl," the soldier said. "Who are you? What are you doing here?"

"My name is Reesa Flowers," Reesa said. "I was . . . abducted and put aboard that ship. But I managed to talk them into freeing me. I . . . what is this place? I was told it was uninhabited."

"It's a military prison, ma'am," the soldier said. "You just stand still, ma'am. I don't know what to do about this."

"What's going to happen to me?"

"I don't know, ma'am. I've got to report it," the soldier said. He turned his head to one side and cupped his hand to his mouth. "Corporal of the Guard, Post Number Five!" he shouted.

"Corporal of the Guard, Post Number Five," Reesa heard repeated in the distance, and then even further away, so faint as to barely be heard, "Corporal of the Guard, Post Number Five."

"He'll be here in a minute, ma'am," the soldier said. "You just stay put."

"I'm not going anywhere, I promise you," Reesa said.

A moment later Reesa heard someone approaching them.

"Halt," the soldier with her called. "Who goes there?"

"Corporal Rogers," a voice called.

"Advance, Corporal Rogers, and be recognized."

The approaching soldier advanced several steps.

"Halt," the soldier called again. Then: "I recognize you, Corporal Rogers."

"What is it, Evans. Why did you sound the alarm?"

"This here girl, Corporal," Evans said, pointing to Reesa as the man came closer.

"What? Who the hell are you?"

Reesa gave the corporal her name and explained how she came to the island.

"Well, ma'am, I don't reckon there's much we can do about that," Corporal Rogers said. "But if you'd like to come on back to the guardhouse, I suppose we could give you some coffee and a place to keep warm 'til morning."

"Will I be able to get back into the city tomorrow?"

"Sure," Corporal Rogers said. "I don't see any reason why not."

"Thank you," Reesa said. She turned to the private who had first challenged her. "And I thank you, too. You have been very nice."

"My pleasure, ma'am," the young soldier said, smiling broadly. "Most of the time out here on guard, there don't nothin' happen. This is somethin' I'll be able to talk about for a long time."

Reesa followed the corporal back along a moonlit path until they reached a small building that was made of rock. A welcome lamp glowed from within.

"What was it, Rogers?" a man asked as they stepped inside. "Was Evans wantin' his mama?" A second man laughed.

"No, sir, Lieutenant," Rogers replied. "Look what I got."

"Holy Jesus," the lieutenant said, seeing Reesa. Jumping to his feet, the lieutenant showed Reesa to a small, but private room where there was a bed, and he offered it to her as a place to sleep. She accepted gratefully, and slept soundly until the next morning. After a hasty cup of coffee served by the awed lieutenant, she was escorted to the ferry back to the city.

Once back in her hotel room Reesa took a most welcome bath. The hot water helped to ease some of the physical abuse she had undergone, but nothing could fill the ache in her heart over the loss of the money. She had not only let Ted down, but had added horrendously to his burden.

Chapter Twenty-One

"Frankly, my dear, I'm afraid there is actually very little that I can do," the police captain said. He thumped his hand against the bowl of his pipe, dumping out the blackened tobacco, then began filling it anew. He was a big man with a red neck, which seemed restricted by the blue tunic of his police uniform. He stuck a match to the bowl of his pipe and began drawing on it as he continued his conversation with Reesa.

"You see we are restricted in our jurisdiction to the actual city limits of San Francisco. Now if these two scoundrels have left town—and if they took as much money as you indicate, I'm certain they have left—then all we can do is get out a wanted poster on them."

"You mean you'll do nothing to get my money back?" Reesa asked in dismay.

"Oh, I didn't say that," the police officer replied. "We'll do all we can. I'm just being realistic when I tell you that what we can do simply won't be enough. I'm afraid you have lost your money."

"I see," Reesa said. She stood up and for a moment had to fight against an overpowering dizziness, which threatened to make her faint.

"Are you all right?" the policeman asked anxiously.

"Yes, I'll be fine," Reesa said. "It's just that this has been quite a blow."

"I'm certain that it has," the police officer said. "Would you like one of my men to escort you back to the hotel?"

"No," she said. "I've nothing left to lose," she added, with a short, bitter laugh.

"I'm sorry, madam," the police officer said, rising. "I'm very sorry indeed."

Reesa left the police station and hailed a carriage to return her to the hotel. There was nothing she could do now except pack up and go home. She dreaded facing Ted with this. He wouldn't blame her, of course, but his dream of building the railroad was over now. There was no hope left.

Reesa put her hand to her head, then leaned against the side of the carriage. She wanted to cry, but there were no tears. She looked out at San Francisco. It was such a beautiful city, and she had hoped to be able to enjoy it while she was here. The trip had started with such excitement: plans of marriage to Ted, plans of building the railroad with him, thoughts of seeing a glamorous city—and now it had all evaporated into a mockery.

As the carriage clattered along the street, Reesa suddenly noticed a large building with

the sign: TITUS LELAND TRUST AND INVEST-
MENTS, INC.

"Stop—stop the carriage!" she shouted.

"Whoa," the driver called to the horses.
"Yes, ma'am. Is something wrong?"

"No," Reesa said. "I've changed my mind. I
want to get out here." She paid the driver, then
left the carriage and started toward the Leland
Building. She had no idea what she was going
to do, but she knew she must try something.

Titus Leland's appearance belied his fifty-
nine years. He had a full head of silver hair; a
face that was weathered, but not haggard;
sharp, piercing eyes; and a trim, youthful body.
His healthy appearance was the result of a full
and active life in his youth. He had been a mer-
chant sailor when he heard of the gold strike in
California and worked his passage to the gold
fields.

He didn't make the big strike, but he did
manage to take over five thousand dollars in
gold dust out of the mountain streams, and he
used that to start his fortune.

His first investment was in a ship, which
was abandoned in the bay when the entire
crew, including officers, went into the hills to
make their fortune. The ship became a naviga-
tion hazard, and the city of San Francisco con-
fiscated it. Titus Leland approached the city
council and agreed to take the ship if the council would pay him $250 to get it out of the way.
To his surprise, the council agreed, and three
days later offered him the same deal on another vessel. Titus outfitted both ships, found

crews from disenchanted sailors-turned-miners, and went into the cargo business bringing goods into the rapidly growing area. Within one year, Leland Shipping Lines had twenty ships.

When the railroad boom started, Titus Leland had enough money to get in on the ground floor. He amassed control of the California Coastal Railroad through a very ingenious maneuver. By the law governing their charter, no one person could buy more than two hundred shares of stock. But that same charter required two million dollars of stock to be sold to the public before a government matching grant could be obtained.

A ten percent down payment was needed to buy a share of stock. Titus hit upon the idea of having his friends buy shares of stock, with him putting up the ten percent down payment. They immediately signed over the stock to him as security for the loan, with the understanding that they would default on the loan, turning stock back to him. Within six months, he owned 750 shares, or seventy-five percent of all stock in the railroad, plus the two million dollar government grant to start building.

Titus did not get involved in the Credit Mobilier scandal. He was offered the opportunity, but saw immediately that it was a sham, and he wanted no part of it. It wasn't that he was so fiercely moral . . . it was just that he considered it poor business. It was his theory that good business practices were founded on solid foundations such as ships of the sea and actual railroad stock, not falsified equipment and phony construction gimmicks. His California Coastal Railroad was an immediate financial success, and Titus Leland had become one of the wealthiest men in the world.

"But what good does it do me?" he had often asked his friends. "I've got a rapscallion of a son who cares about nothing but gambling and a good time. I see no prospects of his ever getting married . . . he'll probably get himself shot by a cuckolded husband long before that . . . and I'll die without a grandchild to carry this on. It all seems such a waste. . . ."

Titus sent Warren to New Mexico to participate in the building of a new railroad with Ted Foster. It had been his hope that Warren would learn something from Ted Foster, a man Titus admired and respected. He was exactly the way Titus had been in his youth, and the old man had no doubt but that Ted would be a success.

But it wasn't working the way he had hoped. He had it on good authority that Warren was spending most of his time in the whorehouses and gambling halls of Albuquerque and not only was he learning nothing from Ted Foster, he didn't even get along with him. Titus was about ready to abandon the entire project. Warren was returning to San Francisco tomorrow, and Titus intended to tell him to stay home. He would grant Ted Foster an extension on the money he had already loaned him, so that he could find financing somewhere else and just pull out of all further business transactions with the railroad.

"Mr. Leland, there is a young lady to see you, sir. A Miss Reesa Flowers."

"Reesa Flowers? I don't know a Reesa Flowers. Who is she, some doxie trying to make a claim against my son? No doubt she is pregnant. Why do they think all they have to do is get pregnant, and they can come here and claim Warren did it to them, and I'll pay them off?"

"You have already paid off a substantial number of them, sir," his secretary, a small owlish-looking man, said.

"Yes; I know. All right, send this girl in."

"Very well, sir."

Titus leaned back in his chair and made a tent with his fingers as he waited for the girl to be shown into his office.

"Thank you for seeing me," Reesa said when she came in.

This girl was different, Titus noticed. She didn't have the look of dissipation about her that marked the other girls.

"What can I do for you?" Titus asked. He started to make a caustic comment about her relationship with Warren, but checked it to see what she had to say.

"Mr. Leland, my name is Reesa Flowers," Reesa began. "I am engaged to Ted Foster." Reesa went on with the story, telling how Ted had run into difficulty because of the trick Joaquin had played on him, and how Warren had offered to advance the loan—but only after extracting a terrible price. She told about discovering a way to increase the government grant by serving the seven previously settled communities, and how she had come to San Francisco to borrow money from Pacific Trust against this new source of revenue. She concluded by telling how the money had been stolen from her the day before, and though she avoided the incident of her abduction and rape, she did explain that the police held out no hope for the return of the money.

"I see," Titus said after Reesa had concluded her story. "You've had a rough time of it. What do you want me to do?"

Reesa took a deep breath. "I want you to lend me the money," she said. "The new source of revenue we'll receive will be enough to cover our loss to Pacific Trust and repay you as well."

"Young lady, are you aware that under the terms of our agreement, I hold as security *all* funds due you by government grant?"

"You mean Ted will have to pay you back all of the money he gets?"

"No. But he cannot use it as collateral for another loan. By the terms of our contract, I could foreclose on him right now, since he violated that agreement by securing a loan from Pacific Trust."

"No," Reesa said. "I didn't know that."

"Who discovered the way to increase the funds?" Titus asked.

"I did," Reesa said, adding quickly, "that wasn't Ted's fault."

"I'd hardly call it a fault, young lady," Titus said. "I find much to admire in that. In fact, I find much to admire in you."

"Well, I . . . I thank you," Reesa said, smiling at the unexpected compliment.

"Miss Flowers, you are a woman with a practical mind, I can see that. I have a business proposition for you. I have a way you can earn that one hundred fifty thousand dollars. It won't be a loan, but an outright bonus."

"How?"

"By doing something for me."

"What is it? Yes, I'll do it," Reesa said.

"You haven't heard the proposition yet."

"What could it be? If you're willing to pay one hundred fifty thousand dollars for it, I'm willing to do it."

"I hope you are as enthusiastic about it after you hear the offer," Titus said. He leaned back in his chair and cleared his throat. "Miss Flowers, I take it you know my son?"

"Yes."

"How do you get along with him?"

"I . . . we used to get along quite well. I must admit there's been a cooling between us of late."

"That's the way my son is," Titus said. "He has no substance, Miss Flowers. He is all fluff. Oh, he's handsome and charming and makes a very good first impression on the ladies. You might even say he's a ladies' man of sorts. But he doesn't have the gumption for the long haul, and it doesn't take women long to realize this."

"I'm sorry," Reesa said. "I didn't mean to offend you."

"Offend me?" Titus laughed. "My dear, I never find honesty offensive." He stood up and walked over to a side cupboard and poured two glasses of sherry. He brought one to Reesa and handed it to her before he resumed his talk.

"Warren's mother died when Warren was quite young. I was living a pretty active life then, and it was a bit too much for her. Warren has never known a good woman's love . . . nor, in fact, been subjected to a good woman's influence. I fear that has greatly deprived him of something important. And in so doing, it has deprived me of my own immortality."

"Your immortality?"

"Yes," Titus said. "My bloodline, Miss Flowers. The blood that flows through me flowed through my father and his father and his father for countless generations. Is it to stop with Warren? It will if Warren has no children."

"What . . . what are you saying?"

"Quite simple, Miss Flowers. Warren is coming to San Francisco tomorrow. I want you to marry him."

"You want me to what?" Reesa blurted, unable to believe what she was hearing.

"I want you to marry him," Titus said again. "If you do, I'll give you the money, and you can give it or loan it to Ted Foster as you see fit. You will also marry into a rather substantial fortune. Enough to cause most women to jump at the chance, I imagine."

"Well, I am not most women," Reesa said angrily.

"Precisely my point," Titus said. "Believe me, I wouldn't make this offer to most women. But you have a rare quality about you that is immediately apparent to anyone with discernment. I feel you would be a very good influence on my son, and what's more important, an exceptional mother for my grandson. What do you say?"

"I say no," Reesa replied.

"I'm sorry to hear that," Titus replied. "I had thought that you loved Ted enough to do this for him."

"Of course, I love Ted," Reesa said. "That's why I'm refusing your offer."

"Look at it this way," Titus invited. "If you agree to marry Warren, Ted will get the money, and he will be able to complete his railroad. If you refuse to marry Warren, I'll foreclose immediately and he'll lose everything. I'll ruin him."

"You . . . you would do that?" Reesa asked in a small voice.

"Yes, my dear. I'm sorry if I have disillusioned you. But I am a businessman, and I play by the rules. You can check on me if you wish. I've never cheated another man, but I do take every legal advantage, and I am a hard fighter."

"I see," Reesa said weakly.

"I want a grandson, Miss Flowers," Titus said. "And I don't mean some bastard conceived by some doxie."

"I can't," Reesa said. "I can't do this to Ted."

"Look at it realistically, Miss Flowers. Do you think you can have any life with Ted Foster if he fails in this venture? He is much too proud of a man to ask that of you."

"He won't have to ask it," Reesa said quietly. "I'll offer it to him."

Titus laughed. "You've measured the man's pride. Do you really think he'll accept your offer?"

"No," Reesa agreed. "He won't accept it."

"Then examine the options," Titus said. "If

you marry my son, Ted Foster will get his money and build his railroad. If you do not marry my son, Ted Foster will lose everything. Including you, Miss Flowers. Realistically, he's not going to be able to marry you either way. But if you agree to my offer, he will at least have his railroad. Now which will it be? The railroad without you, or no railroad, and no you either?"

"You make it sound as if I have no choice," Reesa said.

"You don't have a choice," Titus said. "That is, if you love him."

"What about Warren?" Reesa asked.

"What about him?"

"Have you spoken to him about this? You know as well as I that Warren isn't the marrying kind. He may not go along with this."

"He will be here tomorrow," Titus said. "If he doesn't go along with it, then you are free and clear. If you agree to my proposal, I'll give you the money anyway, whether he wants to get married or not. What do you say?"

"How soon can Ted have the money?" Reesa asked.

"I'll wire my bank in Trinidad and have a courier deliver the cash to him tonight," Titus said.

"And if Warren declines tomorrow, Ted keeps the money?" Reesa asked.

"With no strings attached," Titus promised.

Reesa let out a big sigh. "Very well, Mr. Leland. You've got yourself a deal."

"I'll send you with my clerk to validate the transfer of funds," Titus said. "Warren arrives on the seven-o'clock train tomorrow morning. He should be here by eight."

"I'll be here when he arrives," Reesa said.

Reesa left the office with a very thin, very fidgety clerk, and together they went to a telegraph station. The clerk handed the message to the telegrapher. "Will that be all?" he asked of Reesa.

"No," Reesa said. "I want to stand by the instrument as the message is being sent and wait on the confirmation."

"What good will that do you, miss?" the telegrapher asked. "It'll just be so many clicks to you."

"Nevertheless, I'll feel better if I do," Reesa replied, purposely not telling them that she knew the science.

Reesa listened as the message was sent. It was, as Titus Leland promised, an order to transfer $150,000 by cash from the bank in Trinidad into Ted Foster's hands at End-of-Track. A few moments later, the reply came back confirming the order. The clerk wrote the message on a piece of paper and handed it to Reesa, though as she had read it as it was coming in, she already knew what it said.

"Thank you," she said, taking the message. She looked at the clerk. "That will be all now."

Reesa spent the rest of the day in a daze. She wandered through the city looking at the sights without actually seeing them. She felt as if someone very close to her had just died, but the shock was still too great for her to react to it. She went to an apothecary that evening and bought a sleeping draught to help her through the night.

Reesa was at the office of Titus Leland by seven-thirty the next morning waiting to see Warren. Titus breakfasted daily in his office, and he offered to share the rolls, eggs and coffee with Reesa as she waited. She declined his offer for all but the coffee.

"Mr. Leland, your son is here," his secretary said at eight o'clock.

"Ask him to come in, please," Titus said, wiping his mouth with a linen napkin.

"Hello, Dad; damn, it's good to get back to civilization for a while," Warren said, coming through the door. There he saw Reesa and stopped short. "Reesa! What are *you* doing here? I wondered where you went."

"I came to San Francisco on business," Reesa said.

"Yes? I'll bet it has something to do with the fact that Ted Foster needs money. He's changing his route, Dad, but I've got him right where I want him."

"And where is it that you want him?" Titus asked.

Warren laughed. "Begging for mercy," he said. "I'm going to take that railroad away from him."

"Why?" Reesa asked.

"Why?"

"That seems a fair question," Titus said.

"Because I don't like him," Warren said. "He's such a . . . a *builder*, a dreamer. He makes me sick."

"Because he's all the things you aren't?" Titus asked.

"If you want to say that," Warren replied, "I won't try to deny it. I'm right about why she is here though, aren't I? She asked you for more money. Did you give it to her?"

"I did."

"It figures," Warren said. He laughed it off. "Ah, what the hell. I guess it doesn't makes any difference."

"I made a deal with Miss Flowers," Titus said.

"What kind of deal?"

"I gave her the money on the condition that she would marry you."

"That she would marry me?" Warren asked incredulously. He laughed and looked at her. "Dad, are you serious?"

Reesa felt her heart leap for joy. Warren was about to slough the whole idea off as preposterous.

"Yes," Titus said. "I'm quite serious."

"You want me to marry her?" Warren said. He put his hand on his chin and looked at her. "Sure," he said finally. "Why not? That should get Ted's attention."

Chapter Twenty-Two

When the money was delivered to Ted, he had just about reached the desperation stage. He owed so much for rails (the price had gone from $151 per ton to $163 per ton) that the supplier sent a personal courier with the last shipment to collect the amount due. He also had to order dynamite for blasting. Nitroglycerin was cheaper, but it was also much more unstable. Dynamite was relatively new, but already had proven to be the safest and most effective way for construction blasting. On top of that, he had a payroll to meet, so the $150,000 was put to immediate use.

"Why do you suppose Reesa sent the money on ahead?" Miller asked.

"I think she knew how desperately it was needed," Ted answered. "It is just like her to think of such a thing. Bless her, Miller, she's going to be a wonderful wife!"

" 'Tis going to be a happy day when I see my daughter married," Miller said. "I intend to give her a weddin' the likes of which has never been seen in this part of the country. What do you think of that?"

"I'll leave that up to you and Reesa," Ted laughed. "It's enough for me to have her as my wife. I've no need for fancy weddings or gala balls."

"No need, perhaps, but you'll be appreciatin' it, I'm certain," Miller said.

"Send word to me as soon as she returns," Ted said. "I'm going to Pie Town to get started on the blasting. We should have rails laid to there within two days."

"Aye, lad, I'll deliver her right to you," Miller promised.

Pie Town was a small settlement that had been founded when silver was discovered in the Mangus Mountains. At its peak, it was never larger than a thousand souls, and now that the silver had just about played out, it had decreased in size to fewer than one hundred residents. But it was a previously established settlement, and therefore qualified under the Railroad Grants Act to increase the amount of funds due the railroad.

Pie Town was now enjoying a new boom as word had reached them that the railroad would be coming through. Some of the railroad camp followers, who had been constructing tent cities along the route, moved their operations into many of the abandoned buildings of Pie Town, and there was even talk of hiring a city marshal. As the track had not yet reached Pie Town and Ted wished to be there for the blasting operation, he had to rent a room in the newly reopened hotel, renamed the Railroaders' Hotel.

"I located some dynamite, which was left over from the silver mining," Murdock told Ted as they ate their supper in the hotel dining room that night, a supper consisting of beefsteak, eggs and coffee. The same menu applied to breakfast and lunch as well, and for a moment, Ted envied the fifty or so Chinese who were on the blasting crew, and who were right now camped just out of town eating their own cooking and enjoying its varied fare.

"Good," Ted answered, shoving a fork of scrambled eggs into his mouth. "I have ordered enough to move a mountain, so we shouldn't lack for it."

"Have you heard from Miss Flowers?" Murdock asked.

"Yes, as a matter of fact, I have. I got the money last night. All the bills are paid; we have money for the payroll and enough materials and equipment to get us underway again."

"That's good. You know I didn't want to say anything, but I've had a bad feelin'," Murdock said.

"About what?"

"Well, it's just that Leland left so soon after Miss Flowers did," Murdock said. "I don't know, it was as if he knew what she was going to try and do or somethin' and was bound to make trouble. I don't care an ounce for the son-of-a-bitch."

Ted laughed. "I share your dislike for the man," he said. "But if he had it in his mind to queer the deal, he failed. He reckoned without

231

Reesa's ability to get things done, I guess. I'm awfully anxious for her to return."

"You know what she's doin', don't you?" Murdock said with a knowing grin.

"No, what?"

"Why, hell, boss, it's as plain as the nose on your face," Murdock said. "She's gettin' ready for her weddin'. And, I'll bet she's enjoyin' ever' minute of it."

Murdock Felton was right about one thing. Reesa Flowers was preparing for her wedding. But he was wrong about the other. She wasn't enjoying every minute of it. In fact, she attended to every detail as if her heart would break, and during the fitting of her wedding gown, she had to dismiss the seamstress from her room because the entire affair weighed so heavily on her heart that she was moved to burst into tears.

"But Miss Flowers, the wedding is tomorrow. If you are going to have a wedding gown, I'll have to complete the fitting now," the seamstress complained.

"I said leave," Reesa said again. "I have such a headache that I can't go on with this."

"Very well," the seamstress said in a huff. She gathered her pins and measuring tapes and withdrew from the room, muttering under her breath about the lack of consideration of some people. As she left, she nearly ran over Lyrica, who was at that moment preparing to knock on the door.

"Reesa, it is I," Lyrica said.

When Reesa saw Lyrica, she could no longer

contain her grief. Lyrica was a friendly face to her, a face from the happy time on the train. She broke into tears and fell across her bed, wailing as if her heart were breaking, as indeed it was.

"Reesa, Reesa dear, what is it?" Lyrica asked, her voice mirroring genuine concern.

"Lyrica, oh, it's been awful," she said.

"What is it? What has happened?" Lyrica asked. "You must tell me."

Reesa told her story, beginning with leaving the bank with the money, then being hit over the head and robbed, and then of her awful ordeal on board the ship.

"Oh, God in heaven, how you have suffered," Lyrica cried. Her own heart was breaking, too, now, for she realized that she had been responsible for all this. Not intentionally, for she had specifically told the two thugs not to harm her. But she was responsible for it no less than if she had wielded the club and tied the bonds herself.

"But that isn't the worst of it," Reesa went on.

"But what more could there be?"

Reesa told of being forced into marriage with Warren Leland in order to replace the money she had lost. "The money is there now," Reesa said. "And the railroad has gone on. But I am no longer free to marry my own true love, for I must wed Warren tomorrow."

Lyrica was heartsick. To think that she had caused this sweet girl all this pain, and for nothing! For she had reckoned without Reesa's fierce determination and will. Lyrica began crying.

"Oh, now," Reesa said, seeing the distress of her young friend. "Please, Lyrica, don't cry. Oh, forgive me for burdening you with my troubles."

Reesa's genuine concern for Lyrica's well-being made Lyrica feel all the more guilty, and she was unable to stem the flow of tears for a long while. Finally, after crying into each other's arms like two schoolchildren, the women had spent themselves emotionally and were thus able to compose themselves once more.

"Lyrica, will you be my maid of honor?" Reesa asked.

"Oh, but I can't," Lyrica protested. "Wouldn't you prefer someone else? Someone you've known longer?"

Reesa laughed. "I know no one in San Francisco," she said.

"But I am Mexican," Lyrica said. "To be your maid of honor, would not an *Anglo* be more appropriate?"

"You are my friend," Reesa said. "Nothing is more appropriate than that."

"I . . . yes, Reesa. I would be happy to accept."

"I apologize to you for asking you to do such a dishonorable thing as serve in a wedding where there is no love."

"There is no dishonor," Lyrica said. "I am flattered that you ask me." Privately, she thought that there was indeed dishonor—but it was her dishonor to Reesa that troubled her.

"Will you be married in a church?" Lyrica asked.

"No!" Reesa said resolutely. "I had planned a church wedding with Ted. If that is not to be, then I won't marry anyone in church. A justice of the peace will marry us in Mr. Leland's office tomorrow morning at ten."

"Shall I meet you here?" Lyrica asked.

"No," Reesa said. "Come to the office at ten. I will marry him, and be done with it as quickly as I can."

"Oh, Reesa, how sorry I am that this awful thing has happened to you." Lyrica put her arms around Reesa one more time.

"Thank you for your concern," Reesa said. "And your friendship. It means much to me now."

Lyrica left Reesa's hotel room with the guilt of her sin clutching at her heart like a vise. This was all her fault. She wished she could call back the past few days. God, if there were only some way to undo what she had done! Oh, if she could only see those two men again, she would . . . wait a minute, she thought. An idea! It won't undo what had been done, but it would make her feel better.

Lyrica went to the nearest Western Union office, and sent a telegram to Joaquin. She begged him to come to San Francisco at once. It was, she said, a matter of importance, though it could not be discussed in a wire.

Titus Leland represented wealth, so any occasion that affected him, regardless of the intent to keep it small, was of necessity a major

235

social event. Thus it was that when news traveled through town that his son was to marry, hurriedly puchased wedding gifts began pouring in, and the cream of San Francisco society made plans to attend the ceremony. Railroad barons, mining millionaires, shipping magnates, everyone within traveling distance were present in the Leland Building the next morning. They began coming shortly after nine, and by ten o'clock a sizeable portion of the wealth of the city was present.

Warren stood against the cupboard drinking quietly. He was on his third drink when his father came over to talk to him.

"Don't you feel it is much too early for that?" he asked.

Warren smiled laconically and held the glass aloft. A shaft of early morning sunshine passed through the glass, split into a spectrum burst of color, and projected a rainbow on the wall. "Early or late," he said, "it's all relative. Now on the one hand, you might say it is a bit early for drinking, while on the other, you might say it is a bit late for the charming bride. Assuming, of course, that she comes."

"You think she will not?" Titus asked.

"I don't know," Warren said. "It will be amusing to see whether she has merely taken your money, or if she intends to go through with her end of the bargain."

"Is that all this is to you?" Titus asked. "Amusement?"

"Yes, Father," Warren answered easily. "What is it to you?"

"It's hope, boy. Hope that some of her gumption will rub off on you."

One of the guests walked over to the two Lelands. He stuck his finger between the high-wing collar of his shirt and his neck and pulled it out as if to allow air to enter. He was a big man who looked out of place in his morning coat, but the profits from his gold mine made him wealthy enough to belong with the crowd that had collected in the office.

"Say, Titus, what time is this shindig supposed to get started? I've got a shipment to look after."

"Ten o'clock," Titus replied.

The big man removed a watch and looked at it critically. "The way I make it, that's about two minutes from now. And I ain't seen no sign o' the girl yet."

"She'll be here," Titus said.

"I'll stick around a bit longer if you're sure o' that," the man said.

"Father has faith," Warren said. "If faith can move a mountain, surely it can move Reesa Flowers."

Lyrica stepped into the room then, and the conversation stilled. She was dressed in white and wore a mantilla. She was dazzlingly beautiful and most obviously Spanish.

"Yes, miss, what can I do for you?" Titus asked.

"Excuse me," Lyrica said, speaking with a strong accent. "This is the office of *Señor* Leland, is it not?"

"Yes, it is."

"I am here for the wedding," Lyrica said. "I am the maid of honor."

There was an undercurrent of surprise, which moved through the guests. Warren laughed, but Titus offered the girl a generous smile.

"Come in," he said. "Reesa isn't here yet."

"She is outside," Lyrica said. "She will be here momentarily."

"Well, now," Titus said, looking back at Warren. "Are you still amused?"

"Quite," Warren replied.

Suddenly there was a gasp. It came first from one of the women, then was picked up by others until it spread through all of them like a prairie fire before the wind.

"I'm not late, am I?" Reesa asked calmly.

Titus looked at her, and for a second he was speechless. "Uh, no," he said. "You're right on time."

Warren began laughing, and though his laugh was genuine, it had a hollow ring in the room where so many others just stared in numb shock. Finally, Warren got his breath.

"Come right this way," he said. "I think red becomes you. And it makes a perfect bridal gown for this marriage made in hell."

Chapter Twenty-Three

After the wedding, if indeed such a loveless ceremony could be called a wedding, the bride and groom and the guests adjourned to the decks of the *Star of the West*, the luxurious yacht of Carl Endicott, a business associate and friend of Titus Leland. Reesa would have as soon not gone, as she wished to give no personal seal of approval to what she had done, but she reasoned that the longer she was in a crowd, the longer she could delay the inevitable time alone with Warren Leland.

The boat was luxurious beyond description. It had a polished teak deck, brass fittings, and a richly upholstered salon. Uniformed crewmen buzzed about serving drinks over ice, lighting men's cigars, and helping the ladies to negotiate the ladderways and bulkheads. A string quartet was set up to play lively but unobtrusive music for the background pleasure of the guests.

"Do you like all of this, my dear?" Titus asked Reesa.

"The boat is very beautiful," Reesa agreed. "Would you like it as a wedding gift?"

"What?"

"I imagine Endicott has grown tired of it by now. He tires of his playthings rather quickly," Titus said. "At any rate, I am certain I could persuade him to part with it. I'll buy it for you, and you could use it to take a long honeymoon trip to the Hawaiian Islands. How would that be?"

"No, thank you, Mr. Leland," Reesa replied. "You have already given me my wedding present."

"You mean the hundred fifty thousand," Titus said.

"Exactly."

Titus Leland laughed and put his arm around Reesa. "I knew you were the right girl the moment I laid eyes on you," he said.

Reesa had a strange reaction to the embrace of Titus. She felt in him a passion for life and a virile strength, which were totally lacking in Warren. In fact, Titus reminded her much of Ted. Her skin pinkened as she realized what was happening and, involuntarily, she felt her body stiffen slightly.

Titus noticed Reesa's reaction, and he looked at her with somewhat of a puzzled expression on his face. Then he broke into an easy grin, one which made Reesa blush. It was as if he read her innermost thoughts.

"Don't be afraid of a little feelin', girl," he said quietly, thus intimately. "It's what separates us from the animals."

The yacht took a grand tour around the bay,

and as they passed close to Alcatraz Island, Reesa thought about her terrifying experience offshore there just a few days ago. Was it just a few days ago? It seemed like ages. How different it was to see Alcatraz from the deck of a luxury yacht than it was to wade ashore from the longboat of a rapist's black ship.

It was late in the afternoon, and the sun was slanting long low beams across the bay before Warren and Reesa were put ashore by the celebrants aboard the yacht. As the newly married couple left the deck of the yacht, they were showered with rice and toasted with champagne. Then, to Reesa's surprise, all the champagne glasses were smashed against the deck.

"What are they doing that for?" Reesa asked.

Warren laughed. "With very few exceptions, everyone you see on that deck is a *nouveau riche*. Their parents were all dirt farmers, store clerks, or laborers. Now that these people have money, they look for ways to display their wealth. Among the upper classes in England, glasses are broken after a toast, and they think that following suit gives them class. It is said that if one wants to find a party in San Francisco, go to the sound of crashing glass. To that I would add, do so and you will find a crashing bore."

"You don't like your father's friends very much, do you?" Reesa asked.

"I don't like my father very much," Warren said.

"Why not?"

Warren smiled the same slow smile that

Reesa had come to regard as his trademark. "This way I am seldom disappointed," he said.

A phaeton with a liveried driver was waiting for them, and it took them to the top of Nob Hill, passing one of the new cable cars that had already made San Francisco famous throughout the world. The carriage moved through a large wrought-iron gate, around a curving tree-lined and beautifully landscaped drive, to stop in front of the largest, handsomest house Reesa had ever seen. She looked at it in fascination, absolutely speechless.

"Be it ever so humble," Warren said sarcastically, taking in the house with a wave of the hand.

"Warren, you live here?" Reesa asked, numbed with awe despite herself.

"In a manner of speaking," Warren said. "This is my father's house. In my father's house are many mansions," he added. "For tonight, one of them may be yours."

They walked up the broad steps and through the double doors into the house. A huge foyer greeted them, and a very wide stairway ascended to the second floor where a balcony overlooked the entryway. Reesa was cognizant of polished marble floors, mahogany banisters, rich wall hangings, and a great collection of statuary. Paintings hung on the wall climbing alongside the stairs. Servants seemed to materialize, then melt back into the house almost as if they were ghosts.

"There is an excellent view of the city from up here if you wish to see it," Warren invited.

"Yes," Reesa said. "Yes, I'd like to see it."

Warren led the way upstairs, then down a long hallway and out onto a huge balcony, which ran the full length of the back of the house. The back lawn was exquisitely landscaped with boxed hedges forming geometric patterns, and statues and fountains surrounded by beautiful flowers of every hue. But the most breathtaking sight was of the city of San Francisco. She saw white houses clinging to green hills, and from this vantage point she could see the sparkling blue water of the Golden Gate as well.

"Oh, Warren, it's beautiful," she said.

"I suppose so," Warren replied. "Come, I'll show you your room."

Reesa followed Warren back into the house and down the hallway, wide enough and long enough to have accommodated two of the railway cars where she and her father made their home. At last he halted.

The carved double doors were shut, and when Warren pushed them open to allow Reesa to step into the bedroom, she saw that it, like the rest of the house, was elegant beyond her wildest imagination. A large bay window bowed out, offering substantially the same view as was enjoyed from the balcony. The floor was covered in a very deep, very plush dark blue carpet. The walls were white, carved panels, trimmed in blue and gold. The ceiling was vaulted and decorated with paintings of cherubs, birds and flowers.

A large dresser with a huge mirror sat on one side of the room, flanked by other large pieces of bedroom furniture. There was a small dining area near the window, with a roomy closet-dressing room opposite. A canopied bed dominated the room, and two servant girls stood nervously beside it.

"These girls will take care of anything you might need," Warren said. "I'm sorry, I'm not around enough to remember their names, but it really doesn't matter."

"Of course it matters," Reesa said, remembering the pains Ted had taken to discover the names of the railroad workers. "What are your names?" she asked them.

"My name's Daisy, mum," one of the girls, a pretty young blonde, said.

"And I'm Anne," the other supplied.

Both girls had English accents, and Reesa commented on it.

"Yes, mum," Daisy said. "Mr. Leland hired us from England. Paid our way over, too, he did."

"It was most generous of him, mum," the other added.

"My father is generous to a fault," Warren said sarcastically.

Reesa looked around the room again, then walked over to look behind a door. "What is this?" she asked.

"It's a bathroom, mum," Daisy said. "If you turn those knobs, the water runs right into the tub. There's no need to carry it in buckets."

"Oh, how marvelous," Reesa said, more impressed with that than anything else she had seen.

"Careful, Reesa," Warren warned with a laugh. "You'll get intoxicated by your new wealth, and you'll forget all about your Ted."

"I'll never forget about Ted," Reesa said hotly.

"To be sure," Warren replied with an easy laugh. He walked over to a cabinet and opened the doors, revealing a large selection of liquor. He poured some whiskey into a glass, then looked back at Reesa. "Would you care for a wedding toast?"

"No," Reesa said. "I'm going to take a bath."

Warren laughed. "I rather thought you would," he said. He looked at the two servant girls. "If you would help Mrs. Leland? I'll be back in a short while."

Warren left the room carrying the drink in his hand, still chuckling as if he alone was aware of some hilarious but very private joke.

"Mrs. Leland," Daisy said. "Did you hear what he called you, mum? It must be a grand feelin', hearin' that for the first time."

Instead of Mrs. Foster? Reesa thought. *No, Daisy, it wasn't a grand feeling. It is a feeling of bitter heartbreak.*

Later, after the bath and the toweling had left her body pink and clean, Reesa put on a yellow, silk sleeping gown. The silk clung to her body like a second skin, and as she examined herself in the mirror, she saw every curve and dip of her body. Even the nipples protruded through the silk, forming two sharp points.

"Oh, mum," Daisy breathed. "You are beautiful!"

"Thank you," Reesa said.

Reesa sat at the dresser mirror and brushed

her hair with long luxurious strokes as she waited for Warren. Within a short time, the hair took on the sheen of burnished ebony, and its jet blackness, her suntanned skin, and the pale yellow silk of the nightgown created a picture of loveliness.

The door opened and closed, and Reesa saw Warren come into the room. He walked directly to the dresser and stood behind her, looking at her in the mirror. "You are a gorgeous creature," he said quietly. He put his hands on her shoulders and rubbed his fingers lightly on her soft skin.

Reesa knew these hands, and she knew the skill and subtlety with which they could awaken passions in her. Despite her emotional hunger for Ted, her physical hunger was one which Warren could satisfy.

Warren slid his hands down, slipping them in under the gown and grasping each breast. The firm mounds of flesh burned under his touch, and his fingers moved caressingly out to touch the nipples. They sent tiny jolts of pleasure through her body, and she felt her insides turning to hot lava.

"My father wants you to have his grandson," Warren said. His hands were still working their magic on her body. "Did he tell you that?"

"Yes," Reesa whispered.

Warren pulled his hands back, then turned and walked away from her. The movement was so sudden that for a second Reesa didn't realize what was happening.

"Well, that's something he will never see," Warren said with a cold laugh.

"What? What are you talking about?"

Warren turned to look at Reesa. His face was twisted in hate. "He took my mother from me," Warren said. "He killed her when I was just a child."

"What do you mean he killed your mother? He told me she died."

"She did die," Warren said. "She died of overwork and exhaustion. My father was so busy making his fortune that he worked himself and everyone around him without letup. My mother was a delicate woman, not given to that type of life. He killed her, as surely as if he had shot her. I was only eight years old at the time. From that day to this, I've hated him, and I've looked for some way to repay him." Warren laughed. "And now I've found the way. I'll deny him the one thing he wants more than anything else. You'll never bear his grandchild. Never. I'll give him all the bastard grandchildren he wants, but no wife of mine will ever bear my child."

"How do you propose to prevent it?" Reesa asked.

"Simple, my dear," Warren said. "There are thousands of women who quite willingly warm my bed. I'll merely seek my sexual pleasures elsewhere, and leave you to stew in your own juices."

"Warren, my God, if you felt this way, why in heaven's name did you marry me?" Reesa asked. "If you had said no, your father wouldn't have insisted."

"And let everyone off the hook?" Warren asked. "No, my dear. I find this an exquisite form of torture, both for my father and for Ted."

"And for me," Reesa said.

"I'm sorry," Warren said. "I bear you no personal malice. It is unfortunate that you are caught in the middle. But look at it this way," he added, smiling brightly. "You are a wealthy woman now. I'll never deny you any extravagance, and I know my father won't. Take all the lovers you wish; I certainly intend to. Enjoy life to the fullest. Take Ted as your lover if you wish. It will be pleasure enough for me to deny him the right to marry you. There is only one thing I insist upon. Do not have a child. If you become pregnant, you must get rid of it."

Reesa sat numbed with shock over what she was hearing. She was unable to answer Warren, so stunned was she by his pronouncement. Warren turned back to her just before he left the room.

"Don't wait up for me, dear. This is my wedding night and something there is inside me," he mocked, placing both hands over his heart in the style of an overly dramatic matinee idol, "which cries for love. I'm going to find someone to share my bed on this, my wedding night. Good night."

Reesa sat in silence for several moments after Warren walked out of her bedroom. The heat that had begun to build in her body had turned cold and leaden. She finally turned back to the mirror and resumed brushing her hair, staring numbly at the image in the mirror.

She didn't cry. There were no tears left.

Chapter Twenty-Four

"Fire in the hole!"

The warning drifted down from the rocky walls of the canyon and was picked up and repeated by someone closer. "Fire in the hole!"

The first two warnings were given by the Chinese workers who were placing the charges, and a third warning was given by an American, just to make certain there was no mistake, that rang loud and true through the bright, New Mexico afternoon.

"Fire in the hole!"

There was an expectant intake of breath as everyone waited, for this was the warning that a dynamite charge had been placed and was about to be exploded.

The blast went off with stomach-shaking effectiveness, and tons of rock crashed into the valley below, raising a tremendous cloud of dust.

"Look at that!" Murdock enthused. "That blast was so clean you can just about go in and prepare your roadbed with a broom. I tell you, boss, them little Chinamen are somethin' to behold."

"They are doing an excellent job," Ted agreed. "In fact, it's beginning to look like we'll get to the territorial line as fast this way as we would have had we gone our original route."

"I'm glad Miss Flowers come up with this idea," Murdock said.

At the mention of Reesa's name, Ted's eyes reflected a flicker of worry. Where was she? She had been gone for ten days now and, other than the receipt of the money, he had heard nothing from her. It was beginning to disturb him, and he had even thought of taking off and going to San Francisco to get her. In fact, if he didn't hear anything within three more days, he might just do that. Three more days would punch them through the pass, and the track laying could continue on schedule.

"You aren't gettin' a little worried about her, are you, boss?" Murdock asked when he saw the reaction in Ted's eyes.

"No," Ted said. "I guess not. But I do wish she would come back. I would like her to be here when we cross the Arizona line. It'll be as much a victory for her as it is for us."

"Fire in the hole," they heard again.

"They got that laid in there fast," Ted commented.

"I tell you, boss, them Chinamen could move that whole damn mountain if you wanted 'em to," Murdock said gleefully.

A moment later, there was another explosion, and more of the ledge that blocked construction of the railroad fell into the valley below.

* * *

The bartender picked up the two whiskey glasses and saw that there was nearly an inch of whiskey left in each of them. He shrugged his shoulders, then removed the cap from the whiskey bottle and poured the liquor back into its original container. The two men who had been drinking it wouldn't mind. They were upstairs right now with Angie and Maria. The bartender laughed. Angie and Maria knew their business all right. They had pegged the two galoots as having money from the moment they walked in, and they moved to them like a bee to a flower. It was funny. They were a couple of the ugliest *hombres* he'd ever seen: one was missing an eye, and the other had a terrible scar across his face. But they'd come in Red Wood wearing new suits, the both of them, and spoutin' off about a diggin' they'd uncovered which made 'em their poke.

"Diggin's," the bartender snorted under his breath. "The only diggin' them fellas did was the diggin' it took to bury the *hombre* they took that money off of."

The bartender had no idea where the money came from, but he was ready to wager that it wasn't honestly obtained.

"*Señor*, a whiskey please," someone said.

The bartender looked toward the end of the bar and saw a handsome, well-dressed Mexican. He wore black, with silver and turquoise conchos, and a silver clutch at the neckerchief around his neck. His hatband was made of silver as well.

"We don't . . ." The bartender had started

251

to say, "We don't serve Mexicans," but there was something in the demeanor of the man who spoke to him that caused him to stop in midstatement. It could hve been the man's eyes, cool and appraising, or his manner, confident and assured, or just the way he wore his gun. It was slung low and kicked out, the way a gunfighter wore a gun.

"You were saying?" the Mexican asked.

The bartender cleared his throat. "We don't get many of your kind in here," he said lamely.

"You have no objections to my kind, do you, *Señor?*" the Mexican asked, smiling and holding a fire to the long thin cigar that protruded from his lips.

"No, no, of course not," the bartender said. He started to pour whiskey from the bottle he had just put the leftovers into.

"I prefer a new bottle, *Señor,*" the Mexican said.

"Yes, yes, of course," the bartender replied nervously. Something about this man made him uneasy, and as he started to pour, he saw that his hands were shaking badly.

"Allow me, *Señor,*" the Mexican said, taking the bottle from him. The Mexican poured a glass and sat the bottle back down. "My name is Joaquin Mendoza," he said. "I am seeking someone."

That's it! the bartender thought. That's what made him nervous about this man. He was a man hunter looking for someone. The bartender decided he would not like to be searched for by this man.

"What are you looking for?" the bartender asked.

"There are two of them. I know only their first names. One is Jake and the other, Emmett," Joaquin said. He flicked ashes into a spittoon. "But I know they come in here, *Señor*. I was told this by two people."

"Well, if you don't know anymore than that, how can I help you?" the bartender stammered.

"One man has a patch over his eye. The other has a scar like so," Joaquin said, moving his finger along his face.

The bartender's eyes darted toward the head of the stairs at the room where the two men had gone with the women.

"I see," Joaquin said, smiling easily. "They are upstairs."

"I didn't say that," the bartender insisted.

"You didn't have to, *Señor*," Joaquin said.

"What do you want with them?"

"*Señor*, I believe you already know," Joaquin said. "I want to kill them."

Joaquin said the words quietly, but within seconds it had spread all over the bar, and conversations, poker games, and just plain drinking stopped as the patrons all looked at the handsome Mexican.

"What did you say, mister?" someone asked.

Joaquin looked toward the speaker and saw that he was an older man wearing a badge.

"I see," Joaquin said. "You must be the sheriff."

"That I am. And I'll not allow any cold-blooded killing in my town," the sheriff added—nervously, because he didn't know how

Joaquin was going to take it, but resolutely because he felt it should be said.

"I appreciate that, Sheriff," Joaquin said. "I do not intend to make the kill in cold blood. I will first challenge them and give them an opportunity to give themselves up. But if they go for their guns, I'll have no choice but to defend myself."

"Fair enough," the sheriff said, clearing his throat. He looked around at the others in the barroom. "You heard the gent, fellas. He's promised me that it'll be a fair fight. I aim to let 'im brace the two men when he wants to, and I'll make no move to the contrary, unless in my opinion it ain't all on the up 'n' up."

"That's the way it ought to be done, Sheriff," one of the others agreed.

Joaquin nodded and turned back to the bar.

The piano, which had been playing in the corner, and had stopped for the discourse, now began to play again. However, all eyes were on the top of the stairs, and all conversation directed toward the upcoming gunfight. Within a moment, the piano stopped again, and everyone in the saloon waited.

The waiting grew more strained, and the conversation soon petered out. Now there was absolute silence, and when someone coughed nervously, everyone turned to look at him accusingly. The clock on the wall ticked loudly as the pendulum swung back and forth. Involuntarily, perhaps a dozen or so men looked at the clock as if it were very important to fix the time in their minds, the better for the telling of their stories later.

Whiskey glasses were refilled as quietly as everything else, the drinker merely walking over to the bar and holding his glass out silently.

More people drifted into the saloon, but they were met at the door, and a whispered exchange told them what was going on. Most who wandered in stayed, drawing on their beer or whiskey as silently as the others, and then waiting.

Waiting.

The tension grew almost unbearable. From the room at the top of the stairs, there came the sound of a woman's moan of passion. There wasn't a man in the saloon who didn't know what was going on up there, but that which would have normally elicited peals of embarrassed laughter brought only silence.

One of the men upstairs laughed loudly and another cursed. The women laughed, and then there was the sound of footfalls, as boots struck the floor. The door opened, and the two men came out of the room, laughing and talking to each other. They had started down the stairs before they noticed the deathly silence and the eyes staring up at them.

"Jake, what the hell's goin' on?" one of them said.

"Buenos dias, Señores," Joaquin said pleasantly, stepping away from the bar and looking up toward the two men. "I believe one of you is named Jake and the other Emmett. Am I correct?"

"Who are you? What do you want?" Jake asked. He retreated two steps back up the stairs. Emmett, who was already at the top of the stairs, moved over behind the railing and stood looking down onto the saloon. The women, who had followed them out of the room, let out a gasp of fear and ran back into the room from which they had just come.

"My name is Joaquin Mendoza," Joaquin said. "Of course, that name means nothing to you now. But it is the name of the man who may have to kill you. You took one hundred and fifty thousand dollars, which didn't belong to you, and you beat a young woman, then turned her over to an evil ship captain so that he could have his way with her."

"What's it to you, Mex?" Emmett challenged.

"Let us just say that I want to see justice done," Joaquin said. "Now, I want you both to throw down your guns and come to me with your hands in the air. I am taking you back to San Francisco where you are going to return the money, and then give yourself up to the police."

"You talk like a crazy man," Jake said, laughing shortly.

"Jake, I don't like this," Emmett said. "I don't like this at all."

"Aw, don't worry about it none," Jake said, waving his hand toward Emmett. The two men stood rooted to their position for a moment longer. Everyone in the saloon continued to stare.

"Throw down your guns," Joaquin said again with quiet authority.

"We ain't gonna do it," Jake said.

Joaquin spread his legs slightly, then held his

hand out, ready to draw. "Throw down your guns or use them," he said.

There was a silence the length of a heartbeat, then Jake yelled, "Get 'em, Emmett!"

At the same time Jake yelled, he started for his gun. But Joaquin's gun was out in a move so quick that it was later described as a blur. Joaquin's first shot sent Jake slamming back against the wall, then he tumbled forward and slid down the stairs head first, his gun rattling to the bottom of the stairs before him. Joaquin's second shot caught Emmett right between the eyes, and his face grew blank in death just before he flipped over the banister and crashed back first through a poker table on the floor below. Neither Jake nor Emmett had managed a shot, though both guns had cleared their holsters.

"This here'n's deader'n a doornail," one of the men said, looking at Jake.

"Him, too," another said from near Emmett's body. He poked at him with the toe of his boot.

Joaquin holstered his pistol, then looked at the sheriff. "Sheriff, was it a fair fight?"

"Fair as fair can be, I'd say," one of the other men yelled. He was answered by a host of others, and the sheriff nodded his head in agreement.

"Can I buy you a drink, Joaquin?" someone invited.

Joaquin looked back at them and smiled. "No, thank you. I have some hard riding to do."

"What about the money?" someone called. "Didn't you say them fellas stole a hundred fifty thousand? You'll be wantin' that back, I suppose?"

"I have it back," Joaquin said. "It was in their saddlebags."

"Did you hear that?" Joaquin heard someone ask as he left. "He had the money already, but he braced them two anyway. That took guts, I'll tell you."

"Either that or he hated them two like sin," the sheriff answered.

They were both wrong, Joaquin thought as he forked his horse. It took neither bravery nor hate to do what he did. It took a sense of fair play. Joaquin was merely righting a wrong that Lyrica had done to Reesa.

Chapter Twenty-Five

Ten days after Miss Reesa Flowers stepped onto the crowded, dusty coach at Albuquerque to begin her trip to San Francisco, she, as Mrs. Warren Leland, stepped onto the private car that would take her back. The car was on a side track at the San Francisco railroad terminal, and many of the same people who had come to the wedding were now here to see the newlyweds on their journey. They wandered in and out of the car for some two hours, bearing baskets of fruit and bottles of champagne. The whole thing took on the aura of a party, and little groups would form, talk for a while, explode in a peal of laughter, then move through the car or along the station platform to form new groups, a few moments later to repeat the pattern.

Reesa was aware of the impromptu party going on in the lounge area of the car, but she was in the bedroom with Daisy, folding and packing away her wardrobe. It was an entirely new wardrobe, paid for by Titus Leland "as a wedding present," he said, and picked out by Daisy and Anne.

"Oh, mum, I do hope you like the lovely things Anne and I picked out for you," Daisy said anxiously.

Reesa looked at the girl and smiled. Daisy, too, was a sort of wedding gift, and she was returning to Albuquerque as Reesa's maid. "They are lovely, Daisy."

Daisy smiled in relief. "Thank you, mum," she said. "I told Mister Leland that a fine lady such as yourself would want to select her own wardrobe, but he insisted that Anne and I do it for you."

"He knew that I wouldn't do it," Reesa said.

"Mum, you mean you'd turn down these fine clothes?" Daisy asked in surprise.

"That is exactly what I mean," Reesa said.

"Lord, mum, I've been in this country for two years, and I've yet to understand you Americans."

Reesa smiled. "You mean we, don't you? You're an American now."

"Yes, mum," Daisy answered. "Tell me, mum. What's it like, this Alby . . . Alby . . ."

"Albuquerque?"

"Yes, mum. What's it like there?"

"Oh, I think it's beautiful," Reesa said. "Huge, red mountains with jagged canyons, magnificent sunsets, and the quiet, timeless desert."

"But the desert . . . isn't that just sand, mum?"

"Not at all," Reesa said. "There are cactus

260

and desert flowers, which make it all so beautiful that it's hard to describe."

"That's where Mr. Foster is?" Daisy asked.

"How did you know about Mr. Foster?"

"There's been talk," Daisy said. "Excuse me, mum, for tellin' you, but I thought you might like to know."

"What kind of talk?"

Daisy cleared her throat. "It's been noticed that Mr. Warren spends his nights elsewhere. It did seem a bit odd, but then someone explained that your marrying him in the first place was odd, seeing as your heart belonged to another. A man named Ted Foster."

Reesa looked at the girl for several moments, with a look of total resignation.

"Excuse me, mum," Daisy said in a frightened tone of voice. She was unable to interpret Reesa's expressions. "I had no right to speak."

Reesa smiled. "Don't worry, Daisy. I can't be angry with you for telling the truth. Yes, I am in love with Ted Foster, though circumstances forced me to marry Warren Leland. I'd rather not discuss them right now; anyway, I imagine, since you know everything else, you know the circumstances as well."

"Yes'm," Daisy said. She walked over to Reesa and put her hand on Reesa's shoulder. "Mum, the really terrible thing is, Mr. Foster may never know what an act of love for him your marriage to Mr. Leland really was."

There was a bump as the private car was connected to the rest of the train. Reesa heard laughter and shouted good-byes, and knew that the visitors had left the car and were standing on the platform waving good-bye.

"Here we go, mum," Daisy said excitedly.

The trip back was uneventful, and Reesa passed the time by reading or chatting with Daisy. She had come to like the young servant and to admire her grit. Daisy's mother had died when Daisy was only sixteen years old. Her father was an alcoholic, though in Daisy's quaint words, he was "a gentleman much in his cups," and he arranged for Daisy to take a position with a tavern keeper.

"But it wasn't a servin' girl he was wantin', mum," the girl explained. "It was a doxie, to keep his customers happy. So I ran away. Then I heard that there were jobs like this one in America, so I went to an agency and signed on. And here I am."

When they reached Albuquerque, the usual crowd was gathered at the depot to welcome the train. Reesa looked out at the crowd in a totally different respect now. No longer did it seem large; in fact, by comparison with San Francisco, it was pitifully small. Also, the sense of excitement, the promise of mystery was gone. Reesa had "seen the elephant" as her father would say. There was no mystery left to reveal to her, and she had put away all romance forever by marrying Warren Leland.

Reesa walked from the private car up through the coaches, so that when the train stopped she disembarked with the coach passengers. No sooner had she set foot on the plat-

262

form than she heard a whoop and her name shouted.

"Reesa, we're over here!" Ted shouted.

Reesa saw Ted and her father coming toward her. Before she could say anything, Ted broke into a run and reached her in just a few strides. He grabbed her and kissed her, and despite the awful truth she was going to have to tell him, or perhaps because of it, Reesa allowed herself the kiss, melting into his arms with the pleasure of it and returning it with a fervor to match his own.

"Don't forget your papa," Miller said, laughing behind Ted's shoulder. "Save some of your affection for him."

"Oh, Papa," Reesa said. She was crying now, and she went into his arms, holding him to her as tightly as she could. There was the old, comfortable and familiar smell of him that she had known since childhood: a combination of tobacco, Irish whiskey, train smoke, and just a hint of lye soap.

"There, there," Miller said, holding his daughter and patting her affectionately on the back. "I never could understand what it was that made a woman weep so easily."

"Excuse me, mum, but Mr. Leland is looking for you," Daisy said.

Miller and Ted looked at Daisy in surprise, and then back at Reesa.

"This is Daisy," Reesa said. "She is my friend, and, uh, my maid."

"Your what?" Ted asked with a little laugh.

"She is my wife's maid," Warren said, approaching them then. "Of course, Daisy prefers being called a friend, but what that all boils down to is a maid. You know the old saying, a mule in horse harness is still a mule?"

"Your . . . your *wife*'s maid?" Ted asked, clearly puzzled by the conversation.

"Yes," Warren replied easily. He put his arm around Reesa. "Gentlemen, I'd like you to meet Mrs. Warren Leland."

"Reesa, is this true?" Ted asked in a choked voice.

Reesa hung her head without a word. Tears slid down her face.

A blood vessel began jumping in Ted's temple, and he stared at the two for a moment, then spun on his heel and walked away quickly, shoving the unfortunate people who happened to get in his way to one side.

"I must say, he wasn't a very good sport about it," Warren said with an easy laugh. "I don't believe he even offered his congratulations, did he?"

Reesa looked at her father. His face was flushed, and his eyes flashed in anger. He began shaking, and Reesa was frightened that he might have a seizure of some sort.

"Papa," she said, reaching for him.

"No," Miller said, pushing her away from him. "I am not your papa. And you are no longer my daughter."

"Papa, please!" Reesa begged in one loud sob.

Miller tried to jump back to avoid her and as he did so, he dropped one of his crutches. Reesa reached for it, but Miller grabbed it first, shoving her back angrily. "I don't need your help," he said icily.

"Oh, Papa, don't; don't do this," Reesa said.

Miller settled his crutch, then turned and left, swinging along as quickly as he could manage on the crutches.

"My, they appear to be upset, don't they?" Warren asked, still laughing.

Daisy put her arms around Reesa, and Reesa, taking comfort where she could, cried onto Daisy's shoulder. "Come along, mum," the girl said. "Let's return to the car. I'll fix you a nice cup of tea."

"You do that," Warren suggested, showing no sympathy for Reesa's plight. "I'm going out to End-of-Track to see how the money is being spent. I'll probably get Sally to put me up for the night," he added, "so you needn't wait up for me."

When Warren arrived at End-of-Track, he was amazed by the amount of progress that had been made since he left. The seemingly impossible mountain pass had already been negotiated, and the track passed through Pie Town, Omega, Quemado, and was headed for Red Hill. They were, in fact, only twenty-five miles from the Arizona Territorial line, and the men were laying track at a rate exceeding five miles per day. There seemed little that could stop them from crossing the line before the deadline, and once that line was crossed, the government grant would be paid and Ted Foster's railroad would be a reality.

Warren watched the work for a while. It

seemed odd to him to realize that as long as he had been associated with Ted Foster's railroad, he had never before really watched the actual track laying operation. He had been so busy conducting his personal battle with Ted that he hadn't allowed himself the luxury of watching. Now, however, that battle was over, and Warren considered himself the clear-cut victor. Ted Foster was going to get his railroad built, but Warren, by marrying Reesa, had certainly rendered it a hollow victory for Ted.

"Get that cart up here!" one of the foremen called, and Warren looked back to see a horse-drawn cart being pulled along the section of track, which had been laid only moments earlier. The cart was loaded with sixteen rails, plus the exact number of spikes, bolts and rail couplings, called fishplates, which would be needed for laying the track. The cart was rolled out to the very end of the last pair of rails spiked down.

The bed of the cart was equipped with rollers, and the rails were pulled off easily and quickly, then dropped into place. A team of men walked between the rails using a notched wooden board to space the rails exactly four feet eight and one half inches apart, and then the men with the hammers would drive the spikes home. No sooner was that rail laid than the cart moved out onto them and brought rails for the next section. After all sixteen rails were used, that cart was pushed off the track, and a following cart came with sixteen more units.

Warren started back to his horse to return to the main camp when he saw the Chinese cook beginning to set up the kitchen for their evening meal. He had never before paid any attention to them, but today he saw one girl who made him stop and stare. She was very young, Warren would guess around fifteen or sixteen, and she was exquisitely beautiful. She had high cheekbones, not prominent but well-accented, and even at this distance Warren could see that her eyes sparkled like set jewels, framed by eyelashes that were as beautiful as the most delicate lace. Her skin was smooth and gold, and her movements were as graceful as a lily stirred by the breeze.

"You," Warren called, pointing toward the girl.

The girl looked up and smiled.

"Come here," Warren said.

The girl replied in Chinese and bowed low.

"What the hell, don't you even speak English?" Warren asked. He looked around and saw Ling Cho near one of the empty carts.

"Ling Cho," he called. "Come here."

Ling Cho hurried over. He bowed slightly.

"Ask that girl to come closer," Warren said, pointing at the beautiful Chinese girl.

"She is a cook," Ling Cho said.

"I know she is a cook. What the hell does that mean?"

"She is not an employee of the railroad," Ling Cho explained.

"No, but by damn you are," Warren said. "Now ask her over here."

Ling Cho shouted something in Chinese, and the young girl came to them. She stopped about eight feet away and hung her head, though she looked at Warren through upcast eyes.

"Ask her to hold her head up so I can get a better look at her," Warren said. "She is a beautiful girl."

"Hold your head up, little one," Ling Cho said in Chinese.

"Does he like me?" the girl asked.

"Why should that matter to you?"

"I think he is very handsome. Should he ask to buy me as his wife, Leader, please say yes."

"What is she jabbering about?"

"She is afraid she will be punished for neglecting her work," Ling Cho said.

Warren smiled at the girl. "You tell her I won't let anyone punish her."

"She is not your responsibility to punish or not, sir," Ling Cho said.

"By God, I can make her my responsibility," Warren said. "What is her name?"

"Golden Tears," Ling Cho said.

Warren looked at the girl a bit longer, then smiled at her again. He got up on his horse and touched the brim of his hat just before he rode away. "Good-bye, Golden Tears," he said. "I'll see you later."

"He does want to marry me," Golden Tears said excitedly. "Tell him yes, Leader. He is a very rich man, is he not?"

"He is also married," Ling Cho said.

"But he is rich enough to be able to afford two wives," Golden Tears insisted.

"That is not done in this country," Ling Cho explained. "Besides, you are a peasant Chinese girl. Do you seriously expect someone like Warren Leland would marry you? I do not say this to be cruel, little one, merely to instruct you in the facts of life."

"But he does like me, I know this."

"I do not deny that he likes you, little one. But what he has in his mind is quite different from what you have in your heart. You should avoid this one. Please, listen to me. I am much your elder and say these things for your own good."

"Very well, Leader," Golden Tears said, with an edge of disappointment in her voice.

Chapter Twenty-Six

Warren didn't return that night. In fact, he had been gone for four nights when Reesa heard that the Arizona line would be crossed sometime during the next day, and she made up her mind that she wanted to go to End-of-Track.

"But, mum," Daisy protested.

"I told you to please call me Reesa."

Daisy smiled. "I know you did, mum . . . I mean Reesa. It just takes some getting used to, that's all. But what I was going to say, Reesa, is that you are just asking for more hurt, aren't you?"

"I don't care," Reesa said. "I've been a part of this operation all along, and I'm going to see it through. Now you get the car ready to travel, and I'll go get Sam to pull us out there."

When Reesa first approached Sam, he began to make excuses as to why he couldn't pull her car to End-of-Track.

"Sam, you too?" Reesa asked. "Have you turned against me along with everyone else?"

Sam cleared his throat and looked at the ground. "Reesa, girl, I reckon you got your own life to live, 'n' it ain't really nobody else's business. It's just that no one can understand why you up and married that Leland fella. Especially with him spendin' ever' night since you come back with Sally or one of her girls."

"Regardless of my reasons, it's something done," Reesa said. "Now, Sam, I'm asking you again; please pull my car out to End-of-Track."

Sam sighed. "All right, Reesa. I'll do it. I don't know how Mr. Foster's gonna take it. He might decide to fire me."

"He won't fire you," Reesa promised.

"We'll be leavin' in about an hour," Sam said. "Be in your car."

"I will be, and thanks, Sam. I really appreciate this."

Reesa hurried back to the car where she found Daisy just finishing stowing the items that needed securing for travel. "Are we going to End-of-Track?" she asked.

"Yes," Reesa said, her eyes flashing in excitement over the prospect.

"Oh, that'll be wonderful," Daisy said. "I've never seen men building a railroad before. Are there many?"

"Hundreds," Reesa said.

Reesa was in better spirits as they journeyed to End-of-Track than she had been at any time since the fateful trip to San Francisco. She didn't admit it, even to herself, but the reason for her improved spirit was the prospect of seeing Ted again. Even if Ted hated her and wouldn't speak to her, she would be seeing him,

271

seeing him realize his dream. She knew that she was responsible for his success and she would take a quiet pleasure in that.

Daisy and Reesa were chatting about the scenery through which the train was passing when the train came to a sudden halt. So violent was the stop that lamps and chairs tipped over, and Reesa heard the crashing of dishes in the cupboard.

"Reesa, what is it?" Daisy cried.

"I don't know," Reesa said. "But hang on tight."

Both women were in seats that were secured to the floor, so they were spared the indignity and possible injury of being unceremoniously dumped over.

"I'm going to get out and see what's going on," Reesa said.

"Oh, please be careful," Daisy warned.

Once outside the train, Reesa saw a large bonfire on the track just in front of the engine. Sam was out of the engine arguing with two men on horseback. Reesa hurried up to the front of the train.

"Sam, what is it? Why is that fire on the track?"

"Buenos dias, Señora!" one of the horsemen said. Reesa recognized him as Ronaldo, Joaquin's friend.

"Ronaldo, what are you doing here?"

"I am most sorry for the fire, *Señora*," Ronaldo said. "But Joaquin insisted that we warn the train before anyone was hurt."

"Warn the train? Warn us about what?"

At that moment, there was a stomach-jarring explosion, and Reesa and Sam looked toward the pass to see a tremendous cloud of dust rising. Tons of rock and shale crashed down on the track, closing the pass.

"About that, *Señora*," Ronaldo said. "If the train had continued to go, you would have been hurt in the blast."

"Oh, no; you've cut the track!" Reesa said.

"*Si.* Now the trains cannot run," Ronaldo said. "Engineer, you may drive the train back to Albuquerque. You will not be harmed."

Sam sighed. "You'd better get back on board," he said to Reesa. "I'll take us back."

"No," Reesa said.

"What do you mean, no?" Ronaldo asked. "You have no choice, *Señora*. Your engineer cannot drive the train through the pass, she is blocked."

"I am going to see Joaquin," Reesa said.

"What?" Sam asked, sputtering.

"Ronaldo, take me to see Joaquin, please."

"I don't know, *Señora*, he may not . . ."

Reesa suddenly noticed that Ronaldo was calling her *señora*, rather than *señorita*. "How did you know I was married?" she asked.

Ronaldo smiled. "We know," he answered, without elaborating.

"Well, no matter, I've been back long enough for the world to know," she said. "Ronaldo, please take me to see Joaquin. It's very important."

Ronaldo sighed and said something in Spanish. Finally, he patted his saddle. "Very well, *Señora*," he said. "But when Joaquin grows angry, you must convince him that I did not take you against your will."

"Reesa, girl, don't be crazy," Sam warned.

Reesa climbed onto the horse with Ronaldo and looked back at Sam. "Don't worry about me, Sam, I'll be all right," Reesa said. "You go on back to Albuquerque. You can stop at Hickman and send a telegram to End-of-Track, telling them what has happened. That is if the wire is still up."

"But what are you going to do?"

"I'm going to talk to Joaquin," Reesa said.

Ronaldo and the rider with him slapped their legs against the flanks of their horses, and the animals bolted forward. Reesa was sitting sidesaddle with her leg hooked across the pommel in front of Ronaldo, and it was an uncomfortable ride, but she made no complaint. After a couple of hours, they came to a small ranch, and Ronaldo borrowed an extra horse for Reesa. Thus the remaining journey was made much easier for her, though she was still close to physical exhaustion by the time they reached the *Casa Grande*, the Big House.

"Who is the extra rider?" Joaquin called from the porch. Then he recognized Reesa. "*Caramba,* why have you kidnapped her?"

"I asked to come, Joaquin," Reesa said. She swung down from the horse, and then had to hang on to the saddle for a bit to keep from pitching over, she was so tired.

"You asked to come?" Joaquin said, coming to her assistance. "Why?"

"I want to talk," Reesa said.

Joaquin led Reesa into the big house and

called for a glass of water for her. "Did you eat?" he asked Ronaldo.

"Some jerky," Ronaldo answered.

"Come, *Señora,* we are about to take our evening meal. You will join us. And you, Ronaldo."

"Thank you," Reesa said, following Joaquin gratefully into the dining room, where the spicy aromas were already reminding her of how hungry she was.

"Hello, Reesa," Lyrica said quietly. Sitting beside her at the table was Frederica.

"Lyrica! What are you doing here?"

"Don Esteban is my uncle," Lyrica said.

"Oh, what a wonderful surprise," Reesa exclaimed. "I never expected to see you again."

"*Señora,* you are not as surprised as we," Joaquin said. "Tell me, why did you come here?"

"Joaquin, please. Let her have her dinner before you badger her with questions," Lyrica said.

"Yes, yes, of course," Joaquin agreed. "You must forgive me, *Señora.* Please, eat and then we will find room for you. Tomorrow, when you have rested, we can talk."

"Thank you, Joaquin," Reesa said.

The meal was eaten in a very relaxed atmosphere, with Joaquin and Ronaldo teasing not only each other, but Lyrica and Frederica as well. Even Reesa came in for some good-natured teasing, as Ronaldo told of her storming off the train demanding to be taken to Joaquin.

"Ah, *caramba,*" Ronaldo said. "Her eyes

flashed such fire that I feared for my life if I refused."

"You should not be surprised, Ronaldo," Joaquin teased. "Have you not heard that women with black hair may know great fury?"

After the meal, the diners adjourned to a large room that Reesa would have described as a parlor, though it was decidedly less formal. Although Reesa had been at the big house before, there were many things she did not remember, or had not noticed the previous time. Indian rugs decorated the floor and hung from the walls. There was also a rack of rifles against one wall, and the antlers of antelope and horns of buffalo were mounted on decorative plaques. Don Esteban, Joaquin's father, had not taken the evening meal with them, but he joined them in the room. He was tall and ramrod straight, with silver hair and flashing eyes. It was easy to see where Joaquin and Frederica acquired their handsome looks.

Reesa was introduced to Don Esteban, and he smiled and kissed her hand graciously.

"*Señora*," Don Esteban said. "We are about to listen to a guitar concert. Are you familiar with the guitar?"

"Yes," Reesa said, "of course. Someone was always playing one somewhere as I grew up. A railroad worker or a cowboy." And I heard the guitars the last time I was here," she added hesitantly.

"But they played only chords to help them sing, am I right?" Don Esteban asked.

"Well, yes. What else is a guitar for?"

Don Esteban and the others laughed.

"Did I say something funny?" Reesa asked, a bit piqued.

"Excuse us for laughing, Reesa," Joaquin said. Reesa noticed the familiarity of the first name, but didn't comment. "But you see," Joaquin went on," the Spanish invented the guitar. And we didn't invent it to sing songs to the cows as do the *Anglos*."

"It is a concert instrument when in the right hands," Don Esteban said. "Forgive us for being impolite, but it pains us to see the guitar misused as an instrument."

"Well," Reesa said, now curious as to just what a guitar could do that she hadn't heard before. "I must say that I am looking forward to this."

"Good," Don Esteban said. "Manuel, you may begin."

Manuel, whom Reesa had seen earlier helping to serve the meal, now picked up a battered guitar case and opened it. The case may have been battered, but the guitar inside was exquisitely beautiful. The box was cherry red, giving way to soft yellow. It showed tender care, and the way Manuel handled it, gently and with respect, told the story of his love for the instrument. He strummed the strings lightly, moving through an intricate chord progression that rose from the sound box and wove a pattern of melody as delicate as a lace doily.

Reesa sat quietly, listening in delight. She was amazed that this sound was coming from a guitar. It was as if she were discovering something entirely new. She was long familiar with the guitar, but had never really known it.

Manuel went through the chord progressions a few times and then stopped. He hung his head for a few seconds, then started to play. The music spilled out, a steady, never-wavering beat with two or three poignant minor chords at the ends of phrases, but with an overall, single string melody, weaving in and out of the chords like a thread of gold woven through the finest cloth.

The sound was agony and ecstasy, joy and sorrow, pain and pleasure. It moved into Reesa's soul, and she found herself being carried along with the melody, now rising, now falling. Perhaps it was the moment, the quiet, the softly lit room, the weight of her personal sorrow, but Reesa had never been moved so deeply by music before. She sat spellbound for several seconds after the last exquisite chord faded away.

"Now, she understands," Don Esteban said quietly, as he saw the expression on Reesa's face.

"I will show you to your room," Lyrica invited. "You must be tired."

"Yes," Reesa said. "Thank you, I am."

Casa Grande was a two-story stucco house with red slate shingles on the roof. It was a sprawling house, shaped somewhat like the letter "U," though with the wings at more of an angle. Reesa's room was at the end of the east wing, and she followed Lyrica down the long hallway.

"I can't tell you how good it is to see you here," Reesa said.

"It was a pleasant surprise to see you, too," Lyrica said.

"Tell me, Lyrica, would it be possible to have a bath?" Reesa asked.

Lyrica laughed. "I have already asked for a bath to be drawn for you. I remember you told me on the train of your penchant for bathing."

Lyrica opened the door and motioned for Reesa to enter. The room was large and comfortable, with a huge double window looking out over the lawn. On one side of the room, near the wall, was a large tub. It wasn't the type with running water, as she had enjoyed for the few brief days she had spent in the Leland Mansion in San Francisco, but the steam arising from the water attested to the fact that it was adequately hot and would be very relaxing.

"Thank you," Reesa said when she saw the tub. "Oh, that looks absolutely heavenly."

"Good night, Reesa. I'll see you in the morning," Lyrica said. "Oh, just hang your clothes outside your door. I'll have them cleaned and returned by the time you wake up tomorrow." Lyrica smiled and pulled the door shut.

Reesa walked over to the tub. She saw not only the water, but the towels, soap, toilet water and oils she would use placed on a bench beside the tub. She removed her clothes, hung them outside the door, and slipped gratefully into the water.

After the bath, Reesa toweled herself dry, then walked over to the windows, still nude. She pushed them open and looked outside.

A cluster of trees waved gently in the night

wind, and the leaves of one of them caught a moonbeam and scattered a burst of silver through the darkness. The fragrant scent of carefully nurtured flowers floated in from a nearby garden, and the breeze kissed her naked skin as softly as the touch of silk.

Reesa heard a very light knock on the door.

"Who is it?" she called quietly.

"Joaquin."

Reesa looked around quickly for something with which to cover herself, since Lyrica had taken her clothes. Then, in a sudden rush of bravado, she decided not to bother. After all, he had seen her this way before. And, she admitted to herself, she would not turn away Joaquin's attentions, should he offer them. Besides, to whom did she have to be faithful? Certainly not her husband. And Ted had to be dismissed from her heart forever. There was only herself to worry about now, and Reesa wanted the comfort and the sex Joaquin could offer.

She took a deep breath, as if about to plunge into an icy stream. "Come in," she called.

The door opened and closed, and Reesa looked over to see him standing just inside. His legs were bare beneath the serape he was wearing.

"You won't need that," Reesa said.

Joaquin smiled, took it off, and draped it across a chair.

"I just used it for the walk through the hall," Joaquin said. He came over to her and she could smell the scent of him, mingled with the fragrance of the flowers from outside. His skin shone silver in the moonlight, and as she looked at him, she could see that he was ready for her.

"Do I have to beg you this time?" Reesa asked, smiling at him.

"Please, Reesa. Do not hold that foolish threat against me. I think I was merely saying that to prevent myself from taking you by force. You are so beautiful, and I wanted you so much."

"Oh, Joaquin, why couldn't I have fallen in love with you?" Reesa asked. She put her arms around his neck and pulled his lips down to hers. She could feel the texture of his lips as she kissed him, and her mouth opened hungrily, as if she would consume him.

Soon they were in bed with their naked bodies pressed together. Reesa, who had lost Ted, and been denied the marital bed by the scurrilous acts of her husband, sought now to release the passionate hungers so long enchained. Joaquin became Ted's surrogate, and though each took a full measure of pleasure from the other, they paid back in kind, as eager to give as to receive. During their mutual worshiping at love's altar, the music of the earlier guitar concert seemed to replay itself in Reesa's head, and as the beautiful melody weaved its way once more through her body, so did the delightful wanderings of Joaquin's hands and mouth. Finally, he moved over her and as she felt his weight pressing against her, she opened herself to him, abandoning all thoughts but the momentary quest for pleasure. She was lifted to dizzying heights of sensation, going from peak to peak with such rapidity that it was difficult to tell when one was left and another attained. Finally, a shuddering moan of pleasure told her that Joaquin had joined her in this maelstrom of sensation, and she locked her arms around his naked back, providing him with the cushion he needed to ride out his pleasure.

Later, with the pleasant weight of Joaquin still on her and only their heavy breathing to tell of the experience just past, Reesa closed her mind and her heart to any possible recriminations. She intended to take what joy there was for her now, since there seemed to be nothing else left.

Chapter Twenty-Seven

Lyrica got up in the gray light of early morning and left the house before anyone else had arisen. She hurried to the barn and saddled a horse, then rode out the back trail and headed for the tall mountain just behind the house, known as Mendoza's Peak.

When Lyrica reached the top of Mendoza's Peak, she dismounted and walked out to a rock ledge and stared down at the ranch and the house below. A wispy pall of wood smoke lay in a long, diaphanous haze over the house. Lyrica knew that the cooks were awake and preparing breakfast. The others would just be beginning to stir now as the rich aroma of coffee and bacon would fill the house.

The thought of breakfast made Lyrica hungry, so she took some beef jerky from her saddlebag and unhooked the canteen from the saddle horn. The canteen contained coffee, and the coffee and jerky would make a passable breakfast.

Lyrica had heard the knock on Reesa's door

last night, and she, just one room away, opened her door a crack to peek out. She saw Joaquin standing there wearing only a serape, and she saw him go inside. Lyrica withdrew to her room and pressed her ear to the wall. She heard them when they began to make love, and she returned to her bed and cried into her pillow until there were no tears left. Later, much later, she heard Joaquin leave Reesa's room to return to his own.

Lyrica was unable to sleep that night, so with the coming of first light, she left the house in order to be alone with her anguish and think things out.

It was obvious to her that Joaquin was in love with Reesa. From the time she first arrived at Rancho Sombra de las Montanas, she had heard of the beautiful *Anglo* woman. She knew also that Joaquin's thoughts were often of Reesa. And, when she asked Joaquin to avenge Reesa, he was quick to respond. Even, she thought, happy that he would be able to do something for the American girl.

Lyrica had set up the robbery in the first place in order to win Joaquin's love. But it had gone terribly awry and, in fact, had caused the opposite effect. Joaquin felt sympathy for Reesa, and that strengthened his love for her. Not only that, but Joaquin had been angry with Lyrica for setting in motion the events that had so disrupted Reesa's life.

As Lyrica sat on the rock eating her breakfast and looking down onto the house below, the obvious solution began to present itself. She would help Joaquin win Reesa. Her love for

Joaquin was strong enough that she could make this sacrifice for him. And her sin against Reesa was strong enough that she felt she must do this for penance.

As the solution came to Lyrica, a sadness descended over her and tears began to slide silently down her face. She closed her eyes tightly, crossed herself, and said a little prayer asking for the strength to do what she must do.

Golden bars of the morning sun slashed in through the window and flooded Reesa's pillow with light. It was a combination of this light and the movement of someone in her room that awakened her.

"Good morning, *Señora*," a short, dumpy woman said. Reesa recognized the woman as one of the house servants she had seen the night before. The woman was holding Reesa's dress and underthings.

"It is all clean and pressed," the woman said, smiling broadly.

"Thank you," Reesa said.

The woman hung the clothes on a hook on the closet door and pointed to the dresser. "Here is a basin of hot water, soap and towels, *Señora*," she said. "Breakfast will be served in twenty minutes."

After the woman left, Reesa stretched luxuriously in the bed. It was only then that she realized that she had slept nude last night. So complete was her satisfaction, so delightful her feeling, that when Joaquin left her room the night before Reesa had gone right to sleep without worrying about anything to sleep in.

Reesa blushed, wondering if the maid had noticed her nudity. Perhaps not; she had been under the covers.

It had been good with Joaquin the night before. Even better than with Warren, because Joaquin brought an obvious passion to his bed, and passion, Reesa was convinced, was much better than skill. But, Reesa told herself sadly, only with Ted had the passion been matched with an emotional commitment that went both ways.

But there is no more Ted, she told herself. She was embarked on a new life now. A life of emotional deprivation. Therefore, if she wished to compensate by finding passion where she could, who would dare fault her? Her father? He had disowned her, and Warren was a hedonist of the first degree who would probably enjoy watching Reesa commit adultery, were she to permit such a blasphemy.

Reesa stretched one more time, then hopped out of bed and began dressing. She had just finished and was making a few last brush strokes on her hair when she heard a knock at the door.

"Come in," she called.

Joaquin opened the door and stepped inside. "Good morning, Reesa," he said. "I've come to escort you to breakfast."

"Thank you," Reesa replied. "I'm ready."

Breakfast was the same casual affair as dinner had been the evening before. No one had faint appetites, and even Reesa, who so often restricted her breakfast to a cup of coffee and a biscuit, ate heartily of the veritable banquet offered her.

"Where's Lyrica?" Frederica asked.

"I saw her riding out this morning," Ronaldo said.

"Riding out? Riding where?" Joaquin asked.

"She took some coffee from the kitchen early this morning, *Señor*," one of the servants said as she delivered more eggs. "She said she wanted to go for a ride."

"That's odd," Joaquin said.

"Perhaps not so odd," Frederica said, her eyes fixed on Reesa's face. "After all, her room is right next to Reesa's."

Reesa flushed, and she looked down at her plate in embarrassment. Joaquin spoke angrily in Spanish to his sister.

"I am not being critical, my brother," Frederica replied in English. "It is just that it is obvious to all that Lyrica loves you and to be indiscreet right under her nose is not in the best taste."

"Lyrica loves you?" Reesa asked. "But I thought she was your cousin."

"Her mother married my uncle," Joaquin said. "We are not blood cousins. But I wouldn't worry, Reesa. Lyrica is but a child. She only thinks she loves me."

"Ah, *chijuajua*, some child," Ronaldo said.

"I . . . uh, excuse me," Reesa murmured. She got up from the table and left quickly, burning with embarrassment and guilt.

Lyrica was her friend. How could she have done this to her? She would never forgive herself for satisfying her physical needs in the arms of the man her friend loved.

287

Reesa had no sooner reached her room than she heard an urgent knock on the door.

"Who is it?"

"Reesa, it is Joaquin. Please, let me in. I must talk to you."

"No," Reesa answered.

The door opened and Joaquin stepped inside.

"Go away," Reesa said. "I don't want to talk to you." Reesa walked over to the bed and sat down.

"Please," Joaquin said. He sat beside her, then put his hands on her shoulders. "Listen to me, Reesa."

"All right, I'll listen."

"Perhaps Lyrica does love me. If she does, then it is wrong of me to treat it so lightly, and for that I apologize."

"I'm not the one who should be hearing your apology," Reesa said.

"Yes, you are," Joaquin insisted. "Because I have made you feel as if you have hurt Lyrica, and she is your friend. For this I apologize. But, you should know how I feel, for you are, how do the *Anglos* say it? You are in the same ship."

"In the same boat?"

"*Si.*"

"In what way?"

"I love you, Reesa, the way Lyrica loves me. And, as I don't return Lyrica's love, neither do you return mine."

"Joaquin, you don't love me," Reesa said.

"But I do, Reesa."

"You can't love me," Reesa said with a little laugh. "You know I'm married."

"And your heart belongs to yet another," Joaquin said. "Tell me, does the man you love return the love to you?"

"Yes, Ted loves me," Reesa said. But even as she made the declarative statement, she wondered. Did Ted love her? Was it as deep and honest a love as she had for him? If he truly loved her, could he not see the sacrifice she made for him and love her all the more for it?"

"You say this, but you are not sure," Joaquin said. "Perhaps we are all in the same boat."

"Perhaps so, Joaquin," Reesa said quietly. She put her hand on Joaquin's and squeezed it, then smiled sadly. "Is there nothing we can do?"

"We can wait," Joaquin said. "Now, perhaps you feel like talking about the reason you came to see me?"

Reesa sighed. "I wanted to ask you to let the railroad go through," she said. "But now, I am so confused I don't know what to do. Sometimes I think I should go back to San Francisco and make a life for myself there."

"I will let the railroad go through," Joaquin said quietly.

"Of course, I don't know what I expected by coming out here, I just . . . " Reesa paused in mid-sentence. "Did you say you would let the railroad go through?" she asked.

"*Si*," Joaquin said.

"But why? You've been fighting it so hard, surely you don't intend to change your mind just because I asked you?"

"Reesa, I realize now that the railroad is not going to go away or find another route. If not your Ted, then another will come, and then another and yet another. If we continue to fight the railroad, soon there will be a killing. Then perhaps more killings until there is a war. I do not mind killing a man who should be killed. But the men who work on the railroad are honest men with no evil in their hearts. My men are honest men who believe in what they are doing. To put honest men into a war against each other means that only honest men are killed. That would be a sin. I will make no more effort to stop the railroad."

"Oh, thank you, Joaquin," Reesa breathed.

"But if I do this thing, I feel that the railroad should make . . . concessions," he said, looking for the right word.

"What sort of concessions?"

"The railroad has land grants that extend one mile to either side of the track," Joaquin said. This hurts the people who own small ranches. Some will lose everything they have worked so hard for. Perhaps *Señor* Foster will sell that land to me so that I can return it to the small ranchers," Joaquin offered. "It was land that originally belonged to my family, and we gave it to these ranchers. I do not feel good about buying the land back to give it away a second time, but if *Señor* Foster will not charge too much, perhaps I can do this."

"I'll talk to him," Reesa said. "I'm sure he'll be willing to do as you ask."

"Will he listen to you?" Joaquin asked.

"Yes," Reesa said. "I'll make him listen."

"Good," Joaquin said, smiling broadly. "Then let us call off this fight."

Reesa felt so good over having worked out a deal with Joaquin that she nearly forgot the incident at the breakfast table, and didn't think of it again until she saw Lyrica returning from her ride just before noon. She wondered how best to treat the situation, but Lyrica took the problem out of her hands.

"Reesa," Lyrica said. "I must talk to you."

Reesa felt apprehensive. She didn't want to talk to Lyrica because she was afraid that it would lead to angry words. And she didn't wish to get into an argument with the girl she considered her friend. But there was really no way to avoid the discussion, so she took a deep breath and agreed to go to Lyrica's room to talk with her. She stood just inside the door as Lyrica paced about nervously, obviously seeking a way to begin the conversation. Finally, Reesa decided to begin it for her.

"Lyrica, about last night," she said. "I am truly sorry. I didn't know you were in love with Joaquin."

"But you know now?" Lyrica asked, puzzled by Reesa's statement.

"Yes," Reesa said. "I was told this morning. I—I want to ask for your forgiveness."

"My forgiveness, Reesa? Forgiveness for what?"

"I have hurt you."

"No. I have hurt myself," Lyrica said. "Now, I wish to ask something of you."

"What?"

"I wish to ask that you return Joaquin's love. He loves you very much, Reesa. It would make him very happy if you returned that love."

"Lyrica, loving him as you do, you would ask such a thing?" Reesa asked.

"*Si*," Lyrica said. "I would be happy knowing that he is happy."

"Lyrica, believe me, it doesn't work that way," Reesa said. Tears sprang to her eyes as she thought of the sacrifice Lyrica was willing to make, and compared it to the sacrifice she had made. "I loved Ted enough to give him up. But I have discovered scant reward in that."

"It is different with Joaquin," Lyrica insisted.

"How is it different?"

"Joaquin loves you far more than Ted Foster ever did."

"How can you say such a thing?" Reesa asked. "You don't know Ted."

"But I know Joaquin," Lyrica said. "It was Joaquin who was willing to face down the scarfaced man and the man with one eye. He killed them both to avenge you. Ted didn't do that, Joaquin did."

"What did you say?" Reesa asked in a small, shocked voice.

"The two men who robbed you and gave you to the ship captain," Lyrica said. "They are dead now. Joaquin faced them down and killed them both."

"But . . . but how did he *know* about it?"

"I told him," Lyrica said. "I told him their names and gave him their description."

"But, Lyrica, how did *you* know all that? I only saw one of them, and I didn't know the name of either of them."

"Reesa, please, you must forgive me," Lyrica

said, suddenly realizing that she had said much more than she intended.

"Lyrica, what is it? What is it that you aren't telling me?"

"I sent the men to rob you," Lyrica said. "I told them not to hurt you. I only wanted them to take the money from you. I had no idea they would do what they did. That is why I asked Joaquin to avenge you."

"But . . . *why?*

"I knew that the money was for the railroad," Lyrica explained. "I thought that if you didn't have the money, the railroad wouldn't be built. That would please Joaquin, and perhaps make him love me. But I didn't want to hurt you. I didn't know they would do what they did."

"Lyrica, what they did was nothing," Reesa said. "If that were all that happened I would count myself lucky. It was what came afterward that has done me the greatest hurt. I was forced to marry Warren and give up Ted. And you did this to me. *You!*"

Reesa turned and ran from the room. She sped down the hallway and out the front door. Finally, when she reached a hitching rail in front of the house, she paused to grab her breath.

"What is it, Reesa?" Joaquin asked, following her out the door. "Why did you run out of the house like that?"

Reesa looked at Joaquin with her eyes flashing anger. "Tell me," she said. "Just how much were you willing to pay Ted for the return of the land? One hundred and fifty thousand dollars, perhaps?"

"She told you," Joaquin said.

"Yes," Reesa replied, looking away. "How could she have done this? And you? You let it happen."

"No," Joaquin said. "I knew nothing about it until it had already happened. I have the money now. I was going to tell you about it."

"When?" Reesa asked. "After you used it to cheat Ted out of his land?"

"*Señora,* let us not lose sight of who is cheating whom here!" Joaquin said angrily. "Do not forget, it was my land in the first place."

"I need a horse," Reesa said after a moment. "May I borrow one?"

"*Si,* of course," Joaquin said. "I will ride back to town with you."

"No, that isn't necessary."

"It is a long way back. Much could happen to a woman riding alone."

"I don't care what happens to me anymore," Reesa said dejectedly.

Chapter Twenty-Eight

The soft desert sand was still warm from the heat of the day, though it had been cooled enough by darkness to be comfortable. Thus it provided an adequate mattress for the two lovers who were now approaching the summit of their experience together. The man's breathing started coming in gasps, and the woman's whimpers of passion grew louder as the two of them attained their quest simultaneously, then locked in each other's embrace as they let the waves of passion wash over them.

Later, after the last sensations had spent themselves, the man got up and began getting dressed. The bright moon was shining on the girl who had not yet moved from where she lay beside the ravine.

"It was good," the man said easily. "But it's over now, so you'd better get dressed."

The girl smiled up at him.

"Here," the man said, picking up the girl's clothes and dropping them on her. "Get dressed now."

She continued to smile, but made no move to comply with his request.

"Very well, have it your own way." He reached in his pocket and took out two coins. "Here," he said. "You earned this." He dropped the coins on the dirt beside her.

The girl's face registered surprise, then twisted into an expression of rage. She picked the money up and threw it at him, then stood up and leaped at him, screaming in anger.

"Hey, what the hell? Have you gone crazy?" the man asked, surprised by the girl's sudden move. He fended off her charge, then pushed her back. Thrown off balance, she let out a short scream and fell backwards into the ravine, which cut a deep scar into the desert floor beside where they had lain. Her scream faded as she slid downward. When she reached the bottom, she was perfectly still.

"Are you all right?" the man called out running to the edge of the ravine. "What did you do that for, you crazy . . . " He stopped in mid-sentence as he saw her. There was no need to go on. Even in the moonlight, he could tell that the girl was dead. Her head was grotesquely twisted and her eyes were open and unseeing. Her neck had been broken in the fall.

"My God," the man said quietly. "What the hell did you do that for?"

He instinctively looked around to see if anyone saw or heard what happened, and then realizing that nobody would be there in the dead of night, he walked quickly away.

* * *

The five-thirty call rousted the work crews out of bed, and by six o'clock work was underway. The steel had been ringing for nearly an hour when Warren stepped out of Sally's car and saw Ted and Murdock standing together near the engineering car. He adjusted his hat and tugged at his cuff, then strolled over to join them.

"Well, how goes the mighty railroad builders today?" Warren asked.

"Good morning, Mr. Leland," Murdock said.

" 'Morning, Leland," Ted put in.

"Have you any estimate on when we'll have the pass open?" Warren asked.

"No," Ted said. "Why, are you anxious to get back to Albuquerque?"

"No, no, my dear fellow. But I am anxious to bring my wife out to join me. You know my wife, the former Reesa Flowers?"

"Why do you want her out here?" Ted asked. "Aren't you afraid that will interfere with your visits to Sally's girls?"

"No, not at all," Warren answered. "Reesa is very understanding about that sort of thing."

"I'll just bet," Ted said.

"My—don't tell me you are worried about my wife's sensitive feelings being bruised? I should think that would be the last thing you'd worry about, Foster. After all, she certainly paid no attention to your feelings, did she?"

"I've got some things to do," Ted said, flushing angrily.

"To be sure," Warren said. "Nothing must stop the railroad."

Warren laughed as Ted walked away.

"Mr. Leland, you ought not to ride Mr. Foster like that. His heart was plumb broke when Reesa up and married you."

"How touching," Warren said.

"I. thought I knew Reesa better'n that, too," Murdock went on. "What I can't figure is why she done what she did. I thing they's somethin' to this that none of the rest of us know yet."

"Oh, most astute of you," Warren said sarcastically.

"You know, Mr. Leland, I don't always know what all them words you say mean," Murdock said. "And I ain't none too sure that I like it. But Mr. Foster said let you be, so that's what I aim to do for the time bein'."

The smile left Warren's face, and an evil glint flashed in his eyes. He looked at Murdock coldly. "Don't ever get the wrong idea, Felton," he warned. "I wouldn't even try to fight a giant like you. I'd shoot you at the first move."

"Yes, sir, I reckon you would," Murdock said. "But I reckon two or three of them little bullets in that popshooter you carry wouldn't stop me before I broke your neck."

"Shall we try it then, Mr. Felton?" Warren asked.

"Mr. Felton, Mr. Foster wants to see you," one of the men called from the front of the train.

"I reckon not," Murdock said easily. "At least not now."

Warren watched Murdock walk quickly to the front of the train, and he stuck his hand in his pocket to keep it from shaking. The truth was, Murdock was probably right about not being stopped easily. Especially with the gun Warren carried, a short barrel .25 caliber special. It was potent enough to do the job, and in fact had done so on more than one occasion. But the greatest advantage was in its size. That gave him the advantage of having a concealed weapon, but he had to trade that advantage off in the amount of stopping power of the bullets. And, of course, with Murdock Felton, even the advantage of a concealed weapon was negated, since Murdock, as well as everyone else on the railroad, knew that he carried one.

The shakes stopped, but the nervous sweats did not, and Warren reached for his handkerchief to mop his brow.

Ling Cho watched the work of his crew with satisfaction. Two hundred bodies welded together to function with one mind. His mind, he thought with pride. The Chinese were looked down upon as if they were something less than human. They ran laundries, cafes, or worked as house servants, and that was the extent of their existence. Except for the railroad. They had been proving their worth on the railroads, and through the railroads were leaving behind a monument to their race. And of that Ling Cho was inordinately proud.

A small elderly Chinese man approached Ling Cho, stopped at a respectful distance and waited, as was dictated by the social order of his station, for Ling Cho to recognize him.

"Yes, Wu Tien, what is it?" Ling Cho asked. Wu Tien was one of the cooks on the Chinese kitchen staff.

"Leader, there is much sorrow in the kitchen," Wu Tien said.

"Sorrow? Why is there sorrow?"

"Come," Wu Tien said.

Ling Cho followed Wu Tien along the track and down the elevated roadbed into an area where a collection of crossed poles, suspended pots, fires and smells made up the Chinese kitchen. Wu Tien pointed to an old woman who was crying.

"Old woman, why do you weep so?" Ling Cho asked.

"I weep for my daughter," the old woman answered.

"You weep for Golden Tears? Why?"

"Because she is dead," Wu Tien said. "Come, I will show you."

Ling Cho followed Wu Tien from the camp, and they walked approximately two hundred yards across the desert floor. Finally they came to the edge of a ravine. Wu Tien stopped and pointed. "She is down there," he said.

There, in the bottom of the ravine, Ling Cho saw her. Golden Tears, who had been so beautiful in life, was grotesque in death. She was nude and already her young, hairless body was being discolored by the sun. Scars and cuts on her body were puffed with dried blood, and insects crawled around exploring the strange creature that now lay in their domain. Her eyes were open and bulging, shining with opaque blackness. Her head was twisted sharply to one side, and a large discolored knot showed where the neck had been broken.

Something flashed in the sun near Ling

Cho's feet, and he picked up two coins, examined them curiously, then dropped them in his pocket.

"When did you find her?" Ling Cho asked.

"A short time ago, Leader," Wu Tien said. "Her mother said nothing about the girl being gone for a while, thinking perhaps she was taking a walk as she sometimes did. But then she grew worried, so she came to see me. I searched and found her here."

"Wu Tien, have you noticed any of the Americans, the round eyes, talking to Golden Tears?"

"No, Leader. Do you think a round eye did this thing?"

Ling Cho stuck his hand in his pocket and felt the two coins. "Yes," he said.

"Will you tell the round-eye chief of this?"

"No," Ling Cho said. "If justice is to be done, we must see to it ourselves and in secret."

"But the round-eye chief is an honest man, is he not?"

"Yes, he is honest, as is my friend Murdock Felton. I believe also the one who talks with wires is honest. But Golden Tears is our responsibility. Do you agree?"

"Yes, Leader."

"Tell the mother of Golden Tears to finish with her weeping and say nothing of this," Ling Cho ordered. "And get clothes for the girl's burial from her mother. I will get shovels, and we will bury her here."

"Yes, Leader," Wu Tien said, starting back to the kitchen camp at a trot.

Ling Cho stood there for a moment longer,

looking down at the body of the young girl. He felt heartsick over the tragedy. Golden Tears was such a beautiful girl and filled with such curiosity. Though he had mentioned it to no one, it had been his intention to speak to the mother of Golden Tears after the railroad was completed. He had been paid well for his work on the railroads and had saved his money. He would have had much to offer Golden Tears. Now that could never be.

Ling Cho turned to walk back for the shovels. Just as he started back, he saw something white lying in a bed of prickly pear cactus. He bent to pick it up and saw that it was a handkerchief. The handkerchief was wadded up and stuck together with a sticky substance. Ling Cho smelled it and recognized the pungent odor of semen. The handkerchief had obviously been left there by the guilty party, who had used it to clean himself after the deed.

Ling Cho examined the handkerchief closely and saw a laundry number. He smiled. "So, my friend," he said under his breath. "You have signed your work."

Chapter Twenty-Nine

The rockslide, which Joaquin had brought down into the pass, was causing Ted immense difficulty. The terms of the railroad grant act specified that continuous track be laid for every mile claimed. So it would do little good to reach the Arizona town of Springerville by the deadline if the pass were still blocked.

"The only way you're going to get the rock out of here in time is blast it out," Murdock insisted.

"There is no dynamite available," Ted said.

"Buy some more."

"That's what I mean," Ted said. "The dynamite plant in San Francisco is out of production because of a fire. All the existing stockpiles from Chicago to the west are gone."

"How about black powder?"

"Maybe," Ted said. "But it requires eight times as much black powder to do the job. If we could get that much together, the time required to fuse it and set it is so slow, I don't know if it will do us any good."

"We've got to try," Murdock said. "I don't see that we have much choice left, do you?"

Ted sighed. "No, we have no choice left," he agreed. He pinched the bridge of his nose and leaned back in his chair. "Murdock, why don't you ask Ling Cho to come see me? His men are going to handle it, so we'll need his thinking on this."

"All right, boss," Murdock said, unwinding his huge frame from the chair he had been sitting in. As he started out the door of the engineering car, he saw Ling Cho and Miller approaching the car. "Well, how's that for service?" he asked. "Ling Cho is on his way in here right now."

"Good," Ted said.

Ling Cho and Miller came into the engineering car and exchanged greetings with the two men who were already there.

"Ling Cho, can your men move that rock with black powder?" Ted asked.

"Can do," Ling Cho said. "But much work for black powder, maybe cannot do in time."

"The way I see it, we don't have much of an option," Ted said. "There is no more dynamite available anywhere. We'll have to use black powder."

Ling Cho studied the pass for a long time. "Boss Foster, can you get nitro?"

"Nitroglycerine?" Ted asked. "Are you serious?"

"Nitro very strong stuff," Ling Cho said. "More strong than dynamite."

"And much more dangerous," Ted said. "All you have to do to make nitro go off is sneeze."

"But nitro can do job," Ling Cho said. "Black powder, maybe cannot."

"God, I don't know, Ling Cho," Ted said. "I want this railroad built, but I don't want to build it over bodies of my men."

"Not to worry, Boss Foster. Just Chinamen," Ling Cho said, eyeing Ted carefully.

"What the hell do you mean!" Ted exploded. "Chinamen, Irishmen, German, they are all the same, and I don't want any of them killed."

"There are those who do not feel that Chinamen are the same as other men," Ling Cho explained.

"You know damned well I'm not one of them," Ted said.

"I'm sorry I tested you," Ling Cho apologized. "But not to worry about men. I will set the charges myself."

"Ling Cho, you sure you want to do this?" Murdock asked.

"Yes," Ling Cho said.

"Bring this in and you've earned yourself double wages," Ted promised.

"Don't do it and you're dead," Murdock teased, with an edge of truth to his grim humor.

"I wish now to ask a favor of you," Ling Cho said.

"You've got it," Ted replied, not even inquiring what the favor was.

"Golden Tears has been murdered," Ling Cho said.

"The beautiful girl who works in the kitchen? Who did it?" Ted asked.

"That I do not yet know," Ling Cho said.

"But I believe I will soon be able to find the answer to this question. I want to send a telegram to San Francisco."

"Certainly, send as many as you want," Ted replied. "Would you like me to start an inquiry?"

"No," Ling Cho said quickly. He smiled an apology for being so blunt. "Please to understand, I know you want to help, but I think the fewer people who know this, the easier will be the task of discovering the murderer. I beg of you to say nothing. It should not go beyond the ears here."

"Very well, Ling Cho," Ted said. "If you want it that way. We are pretty much our own law here, so I'll let you handle it however you wish."

"Thank you, Boss Foster," Ling Cho said. He handed a piece of paper to Miller. "If you please, Mr. Flowers, send this message to Ba Wong in San Francisco."

"Ba Wong? Isn't he a Tong chief?" Murdock asked. "Ling Cho, you aren't getting involved with Tongs?"

"Only to ask that he answer a question for me," Ling Cho explained. "I have done many favors for Ba Wong and feel that I can ask a favor of him."

"What's the message?" Miller asked.

"I found a handkerchief near the girl's body," Ling Cho explained. "It has a laundry mark and that is good identification. Ba Wong can determine who the number belongs to."

"Is it a San Francisco number?" Ted asked.

"Yes, it has the Chinese character for San Francisco," Ling Cho explained.

"That shouldn't be too hard," Miller said. "How many of our people would likely have San Francisco laundry marks?"

"About three hundred," Ted said. "I hired most of them from that area, remember?"

"Oh, yes," Miller said. "I see what you mean. Very well, Ling Cho, I'll get this right off."

"No," Ling Cho said. "First, order the nitroglycerine, then send this message. I will examine the best places to use the nitro now. I thank you, gentlemen, for your help."

Murdock and Ted watched Ling Cho leave the car and climb the hill to examine the rubble, which covered the pass.

"He's a hell of a guy, you know that?" Murdock said.

"Yes, he is," Ted agreed. "Murdock, you know most of these men. Who would do such a thing as murder that girl?"

"I don't know, boss," Murdock answered glumly. "I thought I knew them all pretty well, and I swear I can't think of a one who would do it. Of course, get a man liquored up enough, and you never can tell what he might do. I'll tell you this, though. Whoever the son-of-a-bitch is, I'd like to have his neck in my hands right now."

When Reesa returned to Albuquerque, she was bone weary from the long ride, and she went immediately to the car where she and Daisy were living, and straight to bed. Daisy was deliriously happy to see her, not only be-

307

cause she was worried about Reesa, but because she was beginning to worry about herself being ill-equipped to long survive the rigors of living in such an inhospitable country.

Reesa slept the rest of the day and the entire night away without awakening once. Only the aroma of breakfast lured her back to consciousness the next morning, and when she sat up in bed, every bone in her body ached.

"How do you feel, mum . . . I mean, Reesa?" Daisy asked, bringing a hot cup of tea to Reesa while she was still abed.

"Oh," Reesa moaned. "I feel as if I have been run over by a locomotive."

"I am so glad you returned," Daisy said. "I've been frightfully lonely without you."

"Has Warren been in touch?" Reesa asked.

"No, mum. I've heard nothing from anyone. Sam, the railroad engineer, brought the car back here and here I've sat. I've been frightfully worried for fear something had happened to you. Did you see the brigand?"

"The brigand?" Reesa repeated, rubbing the back of her neck.

"Yes, mum. You know, the Mexican fellow who was responsible for blowing up the pass?"

"You mean Joaquin?" Reesa asked, smiling at the English girl's description of him. Then when she recalled what she had discovered about Joaquin, her smile faded. "Yes," she said. "I saw him."

"Oh, what is he like?" Daisy ask. "Is he dashing and romantic?"

"I suppose you could say that," Reesa answered. "Why would you ask such a thing?"

"Oh, I should like ever so much to meet some-one like that," Daisy said. "He could place me on the back of his horse, and we would ride off into the sunset."

"Daisy," Reesa said, laughing. "I didn't know you were given to such romantic fanta-sies."

"Oh, yes, mum; it's the only type entertain-ment a poor girl like myself has." She blushed slightly, realizing that she had divulged one of her fantasies. "Would you like breakfast now?"

"Have you eaten?"

"No, mum."

"Good, then you can eat with me," Reesa re-plied. "After breakfast, we'll go into town, and I'll show you all the sights of Albuquerque."

"Oh, that will be delightful," Daisy said. "I do want to get out of this car. Not that it isn't ever so posh, you understand, and I deeply ap-preciate having such a nice place to live, but . . ."

"I understand," Reesa said. "You're getting what we call cabin fever. You need to get out."

"Yes, mum."

The two women spent the morning shopping, visiting the Emporium, the Ranchers' Mercan-tile (which had a sign advertising "Goods for all mankind"), and any other such shops as took their fancy. They ate lunch in the hotel dining room and were given a private booth in the corner. Thus it was that they were unob-served when a group of men came in for lunch and started a conversation that the two ladies could not help but overhear.

309

"He's ordered nitro," one of the men said.

"Nitro? Why, he's gone plumb loco. Nobody works with nitro anymore. That stuff'll kill you quicker'n anythin' I can think of. Why'd he go and order nitro?"

"They say it's the only way he can clear the pass in time. There isn't any dynamite to be found, 'n' black powder'd be too slow."

"He got anybody kin handle it?"

"That Chinaman's gonna do it for 'em."

The other men laughed. "Hell, if that's all, it won't be no great loss if he does blow himself up. The world's got plenty o' them Chinamen."

"As long as they're blowin' people up, it's too bad they couldn't blow up that goddamn Warren Leland 'n' his new wife."

"What, you mean Reesa Flowers?"

"Reesa Leland now," the first man said derisively.

"Oh, Reesa," Daisy said quickly, putting her hand across the table on Reesa's hand.

"Shh," Reesa warned, placing her fingers across her lips.

"Listen, Reesa's all right. I remember when she and her papa worked here. She's got spunk."

"That ain't all she's got," another said, his voice obviously colored by lechery. "I remember when she used to go down to meet the midnight train."

"Yeah, well, she's like all the rest of them. She sold out to the highest bidder. She married that Leland fella 'cause he's rich."

"I just can't believe that about Reesa. Hell, I've knowed her since she was a little girl, and I

310

tell you if she married Leland, there was a reason behind it!" another said.

"How's Foster takin' it?"

"I guess it's just eatin' away inside of 'em. They say if he was a worker before, why you should see him now. He's drivin' hisself near to death."

"You know what it is, don't you? It's her bein' here in that fancy private car that Leland's got her set up in. It's knowin' that she's so close, and yet so far, in a way of speakin'."

"If the girl had any concern for him at all, if there was ever any love between 'em, why she'd 'a' never left San Francisco."

The conversation of the men changed to other things then, and Reesa felt relieved that she would not be subjected to any more of their painful talk.

"I've a mind to tell them a thing or two," Daisy whispered hotly.

"You'll do no such thing," Reesa said, putting her hand on Daisy to restrain her. "Please, just sit very quietly until they've had their lunch and left. I don't want them to know I'm even here."

"The very nerve of them," Daisy fumed. "If they only knew what you really did for Mr. Foster, they would change their minds."

"Daisy, I'm no longer sure I did the right thing at all," Reesa said. "I fear I made a terrible mistake, and perhaps I've compounded it by coming here. The men are right. We shouldn't have left San Francisco. We're going back tomorrow."

Chapter Thirty

The nitro proved to be almost as difficult to come by as the dynamite. So volatile was the substance that an accidental explosion of the stuff once wiped out a city block in San Francisco, killing fourteen, and shattering windows throughout most of the city. Because of that, San Francisco now had a very strict ordinance prohibiting not only the manufacture, but the very presence of the explosive within its city limits. Many other cities had followed suit, and had it not been for the nearby Heckemeyer Mining Company, which had some on hand, Ted might have had to resort to black powder after all.

Ted bought all the Heckemeyer mines had on hand, and Murdock had a car built especially to transfer it. It was really a classic of ingenuity, and Murdock showed it off proudly.

A second deck was built on an ordinary flatcar. The second deck was mounted on leaf springs so that it would take up whatever shock the flatcar's normal suspension let by. Four poles were erected on the second deck, and an intricate basket of ropes was constructed between the poles. Nestled in the rope basket was a large box. The box was stuffed with cotton, and the idea was to place the nitro container inside the cushion of cotton.

"Your own mother would be safe on this car," Murdock boasted as he showed the car to Ted.

"Well, you don't have to worry about my mother," Ted replied. "Just you. You're going after the stuff."

"I thought you'd say that," Murdock said, grinning through a grimace. "All right, boss, when do you want me to go after it?"

"Right now would be as good a time as any," Ted suggested.

"Boss, someone's ridin' into camp carryin' a white flag," one of the workers shouted.

Ted looked in the direction indicated and saw a coal black horse approaching. The rider was sitting erect and proud and carrying a pole from which fluttered a white flag.

"Son-of-a-bitch, it's Joaquin!" Murdock swore. "Who's got a rifle?"

"Wait a minute," Ted said, putting a restraining hand on Murdock's arm.

"Well, what the hell does he want?" Murdock asked.

"Let's find out. Let him through, boys," Ted called.

There was a mumble of protest and a few exclamations of curiosity as the horseman rode into the camp. He reined his prancing animal just short of Ted.

"You are *Señor* Foster," the rider said.

"Yes."

"I am Joaquin Mendoza," Joaquin said. He smiled broadly. "May I dismount?"

"I suppose so," Ted replied. "But you aren't exactly a welcome sight here, Mendoza. What do you want?"

"I want to go somewhere you and I can talk."

"It's a trick, boss," Murdock said. "Don't listen to him."

Ted looked at Joaquin and smiled. "Murdock, he is here in our camp surrounded by our men. What possible trick could he have up his sleeve?"

"I don't know," Murdock said. "But I don't like it."

"I assure you, *Señor* Felton, I have no trick up my sleeve," Joaquin said easily. "I do have a proposition which I hope will interest *Señor* Foster. It will bring us peace."

"I'll listen to your proposition," Ted said. "In the meantime, Murdock, you take the engine and go get the stuff."

"The stuff?" Murdock asked.

"You know, your special car?"

"Oh, oh, yes," Murdock replied. "I'll get right on that."

"Come into my caboose," Ted invited. He led the way, and Joaquin was right behind him, carrying a pouch of some sort. Once inside, Ted offered Joaquin a chair. "What is your proposition?" he asked.

"As you know, I have expressed an opposition to your railroad," Joaquin started.

Ted laughed and pointed toward the pile of

rock and rubble that covered the rails running into the pass. "Is that what this was? An expression of your opposition?"

Joaquin returned Ted's laughter. "You have a sense of humor," he said. "I like that in a man, whether he be a friend or an enemy."

"But you aren't here to listen to my jokes," Ted said.

"No, *Señor*, I am not. I am here to strike a bargain with you. I want to buy back the land that your railroad has taken from the small ranchers."

"Buy back?" Ted said.

"*Si.* The government land grant gives you land for one mile on each side of the right-of-way. I know the government says it is their land to give. But before it was their land to give, it was in my family for over two hundred years. My family gave it to many other people to bring civilization to this country. Now, with the railroad, those people will have no homes."

"Joaquin, you may not realize that I have had to borrow heavily to build this railroad," Ted explained. "The land grants along the right-of-way have been pledged as collateral. Legally, it is not my land to give to you. Or to sell either."

"But it will be your land when the railroad is completed and the debt repaid?" Joaquin asked.

"Yes," Ted said. "Assuming that I complete the railroad within the prescribed deadline. As you know, I've had some difficulty in making that deadline."

Joaquin smiled. "We will offer you no more

difficulty, *Señor*. When the railroad is completed, will you sell the land then?"

"No," Ted replied.

"I see," Joaquin answered, his mouth a tight line.

"I'll give it to you," Ted said.

Joaquin broke into a big smile. "You will *give* us this land, *Señor*?"

"Yes," Ted said. "It is important to me now, only in that it helps to secure the loan for construction. Once the railroad is completed, I will have no further need of it. Giving it to your people may help this area to develop. That can only be good for the railroad."

Joaquin stood up and grabbed Ted's hand. He began pumping it furiously. "Reesa is right. You are a fine man."

"Reesa?" Ted asked, puzzled. "You've seen Reesa recently.?"

"*Si*," Joaquin answered. "Oh, and that reminds me, this is for you." Joaquin handed the pouch he had been carrying to Ted.

"What is it?" Ted asked.

"Open it, *Señor*."

Ted opened the pouch and looked inside. It was filled with money.

"Look at this," he said. He dumped the money onto a table. "How much is here?"

"Very nearly one hundred and fifty thousand dollars," Joaquin said. "I think almost one hundred had been spent by the time I got it back."

"Got it back? What are you talking about?"

"*Señor*, this is the money Reesa borrowed

from the Pacific Trust Bank," Joaquin explained.

"It can't be," Ted said clearly puzzled by the turn of events. "I've already received that money. That's what we're working with right now."

"No, *Señor*," Joaquin explained. "The money you are working with now is the money Senor Titus Leland paid Reesa to marry his son."

"What?"

"*Si, Señor*," Joaquin said. "This money," he pointed to the money on the table, "was stolen from Reesa after she borrowed it. She went to see Titus Leland to try and borrow more, but he refused to loan her any. Then, when he discovered that you had borrowed from Pacific Trust, he threatened to close your railroad immediately. However, he gave Reesa a choice. She could marry Warren and he would not only call off the foreclosure, but would give her the money you needed, or she could refuse to marry Warren and you would be put out of business that very day."

"And so she—?" Ted started, but he was unable to finish his sentence, so struck was he with shame over the things he had said and thought.

"*Si Señor*. She married another to save you."

"My God," Ted whispered. "How could I have been so blind?"

Joaquin sighed. "It is, perhaps, the fate of those of us who sacrifice for others, that we not be fully appreciated for our efforts."

"What do you mean?" Ted asked.

"Simply this, *Señor*, Reesa loves you so much

that she was willing to give you up for what she thought would be your happiness. And I, I love Reesa so much that I am willing to give her up for her happiness. I am giving her up, *Señor*, by telling you all this. I hope you will not make my sacrifice be in vain."

Ted smiled broadly. "It won't be in vain," Ted said. "I'm going to go after her. Married or not, she's coming with me."

"Good, *Señor*," Joaquin said. He stood up. "Now, I must deliver the good news to my friends, that the land will be returned to them when the railroad is completed."

"Oh," Ted said. "Yes, that's right. Joaquin, I can't go after Reesa now. I must finish the railroad by the deadline or default, and all the holdings, including the right-of-way land grants, will go to my backers. Please, you must do something for me."

"*Si, Señor.* What is it?"

"Go see Reesa. Tell her of our conversation. Tell her that I love her, and I'm coming for her when the railroad is finished."

"*Si, Señor*, I will do this thing. *Adios.*"

Inside the engineering car, Warren Leland stood at the window and peeked through the curtain as Joaquin rode away. There was only one other person in the car with Warren—Miller Flowers, who was sitting near the telegraph instrument.

"I wonder what that Mexican wanted?" Warren asked.

"I suppose Ted will tell us in good time," Miller replied. "Maybe it's good news."

"Good news?"

"Maybe he's decided to quit fighting the railroad."

"Ha," Warren laughed. "I don't think that is likely to happen."

The telegraph began clacking, and Miller transcribed the message. "Hey," he said. "This is a break. We're about to discover who killed Golden Tears."

"What? Who killed who? What are you talking about?" Warren asked.

Quickly, Miller explained about the death of Golden Tears. He told how Ling Cho had found the handkerchief, and wired to San Francisco for an identification check on the laundry number.

"It's about to come in now, as soon as the lines are cleared," Miller said. "Whoever owned that handkerchief killed Golden Tears."

"That's silly," Warren said. "You mean to tell me that you think you can determine the killer just through a handkerchief?"

"It's obvious that whoever left that handkerchief out there killed her," Miller said.

"But a bunch of numbers, what does that prove?"

"The Chinese are very thorough," Miller said. "They've got a number for every customer they've ever had. It's simply a matter of looking it up."

"But that wouldn't be any good in a court of law, would it?"

"It'll be good enough in our court," Miller replied. "We have our own law."

"I . . . Miller, listen, there's something . . ."

"Shhh, it's coming in now," Miller said.

Miller hunched over the instrument, transcribing the dots and dashes. After a moment, he looked up at Warren with an expression of shock on his face. "It's you," he said quietly.

"It was an accident, Miller," Warren said quickly. "I didn't mean to kill her. I don't know what got into the girl. I gave her some money and she went berserk. She attacked me for no good reason. I just tried to shove her away from me and she . . . she fell down that ravine. I swear to you it was an accident!"

"Then why didn't you say something when it happened?" Miller asked.

"I was afraid no one would believe me," Warren said. "Anyway, what difference does it make?" he shrugged. "I mean she was Chinese; it's not like an American girl got killed or anything."

"She was a human being." Miller said. "Same as us."

"Miller, why don't you pretend you never received that wire?" Warren said. "I'd make it worth your while. How much money would you like? Ten thousand? Twenty thousand? After all, you're my father-in-law now, it would be keeping it in the family."

"What in the hell did my daughter ever see in you?" Miller asked, his mouth twisted in a contemptuous snarl. He reached for his crutches. "I'll let Ted decide."

As Miller stood and turned his back to leave, Warren saw a ball peen hammer that had been left on Miller's desk by one of the construction crew. Warren picked the hammer up, then coldly and calculatingly brought it smashing down on Miller's head. He caught Miller as he collapsed, then dragged him out onto the car platform. He looked around quickly, and upon seeing no one, flipped Miller's body over the edge of the platform. Miller's head struck the track, and his crutches fell beside him. Warren smiled. It would look as if the old man had simply lost his balance and pitched off the platform onto the track.

Warren returned to the desk and tore the page off the message pad, slipped it into his pocket, then left the engineering car before anyone else saw him.

Chapter Thirty-One

"I'm sorry, Mrs. Leland," Fred Rule said, as he sorted bills of lading. "But it is against line regulations to attack any private car to a Western Pacific passenger train without specific authorization from our home office in Kansas City."

"Then get permission from the home office," Reesa said.

"I told you, I will send a letter."

"Can't you send a wire?"

"No," Rule said. "The regulations say that permission must be obtained in writing from the home office and authorized by the senior superintendent's signature. A wire is not the same thing."

"I want to leave here now," Reesa insisted.

"I'm sorry. There's nothing I can do."

"Yes, there is," Reesa said. "I'll ship this car to San Francisco as freight. You can clear that here."

"You would have to be attached to a freight train," Rule said.

"I don't care," Reesa said. "Our car has everything that we will need. Besides, it will only be to Denver. Once we reach Denver, we'll change trains and, fortunately, lines as well."

Rule sighed and ran his hand over the top of his head. "Very well, Mrs. Leland," he said. "I'll attach your car to the nine-forty-two freight. Please be ready."

"We will be ready," Reesa said. She returned to the car to tell Daisy the news and to help prepare the car for shipment.

They ate a light supper, then spent the evening talking until about nine-thirty, when Reesa heard the whistle of the approaching freight. "This is it," she told Daisy. "I'd better go see the trainmaster and make sure he notices that we are being shipped."

Reesa stood on the platform as the train approached. The arrival of a freight train didn't create nearly the excitement of a passenger train, so Reesa was practically alone as the giant 2-6-2 engine pounded by, throwing sparks and spraying steam. Car after car of the dark boxcars and flatcars slipped by, until the train finally stopped. Reesa walked back to the only car showing light, the small caboose, and waited for the trainmaster to disembark.

"Well, hello, Reesa," Quince, the trainmaster said with a warm smile. It's been a while since I saw you, lass. How is everything? How is your father?"

"Papa is just fine, Mr. Quince," Reesa said. She handed the trainmaster a shipping order.

"What's this? Don't tell me you're working for the WP again?"

"No," Reesa said. "This is a shipping order to attach my car to this train to pull it to Denver."

"Lass, you want to put a private car on a freight train?"

"Yes," Reesa said. "I've already paid the shipping fee."

"But why, for Christ's sake? There are two more passenger trains leaving here today."

"Mr. Rule said that I can't attach to a passenger train without specific written approval from the home office."

"Hogwash," Quince said. "Station masters do it all up and down the line. The home office never says a thing about it. They welcome the revenue."

"Well, you know what a stickler Mr. Rule is for regulations," Reesa said.

"Come along, lass, we'll talk to him," Quince invited.

Rule was scribbling in a large ledger book when Reesa and Quince went into the depot.

"Rule, what is this business about attaching Reesa's private car to my train?" Quince asked.

"She paid the fare," Rule answered without looking up. "She's entitled to have her car moved."

"Yes, but by a freight? My God, man, there are two passenger trains leaving out of here tonight. Attach her car to one of them."

"That's against regulations," Rule insisted.

"To hell with that," Quince exploded. "That regulation is consistently disregarded by every station master on the line."

"Not by this station master," Rule insisted.

"I'm not sure but what that's been overridden by now anyway," Quince said.

"Until I get a regulation superseding it, I intend to follow it as it is written," Rule replied.

"Rule, do you know what we've got here?" Quince asked. "We've got a forty-car freight, with no provisions to connect to a passenger car. The coupling isn't designed for that. It would be dangerous to attach this girl's car to the end of that train."

"She doesn't have to go," Rule said.

"Reesa, I'd advise you to wait," Quince said.

"No," Reesa replied resolutely. "I intend to get out of here tonight. I don't care if you have to jury-rig the coupling. I just want to leave. Please, hook up our car."

Quince sighed. "Very well, Reesa. I'll pick up your car."

"Thank you," Reesa replied.

"Here you are, boss," Murdock shouted as the engine and special car pulled into camp. He hopped off the car and ran over to Ted. "She rode as safe as a babe in its mother's arms. It's a good thing, too, not only for my sake, but because I'm told there's not another ounce of the stuff this side of Cincinnati."

"I'm glad you made it back all right," Ted said quietly.

"Well, you don't look glad," Murdock said. "What the hell's wrong?"

"In there," Ted said, pointing to the private car which had been his, but which he had given to Miller to use. "Miller's in there."

"In there? Why didn't he come out to meet me?"

"He's dead," Ted said.

Murdock's face registered his shock. "What happened? Did he get sick or what?"

"He fell off the back of the engineering car," Ted said. "His head hit the track."

"Was he out on the platform when the car was being moved?" Murdock asked.

"No, the car hasn't been moved. He just fell off."

"You mean to tell me he just walked out there and fell off?" Murdock said. "I don't believe it. You know how well he handled himself."

"I know," Ted agreed. "It does seem hard to believe. But the evidence speaks for itself."

"Well, I'll be damned," Murdock said. "I really liked the guy. What about Reesa? Shouldn't she be told?"

"Yes," Ted said. "Of course, Warren should tell her, but I don't know where he is. I'll go in first thing in the morning to tell her. There's no sense in upsetting her tonight."

"You're probably right. You want me to go in with you in the mornin'?"

"No. You stay here and supervise the blasting," Ted said.

"Speaking of blasting, where's Ling Cho? I thought sure he'd want to be here to see his new firecrackers."

Ling Cho was at that moment confronting Warren Leland. He had told Warren that he had something of urgent importance to discuss

with him and asked that Warren come to the
tent the Chinese cooks used. They were alone in
the tent, and Ling Cho studied Warren's fea-
tures for a long, silent while before he spoke.

"You killed Miller Flowers," Ling Cho finally said. It wasn't an accusation, it was a
simple statement of fact.

"What? Don't be ridiculous," Warren sputtered. "Why would I kill him? He was my
father-in-law."

"You killed him because he discovered that
you murdered Golden Tears."

"Old man, you've gone crazy," Warren said.

Ling Cho put his hand in his pocket and
withdrew two coins. He showed them to Warren. "I found this money by the girl's body," he
said quietly. His words slid out smoothly as if
lubricated by the finest oils. There was something strange about them, and for a moment
Warren was puzzled. Then he realized what it
was. The man who normally spoke only in
pidgin English was speaking as clearly as an
Oxford scholar.

"You've lost your accent," Warren said.

"I want to be most certain that you understand my every word," Ling Cho said.

"All right, so you found that money by the
girl's body. What does that mean?"

"I know the girl was attracted to you," Ling
Cho said. "And you were quite obviously attracted to her. Her interest was emotional,
yours was carnal. When you finished with her,
you offered to pay her money. She was offended and attacked you, so you fought her off.
In so doing, you broke her neck."

"I don't know what you are talking about," Warren said.

"This is all conjecture, to be sure," Ling Cho went on. "But I found the handkerchief you used to clean yourself with. It had a laundry mark. I believe it was your laundry mark, Mr. Leland. I believe Mr. Flowers received verification of that from San Francisco, and you, somehow, discovered it. So you killed him. But I still have the handkerchief, Mr. Leland, and as soon as another telegrapher is available, I shall ask that the message be conveyed to me."

Warren's hand flashed to his shoulder holster, but even as the gun was coming clear of leather, Ling Cho's hand was there. A very quick thrust of Ling Cho's hand sent Warren's pistol into the air. Ling Cho brought the back of his hand across Warren's face, then so fast as to be almost one blow he slapped Warren's face with the palm of his hand.

"No!" Warren shouted, suddenly terrified by the strange behavior of a man he had so long regarded as practically subhuman.

"Do not worry, Mr. Leland," Ling Cho said. "I do not intend to kill you. That would be too quick, and too painless. I am going to watch you suffer the turning wheels of justice. Before, when there was only the Chinese girl involved, I could not be certain that justice would be done. Now, with the death of an Occidental, I think there is every possibility we will be privileged to watch you hang by the neck until you are dead."

Ling Cho opened the cylinder gate on Warren's pistol and ejected the shells. They fell to the ground, one at a time, until all six lay there.

"Good day, Mr. Leland." Ling Cho returned the pistol to Warren, who slid it back into his holster. He turned and quickly left the tent.

"Ah, there you are, little buddy," Murdock said, stepping into the tent a moment later.

"Murdock, most gratified to see nitro not explode you," Ling Cho said. The words and rhythm of his speech pattern returned to the Ling Cho everyone knew.

"You ain't no more gratified than I am, little buddy. Anyhow, I got the stuff here, 'n' it's ready for you as soon as you are."

"Now I am ready," Ling Cho said. "I have hole prepared for first charge. I will take the nitro I need into position."

"Don't waste any of this stuff, buddy," Murdock said. "This is all there is."

"I should be able to do it in three explosions," Ling Cho said.

"Well, let's get on it," Murdock said, leading Ling Cho to the nitro.

"It's getting a little late in the day," Ted told Ling Cho, as Ling Cho climbed onto the car and looked at the vat of nitro. "Are you sure you don't want to wait until morning?"

"Time is running short, Boss Foster," Ling Cho said. "Maybe do one blast tonight and we catch up."

"All right, Ling Cho. Whatever you say," Ted agreed.

Ling Cho took a detonating container from the package of containers that were designed for that purpose, and prepared to transfer enough for the first charge. He ran a small blue flag up on a pole, then looked back at Ted. "Boss Foster, more better everyone get back from this car until I have nitro I need. When I have the nitro, I will take blue flag down."

"All right, you heard the man," Ted said. "Everybody get back, all the way around the bend in the tracks!"

Everyone in the crew followed Ted's instructions. The engine backed away along with the workers. Word was sent through the rubble-closed pass to the other side, to inform those who were still on the far side of the pass not to come around until they got further word. That included Sally's girls.

"You ever handled nitro, boss?" Murdock asked, as he and Ted watched from a rock ledge. They were so far away that Ling Cho was no more than a small figure in the distance.

"I've assisted," Ted said. "How about you?"

"Are you kiddin'? Could you see me wrappin' these big mitts around a container of nitro? I'd set it off just by holdin' it."

"I've never seen anyone who could work with dynamite better than Ling Cho," Ted said. "If he is that good with nitro, we'll have no worries."

"If he ain't that good, he'll have plenty of worries," Murdock said.

"What's takin' him so long?" someone asked.

"You don't hurry that stuff up," Murdock said. "Hey, boss I nearly forgot. We left Miller back there in his car."

"It shouldn't matter to him," Ted said.

"I don't know," Ted said. "I'm going to hate having to tell Reesa about it, I know that."

"Hey, he's put the flag down," someone said. "Can we go back?"

"Let's go," Ted said.

The crowd of workers moved slowly back down the track, but even before they reached the camp, Ling Cho was already out the other side, climbing up the mountain side to lay in the first charge.

Warren had climbed the mountain when everyone else left the camp. It was easy to slip away in all the confusion, and now he was several hundred feet above the pass and above the point Ling Cho had marked for his first charge.

Nothing had worked out as it should for Warren. He had not wanted to be associated with this foolish railroad venture in the first place, but he took it, because in so doing it allowed him to put a great deal of distance between him and his father.

At the thought of his father, Warren's stomach reacted. He hated his father . . . oh, how he loathed him. He was always holding others up to Warren, extolling the virtues of hard work, honest enterprise, and ambition. Ambition and hard work had killed Warren's mother. Afterwards, there was only his father to goad and taunt, cajole, push and hound him, to mold him after his own image.

But Warren rebelled. He purposely stood for everything his father was against, and hated everything his father stood for. It had been a victory of sorts to marry the girl his father had chosen for him, and then sit back and deny his father the grandchild he so desperately wanted.

Then when things seemed to be going their best, a simple little sexual act with a simple Chinese girl had backfired. It was baffling to Warren. How had it gotten this far? He had been sampling the favors of Chinese girls since the onset of puberty, and it had all been made possible by a few coins. Why was this one different? Did Ling Cho mean to imply that this foolish little girl actually thought that he, Warren, could *love* her? Was the girl that stupid? If so, it was probably a very lucky break for him that the girl had been killed.

But it wasn't lucky that he was caught. He should have paid more attention to what he was doing. Dropping the handkerchief there had been a very careless blunder. But the blunder could be corrected. Miller was dead, and now only Ling Cho remained. And soon, he too would be dead.

Warren checked the boulder beside him and dug the crowbar in beneath it. He had taken the bar from the tool car, intending to use it as a weapon against the Chinaman. But then he got a better idea. If he could dislodge a few boulders and start them toward him, Ling Cho would be trapped. The boulders wouldn't even have to kill him, just make him move out of the way. As volatile as the nitro was, that would be enough. A rapid move would cause the nitro to detonate.

Warren raised up and saw Ling Cho approaching the blasting site. He waited one more minute until Ling Cho was in place, then moved around behind the rock. He began pushing on the bar, straining against it. Finally it began to move, a little at a time, and then all of it. With it went a couple dozen other rocks, not quite as large, but big enough to start an impressive slide.

The slide was large enough to be noticed from ground level. Ted saw it first.

"Oh my God, Murdock, look!" Ted said, pointing to the rocks, which cascaded toward Ling Cho.

"Ling Cho!" Murdock yelled. "Look out!"

There was just time for the echo of Murdock's voice to return to them, haunting in its tone of horror, and then a stomach-jarring explosion erupted on the side of the mountain. Tons of rock and dirt slid down the mountainside, and when the smoke and dust cleared away, Ling Cho was no more.

Chapter Thirty-Two

For the first leg of the trip toward Denver, Quince rode in the private car with Reesa and Daisy. Quince was fifty-one years old, and Reesa had known him since she was a very young girl. She knew him to be an honest and open man, and she had always liked him. They talked about amusing incidents from the past, but Reesa noticed that Quince managed to slip in the fact, more than once, that his wife had died. He said this, ostensibly to Reesa, but in such a way as to ensure that Daisy heard it as well, because despite the difference in their ages, it was obvious that Quince was quite taken with her.

"You must have an awfully responsible job, Mr. Quince," Daisy said. "Rather like being captain of a ship, I would imagine."

"Please, call me Jonas," Quince said. He beamed under the girl's interest and smiled as broadly as a schoolboy who had been noticed by the prettiest girl in class. "Yes, it is rather important—Martha, that's my late wife, Martha, she's dead now, you know . . . I'm a widower. . . ."

Reesa hid a smile from the two of them. This was at least the fourth time he'd mentioned it.

"Martha used to say that having a job this responsible kept me young. And you know, I believe it does. It keeps you alert physically and mentally all the time."

The train slowed to a stop.

"Oh, dear, not again," Reesa said. "Why do you suppose we have stopped?"

Jonas Quince pulled his silver-cased Elgin Engineer's Special watch from his pocket and flipped it open. "We're waiting for the southbound Midnight Flyer," he said. "Passenger trains have the right-of-way on the line. We have to pull over for all of them."

"Well, then shall I serve some tea?" Daisy asked.

"That would be nice," Reesa agreed.

"Thank you, ma'am, I take that most kindly of you," Quince said.

They just had time to finish their tea before they heard the Midnight Flyer approaching on the adjacent track.

"Right on time," Quince said, looking again at his watch.

The engineer of the Midnight Flyer blew his whistle in greeting and the great train rushed by at sixty miles per hour, smoke and steam trailing back in long wisps, great driver wheels pounding at the rails, and sparks flying from the firebox. The blast of air and noise from its passing shook the car like a cork bobbing on water. The lighted windows of the cars streamed by so fast as to be almost one long blur of light. Within a moment, the last car flashed by, and Reesa saw the red and green lamps at the train's end, already receding in the distance.

"Oh, my, how magnificent!" Daisy said. "I do believe that was the most marvelous thing I have ever witnessed!"

"I'll go see the engineer and see if we can't speed up a bit ourselves," Quince said.

"You can't walk up to the engine," Daisy protested. "Suppose he started up while you were still on the ground? You'd be left."

"Oh, I won't be goin' along the ground, ma'am," Quince said. "I'll be going topside." He pointed to the top of the car.

"Topside?"

"He's going to go along the tops of the cars," Reesa explained.

"Oh, my, isn't that a bit dangerous?"

"Certainly," Quince said. "For someone who doesn't know what he's doin'. But not to worry, miss, I been runnin' the cars since before you was born."

Quince stepped outside, and just as the train got underway again, he climbed to the top of the car and started forward.

"Isn't he a wonderful man?" Daisy asked.

"He's very nice," Reesa agreed. "Even if he is pretty old."

"I don't care how old he is," Daisy said. "In England I saw many proper gentlemen married to ladies who weren't a third their age. It's different for women."

"Oh, I wasn't finding fault," Reesa said

quickly. "Besides, it's obvious that he likes you."

"Oh, do you think he does?" Daisy asked. "Oh, Reesa, wouldn't that be just too wonderful?"

Quince reached the engine cab and dropped down to talk with the engineer. The fireman had just restoked the furnace and was looking at the steam pressure. They both turned around when Quince dropped in on them.

"Didn't think you'd come up to visit us with the pretty ladies back there," the engineer teased.

"I've got a job to do just like you," Quince said.

"Hey, what was that?" the fireman suddenly yelled. He pointed ahead of the onrushing engine, and they saw a few random rocks sliding down a rock wall and rolling across the tracks.

"Did they clear the tracks?" the engineer asked anxiously.

"Yeah, I think so."

The engine flashed by the spot where the rocks had fallen, and the three men in the cab breathed more easily.

"Must have been a deer or something kicked a few rocks loose," Quince suggested.

"Yeah, it happens all the time," the engineer replied.

But it wasn't a deer. Two hundred feet above the narrow cut through which the tracks ran, a small normally dry creek bed was straining to hold a raging torrent of water, the result of extraordinarily strong mountain rains. The normally dry creek bed now held ten feet of swiftly moving water, and trees and other debris rushed pell-mell downstream.

The creek bed wasn't large enough to hold the torrent, so in accordance with the forces of nature, the water was enlarging the creek bed, cutting its own channel. Dirt and rock had to be removed to widen the channel, and it was from this action that the few rocks had fallen across the track. In addition to those few rocks, however, a tremendous cut was being hydraulically excavated where the creek made a long sweeping bend. The bend was right above a gigantic overhang, which guarded the entry of the tracks into a long tunnel, known as the Munson Tunnel after its builder. Already rocks were beginning to drop onto the track, though so far the fall was inconsequential.

"I came up here to see if you could get any more out of this hog," Quince said, using the railroader's term for a locomotive.

"Hey, what do you think you're in, a highliner? We ain't pullin' passengers, Quince, we're pullin' freight. We ain't nothin' but a rattler."

"Yeah, but we're ridin' the high iron," Quince said. "And the regs say that any train on the main line may make as much speed as is safe to maintain."

"We'll give 'er what we got, Quince," the engineer said. "You gonna boiler head?"

"No, I'm goin' back to the shack," he said.

"Shack, my ass. You ain't goin' to the caboose," the engineer teased. "You're goin' back to the drone cage where them pretty ladies are."

"I might look in on 'em," Quince admitted.

"Well, you'd better stay up here until we clear Munson Tunnel. Get caught on top of the cars while we're in there, and you'll get swept off."

"Much further?"

"'Bout a quarter of a mile," the engineer said. "The light'll pick it up directly."

The train pounded on down the track, the poles lighting up, then whipping by. Finally the dark maw of the tunnel loomed ahead of them. Quince happened to look up just as they went inside and saw something that made his blood run cold.

"My God!" he shouted. "There's a landslide. Half the damn mountain is coming down!"

The engineer reached for the brakes, and the locomotive wheels locked in place. The walls of the tunnel were painted orange from the glow of sparks, which flew from the sliding wheels.

"No, that's no good, you've got to get us out of here! Open her up full!" Quince yelled.

The engineer released the brakes and slammed the throttle to full open. As the train had still been sliding forward, the application of the throttle allowed it to regain its momentum easily, and it shot ahead again.

Forty cars back the drone cage, or private car, in which Reesa and Daisy were riding, was caught up first in the train's attempt to stop, and then in the continued motion to go forward. That had the effect of "popping the whip," and the car, which had a coupling system designed for passenger use and thus was jury-rigged to the freight, separated from the rest of the train. It continued to roll forward on its own momentum, and for several seconds there was no indication of what had happened. But then it became obvious as the car began to slow. Daisy was looking forward, and she saw it first.

"Reesa, the train has broken away from us!" she shouted.

"What?" Reesa ran to the front of the car, and saw the train pulling away. She also saw the black opening of the tunnel, and knew that they would probably come to a stop somewhere inside. That could be extremely dangerous. If the engineer didn't realize he had lost the car and they were left sitting on the track in the tunnel, the next train through could crash into them.

Reesa was about to voice her fear, when she noticed an even more immediate danger. For this, she didn't have time to shout a warning, just emit a scream. The rock slide hit at about the same time they entered the tunnel, and the car came to a smashing halt.

The sound was unlike anything Reesa had ever heard in her life. It was a terrible, wrenching, smashing sound, which seemed to go on forever. The windows of the car were broken, the top came crashing down, and the furniture was smashed. She and Daisy were knocked to the floor by the shock of the blast, then another crash shook the car, and for Reesa, everything went black.

The rest of the train emerged from the other side, and Quince let out a whoop of relief. "We made it through! Come on, pour on the coal, we've got to get to the next stop so we can send a warning about the tunnel being closed. There won't be any more trains tonight, that's for sure."

"We'll be in Colby's Switch in fifteen minutes," the engineer said. "He has a telegraph there."

"I'd better go back and see if our two passengers are all right," Quince said.

Quince climbed to the top of the first car, then began running toward the rear of the train. It was dark, and the train was making maximum speed, but Quince was at home here as the ordinary person is strolling down the street. He was agile and sure-footed, and he jumped from car to car with ease, until he stood on the last car and gazed down with shock at the sight that greeted him. Reesa's private car wasn't there!

Joaquin was in the Albuquerque station when word came in. The Munson Tunnel was closed by a landslide, and Reesa Leland's private car was trapped inside.

"Is she still alive?" Joaquin asked, when he heard the news.

"They don't know," Rule answered. "There are tons of rock covering them. If they are alive now, chances are they won't be long. They'll smother."

"You've got to send a message for me," Joaquin said.

"No private messages during a company emergency," Rule said.

"But it's to the girl's husband and father at

End-of-Track," Joaquin said. "They must be notified of this!"

"I'm sorry," Rule said. He opened a book of regulations. "It clearly states here that during the time of a company emergency, the wires must be kept clear for emergency messages."

"Damnit, man, this is an emergency message!" Joaquin insisted.

"It is not a company message," Rule said.

Joaquin thought of pulling his pistol and using it to force the man to send a message, but he realized that he couldn't read telegraphy, and there would be no way to verify it. There was only one thing left, and that was to ride out to the pass. Joaquin winced as he thought of it. That was over forty miles, and the only way there was by horse, since there were no engines available.

Joaquin sprang to the saddle and urged Diablo into a gallop. As he rode out of town, bent low over Diablo's neck and raising clouds of dust behind him, he formulated a plan. There were at least two ranches between Albuquerque and the pass where he knew he would be able to change mounts. If he rode Diablo and the other two horses at full speed, he could reach the camp in about two hours. That would put him there by three in the morning. That could present a problem if they had a nervous sentry posted.

Joaquin rode into the first ranch at a full gallop. He rode straight to the corral, yelling as he rode in. By the time he had the saddle off Diablo and had selected another mount, a lantern appeared in the window of the bunkhouse.

342

"Who is there?" someone shouted in Spanish.

"It is I, Joaquin Mendoza. I must cover a great distance quickly. I am leaving my horse here, I must borrow one of yours."

Joaquin had finished saddling the new mount by the time the explanation was completed, and he swung onto the fresh horse. *"Adios!"* he yelled as he galloped away.

"Adios, Joaquin. Go with God!" came the return greeting.

The second transfer went just as smoothly, and almost before Joaquin realized it, he was approaching the camp. He began yelling, calling Ted's name, so that the sentry would not be surprised and shoot out of fear.

"Ted, Ted!" he shouted as the horse pounded into the camp at a full gallop.

The gandy dancers, who were sleeping nearby and who were awakened by the shouts, yelled curses at the man who had disturbed their slumber. The Chinese were also awakened, and Joaquin could hear their voices babbling in excitement and curiosity. Ted appeared at the back door of his caboose.

"Joaquin, what is it?" Ted asked.

Joaquin dismounted and walked over to the car. He was breathing heavily, and his mount was covered with the white foam of a hard sweat.

"Look at your animal!" Ted said. "You must have ridden as if all the demons of hell were after you!"

"I have ridden from Albuquerque in two hours," Joaquin said.

343

"Two hours? That's impossible," someone said.

Joaquin held up his hand. "Please, I've no time to talk of this. I have come about Reesa."

"Reesa? What about her?" Ted asked.

"There has been an accident. I did not get to see her to deliver the message you wanted because she had already left for San Francisco. But there was a wreck."

"A train wreck? My God, is she hurt? Where is she?"

"I don't know if she is hurt," Joaquin said. "She is trapped in a place called the Munson Tunnel. There was a rockslide. They say tons of rocks cover her car. If they don't get her out soon, she will suffocate."

"Boss, how they gonna move that rock?" Murdock asked. He had been awakened by the noise and joined them in time to hear Joaquin's message.

"They'll have to blast it out," Ted said.

"That's just what I mean," Murdock said. "There ain't nothin' left to blast with, remember? We got it all, and we ain't got much of it left."

"He's right," Ted said. "Joaquin, there isn't any dynamite available. We'll have to use our nitro."

"Boss, are you crazy? Who are you gonna get that will work with nitro? You saw what happened to Ling Cho last night. I don't believe I can get any of the Chinamen to work with it now, and I know none of the Irishmen will."

"I'll do it," Ted insisted.

"You've never done it before." Murdock said.

344

"I've assisted," Ted replied. "I know what to do."

"Even if you could do it, you've got to get the stuff there."

"Fire up the engine," Ted ordered. "I'll pull that special car you designed."

"Boss, that car was good for bringing it out here, but I only had to bring it from the Hecke-meyer Mines. That's about twenty miles, and it took me two hours to get it here. You've got more'n one hundred and twenty miles to go. At ten miles an hour, it would be too late by the time you got there."

"I'll pull just the one car," Ted said. "I'll run at full speed. I'll be there in less than two hours."

"You pull that stuff at full speed, and you'll be dead in less than two hours," Murdock said.

"I have no choice," Ted said. "I don't expect anyone to go with me. I'll run the engine my-self."

"You'll need someone to fire it," Murdock said.

"I will fire it," Joaquin offered.

"No offense meant, mister," Murdock said. "But to shovel coal for this kind of a run, it's going to take someone with more muscle than brain. That'll be me, I reckon."

"I am going with you, *Señor*," Joaquin said.

"Thre's no need for you to take that risk," Ted said.

"I am going," Joaquin said again, more reso-lutely than before.

"Very well," Ted said. "I'll be dressed in a moment."

"Perhaps I should tell her father," Joaquin suggested.

"He's dead," Ted said. "I'll tell you about it on the trip."

"I can think of no one else who needs be told, can you, *Señor*?" Joaquin asked pointedly.

"No," Ted said. "I can think of no one else."

Chapter Thirty-Three

When Reesa came to, she heard sobbing.

"Daisy?"

"Reesa, oh, Reesa," Daisy said. "Thank God you aren't dead. When I couldn't get you to answer me, I thought you'd been killed."

It was so dark inside the twisted wreckage of the car that Reesa couldn't see her hand in front of her face. "Where are you?" Reesa asked.

"I'm over here, mum," Daisy answered. "Close to where the settee was, I believe."

"Are you all right?"

"I don't know," Daisy said. "There is something lying across my legs, and I can't move."

"I'll try and get to you," Reesa said. She began inching forward slowly, picking through the rubble and the wreckage, feeling her way with outstretched hands. "Keep talking so I can find you," she said.

"What'll I say?"

"Anything."

"My name is Daisy Waite, and I was born in Tilbury on the Thames. I came to. . . ."

"I'm here," Reesa said, reaching the girl at that moment. She put her hand out and touched Daisy's face. Daisy grabbed her fingers and squeezed tightly.

"Are you in pain?"

"No, mum, not really," Daisy said. "The fact is, I can't feel anything in my legs."

"Well, hang on, Daisy. We'll get out of here."

""How, Reesa?" Daisy asked. Her voice cracked. "I wasn't knocked out the way you were. It sounded like the whole mountain fell in on us."

"Ted will get us out," Reesa said.

"Ted?"

"Yes," Reesa's voice was firm. "He'll come, and he'll get us out of here."

"Oh, Lordy, mum, I wish I had something like that to cling to. But I fear we're going to die in this awful place."

"No," Reesa said calmly. "We won't."

Reesa couldn't explain the calmness she felt. She knew that the odds were very much against their escaping. But somehow, she felt they would. And, just as strongly, she felt that Ted was going to play a part in it.

The throttle was wide open, and the engine was speeding at more than seventy miles per hour.

"This is faster than I've ever been in my life!" Joaquin shouted.

"This is faster than ninety-nine percent of the human race has ever been," Ted replied. "How does our load look? The box hasn't slipped in the ropes, has it?"

Joaquin hopped back to the tender, then climbed up onto the pile of coal so he could see the one trailing car. He returned to the engine and yelled at Ted and Murdock.

"It is still as it was."

"We're going to have to stop in Albuquerque to make certain the tracks are cleared ahead," Murdock said.

"You know Rule," Ted replied. "That son-of-a-bitch probably wouldn't give us clearance anyway. Just go on through."

"But if there's someone ahead of us, we're dead ducks," Murdock said. "And if it's a passenger train, there'll be a lot of innocent people go with us."

"Slow the train down when we reach Albuquerque," Joaquin said. "I will jump off and have a talk with Mr. Rule. He will clear the tracks ahead."

"You think you can talk him into it?" Murdock asked.

Joaquin smiled and patted his pistol. "I think so," he replied.

The train began slowing gradually as they approached Albuquerque, in order to avoid the shock of stopping too quickly. Such a stop could set off the nitro and destroy not only the train, but a goodly portion of Albuquerque as well. By the time they rolled into the yard, they were traveling no faster than a man could walk.

"Son-of-a-bitch," Murdock swore. "The damned switch is closed!"

"I'll open it," Ted said. He pulled the brake

lever and the train stopped. Ted jumped down and ran to the switch, only to find it locked. "Joaquin!" he called.

"Yes," Joaquin answered. He jumped down and ran to Ted.

"Can you use that gun or is it for decoration?"

Joaquin saw the lock, and without a word pulled his pistol and fired a shot. The padlock flew apart, and Ted opened the switch.

"Get that track open ahead," Ted said, starting back toward the train.

Murdock opened the throttle as soon as he saw Ted returning to the engine, so Ted caught it as it was already rolling.

"What is this? What's going on here?" Rule yelled, running out to the track.

"Good morning, *Señor*," Joaquin said. "Perhaps you would be so kind as to return to your telegraph instrument and signal for the track to be cleared between here and the tunnel?"

"I will do no such thing," Rule insisted. "That is an unauthorized locomotive!"

"It is also carrying a great deal of nitroglycerine," Joaquin said. "So I'd advise you to clear the tracks."

"I will not."

Joaquin pulled his pistol and shot the hat from Rule's head.

"All right," Rule shouted in panic. "I'll clear the track. But if any trouble comes down from the home office, I intend to let them know that I was forced into it."

"You do that, *Señor*," Joaquin said, smiling at him.

Ted blew the whistle in a series of short blasts, denoting an emergency, and the abbreviated train was almost up to full speed again by the time it cleared the Albuquerque yard.

The sun was barely full disc up, a bright orange ball still touching the horizon and painting the mountains with various hues of red and gold as they approached the Munson Tunnel. Ted slowed the train down as they came around the final bend.

Suddenly there were three sharp explosions, and a flash of light bathed the engine cab!

"What the—?" Murdock yelled.

"We ran over their warning torpedoes," Ted said. "It's just a signal that the track is closed."

Murdock let out an audible sigh and then smiled. "Boss, I swear I thought the angel Gabriel had come for me."

Ted pulled the brake, and the train came to a full stop about fifteen yards short of where the tunnel entrance used to be. There was nothing there now but a large pile of rubble. Several people, men and women, were crowded around the collapsed entrance, and Ted recognized Jonas Quince. He called to Quince as he hopped down from the engine.

"Mr. Foster, I didn't expect to see you here," Quince said, coming over to him.

"What's the situation?" Ted asked.

"It looks bad," Quince answered. "There are two women trapped inside."

"Just two? How did everyone get out?"

"There wasn't anyone else," Quince said. "Reesa Flowers had a private car, and it was connected to the end of a freight. Her car separated just before we entered the tunnel. It rolled in, then was hit by the landslide."

"Separated? You mean the engineer snapped it off, don't you?" Ted asked angrily.

"It was an accident, Mr. Foster," Quince said. "Believe me, the engineer feels as badly about it as you do."

"I doubt that," Ted replied. He walked up to the entrance, then climbed a pile of rock and looked around. "It's closed solid here, how about the approach from the other end?"

"Completely collapsed," Quince replied. "We'll have to go in from this end."

"Have you heard anything from them? Any contact?"

"No."

"Have you tried?"

"Yes, we've tried."

"Them girls is dead if you want my opinion," a bystander said.

"I don't want your damned opinion," Ted said angrily. He looked at the man. "Are you associated with the railroad in any way?"

"No."

"Then get the hell out of my way," Ted ordered. Ted climbed back down the pile of rubble and looked at the morbid crowd. It surprised him to see so many this early in the morning.

The relief valve on the engine he had brought in popped open and a loud stream of steam shot out. Several of the people who had been standing close to the engine jumped back nervously.

"Are you goin' to try and get 'em outta there, mister?" one woman asked. Ted looked at the woman who spoke. Of an indeterminate age,

352

she could have been anywhere between twenty-five and fifty. She wore a gray dress, which hung shapelessly from her thin frame. Her hair had the color and texture of sunburned grass. Her skin was weathered and wrinkled, and she held a baby clutched against her flat bosom.

Ted felt some of his anger slide away as he looked at the woman. She advertised the difficult life of the frontier by her very appearance. Naturally she was drawn to the scene of the accident. Anything, even something as potentially gruesome as a railway accident, was a welcome respite from the tedious day-to-day struggle of just staying alive.

"Well, are you, mister?" the woman asked again. "Try 'n' get 'em outta there, I mean."

"Yes, ma'am, I'm going to try damned hard," Ted said. "Quince, who is in charge around here?"

"As far as I know, I am," Quince said. "None of the line supervisors have showed up yet."

"Then let's get to work," Ted said.

"Mr. Foster, we've already dug around there. There's nothing we can do until we get some dynamite in. We'll have to blast that stuff out of there."

"You won't find any dynamite this side of the Mississippi River," Ted said. "We'll have to do it ourselves."

"With what?" Quince asked.

"Nitro."

"Where are you going to find nitro? And how would you get it out here in time?"

"I've already got it," Ted said. He pointed to

the flatcar behind the puffing engine. "There it is."

"Good Lord! You mean you were carrying nitro when you came roaring up here?"

"That's right," Ted said. He rubbed his hands together. "I don't suppose you've ever worked with it before."

"Not me, no sir!" Quince said.

"All right, I'll do it," Ted said. He waved back to the engine at Murdock. "Murdock, help me find the best place to set it."

"You sure you can do this?" Quince asked.

"The way I see it, we don't have much choice in the matter," Ted replied.

"I don't know . . . what if something goes wrong?"

"Quince, damnit, if we don't do something, those girls are going to die for lack of air."

"Yes, but we don't even know if they are still alive."

"If they are dead, then it won't make any difference if something goes wrong," Ted said angrily. "Now are you going to help or not?"

"I'll help," Quince said. "What do you want me to do?"

"Keep everyone away from that car," he said. "And when I start laying in the charge, get everyone back out of the way."

"Boss, I think we can move this stuff outta here," Murdock said. He had been examining the rubble. "This ain't no different from what we do every day. Just a matter of movin' a little bit of dirt."

"Where do you think?" Ted asked.

Murdock pointed to two locations. "If we can

touch 'em off here and here," he said, "it should pitch this whole damned pile right off and into the canyon below."

"All right, help me get the holes ready. I'll plant the stuff by myself."

"Let's get started," Murdock said.

The two men worked quickly, digging the holes for the charges, placing them in such a way as to direct the force of the blast where it would do the most good. Finally, after nearly an hour's preparation, they were ready to place the charges.

"All right, Murdock, here goes," Ted said finally. "You back the engine up and keep everyone the hell out of here."

"I'll keep 'em back, don't worry."

Suddenly several dozen rocks came tumbling down from the mountain top above them. They were relatively small rocks, and they bounced harmlessly across the track and the canyon on the other side.

"What was that?" Ted asked.

"That's what caused this collapse in the first place," Quince said. "The creeks are flooding and causing rock slides."

"Damn, that's all we need." The image of Ling Cho being caught in a rockslide as he placed a charge last night came into Ted's mind.

"Maybe you ought to wait," Murdock suggested tentatively.

"Wait for what?"

"Wait for some more of the railroad people to get here. Maybe one of them can handle nitro."

"I'll do it," Ted said.

"Then at least wait and see if there is going to be another rockslide," Murdock warned.

"I don't figure we have time to wait. I've got to get those charges planted now."

"All right, boss," Murdock said, shrugging his shoulders. "It's your funeral."

"Couldn't you have chosen a better expression?" Ted asked with a short, nervous laugh.

Murdock and Quince moved the engine and the curious back down the track, and Ted loaded two detonating containers with the remainder of the nitro. Once they were both loaded, he started climbing back up the hill to place them in the holes he and Murdock had prepared. The footing was difficult, and once he slipped and fell to one knee. He was unable to break his fall with his hands because he was carrying a container of nitro in each hand. Therefore his kness struck a rock sharply, and he felt an excruciating pain shooting through him. When he stood up again, the knee was throbbing angrily, and a quick heat began to build just below the kneecap. It was painful, but he could tell from the movement of the cap that it wasn't broken.

Ted finally got the first charge in place, and the detonating fuse attached. He limped over to the second spot, when he saw a train approaching. The train stopped just behind the engine Murdock had backed out of the way, and a couple of men hopped out and started running down the track toward Ted.

"Get back!" Ted shouted. "Get back, I'm working with nitro!"

"Foster, get down from there," one of the men ordered.

"Who are you?" Ted asked.

"I am Chief Railroad Detective Clyde Matthews. You are not authorized here, and I am ordering you down right now."

"You go to hell," Ted called back. "I'm going to blow this rockslide out of here. There are two women trapped inside, or haven't you been told?"

"I know there are two women in there," Matthews said.

"I intend to get them out."

"We'll get them out."

"How, by digging with your hands?"

"We have two cars of men with us," Matthews answered. "We'll dig them out."

"You don't have time," Ted said. "They may be dying in there. Now get back out of the way so I can plant this last charge."

Matthews pulled his pistol and pointed it up at Ted. "My. Foster, I am ordering you down from there at once."

Ted drew his arm back as if to throw the nitro. He pointed at Matthews and the man who had come with him. "Lay your gun down on the track and get the hell out of here, or I'll throw this at you right now." he said.

"What? Are you crazy?"

"Lay your gun down, Matthews" he said. "You, too," he pointed at the other man.

"I don't have a gun," the other man said.

"Well, you better find one quick, because unless I see one lying there beside his, I'm throwing this thing at you."

357

The other man reached behind his jacket and pulled out a pistol, then laid it on the ground beside Matthews's gun.

"I'm glad you remembered where you left it," Ted said. "Now, get out of here, both of you."

Both men turned and ran back down the track. Ted waited a few moments longer, then planted the second charge and attached the fuse to it as well. He strung the fuse back along the tracks until he was well clear of the area, and then he lit it.

"Lordy, Reesa, what was that?" Daisy asked, as the explosion shook the very ground.

"They're here," Reesa said excitedly. "They're blasting for us. Daisy, I told you Ted would come."

The rock started shifting and sliding, and the two girls could hear the car being ripped open. Dirt and small rocks started streaming in through the rent in the roof of the car.

"That's making it worse!" Daisy cried. "Oh, we're going to be killed!"

The car began tipping and tearing, and more and more dirt fell in. Daisy reached for Reesa and held her tightly. The car tipped completely over, and the two girls went sliding to the opposite side. Whatever had trapped Daisy's legs had now released them.

"Oh, Reesa, my leg, my leg hurts so," Daisy cried suddenly. "I think it's broken. Reesa, we're going to die here." She began to weep as she clung to Reesa.

Finally the sliding rock and dirt stopped.

"I think it's over," Reesa said, her eyes tightly shut.

Daisy was crying softly.

Reesa opened her eyes and saw Daisy. She put her hand down to touch the girl's face. "You'll be all right," she said, rubbing Daisy's cheek gently. "You've got an awfully dirty face though."

"Who wouldn't have a dirty face?" Daisy answered through lessening sobs.

"Dirty face!" Reesa suddenly shouted. "Daisy, I can see you! There's light coming in!"

"What does that mean?"

"If there's light, that means they've blasted through! Daisy, we're saved!"

"Reesa!" Ted's voice called. "Reesa, are you all right?"

"Ted, we're all right, we're all right!" Reesa shouted back.

Reesa heard the sound of wood being pulled apart, and a moment later, she saw Ted's face staring anxiously down at her. She looked up at him, and though tears were streaming down her own grimy face, she was smiling broadly.

"Listen," Ted said, as calmly as if they were sitting on a sofa in her living room, "I just wanted to say that I love you, and whether you are married or not, it makes no difference to me. We'll work something out."

Chapter Thirty-Four

"He is in here," Ted said. "I've arranged for his funeral to be held as soon as you give the word."

Ted watched Reesa walk into the bedroom and look down at the body of her father, who lay on the bed. Ted had hired an undertaker to prepare Miller so that Reesa could view him without undue shock. He had told her of the accident during the ride back to Albuquerque and comforted her tears as best he could. When Ted considered all that Reesa had been through and how well she had withstood it, his admiration of her equaled his love for her. Even watching her kiss Joaquin good-bye at the depot in Albuquerque had not upset him. In fact, it seemed right and proper for her to show affection for him.

As Reesa looked at the still form of her father, she began remembering things about him, little things that now tumbled back into her mind as sharply as if they had just happened.

She could hear a conversation, which had taken place ten years earlier.

"Reesa, girl, we'll be goin' out West I'm thinkin'. There's nothin' left for us here now."

"But, Papa, Mama's grave is here. Are we going to leave her behind?"

"Child, your mama isn't in that grave. She's here in our hearts, and that's where she'll always be. Just like me, when I'm gone. I'll still be right there in your heart."

"Papa, I don't want you to ever die."

"Honey, we've all got to die. We can't go to heaven until we do."

"Where is Warren?" Reesa finally asked.

"I don't know," Ted answered. "I haven't seen him around since last night. In fact, I didn't even bother to try to find him when I heard you were in trouble."

Reesa looked over at Ted. "I'm glad," she said. "Don't you know it was you I wanted to see while I lay trapped in that car?"

Ted put his arms around her. "I'm awfully sorry about your papa," he said.

"I'm sorry he didn't live long enough to see us together like this. I know he would have approved, no matter what."

"Well, have you decided what you are going to do?"

"I'm going to divorce Warren," Reesa said finally.

"What about your church?"

"My conscience is clear," Reesa said. "I was never married to Warren spiritually or physically, Ted. We were never . . . man and wife together."

361

"Somehow I can't see Warren being denied his marital rights," Ted said.

"I didn't deny them," Reesa answered honestly. "He is the one who abandoned the bed. Not once, since we've been married, have we been together."

"Why not?"

"He is a very odd person," Reesa said. She told Ted about Warren's hatred for his father, and how he intended to show that hatred by refusing to provide his father with a grandchild.

"You call him odd? I think he's crazy. Reesa, you'd better let me be with you when you tell him you want the divorce. I'm afraid of what he might do otherwise."

There was a knock on the door then, and both turned to acknowledge it. Murdock was standing just on the other side.

"Yes, Murdock, what is it?" Ted asked.

"Boss, that damn telegraph machine is just going crazy down there, 'n' we don't have anyone here who can answer it."

"Oh, yes, we do," Reesa said.

"Who?" Murdock asked.

Ted smiled. "You're looking at her," he said. "Come on, Reesa, I'll put you to work."

The three walked back to the engineering car, then stepped inside. The instrument was clacking as they reached it, and Reesa sat down behind it.

"What are they saying?" Ted asked.

"They are just trying to get an answer from us," Reesa said. She opened the key and began working the switch. "I'm telling them that our original telegrapher was killed in an accident, and I am just signing on. I'm asking what messages they have," she said.

There was a rather lengthy exchange of messages, then Reesa tore the message off the pad and handed it to Ted.

"It's Titus Leland's bank," Ted said glumly. "They need verification of our intent to satisfy the terms of the railroad grant by the deadline or a statement that such terms can't be met."

"I thought we had three more days, the bloodsuckers," Murdock said.

"We do," Ted said. "But they need to either prepare the transfer of funds, or make arrangements to foreclose."

"What are you going to do, Ted?" Reesa asked.

Ted handed the message back to Reesa and walked over to the door of the car. He looked out at his work camp and at the mountains and desert he had tried to conquer. He sighed. "I don't know yet."

"Can't you blast that rubble away from the pass?" Reesa asked.

"No, ma'am" Murdock said. "We used the last of our nitro in rescuin' you, 'n' there ain't no more anywhere."

"Ted, you sacrificed your railroad for me?"

Ted smiled and returned to Reesa. He put his arms around her. "Darling, believe me, it was no sacrifice. Don't you realize that you are worth more to me than a dozen railroads?"

"Yes, I think I do, now," Reesa said. "I just wish I had realized it earlier, and none of this would have happened."

"What are you gonna tell 'em, boss?" Murdock asked.

"Reesa, tell them evaluation is still in progress. I'll have an answer for them by five o'clock this evening."

Reesa began flashing the message back, and Murdock and Ted left the car to look around.

"Have you got any ideas, boss?" Murdock asked.

"Maybe," Ted said. "Didn't I see a couple of the engineers going in for some coffee a short time ago?"

"Yeah, they're in there."

"I need to talk with them," Ted said.

The two engineers stood when Ted entered the tent. One of the kitchen workers had seen Ted and Murdock approach and met them with a cup of coffee for each.

"How's the girl holdin' up?" one of the engineers asked.

"She's doing fine," Ted said. "In fact, she's working for us now. She took her father's place as a telegrapher."

"It can't be a job with much security," one of the engineers observed.

"All may not be lost," Ted said. "Have the tracks reached Springerville?"

"Yes," one of the engineers replied. "But that does us no good as long as this pass remains closed."

"Then we are going to open this pass," Ted suggested.

"Mr. Foster, we don't have more than a couple hundred pounds of black powder, and that simply won't do the job."

"It won't remove the old rubble," Ted said. "But it will do the job I'm going to ask of it."

"What do you mean?"

"The blast that Ling Cho set off, even though not yet placed, may have opened up another possible route for us. It won't be a very good route; the gradient may just about be at maximum, but we can lay track across it and complete the line."

"You mean as a temporary measure?" one of the engineers asked.

"Sure, why not?" Ted replied. "Look, there is no requirement as to mean gradient ratio, only that a continuous and passable line be built. This section would allow the passage of a locomotive and tender, and perhaps a few cars. Hardly enough to be classified as economical, but it will fulfill the government requirements. Later, after the grant has been paid, we can return here and excavate the original track."

"That might work," one of the engineers said slowly.

"All I need is a track, which will allow a locomotive and a few cars to pass. If we have to, we'll establish this as a precautionary area and reduce speed to five miles per hour. Can you do it?"

One of the engineers opened up his case and removed a tablet and some engineering instruments. He began drawing circles and triangles, and filling the pad with figures. He and the other engineer talked in the strange language of gradients and radials: tepetate earth, abutments and foundations, and mathematical formulas. Finally they looked up at Ted and smiled.

"We can do it."

"You mean our railroad is going to be saved?" Murdock said with a joyous shout.

"I think so," the engineer replied.

"Now the question is, can we do it in three days?" Ted asked.

"That question I can answer," Murdock said. "If these boys'll give me the plans, I'll do it. We'll go on twenty-four-hour shifts."

The two engineers drained the last of their coffee and set their cups down. "We've got to walk our new cut," one of them said.

"I'll get the material and tools ready for construction," Murdock put in. "What are you going to do, boss?"

"Find Warren Leland," Ted said. "We have some important business to discuss, and I don't mean about the railroad."

Within moments after the meeting in the mess tent, word had spread throughout the camp that a way had been found to save the railroad. There was jubilation everywhere, and the men prepared to return to work as soon as so ordered. Laughter and joking filled the air. It was gratifying to Ted to see that the almost oppressive layer of depression that had settled over the camp after the death of Miller and Ling Cho, and the fear that the railroad might be finished, was now gone.

Ted searched everywhere for Warren, but was unable to find him. Finally he returned to the engineering car to speak with Reesa. "You haven't seen Warren, have you?" he asked as he stepped inside.

"No," Reesa said. "Why, have you spoken to him?"

"That's just it. I can't find him anywhere."

"I imagine he'll turn up soon," Reesa said. She was busy cleaning the engineering car. "Honestly, I don't think any of you ever picked up a thing," she said. "It's too bad poor Daisy is laid up with a broken leg. I could use her help out here."

"I guess we just sort of let things get away from us," Ted said.

"At least the messages were filed," Reesa said, tearing the message from the pad, which she had received only that morning. "Thank goodness Dad was always very particular with that. I think it was because he knew he was so sloppy with everything else that . . . wait a minute, this is odd."

"What?"

"Message number two four five is missing."

"Two four five?"

"Yes, see, every message is numbered in sequence, and placed here on this spindle. The last message up here is two four four, and the one I took today is two four six. Where is two four five?"

"Maybe there was a numbering error."

"No, these pads are preprinted with the numbers," Reesa said. She began looking around on the desk and in the wastebasket. "Message two four five is gone."

"What is the last message received before this?"

Reesa took down message two four four. "It concerns a shipment of railroad ties," she said.

"Reesa, that's the last message we received, I swear it is. Your dad showed it to me not more than an hour or so before he was killed."

"Maybe he got another message and was bringing it to you when he . . . when he fell," she said, fighting hard not to reopen the hurt of her father's death.

"It wasn't on him," Ted said.

Reesa looked at message 246 and then held it against the light, in such a way as to see indentations on the paper. She sat down at the desk and began running a pencil over the page lightly, covering the whole page in gray-black lead. Soon, white marks began to appear where the indentations were, then words and figures. They were able to read: *27520287 is laundry number belonging to* . . . and then it stopped.

"That doesn't make sense," Reesa said.

"I'm afraid it does," Ted said glumly.

"What?"

"It means your father was murdered."

"Murdered? Why? Who would want to . . . ?"

"Whoever that laundry number belongs to," Ted said. He explained about the murder of Golden Tears, and the handkerchief that had been discovered near the scene bearing the laundry number.

"When that message came back, whoever it was discovered it and killed your father," Ted said.

"But who could it be? Papa didn't write it down, and no one would know unless they could read telegraphy."

"There are over four hundred men in this camp, Reesa," Ted said. "There is every possibility that some of them can read telegraphy, and we just don't know about it."

"I'm going to see if I can find out what name is missing," Reesa said.

"How?"

"By finding the telegrapher who originated the message. He'll have a copy."

There was an urgent knock on the door, and Ted looked around to see one of the engineers. "We've got a problem, Mr. Foster."

"With laying the temporary track?"

"No, sir, nothing like that. It's something else."

"What?"

"I'd rather talk with you alone," the engineer said awkwardly.

"You go ahead, darling," Reesa said grimly. "I'm going to try and get to the bottom of this mystery."

Ted left the engineering car and walked a little ways with the engineer. The man was silent for several moments.

"Well, what is it?" Ted finally asked.

"We found Mr. Leland."

"Good, where is he? I need to talk to him."

"There won't be any talkin', I'm afraid," the engineer said.

"Why? What do you mean?"

"We found him when we were walking the new route. He's dead."

"Dead? How? Where is he?"

"Come along, have a look for yourself," the engineer said.

Ted followed the engineer up the side of the mountains, across the pile of robble, until he saw a small cluster of people standing around looking down at something."

"It looks like he was killed in the explosion that killed Ling Cho," the other engineer who had waited by the body said. "He's been crushed by rocks."

Ted sighed. "It looks like you're right," he said. "The question is, what the hell was he doing up here?"

"I've got an answer to that, too," the engineer said.

Ted turned to look at him. "What?"

The man led Ted a few feet away from the body and pointed to a crowbar lying on the ground. "Look," he said. "Mr. Leland used the crowbar to start a rockslide. Mr. Foster, he caused the rockslide that set off Ling Cho's blast, then he got caught in it himself. He killed Ling Cho."

"I see," Ted said quietly.

"But why?"

"Why? For the same reason he killed Miller Flowers," Ted replied.

"Should we bury him?" someone asked.

"No," Ted said. "Have one of the carpenters build a coffin for shipping. We'll send his body back to San Francisco. His father will want to bury him, I'm sure."

"If this son-of-a-bitch killed Miller, he don't deserve no decent burial," someone said.

"Look, he's dead," Ted said sharply. "It doesn't make any difference to him now what we do. But his father is still alive, and his father is innocent. So we'll have some concern for him."

"Yeah, I guess you're right," the man said. "All right, we'll send the son-of-a-bitch back."

Ted climbed back down the mountain and went into the engineering car to tell Reesa about Warren. When he got there, he discovered her crying.

"Reesa, what is it?" he asked, slipping his arms around her.

"I've just discovered whose name is missing. Ted, I know who murdered my father."

"It was Warren," Ted said quietly.

"It was Warren," Reesa went on. "How could he do such a . . . you knew?" she asked, suddenly realizing what he had said.

"I didn't know until a few minutes ago, when I discovered that he killed Ling Cho. I knew it had to be for the same reason."

"My God, you mean he killed that poor little Chinese girl, and my father, and Ling Cho? Ted, what sort of monster is he?"

"He's a dead monster," Ted said.

"What do you mean?"

Ted sighed, and held Reesa closer. "It's all over, darling. We've just found Warren's body. He was killed in the explosion that he set off to kill Ling Cho."

"Oh, Ted, I was such a fool," she whispered against his chest. "I not only messed up our lives, but I got three innocent people killed, including my own father."

"You did no such thing," Ted said firmly, "and I won't let you think like that. We have to take life as it comes and deal with it in the way

371

we think best. We've both plodded through, but the important thing is, we have arrived here at this point, at the same time. We are together now, darling, and we'll be together forever. That's all that counts, isn't it?"

"Yes, darling. That's all that counts," Reesa said.

PREVIEW

FRANCESCA

Angelica Aimes

This is the second novel by Angelica Aimes, a new and exciting writer. As with *Samantha,* her first best-seller, the author has woven a colorful, exciting and absorbing story of love and passion, romance and betrayal, introducing the reader to a heroine who will be long remembered. *Francesca* is the story of two beautiful young cousins who could not be closer if they were sisters—until a man they both wanted came along. . . . The following scene is excerpted from the first chapter. It is the scene which changes the life of the unforgettable Francesca.*

Ever since Francesca could remember, she had been certain that she would one day marry Malcolm. They had carved their initials on the elm in the garden when she was eight, and Francesca had never even thought of an-other boy since then. During the last two years, with her beloved cousin Clarissa away at school, Malcolm and she had grown even closer. Yet an element of shyness had developed between them, as Francesca became more and more aware of the unfamiliar stirrings within her body when they were together.

Tonight they were alone, she and Malcolm, in the candlelit, fire-warmed study. He had been away on family business and both had realized how painful their separation had been. Now he stood before her and held out his hands to her.

"Please, Francesca, let me embrace you," he whispered ardently. "I have waited so long for a moment when we could be alone together and I could take you in my arms and feel the warmth of your body light up my own. I want to hold you forever, Francesca, and never let you go. I never want a day to pass without you in my arms." As he spoke, he drew her to him, clasping her firmly against his strong, lean body.

She had never been in a man's arms before. She had never felt a man's embrace, and now, after the lonely days without him, any natural caution she may have had was lost. Malcolm's warm breath in her ear sent shivers of excitement coursing through her. His lean body, pressing tightly against her own, banished every thought from her head. Before she knew what was happening, her eager lips were encircled by his as she answered him with all the abandon of a first love.

Emboldened by the passion of her response, Malcolm pressed her closer to him until their bodies were as one as their lips joined in a long, lingering embrace. For the first time Francesca tasted a man's special flavor, and with her generous, unrestrained kiss she gave Malcolm her heart, her soul, and every fibre of her innocent, trusting nature.

Overwhelmed by the unexpected gift of love, Malcolm hesitated. Her kiss had aroused an ardor that no other kisses, however passionate, could satisfy. Moved as much by the deep emotion he had awakened in her as by his own desire, he drew his lips from hers. "Francesca," he asked earnestly, "am I the first man you have ever kissed?"

She nodded, suddenly embarrassed and afraid that her kiss had disappointed him.

"The first man, the only man?" he asked wondrously. Again she nodded shyly.

"Oh, Francesca, Francesca," he cried, overcome by the passion of the innocent girl, "then you long for me as I do for you! You love me!"

"Yes, Malcolm, yes," she whispered, but her words were lost in the torrent of kisses he showered on her mouth and eyes and neck.

"I knew you cared for me, but I thought it was as an old friend—a brother, almost," he marveled. "I never dared hope that I could be anything else to you!"

Francesca smiled at him. Love lit her face and glowed from her eyes. "I love you, Malcolm," she said simply. "I think I have loved you since you helped me up when I fell off my horse and kissed my forehead where I had bumped it—when I was five." She stroked his cheek tenderly. "Kiss me again, my love," she whispered.

"I never want to stop kissing you," he answered. "I never want to let you out of my arms." And again his lips enveloped hers and he thrust his tongue deeply into her mouth. She accepted it eagerly and answered it with her own.

Malcolm had gone much further than he had intended to when he called on Francesca that evening, much further than he had ever dreamed possible. Now, almost before he knew what he was saying, the words came pouring out of his mouth.

"Francesca," he heard himself ask as if in a dream, "will you marry me? Please say you will be my wife. I love you as I have never loved another woman. Tell me you love me, Francesca. Tell me you will be mine." He had gone too far to turn back now, even if he had wanted to. He had to possess her. His body was bursting with desire.

"I do with my whole heart and I will forever and ever," she answered and, as if to seal her promise, she surrendered herself to his lips. He consumed her with a kiss that, in its intensity and abandon, he believed gave him claim to even more.

He drew away from her and, taking her face in his hands, he gazed intently into her dark, velvet eyes. "Francesca, how can I be sure you love me?" he asked her. "What will you do to show me that you love me truly and totally, me and no other?"

"I will do anything, Malcolm," she replied, "anything you want, to prove my love; anything you ask." His questioning voice had surprised and upset her. "Do you want me to wake up Uncle Jeremy and tell him? Or rush out into the street and shout my love so that all of London will know it?"

Malcolm smiled at Francesca tenderly. "All that," he said, "and neither. It is something much slighter, but much more important to me. Something you can do now, just for me, that will remain forever between us. It will be ours alone."

"What is it, Malcolm," she asked, uncertain of what he wanted.

He whispered his desire in her ear and his words sent shivers up her spine. "Let me look on your beauty, just for a moment. I will not touch you," he added hurriedly. "That is my solemn promise. I want you to give your beauty to me, to pledge it to me with this act, as proof of your love. Only this and nothing more."

"But Malcolm, I have never . . ."

He interrupted her roughly. "A moment ago you pledged your love to me. Now you deny me the one small thing I ask of you to prove the truth of your words. How can I believe in such a love? There is nothing I would not do for you, nothing I would not sacrifice. If you asked me to give my life, I would. But you will not even allow me a glimpse of your beauty."

"No, no," Francesca protested. "I would do anything you asked, anything to prove that I love you. It's just . . . I have never . . ."

"I know, I know, darling." Malcolm spoke more gently now. "You are shy. No man has ever gazed on your loveliness before—and no man but I ever shall again." He stroked her golden hair. "Don't be afraid, Francesca."

"What . . ." Francesca hesitated. "How much do you want to see?" she whispered, and Malcolm knew he had won.

He kissed her lightly, lingeringly, on the lips. "I want to see all of you," he murmured. "I will snuff out the candles and turn away and not look until you call me."

Francesca hesitated for a moment and then, turning away from him, she began to undress with shaking fingers. While she was disrobing, Malcolm turned the key in the library door and snuffed out the candles. Quickly, quietly, he stripped off his own clothes. He stood in the shadows by the door until he heard her call him softly. Then he stepped forward.

He was unprepared for what he saw. Francesca stood quietly, her head bowed, while the glow of the fire bathed her long, slender body in its reddish light. Her skin was as smooth and creamy as a calla lily. Her breasts were small but firm and perfectly shaped. Hip bones angled out from her tall, slim body as if standing guard on each side of her smooth, flat belly.

His eyes lingered longingly on her nakedness. Finally he stepped from the shadows. "Please," he whispered, his voice hoarse with desire, "I beg of you, release me from my promise. Let me hold you. Just for a moment, let me feel your flesh pressed against mine."

He came slowly toward her until he stood only inches away. Then he took her hands and gently, almost imperceptibly, drew her to him. His eager fingers stroked her back seductively as his yearning body pressed against hers.

As his strong arms entwined her and his lean, muscular body met hers, Francesca thought, this must be heaven. Soon his lips, his mouth, his tongue were again searching hers and his body was sending strange and wonderful feelings surging through her limbs.

"Oh, Francesca, my love, my life," Malcolm murmured, "don't make me wait another second. Be my wife, my happiness, now, forever, this very night unto eternity. Let me take you; let me make you mine."

"But Malcolm," Francesca whispered, "how can we do this before we are married?" Even as she spoke, Francesca could feel Malcolm's hot breath on her neck and it was difficult for her to concentrate on anything or to remember what was right and what was wrong.

"You are right, my darling, you are right, and sweet and pure. We will be married first," Malcolm said. He knelt down in front of her and said, "I do solemnly swear to make Francesca Fairchild my wife in a holy act of matrimony, right here, right now." He drew her down until she was kneeling in front of him, and he kissed her lips softly.

"Do you love me, Malcolm?" Francesca asked, and all her hopes and fears and dreams were posed in those four simple words.

"I do," he answered, pressing her backward until she was lying outstretched, and there, on Uncle Jeremy's Oriental carpet, as the fire flickered and danced in the grate, Malcolm had his way.

Shortly thereafter Clarissa returned to London, after two years on the Continent. She laughed off Francesca's news, that she was engaged to Malcolm, the handsome Lord Harrod, lionized by every ambitious beauty in town. Her two years abroad had given her an exciting, daring demeanor that entranced Malcolm. He was so dazzled by the petite beauty with the delicacy of a porcelain figurine and the promise of a nymphet that he never looked back. His pledge to Francesca was forgotten, his vows sheepishly renounced.

Although she was prettier, Francesca could not compete with Clarissa. She did not know how. Even if she had had the glamorous airs and flirtatious tricks that turned a man's heart, she would not stand in her beloved cousin Clarissa's way. And so she would leave London—go as far away as possible. Although it was beneath her social station, she would take the position as governess-teacher to the many children of the barbarian prince Elfi Bey, in Cairo. There, she might be able to forget her broken heart—and her secret shame.

As the *S.S. Georgiana* sailed eastward through the Mediterranean Sea, Francesca thought of Malcolm, and hoped that there was something special, something locked away in a far corner of his heart, that would remain forever theirs. She could not know, could not even imagine, what fate held in store for her. Perhaps it was just as well, for in Cairo she would experience pride and passion, ecstasy and humiliation, and the kind of love that changes a trusting girl into an erotic and exotic woman.

* * *

You have just read one exciting sequence from Francesca *by Angelica Aimes, which will be published by Pinnacle Books in December, 1978.*